THE GOLDEN BOMB

THE GOLDEN BOMB:

PHANTASTIC GERMAN EXPRESSIONIST STORIES

Edited by
Malcolm Green

Polygon
Edinburgh

©Introduction and Editorial selection
Malcolm Green 1993

The acknowledgements on page 299-301 are an extension of the copyright page.

Published by Polygon
22 George Square
Edinburgh

Set in 10 on 14pt Monotype Weiss by ROM-Data Corporation Ltd., Falmouth, Cornwall, England.
Printed and bound in Great Britain by
Hartnolls Ltd, Bodmin, Cornwall

British Cataloguing in Publication Data.

Golden Bomb: Phantastic German
Expressionist Stories
I. Green, Malcolm
833.0108 [FS]

ISBN 0748 66058 5

The publisher acknowledges subsidy
from the Scottish Arts Council towards
the publication of this volume.

CONTENTS

Malcolm Green *Introduction*   1

Franz Held *The Golden Bomb*   29
Oskar Panizza *The Crime in Tavistock Square*   36
Albert Mombert *Ice*   46
Paul Scheerbart *Cascading Comets*   50
Alfred Döblin *The Murder of a Buttercup*   55
Albert Ehrenstein *Tubutsch*   69
Carl Einstein *Herr Giorgio Bebuquin*   97
Gustav Meyrink *The Ring of Saturn*   108
Georg Heym *The Dissection*   119
Ferdinand Hardekopf *The Mental Link*   122
Wassily Kandinsky *Bassoon*   126
Mynona *A Child's Heroic Deed*   128
Hans Arp *Wintergarten*   131
Alfred Wolfenstein *Far Greater than Every Magic*   134
Paul Zech *The Terrace at the Pole*   143

Else Lasker-Schüler *If My Heart were Healthy*	150
Georg Trakl *Dream and Dementia*	155
Alfred Lichtenstein *Conversation about Legs*	161
Theodor Däubler *The Propeller*	165
Heinrich Nowak *The Solar Plague*	169
Gottfried Benn *The Island*	203
Hans Flesch-Brunningen *The Metaphysical Canary*	213
Hugo Ball *Grand Hotel Metaphysics*	218
Conrad Felixmüller *Military Orderly Felixmüller, XI Arnsdorf*	224
Heinrich Schaefer *Two Sketches*	229
Wieland Herzfelde *Strenge from Leipzig*	232
Kurt Schwitters *The Onion Merzpoem 8*	238
Franz Kafka *The Vulture*	246
Iwan Goll *The Eurococccus (Extract)*	248
Robert Musil *The Giant Agoag*	266
Hermann Ungar *Something Behind This*	270
Notes	274
The Periodicals	279
Biographies	281

Malcolm Green

INTRODUCTION

'It is popularly said that when someone is hanged, he relives his whole life in the very last moment. That can't be anything but Expressionism!'

Theodor Däubler

I doubt that such a delightful definition of Expressionism could ever be bettered, implying, as it does, that the movement was extremely subjective and all things to all men. Right from the start Expressionism was a protean beast, and it is virtually impossible to pin-point more than family resemblances in what was in fact a rather rag-bag 'movement' which encompassed the naïvely ecstatic and the cynically sceptical, the extreme individualism of the Nietzschian ego and the ethical idealism of socialist brotherhood, revelations of the apocalypse and utopian hymns, social critique and hermetic vision, a glorification of primal instincts and the ideal of the spirit, socialism and anti-liberal nihilism, and much more. As one writer has commented, perhaps the main stylistic feature of the movement was a fear that it might seem bourgeois.[1]

Given this breadth of intentions, the aim of this anthology is not to try to do justice to the whole of the movement by giving a representative selection of the writing, but to tease out several strands which went to make up Expressionism: the 'fantastic, grotesque, speculative', seen already in the 1890s, then among the early Expressionists and early Dada, and later in Surrealism. To this end I have chosen a number of precursors, true Expressionists and, as in the case of Meyrink and Kafka, writers sufficiently close to be often mistaken as such and who not only wrote some of the most exciting prose in this epoch, but also reveal a number of links which help illuminate these three aspects.

Before looking at the writers, let me present an overview of Expressionism. Historically speaking, Expressionism was the first and last major art movement in Germany, embracing all of the arts and showing a political, *avant-garde* consciousness. It can be roughly dated from the first art group Die Brücke, founded in 1906, to the last Expressionist films made as late as 1926. Literary Expressionism started around 1909 in Berlin, and although it had petered out by the beginning of the next decade, it left a heritage which can be traced to the end of the 1920s, and a somewhat vague stylistic concept which is still occasionally used in literary criticism, albeit less frequently than for other art forms.

Centred at first in Berlin and Munich, the movement spread quickly to Prague, Alsace, Zurich, Vienna, Dresden, Leipzig, Heidelberg, Kiel and Hamburg, and produced not only a plethora of artists and writers (some 350), but also an autonomous communications network via its own periodicals (roughly one hundred in all), clubs, cafés and galleries. Although a number of socio-political and cultural reasons can be established for the sudden change in awareness which generally characterises Expressionism, most interpretations

Malcolm Green / INTRODUCTION

fail to explain the sudden explosion of creativity which was packed into little over a decade.

Concentrating now on literary Expressionism, one can roughly divide it into two phases. The early Expressionists picked up the same themes as the art movement — suffering, sickness, madness, loneliness, brutal eroticism, anxiety and above all the city, with its frantic pace and its low life, cafés, prostitutes, variétés etc. — writing with a mixture of protest and fascination, embracing ugliness without sentimentality. But despite the aggressive, polemical, anti-authoritarian tenor of the early Expressionists, with their calls for a heroic 'New Man', who would cast off the chains of societal mores and look the world in the eye with Nietzschian subjectivity, and their individualistic *weltschmerz*, it would be hard to overlook a frequent absurdist streak and black humour. The first phase can be seen as a youthful assault on reality and the art of a paternalistic society. At this stage it had little unifying theory, and can be viewed more as a number of growing pockets of resistance. One other major theme in this early poetry and prose should be singled out here: their sombre visions of the end of the world or of imminent catastrophe which are particularly linked with the poems of Georg Heym, but also hinted at in the stories here from Alfred Wolfenstein and Paul Zech. The writing is often described as prophetic of the war which brought this phase to an end.

Many of the Expressionists openly greeted the war, naïvely considering it to be a great collective adventure, or in other cases as the only way of purging bourgeois stuffiness. Others, in turn, volunteered in the ingenuous belief that they would be protecting their own cultural interests, while yet others saw no choice but to flee to Switzerland, where the seeds of Dada were to be sown. Although Expressionism became somewhat marginalised during the war, and the periodicals were forced to moderate their tone (often allowing visual art to speak where the word was censored) or fold altogether, Expressionist galleries continued to hold exhibitions, and new magazines did continue to appear. By the middle of the war, as the grim reality became apparent, we see the beginning of the second phase, which is typified by an increasing emphasis on the themes of pacifism and universal brotherhood. This was accompanied at first by a period of reflection and consolidation, when theorists and manifestos blossomed and decided what Expressionism was or should be, then to become increasingly politicised with the progress of the war and the 1917 Revolution in Russia. Now with a concrete target at hand, the writing shifted from the earlier mud-slinging and 'screams of the isolated individual' and picked up increasingly on themes of internationalism, solidarity and struggle (although just as often mawkish meliorism), proclaimed in revolutionary ecstatic tones and accompanied by the 'holy narcotic', as Marcuse put it, of 'oh man!' appeals to take one's brothers into one's arms (shown in this anthology at the end of Conrad Felixmüller's piece).

This political activism culminated in the participation in the November Revolution of 1918 in Berlin and Munich, but hopes were dashed as the Revolution was quashed by state terror, and the workers' councils were replaced by Weimar democracy. There followed a period of 'sobering up', where the Expressionists realised that their activism had been too nebulous and lacked a unified programme, and that their heady writing was starting to seem sadly ineffective. With the start of the new decade which introduced an admittedly short-lived period of democracy and comfortable capitalism, where Expressionism boomed in films and on the stage, the literary impulse was already making way for 'Neue Sachlichkeit' (New Objectivity). This was not least because 'Expressionism' was starting to be marketed as an acceptable 'style' by major publishing houses. A Dada broadside against Expressionism, published in the *Dada Almanach* in 1920, met with no response: the spirit was gone.

Having given a sketch of the time span occupied by literary Expressionism, I would like to return to the question of the

Malcolm Green / **INTRODUCTION**

movement's social and cultural roots, and the central question: What was Expressionism?

The word itself was first adopted in 1911, used by painters and writers to indicate a break with Impressionism. However, in some way the name seems to have been a stop-gap solution which does not capture more than a common sense of identity, and before the war it was far more usual to speak of the 'New Poetry'. Furthermore, even in the later manifestos written by leading theoreticians, the name largely remained couched in terms of contrasts with the old art forms and, as we shall see later, early Expressionism owes a significant debt to the very movements they rejected. But to return to the polemic: Impressionism[2] was seen as vacuous and bourgeois, being too wrapped up in aestheticism and beauty, melancholy and resignation, to say anything valid about the reality of a rapidly-changing world. Indeed, the changes in the Wilhelminian socio-economic order, with the turmoil and intensity produced by centralisation and the racing tempo of the vast cities, and the break in the security of the individual's place in the world announced by natural science (Planck, Einstein and Darwin), psychology (Freud, Bergson) and philosophy (above all Nietzsche and the neo-Kantians), are often seen as a major driving power behind the movement.[3] The individual was alienated in the midst of these changes and ontological uncertainties: man was no longer the centre and measure of all things, and there was a growing gap between science and morals, knowledge and experience, so that rationality, intelligence, objectivity and the order of civilisation were called into increasing doubt.

The Expressionists' reaction to this personally felt crisis, their attack on the prevailing reality, came in the form of a passionate reaffirmation of subjective individuality (characteristically in the ideal form of the New Man who could tackle self-transformation, subjective truth and the multiplicity of the self), the attempt to overcome the traditional distinctions between rational/irrational, material/ideal, and an immediacy which united the artist with his product. Thus, with such key words as 'eruption', 'explosion' and 'intensity', they rejected the old artist's *l'art pour l'art* separation between art and life by discarding interpretative psychology and representationalism. To paraphrase this approach: the Expressionist poet is convulsive, delirious, revelationary; he does not see, he beholds; he does not describe, he experiences; he does not represent, he forms anew; he does not accept, he seeks. In turn, this new autonomy of perception, with its delirious intoxication and the possibility of getting to the 'root of things', as Gottfried Benn, a major theorist, put it, brought about a revolution in the language: the Expressionists' language was one of simultaneity and new rhythms, designed to capture the complexity of the throbbing city which represented their reality, the whole contents of the helter-skelter world of their experience, all at once. This urgency is a major characteristic of the new crisis consciousness, one which cuts it off from the writing of the nineteenth century. Thus, although such typically Expressionist features as the literary grotesque, savage criticism of the bourgeois, irrational praise of the individual, the city as a central theme, socialism, premonitions of war, overcoming the gap between art and artist etc., can already be found in a number of writers in the preceding decades, this was largely accompanied by 'outsiderism' or a notion of steady social reform. Expressionism wanted a radical break, an awakening, a new start. It challenged the idea of reform in a society which could offer no way forward now that progress itself was in question, posing its New Man in the place of a new society. And the New Man needed a new language. Expressionism was mostly optimistic about this direct, revelatory form of writing: they believed in the power of words freed from the worn-out cliches of the newspapers and dusty poetasters to communicate the new message.

A note of caution however: as we shall see later, a number of the early writers, such as Ehrenstein or Lichtenstein, were anything but

Malcolm Green / **INTRODUCTION**

winged, intoxicated prophets of the New Man, being far more aware of their isolation and the cruel trick played on them by existence. On the one hand we see a vital renewal of subjectivity, on the other a personal crisis in the same, with a consequent fragmentation of the self which can be found in a lot of Expressionist writing. Between problem and answer, we are now back to the protean nature of Expressionism. It is necessary to go beyond these 'winged' generalisations, largely promulgated by the theorists of the later phase, and take a closer look at the context in which the early Expressionists were forging their New Poetry.

As I have already mentioned, the polemical rejection of the 'old guard' does not really hold. A development from, or debt to, the French Symbolists, Art Nouveau or neo-Romanticism can be seen in such different writers as Alfred Döblin, Gottfried Benn, Carl Einstein, Hans Arp, Ferdinand Hardekopf and Georg Heym. For all of Heym's famous apocalyptic visions, for instance, a look at his story 'The Dissection' reveals a nicely *fin de siècle* mingling of eroticism and death with a very Art Nouveau dream section. Moreover, Heym's piece uses a fantastic motif (as do his most famous, 'truly' Expressionist stories), and some of his stories were almost worthy of the most renowned fantasy writer of the time, Gustav Meyrink. The 'sudden radical break' with the past, which the phenomenon of Expressionism seems to suggest, becomes more hazy when one looks at what the early writers actually read beside the 'major' textbook influences, such as Nietzsche, Strindberg, Rimbaud, Dostoyevsky and Wedekind. At the so-called Neopathetic Cabarets — a mixture of philosophy, chansons and pranks — held in the pre-war years by the New Club in Berlin, we find readings not only of early Expressionist writing (Heym, Lichtenstein, Hardekopf, van Hoddis, Einstein (reading *Bebuquin*) and the older Bohemians Else Lasker-Schüler and Mynona), but also Rilke, the arch-decadent Przybyszewski (read by Ferdinand Hardekopf, who wrote of him: 'O I love him, I am his creation') and neo-Romantic Meyrink. In his letters to his friends, the club's founder, Erwin Loewenson, recommends not only the top aesthetes Stefan George and Hugo von Hoffmansthal, but also Poe, Meyrink and the popular trash horror writer H.H. Ewers, as well as Huysmans and Wilde. Adding to this Ball's admiration of Brummel and d'Aurevilly, Benn's love of Huysmans and Maeterlink, their mutual love of Wilde, Einstein's eulogy on William Beckford's *Vathek* and praise of Mallarmé's *Hérodiade* and Flaubert's *Herodias*, the publication of Maupassant, Herman Bang, Przybyszewski, Lafcadio Hearn, Verlaine, Schwob, etc. (the list of Decadents, Symbolists and such kindred spirits could be extended at length) in the central Expressionist periodicals *Der Sturm* and *Die Aktion*, one starts to suspect that the young Expressionists first checked their poses before finding the objects for their rebellion.

Not wishing to become guilty of polemic myself, I do believe however that an antidote is still required to a prevalent attitude which considers it is defending Expressionism by stepping round the dandyish, decadent aspect of the movement. Much of this can be viewed charitably as a reaction against the communist literary theorists of the thirties, most particularly Georg Lukács, who claimed that Expressionism was a Bohemian, mystic-escapist affair which not only lacked any genuine political consciousness, but was one of the bourgeois ideological currents which culminated in fascism. This sort of thinking, which considers Expressionism to be negatively 'decadent' in a perversely similar way that the Nazis did, requires no consideration here. But global misrepresentations, such as 'the Expressionists knew no irony' (I forget from whom I quote), are still being written and are plainly false. Despite, or perhaps because of their often radical political stance, the pre-war Expressionists' attack on reality not infrequently centred on snapping the solid citizen's mind with what reads like a mixture of public school archness and malicious glee, and at least Ball, Benn, Lichtenstein and Einstein disported themselves with a consciously

Malcolm Green / INTRODUCTION

dandyish air. Lacking a real programme and a serious target before the war, irony, Bohemianism and nihilistic cynicism were a clear choice of weapons. The results can be confusing: Heym's poem 'War' is a masterpiece of the 'black vision of things to come', but at the same time he welcomed war in what seems nothing more than a fit of ennui, and there is very strong evidence that the poem which is forever interpreted as portending the end of a well-ordered, bourgeois existence, Jakob van Hoddis's 'The End of the World', was 'nothing more' than an ironic jab at the fears that were aroused by Halley's Comet! With the early Expressionists we have a consciousness centring on 'Neopathos,[4] paradox, philosophy and fantasy ...', as one reviewer wrote of the Neopathetic Cabaret in 1913 — which are more or less the three aspects I have set out to investigate in this book.

The grotesque, in the form of the so-called 'literary grotesque', was a flourishing humourous genre around the turn of the century, and the early Expressionists, including writers like Heym, Benn, Hardekopf, Iwan Goll and Heinrich Nowak, honed it to perfection in their poetry. But unlike the smug, moralising, satirical or whimsical versions written by their contemporaries, the Expressionist grotesque was black, paradoxical and disquieting. It did not merely shock by ridiculing the holy bourgeois trinity of morality, seriousness and rationality, weaving in absurd, fantastic, incongruous elements and subversive urges, but in its best examples normality is completely suspended and the humour non-sequitur, where no one has the last laugh for no criticism is possible. Thus while the humour of Mynona, Alfred Döblin, Robert Musil, Hans Flesch-Brunningen and fellow traveller Gustav Meyrink revels in paradox and offence, Lichtenstein and Ehrenstein were thoroughly unnerving in their tightrope act between comic self-hate and their demonstration of the tragedy of existence. They played with the borderline between self and world, showing an existential unfairness which is beyond good and evil and protest, making a mockery of the bourgeois notion of character. Seen in this light, it is clear why the grotesque was the humourous form for a generation which rejected the normal interpretative, psychologising narrative and replaced the swindle of identifiable characters with 'snap-shot' fragments. In keeping with a generation where ego was experienced as fragmented, the Expressionist grotesque highlights the arbitrariness of one's perception and experience of the world, and very often turned full circle on the author: the subjective writer shows his own deformed, neurotic, crazed reality, where the safe distinctions between self and other, inner tensions and external causality, is dissolving. The paradox is not simply rooted in either the man or his environment, but the fact that both exist with different demands, to the extent that everything is tragic or funny. From here it is only a small step to the 'horror story', or to the Kafka of *Metamorphosis* or 'The Vulture' in this collection.

Three of the four precursors at the beginning of this book, Franz Held, Oskar Panizza and Paul Scheerbart, used the grotesque as a vehicle for their attacks. Held and Panizza were both active in the early Modern Movement in the 1890s, and both suffered for their convictions (blasphemy trials which led to them both emigrating). With Held's ridiculing of science and pompousness, his gloating vision of the downfall of Europe brought about by a series of supernatural metamorphoses, and his word conglomerates which prefigure the Expressionist experiments, it is little wonder that the text was republished in *Die Aktion* after the author's death. Here grotesque fantasy is used to produce an immoral marriage of the sentient and insentient.

Panizza is less frequently considered a precursor, but his typically brilliant mixture of fantastic invention, black humour and invective was greatly appreciated by Hugo Ball, for instance, and the early Expressionist and later Dadaist, Richard Huelsenbeck writing in his autobiography about *Revolution*, an early Expressionist magazine which published a large number of the writers in this book, said:

Malcolm Green / **INTRODUCTION**

'Our magazine was in the spirit of Panizza'. Other testimonies abound; scarcely any of the Expressionists could have failed to know this exemplary subversive, and the themes of psychoticism and the dissociation of the ego, the frailty and hypocrisy of our belief systems and morals, which are shown in 'The Crime in Tavistock Square', are not merely proto-Expressionist, but attracted the Surrealists, who published the piece in *La Brèche* in the mid-sixties. As with Held, we see here a threatening human aspect in the outside world, this time nature, as experienced in the mind of the beholder. And lurking behind this satire are Panizza's own philosophical preoccupations with a modified Stirnerian solipsism, which also attracted the attention of the late Expressionist anarchists connected with the Stirner Society.

Paul Scheerbart, the most Bohemian of the precursors I have included, was a master of the 'cosmic grotesque' — bizarre sci-fi worlds in a few ironic lines — and it earned him one of the warmest places of welcome among the movement. Dozens of his short vignettes were published in a variety of Expressionist magazines, and he was friends with a number of the early Expressionists. But despite an apparent clownishness, he could write: 'You have no clue that my jokes contain a dangerous scorn', and his 'Cascading Comets' is certainly not one of his cosiest pieces. Here we see the early Expressionist themes of the hollowness of bourgeois complacency and apocalypse, in the form of a fantastic intervention. Scheerbart's speculative side did not reside solely in his famous belief in the life of the heavenly bodies, but also in his efforts to refute the Kant-Laplace gravitational theory of the universe, his attempts to construct perpetual motion machines, his radical plans for a new society based on glass architecture, and much more.

While these authors had a central place among the 'modern' free-thinkers and anti-bourgeois writers at the end of the last century, Mombert represents a slightly different link. His poetry conjured up the ecstatic convulsions of the ego which form a never-ending cosmic music, thus overcoming the fabric of reality to open itself up to the chaos of the infinite. The rapture and solitude of this ego, along with Mombert's use of rhythm, make him one of the more frequently named 'influences'. Here we have a fairy-tale on the loneliness of the ego and its anti-intellectual urge back to primal nature, a longing for a state which was close to the Expressionists' desire. Not a humouresque or grotesque, this fantasy can also be understood as a parable for Mombert's own renewal of the Gnostic tradition, thus falling in with the speculative aspect and, with that, bringing us to the early Expressionists.

Theodor Däubler was an acclaimed and admired Expressionist in his time, but in retrospect he is often classed as 'pre-Expressionist', and Musil, writing in 1919, was not alone in seeing that his work could 'also have appeared twenty-five years earlier', thus placing him with the Impressionists. A true wandering Bohemian, Däubler represents the most idealistic, indeed religious part of this collection. Under the influence of Giordano Bruno's writings, he experienced at the age of fourteen what he termed the 'northern lights vision', seeing all of reality and history as a poetic text pointing the way towards Gnostic union. His major work (of which 'The Propeller', which I have included here, can be seen as a highly poetic mini-version), the 30,000 verse epic *Northern Lights*, is based entirely on this vision, which was worked into the fundamental myth that the earth has torn itself away from the sun and now longs for its return. This reunion with the central light of the universe, which can only be achieved if matter dematerialises into light and spirit, has already been attempted. The attempt failed, and the spirit froze to form a satellite, the moon. But now a new attempt is being heralded by the northern lights. Däubler was an irrationalist, believing that it is the emotions, or rather love, which governs the course of history, and he saw no separation between the animate and inanimate, rejecting, as he did, the inanimate universe of science which is reduced to matter and energy and lacks any cognate

Malcolm Green / INTRODUCTION

subject, believing that it will come to know itself through man (one hundred years before Stephen Hawkins theory!), hermaphroditically reunited as he was before the sexes split.

If Däubler (like Mombert) sounds like an odd bedfellow for the Expressionists, his irrationalism, his belief in overcoming the boundary between matter and spirit, and his vision of the new dawn of mankind were right up their street. Furthermore, his belief in the magic of the word and rhyme, and his linguistic experiments, did not merely anticipate those of the Expressionists — he was a real visionary (who heard poetic voices dictating his verse within him), just as the Expressionists often wished to be. On top of which, one can find a number of writers with views surprisingly close to his in this book.

Robert Musil also professed a form of Gnosticism, believing in a progressive spiritualisation of all living and dead matter (although I suspect that this is not what he is trying to show in his grotesque 'The Giant Agoag'), and parallel to Däubler's poetic anti-scientism, he considered meaningful connection to be a more important principle than causality, and placed analogy above logical conclusions. On a less anecdotal level, the celebrated grotesque writer Mynona (the pseudonym for Salomo Friedlaender) also showed strong parallels with Däubler. He too championed German Idealism, and his grotesques centred constantly around the desire to replace the scientific world-view with magic, fantasy and imagination. To this end he wished to destroy the barriers formed by scientific categories, especially between animate and inanimate, and the text 'A Child's Heroic Deed' is a keen parody of the enemy's way of thinking. Such typical statements as: 'Man projects his own lifelessness as natural laws' and 'People are eager to establish natural laws rather than recognise their intrinsic, inner, inexhaustible creative freedom', are akin to Däubler's views, both sharing the belief that the experienced poles in this universe are intrinsic states and not shades of one another (such that black is black and not a lack of white), only to be united in the nothingness which is the 'indifferent creative self' (Mynona), or a 'point beyond identity' (Däubler).

Turning now from other-worldly speculations, Carl Einstein presents this aspect in a very non-transcendental framework: his novella *Bebuquin* (the first four chapters included here were published earlier under the present title as a finished work) signalised the end of the novel form. The author put an end to the possibility of the psychologising, narrative preoccupations of mimetic writing, introducing a hero whose ego was already fragmented into several alternative egos, and whose world is an aphoristic collage of events. The figures in the story are looking for the ironically-termed 'wondrous', a unity of experience and explanation outside of human experience, and fail because the two can never be made congruent with one another. Einstein's characters are condemned to follow the shape of their thoughts and self-reflection, so that the fantastic gets raised inevitably to the level of logic, and this logic gets 'logicised' to its illogical ends. Here Einstein is showing that the human urge to unify and form a mental picture can never produce anything which corresponds with reality, but at the same time Einstein believed that we have to live with this urge. With true Nietzschean heroism, he construes human thought as an aesthetic riddle, as abstract as maths, a plaything worthy of a *des Esseintes*. Thus, rid of the naturalist novel form, Einstein proposed a dandyist 'literature for discriminating bachelors.'[5] He considered that it is the writer's duty to create an autonomous, imaginative poetic world, void of causality, associations and explanation, and as models of absolute writing he forwarded Mallarmé's *Hérodiade*, Flaubert's *Herodias*, Beardsley's *Under the Hill* and William Beckford's *Vathek*. For Einstein 'Beckford is the father of the present day writers who produce, without narrative development, in the fever of their often intellectual caprices; at the bottom of this artifice, where the material continues to grow, as it were, from ornamental literary associations,

Malcolm Green / **INTRODUCTION**

is an aesthetic pessimism, an anaesthetic for all that lives, a particularly nervous sensibility.'

Again we have an approach, in this case *l'art pour l'art* dandyism, which might seem a far cry from Expressionism (despite Einstein's rejection of objective truth, the use of monologic reflection, the livid scenery and the ironic search for a New Man we see in *Bebuquin*). However, the book was to have a broad influence on the early generation, most notably the fellow dandyish writers Lichtenstein, who took Bebuquin-Einstein's axiom: 'One must have the courage to live one's private madness, to take one's own death in one's hands and enforce it' for his own, and more radically (perhaps simply because unlike Lichtenstein, they survived the early war years), Hugo Ball and later Gottfried Benn.

When Hugo Ball, an incendiary early Expressionist, moved to Zurich in 1915, he was still greatly inspired by his contact with Wassily Kandinsky, who had desired a total, abstract theatre. (Kandinsky's piece 'Bassoon' is in fact a short play text.) Kandinsky envisaged the rebirth of art and society by uniting all artistic means and forces on one stage, and, taking this a step further, Ball saw the possibility of overthrowing rationality completely and creating a *Gesamtkunstwerk* which would break in on the unconscious, taking Kandinsky's societal rebirth to the level of man. The result was Dada, an unwieldy beast as it first manifested itself in Exile Switzerland in 1916 in the form of Cabaret Voltaire; it included recitals of works from 'revolutionary' writers — Frank Wedekind, the Expressionists Else Lasker-Schüler, Hardekopf, Lichtenstein, van Hoddis and Mynona, and the Dadaists Tzara, Marcel Janco and Hans Arp, as well as Expressionist dance and music from, among others, Reger, Liszt, Saint-Saens, Scriabin, Rachmaninoff, and even the occasional Russian balalaika orchestra! The Gallery Dada, a year later, featured recitals not only of Ball's shamanistic invocations, but also texts by Mynona, the Expressionist poet August Stramm and fellow exile and Dada friend, Albert Ehrenstein, and the earlier Zurich Dada publications also included the work of Ferdinand Hardekopf. The 'mad axeman' image of Dada, which was typified by Picabia and Sterner in Zurich and the post-war Berlin group, took a while to develop: for all the later polemic against the wet, wordy world-improver Expressionists, in its inceptions Dada drew strongly on the sort of early Expressionists who appear in this book.

Thus, although Ball could generalise with amusement in his diaries that the Dadaists were the aesthetically inclined species, whereas the Expressionists were the 'morallers', his other major inspiration beside Kandinsky was Einstein, and Ball's novel *Tenderenda* bears tribute to the influence of Einstein's *Bebuquin* and his essays. Here Ball assembled a number of fairly self-contained tableaus interspersed with 'hymns' and Dadaist ('shamanic') incantations to produce a truly 'absolute prose' work, 'a magical-archaic world, a lawless and thus enchanted world going to the point of absurdity', as he described it. Written between 1915 and 1920, *Tenderenda* charts the gradual emergence of Dada (he wrote in his diary: 'Dadaism — a masque, a peal of laughter? And behind that a synthesis of the romantic, dandyist and — demonist theories of the nineteenth century?') from the 'dandyhood of poverty', the boheme, and his subsequent (suitably dandyish) conversion to Catholicism. This wilful, non-representational book, which works hard to avoid a recognisable story-line, underlines the author's rejection of the utility and applicability of intelligence ('we are fantasts, we no longer believe in intelligence') and language debased to journalese. He deliberately availed himself of the absurd non-sequitur, while at the same time looking behind language for an inner mesh of language and meaning, reality as a series of resonances and distortions. In his diary he wrote: 'The important thing is to write unassailable sentences which withstand any criticism ... By eliminating the assailable syntax or associations, one upholds the sum of that which constitutes taste, tact and rhythm, and points to the author's style and loftiness.' *Tenderenda* and *Bebuquin*, both absolute prose, remain

Malcolm Green / **INTRODUCTION**

two of the most singular works of this century. The chapter I have chosen for this anthology from Ball's novel, 'Grand Hotel Metaphysics', is his highly idiosyncratic portrayal of the birth of Dada.

While Ball's search for meaning wandered from anarchism to Catholic conversion, Gottfried Benn's search for the 'new myth' crystallised in his concept of the 'southern' (a quite unintentional pole to Däubler's 'northern'!). In the text I have included, 'The Island', which is the key story in a cycle entitled *Brains*, we see Doctor Rönne's first major doubts about his life as a scientist. In lengthy passages, where Rönne reflects on the history of ideas, its development in the 'north' via Descartes to a water-tight system (here physiological psychology, where man has become reduced to a bundle of mental categories), Benn shows typical Expressionist self-alienation and a sense of the depersonal as a result of, in this case, the overdevelopment of the mind. Benn's answer is a myth of the 'Mediterranean Antique', a symbol of the immediate, acausal, exotic, pre-lingual and pre-logical which overcome the linguistic reflex to yield a drug-like, direct experience, a primitive communication with the object where self and other is dissolved. As such, Benn addresses both sides of the question of self: the trials of the modern dissociated ego, and the attempt to replace this with a new subjectivity. This is underlined by Benn's use of two different languages; a cold, very distant, reduced intellectual language to describe the empty, indifferent, senseless world of empiricism in which Rönne is trapped, and a rich Art Nouveau prose, partly in direct speech, to evoke a hallucinatory reality (a field of poppies, for instance, or a dream of mythical existence in the South Seas). With the almost solipsistic subjectivity Benn invested in his language (e.g. his transitive use of verbs, as in the famous example: 'An olive *happened* to him', where he attempted to convey the subjective 'itness' of the world), he was already stepping out on the path towards an acausal, autonomous poetry as Einstein wanted.

An acausal prose was also important to a number of the other writers in this anthology, such as Schwitters and Arp (who were important forefathers of 'concrete' or 'abstract poetry'), and can be seen in the majority of the pieces from the true Expressionists, in particular Trakl, Hardekopf, Herzfelde, Conrad Felixmüller and Paul Zech, with their various minglings of dream, delirium and vision with reality. Even if the aim is not as apparently refined as 'absolute poetry', the autonomous character of the subjective vision, which registers urges rather than intellectual frameworks, is a typical Expressionist characteristic. Similarly, the speculative is rarely missing, whether in the metaphysical notion of the New Man, or more concretely in the various reflections Ehrenstein, for instance, puts in Tubutsch's mouth on the arbitrariness of time and identity and the Nietschean recurrence of the same, or in Zech's quasi 'absolute philosophy' (which I have attempted to paraphrase in the notes on the authors) in 'The Terrace at the Pole'.

Gottfried Benn was also one of a number of writers who saw a strong similarity between Expressionist and Baroque writing, describing the former as 'faecal Baroque'.[6] The comparison is convincing on a number of counts — the love of sharp contrasts, the ecstatic style, the subjectivism, the daring imagery and extreme metaphors, a belief in inherent power in language and the consequent experiments which explored the 'inner rhythms' and took both towards concrete poetry and, in connection with this anthology, a love of wit and acumen — but above all in their conception of a mutable, malleable world created not of relations and relationships, but small, easily deformed chunks of reality tending to the unreal, pure abstraction and pure poetry.[7] A longing for the absolute, a reality behind appearances can often be seen in the background of both. Nature was seen by the Expressionists as amoral and seething with incomprehensible supernatural powers, or even as so alien to man's experience as to be a matter of indifference. It was no longer a source of rest and inspiration: with his blind urges or his fragmented

Malcolm Green / **INTRODUCTION**

subjectivity, Expressionist Man was left to grasp the flashes of his inner world, one moment in the turmoil of existence, and project them onto an uncertain fabric. Seen in this light, it is perhaps no wonder that the writing we are considering has a strong fantastic element. Indeed, fantastic metaphors[8] and the supernatural abound among even the most slice-of-life Expressionists: the Expressionist world is populated by machines turned into creatures; psychotic delusions; horrifying objects which, as in the case of *Bebuquin*, are 'forever trying to suck him up'; bizarre metamorphoses, as we already saw in the stories from Held, Panizza and Scheerbart; astral flights, as in Wolfenstein's 'Far Greater than Every Magic' or Hans Flesch-Brunningen's 'Metaphysical Canary', indeed, the whole gamut of tricks one finds in the fantasy genre.

That this element in Expressionism is largely overlooked is perhaps not surprising: fantasy writing is often considered escapist, decadent and anti-rationalist (in the negative sense) and resigned, and it is probable that many literary critics are wary of blurring the division between Expressionism and the enormous upsurge in horror and fantasy writing which took place in the same period, a problem the writers did not necessarily have at the time, as evinced by the tastes of the New Club. Fantasy in Expressionism does, however, tend to have a more serious function: even in the sheer delight or conceit that some writers (Mynona, Meyrink, Flesch-Brunningen, Ball, Schwitters, Lasker-Schüler) showed in simply taking ideas for a ride and letting loose a stream of wild associations, we see a radical denial of a society which cannot go forward and from which one cannot simply escape. Reason, good and evil, technology have no place in these worlds; the normal categories are suspended or distorted into the monsterous, and the freedom is seized to present the impossible and create new models which require no rational explanation because, if successful, their laws are self-evident.

Fantasy, then, was also a willing vehicle for polemics and

speculation, whether to put forward a belief in a magical world (Mynona), to illustrate the outbreak of a new, pre-linguistic reality (Benn), to create a new authority in the fabulous figures of the New Man (Felixmüller, Wolfenstein, Zech), or simply to show that the grotesquely nonsensical describes the world best (Ehrenstein and Kafka). And if we recall Einstein's models for absolute prose, fantasy is an intrinsic element: beside Beckford's *Vathek*, Einstein's models included Beardsley's *Under the Hill* and Swift's *Gulliver's Travels*, and both *Bebuquin* and *Tenderenda* speak for themselves.

But sometimes the texts seem to lose any polemical or programmatic character and the fantasy becomes strangely pregnant yet non-sequitor, as in Heinrich Schaefer's 'Sketches', Hardekopf's reverie, Hermann Ungar's 'Something Behind This', Kandinsky's 'Bassoon' or Trakl's 'Dream and Dementia'; the fantasy becomes autonomous, time starts to dislocate, a poetic consciousness is revealed in the surrounding objects, perception becomes synaesthesic and dream and reality are no longer separated. Here we see a writing which is approaching Surrealism, and in a number of cases, as in Trakl, who wanted to open up the unconscious, and rejected the poetic ego, the aims were stated in very similar terms. One can find a lot of parallels between Surrealism and Expressionism, such as the identification with the city; the celebration of the irrational, convulsive and chaotic; the interest in dream, hermeticism and madness; the black humour, the arch poses and wilful provocation; the demands for revolt, liberty and love; and both agreed that the poet's word and image have an existential function, and are even magical.[9] Above all, in both movements we see the attempt to overcome the distinctions between material-ideal, rational-irrational, objectivism-subjectivism. However, unlike Surrealism, Expressionism was largely anti-materialist and, in partial agreement with Lukács's criticism, it never found an ideology or alternative (such as the Surrealist method of automatic writing). In addition, Surrealism was never conceived of as a vehicle for strong emotions.

Malcolm Green / INTRODUCTION

Indeed, it would be simply glib to say that, on the basis of a few outstanding examples, Expressionism was proto-Surrealist: one could quite justifiably present Expressionism in the light of radical Christianity/Judaism, the roots of concrete poetry, nihilism, social verism, drug abuse, rural Expressionism (less justifiably, but the term does exist!) or even maudlin sentimentality (a lot of the Expressionist poetry collections had titles like *God's Violin* or *Affections!*). All this existed as well, and was anything but Surrealism. But at the same time it would be equally tendentious to say that, for all its gnostics, *l'art pour l'art* poetry, dandies, cynics, artificial paradises, calculated effects, drugs and so on, Expressionism was little more than a decadent hangover. We are back to the earlier question: What was Expressionism, and with that, is there a common ground between *fin de siècle*, Expressionism and Surrealism? The answer to the second question is easier: the common ground is a more or less explicit awareness of the gap between our experience and our knowledge of the world, one which is of great significance to the 'modern', not only during its inceptions in the last century, but also after the Second World War among such writers as Konrad Bayer and the rest of the Vienna Group in the late fifties, and a handful of battling writers in recent German letters. We are dealing here with a writing centred around a tension between self and society, self and object, or even self and self, the conscious and unconscious, and the many attempts at a solution.

In his book *Mannerismus in der Literatur*, Hocke claims that there is a recurring, anti-classical and anti-naturalistic 'constant' in European intellectual history which he terms 'mannerism'. He describes the mannerist writer, a generally neglected but fundamental European type, as a 'problematic person', the doubter and despairer who 'seeing the contradictions in his experience of this world ... as an 'absurd' whole, wants to make the opposites visible as a higher unity by means of manneristic art, and thus overcome their discord.' In Hocke's view, the mannerist arts 'are first and foremost involved with human tensions, which are to become visible by deformations, exaggerations or riddles', and span 'artistic nurturing of logistic acumen and demonic-vital expressive drive; painstaking, often far too painstaking, intellectual search and nervous frenzy in metaphoric chains of associations; calculation and hallucination; subjectivity and opportunism with regard to (anti-classical) conventions; delicate beauty and frightening strangeness; drug-like fascination and almost prayerful evocation; a tendency to stagger and amaze and a relaxed receptiveness to dreams; idyllic chastity and brutal sexuality; grotesque superstition and pious devoutness.' Here we have a viewpoint which lends a lot of support to the notion that there is common ground behind these various epochs, underlying, as it does, the concern with 'expressing', or 'overcoming', as with the Dada suspension of the question of identity of self and things, or Surrealism with its automatism, the human tensions involved. Furthermore, Hocke notes that by turning away from the classical world of proportion and seamless perfection and the artist's 'pinpoint' perspective, the artist explores the 'fault' in reality in the role of interpreter and inventor. With this he becomes 'embedded' in his reality, for his actions and consciousness no longer merely determine, they are an inseparable part of his creation. Thus, with this sometimes highly wilful mixture of calculation, artifice and emotion, he creates his own rules which also affect himself, and with this self-referentiality, his emotional life, the subjective, the painful inner limits and the underlying fears and desires, are brought to the fore with unusual intensity. Hence, in the search for new methods and languages which bridge the gap between creator and created, whether by Bohemianism, reformism, drugs, the highly self-referential absolute writing, psychic automatism, a primal, pre-lingual experience, reduced syntax or a scream, we see a further common denominator.

Turning to the first question, it is difficult at first to see Expressionism as anything but a microcosm of this 'mannerism'. This is

Malcolm Green / **INTRODUCTION**

further compounded by the protean nature of Expressionism which I have often referred to. However, as I said earlier, Expressionism distinguished itself through its 'urgency', the sudden explosion of creativity on all fronts, a rapid dissemination of new ideas, the acuteness of the sense of personal and societal crisis and the need to reaffirm the self, and its desire to break with the past, start afresh and address the problems directly, embracing the chaos rather than turning away from the world. This was combined with a naïve belief in radical change which failed to produce any viable ideology and, perhaps because of the extreme subjective emphasis of its solutions, was vague in its self-definitions and too global in the definition of its targets. Central, however, was the ideal of the New Man — whether a morally chastened man of action, an Einsteinian poet who could deal with the multiplicity of the self, or the man who followed his primal urges — and the renewal of language. As I have mentioned, the metaphysics of the New Man was to go hand in hand with a new language, and in connection with this it should be pointed out that the examples of speculative writing I have included are all concerned to a greater or lesser extent with the limits of language and analytic categories, as well as the possibilities (or in the case of Einstein, non-possibilities) of going beyond. Also characteristic of the Expressionists is an overabundance of theory which, rather like Münchhausen who tried to lift himself up by his bootstraps, championed the synthetic, anti-analytic and anti-rational. However, this apparent paralogia in the Expressionist polemics points to an essential characteristic of Expressionist writing: with its highly subjective nature which circles constantly around the pre-linguistic and as yet inexpressible, we find a meta-language. The typical Expressionist writing is one of movement or gesture. As ever, this had two sides, namely the attempt to liberate and renew communication, and the desire to control communication through archness and provocative disregard for convention. Although we will find plenty of both in these pages, the latter aspect brings us once more to the frequently dandyish stance adopted by the early Expressionists at a point when the polemic had not yet concretised. I said earlier that one starts to suspect that the young Expressionists first checked their poses before finding the objects for their rebellion, but now we can see this positively by looking more closely at the example of the dandy.[10] Not only is the *use* of language more important for him than the actual weight of its contents, he is also emphasising his own, often incommunicable subjectivity. Here we have a precedent for the gestural use of language in Expressionism, as well as for the anti-psychological and grotesque/fantastic writing we have been looking at: both remove the normal interpretative framework, substituting a highly subjective one which revolves around the pre-linguistic gesture. One could continue: the artifice, autonomy, 'absolute' quality of the dandyish gesture has already been shown in the extreme of absolute poetry, and the heroic stance Baudelaire recognised in the Dandy, as well as what he describes as the central issue of the dandy's nature, 'the disappearance and centralisation of the ego', will already sound familiar in the Expressionist context. The dandy's stance highlights the question of subject and object, blending as it does the creator and created, just as the Expressionists attempted to unite the artist and his product. Dandyism proper was not central to Expressionism, but the early experiments with the pose were a sign of the gestural language which was starting to permeate their writing, and which is reflected in this anthology. Besides occasional dandyism, the writers here distinguish themselves through an irony, a fine, cerebral over-sensitivity, an other-wordliness or even detachment, or an amoral, subversive, sensual play with ideas which contrasts with the generalised image of the suffering, vigorous, 'grainy', screaming, immediate, impulsive, black on white 'expressive' writer or 'awakener', which the very name Expressionism implies. Subjectivity? Yes — but a subjectivity which is suspicious of easy answers.

Malcolm Green / **INTRODUCTION**

A Closing Word

Many of the texts in this anthology are 'difficult', and have often a conciseness which is easy in German but cannot always be rendered into English. I have tried to do justice to the original word amalgams, dropped articles and bumpiness of the originals, and also avoid over-interpretation: what is unclear to the informed German reader has been left as originally ambiguous as possible. The few textual notes which seemed necessary can be found at the end of the book.

Finally, I have attempted to arrange these texts chronologically, dating them from the year they were written rather than the year they were first published. Although this principle is flawed, it does mean that posthumous works can be included (Ball, Kafka), and allows one to look inside the consciousness of a movement, rather than the history of its manifestations. Important in this context are, for example, the pieces from Ehrenstein and Einstein, written before the literary movement started, and Döblin's 'classic', 'The Murder of a Buttercup', which was written well before the first Expressionist painter set up his easel.

Notes

1 Arnold Armin, *Die Literatur des Expressionismus* (Stuttgart, Berlin: Köln, Mainz 1971).
2 Although historical Impressionism was the central target for the Expressionists' attacks, individual salvos were fired at neo-Romanticism, Art Nouveau and *fin-de-siècle* Symbolism and Decadence. I have used the word Impressionism here to summarise these various movements, which are often lumped together

under the title 'Stylistically Oriented Arts'. Common to them all is an optical orientation and the desire to register the minutest of subjective impressions.

3 One must be cautious before assuming that the changes in philosophy and the social and natural sciences were directly causal for the Expressionist consciousness. Although some writers knew Nietzsche's writings, for instance, it is probably more correct to say that the ideas were 'in the air'.

4 For an early Expressionist definition of this concept, I quote Kurt Hiller, the co-founder of the New Club, in his opening speech for the first Neopathetic Cabaret in 1910: 'Our concept of pathos is more or less the same as Nietzsche's: pathos not as the solemn pose held by the sons of the prophets, but rather as universal gaiety, as panicky laughter.'

5 Carl Einstein, 'Über den Roman', in the pivotal Expressionist magazine *Die Aktion*, 1912.

6 Although, generally speaking, Baroque art supported the status quo and has little in common with Expressionism, we can interpret the use of the word here as referring to the early 'mannerist' period. As Gustav Rene Hocke points out in his book *Mannierismus in der Literatur* (Hamburg, 1957) the reappraisal and interest during the twenties and thereafter in a literature previously condemned as florid and fustian centred almost entirely on the mannerist writing, which exhibited the characteristics listed here.

7 Einstein, writing in his essay *Vathek*, in which William Beckford's book is held up as a prize example of absolute writing, says: 'In *Vathek* we find a stylised rationality which is estranged from the organic.'

8 A common feature of Expressionist writing is the concretisation of the image, where an object is not given attributes in the 'like a ...' manner, but identified as the same.

9 Despite the presence of several German speakers in the Surrealist Group, German writing is very under-represented in

their excavations. The Expressionists remained virtually un-
discovered by them, whereas Panizza and Meyrink were justly
acclaimed.
10 I would like to point to W. Ihrig's excellent book *Literarische
Avantegarde und Dandysmus* (Literary Avant-garde and Dandyism)
(Frankfurt am Main, 1988), which tackles the role of the dandy
with great lucidity.

Franz Held

THE GOLDEN BOMB

(Ca.1890)

Resting unrestrained in its own strength, the joyously muscular statue of the Man-for-himself towered up with its full brazen nakedness in the Luxembourg Museum.

The artist (he was called Daru, I think — at the time I am telling this all of the catalogues have been lost ...), the sculptor had named his work 'L'âge de fer'. A mighty outstretched arm supports itself confidently on a spear. A conquered foe lies under the deadly, crushing weight of its right foot.

Grand Boulevard. In front of the Café Americain. A cold, merciless, winter night.

THE GOLDEN BOMB

A long, tired row of cabs stands in front of the windows of the silky venality. Half dead, patent shoe-tripping misery-men are driving fur-flattered salary girls in through the carriage doors. The brawny, shyly-despairing unemployed are shoving themselves down the dark side streets. Science calls this the 'survival of the fittest'.

The tattered work-willing are begging immaculately dressed whore-mongers for alms.

With piggish callousness, a gross, morbidly plump face in a red and blue striped silk neckerchief turns away a beggar-woman who is pressing an ashen pale child to her flat breast.

Did the man walking behind notice, with his steely Roman face?

On a bench, beneath the boulevard's snow-clad trees, on a corner by the sparkling café, is a ragged old man, slumped over as if paralysed. Body and thigh forming an acute angle. A stiff but crumpled hat lies in the snow next to the motionless form.

'Just watch this, Jeanne! I'll give this scab enough to booze with for a month. That'll be very rigoló … !'

And the fat man really does throw a gold coin into the shabby hat on the ground. The demi-mondaine screeches with laughter.

The man with the Roman face has followed the whole procedure. Once the pair have boarded the carriage, he shakes the old man to try to make him aware of his luck, before the gold piece is taken away by a passer-by (the mégo-'cigarette end' collector's hook is poking about nearby). But the old man can't be roused. His face is blue and swollen. Weakened by hunger, he has simply frozen to death on the bench.

The man with the Roman head takes the gold coin out of the dead man's hat and carries it off to his secret atelier where he has just finished making a dynamite bomb that same evening.

He gilds his bomb with the molten Louis-d'or.

The tool of destruction is round, a return to the 'cocotte en fonte' variety, for the 'marmite' type was already too well known to the police. No fuse, a percussion bomb. The next evening in the Café Americain. The market is in full swing, thoroughbred fillies are setting off their charms in flattering wraps and poses. Yesterday's dynamitard is scarcely recognisable as the fine gentleman who is now just entering.

With chamois-coloured kid gloves, he's carrying a spherical object, wrapped with a carefulness only matched by the cuteness of its teasingly frilled, blood-red tissue paper. He sits down on a plush sofa.

The demi-mondaine next to him assumes that there must be a bonbonnière in the red wrapped ball and insinuates herself on him with ingeniously lascivious witticisms. He lets her lift a corner of the tissue paper ...

She sees the large golden sphere. Her eyes flash with mad greed. Her thoughts stand still at the sight of this enormous lump of gold which must weigh in at a million at least. The women sitting nearby also crowd around the table, giving this icy cold Croesus-face their most inviting looks. He moves his hand over to the golden sphere with an elegant nonchalance — who will he give it to?!

A flash as bright as day. A roar like a collapsing mountain ...

The front of the café is torn clean away. Right across the boulevard, as far as the Maison doreé, lie supple, shapely legs in tasty, blood-speckled lacy knickers; headless and limbless torsos, with wild breasts bursting from their torn sateen corsets. Like the torsos of statues of Venus. All around lie extremities of the highest note, just like that, within the reach of just any old down-at-the-heel Sans-le-sou layabout.

Horror. Trials. A few mistaken executions. But the perpetrator doesn't get caught.

Vendettas and fusillades of repression. In one go the military court sentences twenty new bomb-throwers to the guillotine.

This time the thrower of that particular bomb was among the culprits (in memory of his ingenious idea, his fellow conspirators had honoured him with the name 'Tête-dorée').

The grey inner courtyard of La Roquette prison, opened to the public for the executions, sees an unheard orgy of greedy gaping and adverts for the demi-mondaines.

Ecole de Medécine, near the merry Boul. 'Mich'. The twenty severed heads lie on a marble table in the anatomical hall of France's most famous physiologist (Grand Cross of the Legion of Honour). Tête dorée is the first. All of them are men's heads, with one exception. This one had belonged to a merely theoretical anarchist, a woman who had condemned all acts of violence. But the court hadn't believed her.

There stands the scrawny scholar with the fine, dissecting-knife coldness of his face, talking excitedly among a large group of colleagues. He's giving a description of the highly interesting experiment to which he has invited them all.

He wants to place the decapitated heads under the influence of a very strong galvano-electric current. His secret: how the current will be carried into the very finest of the cerebral ganglia.

The gentlemen are all highly animated after a lavish breakfast. The stale smell of blood overwhelms the exquisite aroma of their Egyptian cigarettes. The cosy wreathes of blue smoke drift off over the gaunt, dead faces — the dissecting table is right beside a very large, wide open window. The smoke draws off into the open air, out into the heavy, thunder-laden July sky.

Twenty copper wires run out of a single mighty battery, one into each of the holes in the gaping, brownish-red spinal columns. Even if nineteen of the brains don't react, the twentieth might be just the right one.

Now!

The current surges into the nerve branchings of the cortices, and then on into the twistings of the grey matter. Now it's entering Tête-dorée's cerebrum ...

Up until now, the lifeless head had maintained a deep, peaceful expression. Now, as the facial muscles slowly set themselves back into action ('only reflexes!' the legionnaire reassures his gawping, horror-struck colleagues), those hollow, yellowed cheeks, covered with a prickly stubble from the trimmed black goatee, and that bloodless cramped mouth, are twisted once more into their old expression of fanatical disgust and frozen rage.

Tête-dorée raises his lids — all the doctors turn ashen grey — and gives the deeply bowed, peering legionnaire a look of white, satanic hate.

The other nineteen pairs of eyelids just twitch quietly at first. But now the nobly formed woman's head opens its eyes. Therein lies something of the transfigured blue of a soft sky as it shines down on the blood-soaked earth.

What's that?! No doubt about it — the raging head wants to open its lips!

The doctors reach for their fortifying nerve tonics. Some of them land their breakfasts back up in front of them.

The compassionate head moves its lips too, imploringly, entreatingly. The tender woman's mouth now manages to choke out a few words:

'Madness! Repent yourselves!'

But the wrathful head, jaws stretched wide open, sticks out a scornful tongue at the doctors, and all the other male heads follow suit.

The doctors huddle together, stricken pale. One goes crazy and jumps out of the window, three storeys down to the street.

Tête-dorée also now manages to spit out a word-like groan. At first a dull, croaking, chewing, gurgling rattle. Now he's clearly crowing out the word 'Dogs!'. And all the other eighteen corpses's gullets repeat 'Dogs!' after him with a snort.

The scholar had an apparatus at the ready, with which he could galvano-plastically coat the faces in gold in order to pin-point certain of the more elusive muscular contractions. (Besides this, the contrivance was used to make moulds from whole corpses for the construction of monuments.)

He sets the machine in action, so as to bung up these ghastly gobs. But seized by a stroke he can no longer turn off the current. So the heads get coated with a thick crust of gold — and they are transformed into golden balls.

The rest of the doctors have also collapsed dead to the floor.

For a while the twenty brains remain fully active, despite their metallic encapsulation. But they haven't any blood. Thus they are forced to repeat automatically the acts of the last seconds of their lives. So they hop about the marble slab with a lightheartedness the half of which they had had to stifle in the guillotine basket. And then (with the exception of the woman's head) they spring out of the window like rubber balls ...

They fall with enormous speed, as if they had been filled with lead. In fact the influence of the electricity has turned their brain matter into — dynamite.

And they crash down onto roofs and pavings. An explosion, the streets are blasted, split, hurled, rattling, smoking, far and wide.

Fires have broken out all over, melting the skull fragments of the golden bombs. There, like dancing beads of quicksilver, all the little golden heads roll together into one gigantic golden head. It grows, swollen up from inside like a balloon. Is it inflating itself by snorting back its snarls of revenge?

A river of gold flows out of the burning Banque de France, up to the golden head which greedily slurps it up. Now it is as tall as the dome of the Panthéon. In a mammoth rage, the bristly, yellow Goliath's head (with stubble formed from the thorn-like church spires it has speared up) stares out from its red, flaming sockets. Slowly the two bulging, cratered lips push themselves carefully apart — a mountain splitting bang ...

Paris is over.

But as the other heads had danced out of the window, the compassionate one had sprouted a pair of dove's wings. A winged, golden sphere, it flew up to the new moon and whispered the whole shocking story into its ear, so that the moon blanched with shock. Now the new moon has become a full moon — up above a destroyed Paris whose once towering monuments have been stamped flat beyond recognition, as was Ravachol's grave by the police — a colossus has formed, as tall as Notre Dame, from the hundreds of thousands of severed heads. With a hop it sets off for the great cities of Europe. First, off to London.

Now the full moon spreads out its web of moon-beams, spun out of self-interest held in check by good common sense, around the temerous monster — and it sinks to the ground.

Up out of the rubble grows the joyously muscular statue of the Man-for-himself as nature had intended. Its crushing right foot presses down on the neck of a foe.

The conquered enemy is wearing the robes of the public prosecutor.

Oskar Panizza

THE CRIME IN TAVISTOCK SQUARE

(1891)

> We should always take care not just to find man guilty; sin is lurking everywhere, in all nature, hidden by a fine veil
>
> *Swedenborg*

About ten years ago my father, wishing to see me educated in both the English administration of justice and the English language, sent me to London. With the help of a number of letters of introduction, which were not completely without effect, I succeeded in ending up under the wing of a secretary of state in the Ministry of Justice who, as I well knew, maintained excellent relations with the Minister himself. 'Young man!' said the former at the end of an interview he granted me, 'I know that as a German you will above all be thirsting for knowledge, and since you will be finding out about lower court practice primarily here with us, I will

Oskar Panizza / THE CRIME IN TAVISTOCK SQUARE

refer you to *Sir Edward Thomacksin*, the chief of the *metropolitan police station in Marylebone Street*. Don't let yourself be put off by the old chap's couple of quirks; he is a fount of knowledge and acquainted with something of your system over in Germany, and in no time at all you'll find yourself familiar with the procedures of civil law. And so it just remains for me to say — all the best!' I gave a bow and the audience was over. For those unfamiliar with English ways, I would just like to note that every offence in England, however great or small, every crime or infringement of the law is first dealt with at the *police station* of the district in question; and there it is decided whether the matter can be dealt with on the spot, or must be referred to a higher court, *the assizes*. Should the crime be of a simple nature, then a sentence is passed at once and the important question is decided, namely whether the culprit is to be placed under arrest or set free. If it is of a more serious nature, he is generally kept in custody and handed over to the higher court.

Mr Edward Thomacksin — or *Sir Edward* as they say there — was an original in the best sense of the word. For me the man was more of a mine of information about the English character than its jurisdiction, which I must admit, after two weeks was of no more interest to me than the jurisdiction of any other country. He was a tall, gaunt man with a clean-shaven face, a thin, snapping fish mouth, a long nose with large nostrils and greyish-blue invigilating eyes behind which a treasure of ardent thoughts was always at the ready. Forever dressed in the same worn-out black coat, his sole aspiration in his duty was not so much to judge according to right and righteousness, but rather to collect material for his special views and projects with respect to the condition and education of the human heart. Given this purely spiritual viewpoint, one could to some extent forgive the arbitrary manner in which he executed his duty. He was an inquisitor. And the punishing of a man for his improvement was not as important to him as the analysis of the inner springs of action within the offender's personality. The first time I met him, he stared at me for several minutes with an almost ferocious look, and said with a wary eye, hesitantly and with strong emphasis: 'Young friend, I am not sure that your eye exhibits enough good sense to be up to the moral task that awaits you here!' This first address left me not a little perplexed, and the days that followed brought more surprises of the same sort. But soon I had grown used to his peculiar way of expressing himself. With the open-heartedness characteristic of the English, he had, in the course of the first weeks, initiated me into his entire philosophical system. He was a follower of Swedenborg. He believed in a process of progressive purification of humanity which ineluctably led to Godliness. He had his own highly personal opinions and suggestions as to how this result was to be obtained. For him it was sensual pleasure and everything to do with it which stood in the way of the desired spiritualisation of humanity. This *lust*, as he referred to it, was what he aimed to destroy.

When he spoke the word '*lust*', his face took on an unspeakably hard and wild expression; his grey merciless eyes gave me a look as if they had been worked from marble and his drawn lips showed the hardness of the hangman. 'Young man!' he said to me one day during an hour of the most confidential conversation in which I felt he was sharing his most intimate thoughts with me, 'if I could eliminate the factor of sensual pleasure from the calculus of the human reproductive act, then we would have won. Swedenborg was a good man; but his aims remained hanging in the air. I believe I have given you the outline for the most certain and effective means of attaining the greatest possible likeness to God. I am now nearly seventy and will consider my life's task complete when I know that my fellow men have stepped onto the path I have indicated. We must remove *lust*, the bestial component, from the act of reproduction, without disturbing propagation itself; the path must pass between these two rocks ... Study, young man, study, so that we may reach our target! My mathematical and scientific library, apart from my collected manuscripts, is at your disposal'. But for this, *Mr Thomacksin* was a warm, friendly man, kind-hearted. He dealt with every offence with the greatest leniency; but woe betide if an incident arose out of the sexual realms and its outrages! Then he let the full weight of the law descend and, I believe, he even happily transcended the legally prescribed limits. He treated thieves with a touching leniency. If somebody had merely stolen a loaf of bread, he left without a fine, so long as he was simply poor. 'He was quite right!' he said to me once during a court sitting as he let a bread thief from *Mincing Lane* not only go free, but with a gift of money, 'He was quite right; he has to live and eat too, otherwise he won't be able to think; and to improve himself he must first of all do some excellent thinking! He was absolutely right! Why do the bakers make their bread with such an appealing crust! I also liked the fact that he chose such a fine shop.'

Before I touch further on the curious case which is the subject of the present story, I must draw a quick sketch of another person from *Sir Edward's* milieu, one who, although he held a subordinate position in the police force, is a major figure in the episode I am about to put before you. Jonathan was from the lower ranks of the police, one of those who walked the beat in the local area. He was a fine, young blond lad of delicate appearance, with large shining eyes, a girlish, insinuating voice, lily-white hands, in short the sort of person who, it is obvious from the first glance, is made of superior human material, and stood out noticeably from the majority of the coarser sort of police. As I heard it, *Sir Edward* had had the man transferred from an unimportant job in order to work in his district as a *policeman*. The fact was that in his work the chief liked dealing with nobody more than Jonathan; and that Jonathan, whose way of life was so completely at variance with that of his colleagues, was only able to keep in with them because he was sometimes able to provide them with otherwise unobtainable privileges and alleviation of duty through his intercession with *Sir Edward*. And if I might venture a personal opinion, then it seemed to me that Jonathan was not just an obedient and dutiful servant, but that he had also taken the peculiar doctrines of his chief for his own, and that with a certain amount of enthusiasm.

It must have been about six or eight weeks later; I was watching the proceedings of the law courts in *Marylebone Street* day in, day out, with enormous interest — less on account of the difficult points of law, the somewhat trifling offences of city vagrancy which were being adjudicated, than for the original rulings which my chief chose to make, often against popular opinion and the strict paragraphs of the law. Not infrequently I would be astonished at the fine instinct and perceptiveness of *Mr Thomacksin* who, immoveable, knew well how to disarm the misdoers engaged in bashfully disavowing their deeds, with a particular and never-failing method. Generally one could tell from the faces of the policemen and the voices from the ante-room just what sort of case was at hand. For there, in the ante-room, the court messenger, or the policeman just returned from his beat, would convey the criminal news to his comrades with a few catchphrases; and usually there would be a few older sergeants who would pass an infallible judgement as to the nature of the person in connection with the facts at hand, such that when he was at last brought before *Sir Edward*, a sort of atmosphere or aura had already formed around the invisible core of the complicated incident which was to be cleared up.

Mr Thomacksin and I were sitting in the law court one afternoon, engaged in animated conversation — as always when nothing new or essential was at hand but while the building was still open. It was that time between spring and summer when dusk still arrives early, and the gas flames, covered with enormous shades which threw dark shadows over the chief and messengers alike, had just been lit. The chief had just taken up his favourite theme: Swedenborg, his good ideas, but his doing things by halves when it came to the practise; complete confusion as to the ways and means; and the method

Oskar Panizza / THE CRIME IN TAVISTOCK SQUARE

which he, *Mr Edward Thomacksin*, had discovered after thorough investigations. 'Cut them out, the sensual pleasures, those horns on which everything ends up torn and bloodied, and then everything will be fine,' he shouted emphatically, and then he began to quote a long chapter from Darwin which explained that a function which has been left to itself over the centuries and taken on quite unforseen characteristics can, through planned suppression, be eradicated in a few decades ... At this moment we were interrupted by a confused murmuring from the ante-room. *'Don't! Don't! Don't! None of your stories! No slander!'* In this way the opinions of one policeman were being thrown back and forth among the others. The chief furrowed his brow at this disturbance. At last the door opened and Jonathan entered in the prescribed outfit, complete with black cloth helmet, a hand axe and a lantern in his hand. *Sir Edward* turned round. He was always more friendly to Jonathan than to the others. 'What's the matter?' he called out, then added, 'I have important matters to discuss with my young friend here; don't bother me with trifles! ... Has somebody put their hand in the wrong pocket again?' 'No, *Sir!*' said Jonathan, deeply excited, 'something extraordinary has occurred!' *Sir Edward* now turned to look straight at the speaker. The ring of conviction and vibration in his voice were signs which no-one with the knowledge of men possessed by the chief could miss. 'Where have you come from, Jonathan?' he asked. 'I've come from home, *Sir*,' answered the young man, 'I've hesitated all day and thought about whether I should officially report my observations from last night, but with my trust in your lordship, my trust in your wisdom, *Sir*, and my duty, I must lay a charge.' 'What's happened? Speak up man!' cried *Mr Thomacksin*, and he straightened himself in his chair. From the ante-room there came a low muttering and suppressed laughter. '*Sir*,' Jonathan started, 'as I was walking my beat last night, through *Tavistock Square*, I shone my lamp through the twigs, and I saw ... how shall I put it ... it's impossible to put into words, *Sir* ...' 'The Devil take you and your lamp if you're going to

41

say you didn't see anything!' 'I did see something!' 'What did you see?' 'It was in the southern corner of the park, where a clump of roses and magnolias stand next to each other!' 'What was going on? Did you see someone beneath them?' 'I didn't see anybody, Sir, the clump was on its own.' 'The Devil, then what was the matter?' 'Sir, there was giggling coming from the hedges!' 'There was giggling coming from the hedges? Good, did you catch the giggler?' 'No, Sir!' 'Wouldn't have advised it either, Johnny! Everybody in England is allowed to giggle beneath rose and magnolia bushes, if they have any.' 'Sir, that wasn't it! It wasn't human giggling; it was something suspicious, and glittering stuff fell to the ground from the large flower-cups of the magnolias, and an unchaste odour emanated from the place; and like a bolt of lightning the thought went through my head, Sir!' 'Jonathan, I don't understand you. Take heed of what you're saying!' The policeman stood there in a fever of emotion, his eyes glowed; the young, blond, delicate man stood there in his rough black uniform like a young preacher. 'Sir, it was an inconceivable event!' the policeman continued, 'I may not be able to give you all the details to support my opinion ...' 'Tell me your opinion, Jonathan, and leave out the details.' The policeman struggled with his feelings but only came out with — 'I can't!' 'Of course you can tell me your opinion, Jonathan,' said *Mr Thomacksin*. 'Sir, the English language is not able to grasp these abominations!' At this point, *Sir Edward* turned to me, showing two rows of bared teeth, and said, quietly. 'You see what calibre of man we have! What a classical turn of phrase! A wonderful lad! Eh? ... I have taken trouble in training him ...' Then louder, to Jonathan, 'Right my lad, now tell me straight what you saw!' 'Sir,' the young policeman continued in his fever, 'it was under the roses and magnolias ...' 'I know that already, Jonathan; what happened?' '... Movements, like those ... policemen often make at night in their beds ...' 'Johnny,' the chief spoke with paternal warmth to his subordinate, 'locomotives make certain movements, and policemen make other particular movements at night in bed, that's no criterion, you must express yourself exactly. What did you see?' 'Sir, it was sickening; a crime against nature: I stood rooted to the spot; I couldn't help myself!' 'Didn't you think to whistle?' 'Sir, there was nothing to whistle about!' 'You could have whistled all the same!' 'Sir, it wasn't a case for whistling!' 'But with the strangeness of the case, as you put it, it would still have been advisable to inform your colleagues on the next corner by whistling!' 'Sir, the matter was so little suited to such action, that the very possibility of using my whistle was ruled out directly!' 'Johnny, now listen: the predisposition of the matter does not bear any relation to the possibility of putting the whistle to your lips!' 'Very good, Sir, the possibility of whistling was not ruled out; but on the one hand I did not consider the event necessitated calling for material assistance; on the other hand, it went well beyond the point of merely whistling for help! In other words, it was *extraordinary*, but not dangerous — apart from which, had I attempted to blow a note, it would have stuck in my throat.' With this the judge turned his head to me again with that peculiar expression which exposed both rows of his teeth, commenting quietly: 'A splendid chap! He could be a theologist, a sophist, a follower of Swedenborg, anything. I don't consider that his career has been finally decided upon. Have you his like in Germany?' I said no with a shake of my head. *Sir Edward* then carried on adroitly in a loud voice: 'Well then, Johnny, you didn't whistle, that much seems certain; now get to the point and tell us, what did you see?' 'Sir, I must repeat what I've said already, it ...' 'What you've said up to now,' interrupted the judge, 'is absolutely nothing; nobody can make head or tail of it. You must get to grips with the facts of the case; and most importantly tell us the scoundrels' names!' 'Sir, it's not a matter of scoundrels in the normal sense of the word.' 'In what sense then?' the chief put in abruptly. 'In the sense of the Sublimely-Inhuman!' Once again *Sir Edward* nodded his head at me and whispered: 'That is Swedenborg!' then out loud 'Why didn't you set to?' 'I was afraid of disturbing them

Sir. First of all I wanted to watch the abomination to the end!' 'What abomination?' 'I don't know!' 'What form did it take?' 'It was madness.' 'What sort of madness?' 'There were contacts, *Sir,*' the policeman shouted and he took a deep gulp of air, 'such as are not allowed before God and the world, there were fondlings, denudations, emptyings, there were giggles, slurring, a renunciation, an entwining, a sort of kissing ... a kissing, *Sir* ...' 'Yes, in the name of three Devils, didn't you see anybody? Didn't you use your lamp?' '*Sir,* there was no one there. The roses and magnolias were alone. And the noises and touchings were not human either.' 'Not human?' asked the chief, 'but what was it then?' '*Sir,*' the fanatical young policeman cried and sobbed, 'the roses and magnolias in *Tavistock Square* were practising self-conception — it was veritable botanical onanism!'

At this, *Mr Edward Thomacksin,* chief of *Marylebone Street police station,* sprang up as if he had been bitten by a tarantula. For a moment the gaunt old man stared, glassy eyed, at the defiant young policeman, his thoughts, it seems, taking a new turn as a result of young Jonathan's account. Then, realising that there could be no mistake, the despairing Swedenborgian stretched out his arms stiffly and with an altered, wailing voice such as I had never heard from him before, he cried out to the ceiling: '*Lord, holy Lord,* turn away thine eye from thy creation! The roses, chastest of all flowers, have blithely copied the most abominable of mankind's crimes. Lord, they no longer await your permission to commit this infernal deed. Thou hast given them the ability to propagate. But that is not enough for them. They want to sin at any price. Lord, despatch a new flood, and damn thy creation, or the world will fall apart!' Then *Thomacksin* fell to the floor sobbing, his face as white as mortar, and he had to be carried out.

Shortly after this incident I left London, and had quite forgotten the affair. Only many years later did I accidentally have the opportunity to talk with a friend about the latest news from London. *Sir Edward,* I heard, had shortly after received a highly influential and remunerative position as a high court judge and was prospering. He had also become very fat. It was only poor Jonathan who landed in the madhouse.

Alfred Mombert

ICE

(1901)

I lay in twilight, a breathing wave on the sea. I dreamed. In a long, pleated, moiré robe of deep lustrous blues and reds. Foaming, flashing braids encircled its seams and ran over my breast. My hair flowed untied, white-wavy spindrift. All around me was the sea, endless, clear as glass, green. And for ages I lay there in peace.

But with time I started to think. I thought: 'How glorious it would be to rest on those clear, green meadows among the white blossoms.'

And now a deeper swell rose up in the rocking surface of the sea. It pitched, it sank sloping down to one side. And we, the billows, slowly started to slide down in that direction. One after the other.

Alfred Mombert / ICE

I lay tenderly bedded between forms as clear as glass: I was holding white blossoms between my fingers, as if in a vase. With a gentle spin I glided onto green, crystal meadows. And everything was so clear and transparent, that I myself became transparent: clear translucent ice.

I glided softly ...
into the 'Ice works: Bender and Sons.'

One Mr Bender said: 'Ten pounds of ice must be dispatched immediately.'

At once I was on my way, carried in a bucket. Soon enough I lay in a refrigerator at home. Deep in thought. They had closed the lid on top of me. I could feel the grey, woollen cloths. I thought: 'Now the cottager is lighting the fire.' 'Her clogs are clattering.' 'Pots are being shifted.' 'The tap is running, now the water will be put on the stove.' 'The kitchen stool is always in the way.'

A rattling, scraping, crackling, buzzing.

Suddenly I noticed that I was melting away at the bottom. I was melting: very slowly, but steadily. I thought: Yes, now I understand, that's just the way ice melts every day. It's much warmer here than at sea. Steadily: drip, drip, drip, onto the iron plate below, drop by drop. How will it all end. What will become of me. Dread fear. I seized up, I iced myself together. If only a very tiny, minute little piece of the poor dear thing would survive. Just a tiny piece. I gave a crack and then I hurt all over. And I became cloudy, grimy, earthen-yellow, appalling.

In the end I was in a truly dreadful state; I exuded the hideous stench of mortal fear. Someone said: 'We've never had a piece of ice like that before. That's not even real ice.'

I was returned to the factory as 'unusable.'

I now lay in a large, moss-covered building; without a roof. Between thick, ancient, brick walls. Very small and miserably exhausted. Stacked above and below me were large blocks of ice; a lot of them. I could see through them in every direction. A lot of men in white coats and green aprons were walking back and forth along the gangways between. They worked with sharp axes. But one of them was wearing a deep blue pleated coat and moved more nobly than the rest. Otherwise they were simply white ice-men. And a night came with ghastly black clouds. It raged and stormed. And then the sea came roaring up to the factory. I heard the voice of the sea from the centre of the storm; wild-rattling silver chains. I couldn't stand it any more, poor little thing that I was. I wept. I wept scorching tears. The sea looked at me, peered through the multitude of clear ice-blocks which could not conceal me. I knew: it had come because of me. Its penetrating gaze alighted on me, a miserable, filthy scrap of ice.

Everyone was up and on the move. For the sea was there. I heard the booming voice of the factory chief giving orders. It all seemed very serious, solemn. And now the negotiations started between the sea and the factory chief. On the one side a human voice, sharp and clear, defying the storm. On the other came a dull raging and roaring from out of the night, rattling chains shaking horrifically backwards and forwards.

The sea demanded I return to its empire as its charge. Its wrath was terrible. It didn't want me back in the miserable state I was in, and threatened to destroy the entire factory.

I lay there between the blocks of ice and wept, wept with unbearable joy, shaken by convulsive home-sickness for the sea. Everything around me started to crash and collapse. The factory chief stood tall with an enormous axe in his hands. The axe sparkled harshly above me. I fell in a faint.

Waking, I hung far away in the dawn, washed to the edge of the sea, far away among green billows. I hung there very tired and weak. Although everything about me whispered and roared, I was mute, voiceless. A small sheet of clear, mute ice. I now woke and slept contentedly in the waves green-dawning play of light. Green-dawning ages.

Alfred Mombert / ICE

Then came an epoch during which the silver tip of a mountain range emerged from the distant depths of the sea. The mountains grew and rose, many silver years long, while my gaze was glued motionlessly to them. Its image reflecting ever onwards through my silent layers. It grew steadily closer and very vivid, with its thick, snow-glistening faces and glades and waterfalls. I remained quite silent and was content. One day the mountain range arrived. I clung to it. It pulled me from out of the glassy currents. The sun rose. I floated up on high; high above all baseness.

I hung free, a heavenly sparkling icicle, from the frozen ice face. Lit through and through by fine beams of light. In the depths were immeasurable fields of glistening snow; far below was the sea, the dancing, rejoicing sea.

'Gold and crystal' — said a little girl who sat below in a skiff.

A gentle clinking. Up here a splinter of clear crystal cracked from me with a chink, fell with an inner play of sparkling colours into the field of light. Through golden aureoles of light. Into the sea. Yet another splinter. And another. Flashing down into the sea.

I jingled in the most sublime of lights.

And from the depths resounded the silver chains, which were resting there on the floor.

Paul Scheerbart

CASCADING COMETS

(1902)

What's happening?
It's getting so close and constantly darker.
There are flashes of lightning but no thunder.
Now there is a whistling up above, piercing like locomotives afraid to enter a tunnel.
And now hailstones are plummeting down, large hailstones and small hailstones. They are not round but pointed with edges, like badly hewn sugar.
But it is not sugar — it tastes cool and appetising.
And now there is a roar from the clouds above.

Paul Scheerbart / CASCADING COMETS

The clouds flash past like lightning.

A storm whirls across the land.

The trees snap, the roof tiles fly away along with flower pots, people's hats and the fluttering crows, far off — into the open country.

And it is hailing and raining.

The rain tastes as cool and appetising as the hailstones.

There is something strange about this hail and rain.

The professors drive up to the town hall in their finest coaches and hold lengthy discussions; all the professors have hailstones in their hands, some even have bottles filled with the new rainwater.

The professors hold splendid discourses, and all the while it is raining and hailing outside, harder and harder.

And the storm wails — wails.

In the town hall the clever professors explain that it is not ordinary hail — nor is it ordinary rain.

And they all take a taste of the hailstones and drink the rainwater.

And they say that they contain a new substance — a comet must have exploded in the sky — it definitely must have been a comet.

The new substance is Comet Salt.

But it has such an odd effect.

Whoever tastes the new salt feels a sort of softness which permeates every limb, and their thoughts become so simple.

The Comet Salt is as seductive as alcohol.

But the Comet Salt does not burn the back of the mouth or the belly below, does not inflame — it makes one satisfied — quiescent.

Soon the people with the salt in their stomachs can no longer collect their thoughts. For them it is as if everything were gone.

And then they remain standing and go no further, their limbs become stiff and hard as wood, and the upheld arm will not fall again; the hand which has raised a hat in greeting remains holding the hat in the air.

Gradually the storm abates and the weather improves again.

Now in the bright sunshine one can at last see the extent of the whole matter.

On the parade ground are ten wet soldiers standing bolt upright on one leg, and the raised legs will not go back down again. A baker's wife gives one of the soldiers a shove sideways and all ten of them fall like wooden soldiers from a toy box.

The air is quiet once more.

And the people lick the Comet Salt which covers the ground in piles. The animals lick the Comet Salt as well.

And one by one all the people and animals, in the streets and in their homes, remain standing, sitting or lying in strange positions.

The dogs' mouths remain open.

The birds turn somersaults in the air and fall with stiffened wings onto the heaps of salt, and move no more.

A funeral procession stands in front of a church and can go no further.

The trees similarly become stiff. The weeping willows and the weeping birches freeze in the positions they've been blown into by the wind — branches blown wide apart — as if the great storm were still raging.

And the air is so still.

And the people and animals are also so still, as if they no longer know what to say. A policeman sits motionless on a bench beside a tramp — they look at one another ceaselessly.

A regiment of decorated night-watchmen stands in front of the town hall, continually ready for inspection.

The children are no more to be heard in school — they all are so quiet.

And in the town hall the professors are sitting around like wax dummies.

The Mayor, who had not touched the salt, drags himself wearily home, drinks a glass of water in an easy chair by his writing desk

Paul Scheerbart / CASCADING COMETS

and sees his wife by the oven — she is as motionless as a departed spirit.

The Mayor throws his hands to his face and gives a sudden cry of anguish.

'Franziska! It's the new era!'

But he can no longer close his mouth — the salt has got to him too — it was in the drinking glass.

The terrible Comet Salt is everywhere!

The king sits on his throne in his residence and clasps his sceptre — but he no longer rules — for all his subjects are as stiff as himself.

However, none of the paralysed loses consciousness; their brains just function a little slower.

Their eyes retain their sight.

Their ears hear; but there is not that much to be heard.

A whole load of salt pillars on every corner and along the middle of the road!

Living pillars of salt!

They sit as if permanently lost in thought — stand as if they had forgotten something — lie, as if in the act of composing a fine poem — not one of them moves a finger.

The whole surface of the earth has become completely rigid.

*

And after seven days the heavens turn dark once again.

And a storm comes once again.

And the storm whirls the animals and people together like withered leaves.

Chimney sweeps fall from the roofs; workers and soldiers, women and children, roll around the alleys like barrels, their limbs snapping off without bleeding.

*

And then it becomes still again.
    And gradually everything changes.
    The houses slowly collapse.
    The branches of the trees fall off like icicles.
    Pillars burst, monuments and towers fall apart with a crash.
    And then a dark dust trickles down onto the earth.
    The dust covers everything — even the waters and the seas.
    Another comet must have exploded. The dust-covered globe continues to turn.

Alfred Döblin

THE MURDER OF A BUTTERCUP

(1904)

Walking up the broad path through the fir trees to St Ottilien, the gentleman in black first of all counted his footsteps, one, two, three — up to a hundred and back again. With each step he swayed his hips so vigourously to the left and right that he sometimes staggered. Then he gave up his counting.

His friendly bulging hazel eyes stared at the ground passing beneath his feet, and his arms swung from his shoulders so that his white cuffs fell halfway over his hands. Whenever the reddish-yellow evening sun shone through the trees and made him blink, his head twitched and his hands made hasty, indignant, defensive movements. The thin cane in his right hand bobbed along the grasses and flowers on the edge of the path and amused itself with the blossoms.

As the gentleman continued in his calm and carefree way it got entangled in the sparse weeds. The serious-minded gentleman did not think to stop, but strolled on giving the handle a slight tug. But he was held firmly; he gave an injured look over his shoulder, tore, at first in vain and then successfully, the cane free with both fists, and stepped back breathlessly, giving two swift glances at the cane and the grass so that the gold chain on his black waistcoat bobbed up and down.

Quite beside himself, the portly man stopped for a moment. His stiff hat was perched on the back of his head. He fixed his gaze on the tangled flowers, then charged at the mute vegetation with his cane raised high, thrashing away at it, his face a bloody red. Blows whistled to the left and right. Leaves and stalks sailed over the path.

The gentleman gave a loud snort and walked on, his eyes flashing. The trees strode quickly past; the gentleman paid attention to nothing. He had a snub nose and a flat, beardless face — an aging baby face with a sweet little mouth.

At a sharp corner where the path rose up he realised it was time to pay attention again. Marching more calmly, he wiped the sweat irritably from his nose and in doing so, he felt that his face was completely distorted, that his chest was wheezing heavily. He started at the thought that someone might see him — one of his business friends perhaps, or a lady. He stroked his face and, with a furtive hand movement, convinced himself that it was smooth.

He was walking quite calmly. So why was he wheezing? He gave a bashful smile. He had leapt at the flowers and butchered them with his cane, yes, beaten away with those powerful but well aimed sweeps of the hand he was accustomed to administer to his apprentices' ears if they were not sufficiently skilful at catching the flies in his office and presenting them to him arranged in order of size.

Alfred Döblin / THE MURDER OF A BUTTERCUP

The serious man kept shaking his head at the strange occurrence. 'People get nervous in town. The town makes me nervous'; he gave a contemplative sway of the hips, doffed his trilby and fanned the pine air over his shock of hair.

After a while he was back to counting his steps, one, two, three. One foot placed in front of the other, his arms swinging from his shoulders. Suddenly, as his vacant gaze was running along the edge of the path, Mr Michael Fischer saw a squat figure, his own self, step from the grass and charge at the flowers, knocking the head of a buttercup clean off. The earlier occurrence on the shady path was taking place there and then, tangibly in front of him. This flower matched the other one to a 'T'. It attracted his gaze, his hand, his cane. His arm rose up, the cane whistled, whack, the head flew off. The head spun through the air, disappeared in the grass. The merchant's heart beat furiously. The severed head now sank clumsily into the grass and started to burrow. Deeper, ever deeper, through the cover of the grass into the ground. Now it rushed into the bowels of the earth and there was nothing that could have stopped it. And the top of its stump started to drip — white blood gushing from its neck — into the hole, just a little at first, like the saliva running from the corners of a paralytic's mouth, then in a thick yellow foaming stream which flowed slimily up to Mr Michael who vainly tried to make his escape, hopping to the right and the left, trying to jump over it as it washed against his feet.

Mr Michael mechanically placed his hat on his sweat-covered head, pressed his hands with the cane against his chest. 'What's happened?' he asked after a while. 'I'm not drunk. The head mustn't disappear, it must remain here, it must remain here on the grass. I'm positive that it's lying quite calmly now in the grass. And the blood — I don't recall this flower, I don't remember the slightest thing.'

He was astonished, disturbed, distrusted himself. He was completely aghast at his own frenzied agitation, brooded in horror on the flower, the fallen head, the bleeding stalk. He was still jumping over the slimy river. Suppose someone were to see him, one of his business friends or a lady.

Mr Michael Fischer puffed out his chest and grasped his cane in his right hand. He looked at his coat and straightened his posture. He was going to bring these wilful thoughts to heel: self control. He, the chief, would master this insubordination. One must be firm with these people: 'What can I do for you, good sir? Behaviour of this sort is anything but normal in my firm. Boy, throw this fellow out.' At the same time he was standing still and waving his cane about madly in the air. Mr Fischer had adopted a cool, deprecatory air; now he would see. Indeed his superiority was so great that, once he had reached the main road on the hill above, he even mocked his own timidity. What a joke if next day there was a red poster hanging on every billboard in Freiburg saying: 'Adult buttercup murdered on the path between Immental and St Ottilien between seven and nine in the evening. Wanted for questioning' etcetera. The flabby gent in black mocked himself while savouring the cool evening air. Down below the nannies and courting couples would find the evidence of his deed. There will be screams and people will run home in terror. And the police inspectors would think about him, the murderer who was laughing slyly up his sleeve. Mr Michael thrilled with awe at his own recklessness, he had never imagined he could be so base, but the proof of his rash energy lay there below for the whole town to see.

The stump rose stiffly in the air, white blood trickling from its throat.

Mr Michael stretched out his hands in a feeble gesture of self-defence.

It had congealed at the top, thick and sticky so that ants had become stuck to it.

Mr Michael ran his hand over his temples and gave a loud snort.

And beside him was the head, rotting in the grass. It will get squashed, decompose in the rain, putrefy. It will end up a yellow,

Alfred Döblin / THE MURDER OF A BUTTERCUP

stinking mush, iridescent greenish-yellowish, as slimy as vomit. It rises up, alive, streams towards him, straight to Mr Michael, wants to drown him, splashes against his body, sprays his nose. He jumps, can do no more than hop about on tiptoe.

The sensitive gentleman shuddered. He had a disgusting taste in his mouth. Was so revolted he could not swallow, vomited without stop. He carried on further, stumbling all the while, hopping nervously, his lips pale blue.

'I refuse, absolutely refuse, to enter into any relations whatsoever with your firm.'

He pressed his handkerchief to his nose. The head had got to go, the stalk had to be covered, stamped flat, interred. The smell of the plant's corpse filled the forest. The smell accompanied Mr Michael; grew more and more intense. Another flower must be planted on the spot, a sweet scented one, a bed of carnations. The cadaver in the middle of the forest had got to go. Go!

Just as Mr Michael Fischer was about to stop, the thought shot through his head that it would be ridiculous to turn back. More than ridiculous. What did the buttercup matter to him? Bitter rage blazed up in him as he realised that he had nearly been taken in. He should have pulled himself together, bitten his index finger: 'Watch out, I'm telling you, just watch out you scoundrel, you bastard.' And at the same time a gigantic fear descended on him from behind.

The plump sullen man looked round shyly, plunged his hand into his pocket, pulled out a clasp knife and opened it.

Meanwhile his feet walked on. His feet started to annoy him. Even they wanted to establish themselves as his master. He was outraged by the way they carried on marching so wilfully. He would soon tighten the reins on these horses. Then they would get it. A sharp prick in their flanks would tame them right enough. They kept carrying him onwards. It almost looked as if he was walking away from the scene of the murder. Nobody must be allowed to think that. The rustling of birds, a distant whimpering, hung in the air and rose up from below. 'Stop, stop!' he screamed at his feet, and then he stabbed his knife into a tree.

He threw his arms around the trunk and rubbed his cheeks on the bark. His hands fingered the air, as if he were kneading something: 'We are not going to be made to eat humble pie.' His forehead creased with strain, the deathly pale gentleman studied the cracks in the tree, ducking down as if something was about to jump over him from behind. Again and again he heard the ringing of the telegraph wires connecting himself with the scene, even though he wanted to tangle and trample them with his feet. He tried to evade the fact that his rage had already subsided, that a gentle lust flickered inside him, a lust to be indulged. In the recesses of his heart he lusted for the flower and the scene of the murder.

Mr Michael gave a tentative sway of the knees, sniffed the air, cocked his ear in every direction, whispered anxiously: 'All I want to do is to bury the head quickly, that's all. Then everything'll be alright. But quickly, please, quickly.' He closed his eyes in misery, turned on his heels as if by mistake. Then he strolled off as if nothing had happened, straight on down the hill, nonchalantly, as if out for a walk, whistling quietly and stroking the tree trunks along the path as he gave a deep sigh of relief. With that he smiled and his little mouth became round as a hole. He sang a song which suddenly occurred to him: 'Bunny in the burrow, sleeping so sound.' He imitated his earlier capering, hip-swaying, arm-swinging. He had slipped his cane right up his sleeve in order to hide his guilt. Occasionally he crept to one side at a bend in the path; was someone watching?

Perhaps it was really still alive; yes, how could he be sure that it was already dead? The thought darted through his mind that he could heal the injured flower by bracing it with splints and placing some sort of plaster around the head and the stalk. He hastened his step, forgot his posture, ran. All at once he started to tremble in anticipation. And at a turning he fell flat across a felled tree, bumped his chest and chin and groaned out loud. As he collected himself, he forgot his hat in the grass; the broken cane had torn his jacket sleeve on the inside; he didn't notice a thing. Ah-ha, something was trying to stop him, but nothing was going to get in his way; he would find the flower alright. He clambered back on his feet. Where was the spot? He must find the spot. If only he could call the flower. But what was its name? He didn't even know its name. Ellen? Perhaps she was called Ellen, yes, no doubt about it, Ellen. He whispered to the grass, bent over to give the flowers an encouraging pat.

'Is Ellen there? Where's Ellen? Well, friends? She's injured, her head, well — just below her head. Maybe you've not heard about it yet. I want to help her; I'm a doctor, first-aider. So, where is she? You can trust me, no problem, honest.'

But how was he-who-had-destroyed-her going to recognise her? Perhaps he was touching her that very moment with his hand, perhaps she was breathing her last right next to him. That couldn't be true.

He roared: 'Out with her. Don't upset me, you dogs. I'm a first-aider. Don't you understand German?'

He lay down flat on the ground, searched, then burrowed blindly in the grass, tearing at the flowers and screwing them up while his mouth hung open and his eyes flickered straight ahead. For a long while he was lost in his broody meditation.

'Hand her over. There are conditions to be made. Preliminaries. The doctor has a right to his patient. Laws must be passed.'

The trees beside the path and on all sides stood pitch black against the grey sky. It was too late. Doubtlessly the head had already shrivelled up. The thought of final death filled him with horror and made his shoulders shake.

The rotund, black figure got up from the grass and teetered along the edge of the path down the hill.

She was dead. By his hand.

He heaved a sigh and rubbed his forehead pensively.

They would come at him from all sides. Let them, he couldn't care less. It was all the same to him. They would hack off his head, tear off his ears, thrust his hands into glowing coals. There was nothing more he could do. He knew that it would be fun for them all, but he wouldn't let out a squeak, wouldn't let these miserable hangmen have the pleasure. They had no right to punish him, they were also corrupt. Good, he had killed the flower, but that wasn't their business. No way, he had a perfect right to do so and he would stick to it whatever they might say. It was his right to kill flowers and he didn't feel bound to give any more account than that. As many flowers as he wanted, within a radius of a thousand miles, north, south, west and east, even if they smirked at him. And if they kept on laughing like that he would go for their throats.

He stood still; his gaze poisoned in the sombre darkness of the fir trees. His lips were swollen thick with blood. Then he hurried on further.

He had to give his condolences to the dead flower's sisters, here in the forest. He explained that the mishap had occurred almost without his doing, recalled the lamentable prostration which had overcome him after so much climbing. And the heat. But basically buttercups were a matter of the greatest indifference to him.

He shrugged his shoulders again in despair: 'What else are they going to do to me?' He ran his grimy fingers across his cheeks; he was completely bemused.

What on earth had that all been about; for God's sake, what was he doing here?

He wanted to take the shortest route and slip away, straight down through the trees, take stock of himself, cool and collected. Very slowly, one point at a time.

He gropes from tree to tree, so as not to slide over on the slippery ground. The flower, he thinks deviously, can stay there on the path. There are plenty of dead weeds like that in the world.

Alfred Döblin / **THE MURDER OF A BUTTERCUP**

But he is filled with horror as he sees a round drop of clear pale resin exuding from the trunk he touches; the tree is crying. Fleeing into the darkness of a path, he soon notices that the way is becoming strangely narrow, as if the forest was trying to lure him into a trap. The trees are forming a court of law.

He must get out.

Once again he runs into a low pine tree; it rains blows on him with its raised hands. He breaks through by force, blood streams down his face. He vomits, lashes out on all sides, kicks the trees with loud screams, slides tumbling down on the seat of his pants, finally falling head over heels down the final slope at the edge of the forest, towards the lights of the village, his tattered coat over his head, while the hill behind him rumbles threateningly, shakes its fists, and all around there's a crashing and crackling from the trees which are running after him and hurling insults.

The fat gentleman stood motionless by the gas lamp in front of the village church. He no longer had a hat on his head, black earth and pine needles clung to his tousled shock of hair and he didn't even shake them off. He gave a heavy sigh. He slowly took the skirts of his coat in both hands and pressed them to his face as drops of warm blood started to trickle down his nose and onto his boots. Then he raised his hands to the light and puzzled over the thick blue veins on their backs. He ran his finger over the thick bundles but could not smooth them flat. He tottered off home down the narrow alleyways, accompanied by the song and the wail of the passing trams.

Now he sat, quite feeble-minded, in his bedroom, talking away loudly, saying: 'I'm sitting here, I'm sitting here,' and looked around his room in despair. He paced up and down, took off his things and hid them at the back of the wardrobe. He put on another black suit and read the paper on the sofa. It crumpled in his hands as he read it; something had happened, something had happened. And the next day it hit him with its full force as he was sitting at his desk.

He was rooted to the spot, couldn't even manage a curse, a pall of silence descended on him.

Nervously agitated, he kept telling himself that it must all have been a dream; but the scratches on his forehead were real. In that case there are things in the world which are beyond belief. The trees had struck him, the death had been accompanied by a howl. He sat there lost in thought and, to the amazement of the staff, he didn't once look up at the buzzing flies. Then he set about harassing the apprentices with a grim expression, paced up and down and neglected his work. He could be seen hitting the table with his fist, puffing up his cheeks and screaming that he was going to straighten up his firm once and for all — and not just that! Just wait and see. He wasn't going to be taken for a ride, not by anybody.

The next morning, as he was doing the books, he suddenly insisted that the buttercup should be given ten marks from his account. He gave a start, meditated bitterly on his powerlessness, and asked the signatory to carry out the transaction. That afternoon, cloaked in icy silence, he put the sum into a special box himself; he even felt bound to open an account for the flower; he had grown weary, wanted peace and quiet. Soon he felt compelled to make her an offertory of food and drink. Each day a small dish was set next to Mr Michael's place. The landlady had clasped her hands in indignation as he ordered this extra place, but the gentleman forbade any criticism with an unprecedented outburst of rage.

He did penance, penance for his secret guilt. He performed devotions to the buttercup, and now the quiet merchant claimed that each and every one of us has his own religion; one must adopt a personal attitude toward an ineffable god. There are things which not everyone can understand. An expression of suffering had cast itself over the seriousness of his monkey-like face; he had also lost some of his corpulence, his eyes were drawn. Like a conscience, the flower kept a stern eye on all his actions, from the most important to the most trifling.

Alfred Döblin / THE MURDER OF A BUTTERCUP

During this time the sun often shone on the town, the cathedral and the castle on the hill, shining with the glory of life. Then one morning the embittered man was standing at the window when he burst into tears, crying for the first time since his childhood. Quite suddenly, weeping until his heart nearly broke. That hateful flower, Ellen, was robbing him of all this beauty, for she was accusing him with each one of the world's beauties. The sunbeams danced, she couldn't see them; she was not permitted to smell the scent of the white jasmine. No one would study the scene of her ignominious death, no prayers would be said for her there: she could throw this all in his face, regardless how laughable it might be and how much he wrung his hands. She had been denied everything: the moonlight, the nuptial bliss of the summer, the quiet life in the company of the cuckoo, the afternoon walks, the perambulators. He pursed his small lips; he wanted to hold the people back as they walked up the hill. If only the world would end with a sigh, so that the flower would shut up. Yes, he even thought of suicide in order to end his plight once and for all.

Occasionally he treated her with bitterness, disparagingly, took a short run up and forced her against the wall. He betrayed her in tiny ways, quickly knocking over her dish as if by mistake, making mistakes with her account to her disadvantage, sometimes treating her with the cunning he normally reserved for his business competitors. On the anniversary of her death he acted as if he had completely forgotten. Only as she seemed to become more insistent on a silent commemoration did he dedicate half a day to her memory.

One day at a social gathering everyone was asked to name their favourite dishes. When it was Mr Michael's turn he answered with cool deliberation: 'Buttercups; buttercups are my favourite dish.' His answer was greeted with gales of laughter, while Mr Michael squirmed on his chair, listening to them with clenched teeth while revelling at the buttercup's rage. He felt like some ghastly dragon which contentedly gobbles up everything alive, wild Japanese images and hara-kiri raced through his mind. Even then he secretly expected severe punishment from her.

He fought a ceaseless guerilla war of this sort against her, constantly hovering between agony and rapture; he anxiously relished the raging screams he sometimes imagined he could hear. Every day he dreamt up new perfidies, and he was often in such a state of agitation that he had to leave his office and enter his room so that he could forge his new plans undisturbed. And so the secret war carried on and no one knew a thing about it.

The flower belonged to him, to the comforts of his life. He thought back with amazement to the time when he had lived without it. From then on he often went for walks through the forest to St Ottilien, wearing an expression of defiance. And one sunny evening, as he was resting on a sawn-off tree stump, the thought flashed through his mind that Ellen, his buttercup, had stood on the very spot he was sitting. It could only have been here. The portly gentleman was seized by a fretful, melancholy devotion. How things had changed! From that evening till now. Stooping over, he allowed his friendly, slightly troubled gaze to wander over the weeds, Ellen's sisters, or perhaps even her daughters. After long contemplation a rascally look flashed across his smooth features. Now his darling flower was in for it! If he dug up one of the buttercups, one of the dead flower's daughters, planted it at home, tended it with loving care, the old girl would have a young rival. Yes, if he was right in his thinking, he could completely atone for the old girl's death. He was saving this flower's life and making recompense for the death of the mother, for in all probability this daughter would go to ground here. Oh, that would annoy the old girl, put her out of harm's way once and for all. The legally versed merchant recalled a section on the compensation of debts. He dug up a little plant with his clasp knife, carried it home carefully in his bare hands and planted it in a magnificently gilded porcelain pot, then placing it on a mosaic-topped table in his bedroom. He took

Alfred Döblin / THE MURDER OF A BUTTERCUP

a piece of charcoal and scribbled on the bottom of the pot: 'Article 2403, Section 5.'

Each day the happy fellow watered the plant with malicious devotion and made his offertory to Ellen, the departed. She was legally bound to back down, perhaps even under police jurisdiction, and no longer received her bowl, her food, her money. Often, as he lay on his sofa, he believed he could hear her long whines and moans. Mr Michael's self-esteem grew in a most unforeseeable way. Sometimes he had slight attacks of megalomania. He had never been so merry in all his life.

One evening, as he reached the door to his home after strolling complacently from his chambers, his landlady calmly announced that the bedside table had fallen over while she had been doing the cleaning and the pot had smashed. She had had the horrible filthy plant thrown into the dustbin with all the broken pieces. The dry, somewhat disdainful way in which she reported the accident left little doubt that the event had been just to her liking.

The portly gentleman slammed the door to, clapped his stubby hands and, with a loud squeal of delight, grabbed the surprised female by the hips and lifted her into the air — or as far as his strength and the height of the ceiling allowed. Then he sauntered from the corridor into his bedroom, his eyes flickering, full of excitement; he snorted loud and stamped his feet; his lips trembled.

No one could hold anything against him; not even in his most secret thoughts had he wished the death of this flower, he had never given anyone even the teensiest hint of such a thought. The old girl, the mother-in-law, could curse and say what she liked. He had nothing to do with her any more. They were divorced. He was now rid of the whole buttercup crew. Luck and right were on his side. There could be no question about it. He had outwitted the forest.

He wanted to make straight for St Ottilien, to that stupid, surly forest. He was already swinging his black cane in his thoughts. The flowers, the tadpoles, even the toads had better believe him now.

He could murder as much as he liked. He didn't care two hoots for the buttercups.

Bubbling over with spiteful glee, the fat, sprucely dressed merchant rolled about in laughter on his sofa.

Then he jumped up, clapped his hat over his head and rushed past his flabbergasted landlady into the street.

He laughed until he burst. And with that he vanished into the darkness of the mountain forest.

Albert Ehrenstein

TUBUTSCH

(1907)

My name is Tubutsch, Karl Tubutsch. I only mention this because I have very few possessions apart from my name ...

It's not the melancholy and bitterness of autumn, nor the feeling one gets after completing a major work, nor the dullness with which one dimly awakes after a long, serious illness: I just can't understand how I have sunk into this state. Inside and outside of me is governed by a complete emptiness, a desolation. I've become an empty shell and don't know how. Just who or what has brought about this ghastliness: the great nameless magician, the reflection in a mirror, the fall of a bird's feather, the laugh of a child, the death of two flies:

it is futile to search for it, or even to want to search; as foolish as attempting to track down any cause in this world. All I can see is the effect and its consequence; one can establish that my soul has lost its balance, something in it is buckled and broken, the inner fountains have dried up. I can't even guess at the reason for this, the reason for my own particular case, and the worst of it is, I can't see anything which might change my hopeless state, not even slightly. For my inner emptiness is complete, systematic as it were, the result of a lamentable lack of any sort of chaotic elements. The days slip by, as do the weeks and the months. No, no! just the days. I don't believe that there are such things as weeks, months and years, there are only days, days which keep plunging into one another, days which I am unable to hold onto by some experience or other.

Were someone to ask what happened to me yesterday, I would answer. 'Yesterday? Yesterday one of my shoelaces snapped.' Years ago I used to be furious if one of my shoelaces snapped or one of my buttons fell off, I invented a special demon to preside over this department and even gave him a name. Gorymaaz, if I remember correctly. Now I thank God if one of my shoelaces snaps on the street. For only then do I have some degree of justification to enter a shop, request a shoelace, answer the question as to whether I would like something else with: 'Nothing!', pay at the till and depart. Or else: I purchase the goods from one of the lads who keep on shouting 'Four for five bob' and get stared at by numerous passers-by who take me for a public benefactor. In any case, a few minutes pass by in this way and, all said and done, that's something after all ...

It shouldn't be said that I have a special aptitude for feeling bored. That's not true. Since time immemorial I have possessed an exceptional ability, have been endowed with the talent for killing time, for coming up with the most exotic of imaginable occupations.

By way of proof: not long ago, as I was on my way to Ganster Lane, I walked up to a policeman, desirous of information, even though I did not know the whereabouts of the aforementioned thoroughfare. And thereupon I made an important discovery which seems to portend the toppling of a number of universal laws. The policeman smelt of rose water. Just think: a perfumed policeman. What a *contradictio in adjecto!* At first I didn't believe my nose. Doubts rose up inside me as to the authenticity of this law enforcer. Perhaps an artful criminal, a usurper, had clad himself in the uniform of a policeman in order to elude his pursuers. Only when I received my information was I convinced of his authenticity. It was so Delphic. Now it was up to me to find out whether all law enforcers — perhaps on account of a new regulation, say — had to disseminate pleasant odours, or whether he was the sole example with this characteristic and had acted, as it were, on his own initiative. Without batting an eyelid, I set myself this far-reaching task. A dissertation, or better still an essay: 'On policemen and their odours' swam before my eyes ... One policeman after another was sniffed at without finding a single further stain on their station, although I did ascertain that not one of them trimmed his moustaches in the English fashion. An observation whose importance for science can only be compared with one which I recently arrived at after unspeakable difficulties. Namely that not one single mammal is coloured green.

As to whether that particular policeman came by his odour from a servant-girl or from some other fault of his own ... I lacked the courage to ascertain. And nothing became of the treatise *De odoribus polyporum.* I didn't dare ask him. For such a remarkable law officer, an officer of the law who smelt of roses, might well have read *Crime and Punishment,* if not *Raskolnikoff.* And knowing what a thrilling sensation many a criminal experiences at the idea of torturing himself and playing hide and seek with the authorities, he might simply have arrested me as some wrongdoer circling the showplace of my misdeed. And I would be faced with having to make my confession, the shameful confession of my innocence.

A cowardice similar to that with the policeman also hindered me in getting to the bottom of other mysteries, the sensing and pursuit of which is my sole occupation and interest in life. On my forays I often passed by an old greengrocer, a woman in her middle years with a coarse appearance and a down to earth way of expressing herself. She deals mainly in green peas. She bestowed a customer, who had sampled her ware and left with a shrug of the shoulders without making a purchase, with appellations which, in their just and multifarious nature, were not second to those given to an oriental ruler. But an old sparrow nibbled at the peas every day unpunished, was never chased away, pecked at the pods and banqueted on the fruit, and I was never able to summon up the courage to ask the vegetable dealer whether or not she was a widow. For there is no escaping the thought: the sparrow is none other than her deceased spouse who comes and visits her and — oh omniscient unconsciousness — is fed by her!

Thanks to my timidity I shall never get to the bottom of this question ...

Likewise the sign above the cobbler's. 'Engelbert Kokoschnigg, Master Shoemaker. At the sign of the Two Lions. Established 1891.' Universal riddles are hard to solve. For weeks on end I racked my brains in vain; why did the esteemed craftsman display a sign which was only befitting for an innkeeper? Had the contracting of marriage, which had presumably coincided with the founding of this business, been lauded in the form of this encroachment, so that one of the roaring lions was the cobbler's wife? Or had a world famous lion-tamer visited Vienna that year, drawing these citizens along with him in the wake of his fame?

Should I wish to put an end to this unbearable dilemma, by interviewing the master craftsman in person, I would necessarily be obliged to have him make me a pair of shoes. And that in turn, quite apart from my ever more chronic lack of the customary legal tender, would be black treason against my own personal shoemaker, old Peter Kekrevishy, who has so often whiled away my time with his tales. All well and good, both he and his handiwork have a somewhat old-time charm about them, he still greets me with 'Good day to you!' and when I ask him for something he says: 'Yes, my heart!' But he is as kindly as the canary which overhears us from its coconut shell, interrupts us with its song and then rewards itself by directing a peck of its beak to its sugar. And the cobbler's tales are also like a song, like the quiet song of resignation. Klausenburg is his birthplace, he finished the lower school there, and was the best pupil when his father died. Then his guardian, a butcher, did not let him continue his studies. The lad had to help at the chopping block during his vacations, and when he applied for the high school, the principal would not have him since his fellow pupils would be forever teasing someone who did the meat round, and the decorum of the school had to be safeguarded ... The guardian had then apprenticed him to a cobbler, because the butcher's lads also wouldn't tolerate a secondary school pupil among them, and then he found the profession far too disgusting. All that bloodletting! But in the year of 1848[1], when the citizens of Klausenburg decided that it was time they also had their own to-do, he had done his bit, albeit with the local band ... A fellow student, who had been awarded worse marks than him, became the director of the observatory in Vienna, and a few steps away from it, in a dingy little room stinking of gruel, sits a man whose wife goes charring and whose only daughter is married in Agram. A man too old, too gentle, too poor to be able to afford a helper, a man who after much pleading, must be glad when his customers don't walk out on him because he is so slow. Now his wife has managed to find him a small sideline. Every day I see the weak little man with his shaking hands taking a paralytic out in her wheelchair. For which he receives a little pocket money and is not even allowed a small glass of wine on Sundays, no! But instead he may chose a book from the paralytic's library and completely wreck his half-blind eyes reading the tiny print, while another — Counsellor to the Court, Baron, Commander of the

Order of Franz Josef etc. — gets paid for summoning down the eternal stars to the earth, drives about in a proper carriage, lives right in the lap of luxury — for no better reason than that he didn't have a butcher for a guardian.

This is my only social contact, an old cobbler and — of course! — a ruined hat-maker who is in no way remarkable except that he made it to Mexico under Emperor Max. He has nothing to say about this land except that it was very hot. Be that as it may, in my eyes he is a man of importance, I have no one else among my acquaintances who has gone further than him ... and there is something exotic in the air when he says: 'Yes, in Velacruz!' and I ask dutifully what it was about this place and he cracks his only joke: 'Yes, in Velacruz, they ain't gotta slivovitz to match the likes of ours' ... I am always loyal and laugh, can't spoil things with him. He is the ombudsman for the poor, and maybe he will at last help me gain Viennese citizenship. I could do with a little sinecure one day.

. . I used to have one more acquaintance, a bow legged Doctor Philosophiae who also completed the course at the export academy and knows an unbelievable number of languages. His name is Schmecker, he's employed at the central bank, works for all he's worth, and doesn't allow himself a holiday. For that reason I once said to him; 'Yes, my friend, there are a few drawbacks when you want to end your days as a bank manager.' He really will become a bank manager, but that 'end your days' has spoilt his fun in advance, and if he sees me approaching in the distance, he looks away when I draw near.

I also used to have a distant relative, Norbert Schigut, the representative. Once he met me unannounced on the street and imparted to me triumphantly, without any invitation on my behalf — he clearly wanted to forestall any rumours — that although his wife had recently walked out on him, she was back again shortly after, full of remorse. This often happens, I remarked. As for myself, I had always written with a dip pen, had changed to a fountain pen, only

Albert Ehrenstein / **TUBUTSCH**

to clasp my quill once more in disappointment, without that being reason enough to give up the hope of one day coming into possession of a typewriter. He ingenuously replied that this had probably been due to the poor quality of the fountain pen, and by happy chance he was just at that moment representing a first class make of fountain pens from America. I fell into a never-ending fit of laughter, although still able to consider whether I shouldn't wrap up a bit of this laughter and save it for gloomier times, but the peculiar fellow went his way, insulted, as if my laughing had been intended as an attack on his commercial honour. Since then we are relatives no longer.

I wander around the large city alone. No one pays me any attention. At most a pinscher barks at me as it nervously paces back and forth on the roof of one of the passing delivery vans. Often I'd like to bark right back. Unfortunately decorum doesn't allow it. One must retain a sense of propriety. And so I can't even enter into closer relations with this pinscher.

I used to write. But the last time I cast a look into my inkwell, there were two dead flies inside. Drowned.

Just what had taken place, the double suicide of two lovers ... or an avalanche in the glass mountains brought about by rolling dust particles ... could no longer be established. The word 'fame' exploded inside my head; who knows what these flies had meant to their people! I was overcome by horror, and I went outdoors to shake it off, ended up near the Kahlenberg line and saw, next to a miserable hovel belonging to one of the railway employees: two cockerels — an old one and a young one — fighting for world dominion on a dung heap. I returned home, completely taken up by this event, and the next day I was highly surprised that none of the papers had printed even the smallest report about this titanic contest for the hegemony of the dung heap. Not to mention the shocking news of the two deceased flies, which must have occurred too late for the stop press.

The two cockerels had battled to the last, it hadn't been one of those faked show fights, there was no doubt that it had been fair and square, but not a word! Perhaps for that very reason ... which should have been precisely mine for dutifully informing every newspaper in the world. But given the diametrically opposed views of the world which separate me from the editors of the popular illustrated weeklies, and the differences in the things which we are both structured to view as important, it was pretty questionable as to whether I would succeed in making my opinion heard. Of course, if the two splattered flies had been the owners of a plum-jam mine, and been called Pollak, or one cockerel had been the Austrian champion ... the chess master Papabile, and the other the presumptive world champion, then one would not be able to walk the streets without being ambushed every two steps by the every-day faces of these two heroes staring out from the shop windows. Better to keep to ourselves and deal with our own affairs. With regard to the cockerels, there was nothing more I could do for them, and anyway as an author it's not in my nature to take sides and forcibly intervene in the course of battle. Just as it is not in my nature to desecrate the slumber of the two flies which had fallen into death's bitter inkwell by exhuming and cremating them ... I left them on the spot where fate had cast them. Given that the boldest of heroic deeds go unmentioned, who will be surprised at my decision to write my notes as of now in pencil, so, as it were, to make them even more transitory. One could more readily accuse me of egocentricity in my reverential approach to the flies. For what could be better suited to my mood than the smell of their decomposing which other hardier constitutions probably wouldn't even notice?

I have now made the effort and bought myself a street directory. I should have done it long ago. People like myself whose centre of gravity lies outside themselves, somewhere out there in the universe ...

Albert Ehrenstein / TUBUTSCH

who yield like wax to every impression ... must continually feed their sensorium, even if just with shop signs, in order to keep from falling into the gaping void.

I travel on a small scale. The Tirol is a pretty land but soon the Baedeckers will start blossoming on the trees, and the majority take their milieu with them when they travel ... in the shape of their relations and friends. In fact it's a matter of complete indifference whence we travel, we always go along quite regardless. Can't leave ourselves at home. This sort of travelling doesn't agree with me. If at all, then through time. I would like to talk with a lord from the fourteenth century, would like to pay a call on Mr Menemptar, the early Egyptian poet, booming lyricist and world-famous author of the hymn-cycle 'Songs to the crocodile of the Nile,' but sad to say I am in such bad shape that I couldn't manage to force the sterling lad to appear in a vision or hallucination. Technicians! Bring me the tramway to the past. No, not until a conductor ... the globe dangling from his watch chain ... shouts out: 'Cambrian Era! All change!' I won't take part until then. Ah, but not even then, for no sooner has something of this sort come into being then Mr Pollak is in on it too, leaving his sandwich wrappers strewn around the Cambrian Era. And it really doesn't deserve that. I see now that it's better for me to go for a walk along Linz Street, because it's the second longest street in Vienna ... I'd also like to be the second longest street in Vienna ... things would be easier then.

What's there to look at? Not a lot. Next to a shop selling umbrellas is a corner shop selling books, paper banners trumpeting the praises of the latest tome, along with others announcing that fresh herrings have arrived at last. Some may like to refer to this as the ingenious arrangement of the non-oriental capital, the rest, more down to earth, go crazy with the disorder. But I myself haven't a clue which are umbrellas, which are books and which are herrings: all the differences swim before my eyes, they have become too minimal for me so that all I can see within this apparent diversity of objects is insignificant gradations in one and the same material ... gradations which eternally recur while it is simply the human means of expression which changes. And then I say, laying a book aside: 'I must have seen this hat somewhere before,' or eating a mince-loaf suddenly gives me the idea that I am in fact dealing with a fashionable talent which is at the conceptional and material roots of this sort of mode of perception and remains unchanging, for otherwise the perceptions would be an impossibility. And people think that I am paradoxical? I've simply learnt from a drunk.

It was evening, I was walking back down Linz Street so as to note the houses in reverse order, when a swaying figure staggered up to me and asked: 'Where on earth are we?' I replied that we were at that moment on the second longest street in Vienna, Linz Street. 'Linz Street, can't be,' his voice resounded. 'You've doubtlessly consumed rather too much Schopenhauer, my good man!' 'You're absolutely on the wrong track there ... it was Zöblinger Riesling,' this unknown portrayer of Toby Belch replied, and I mused as to whether Schopenhauer had not also arrived at his famous theory under Dionysus's sway. Similar to the way in which he had apparently earlier turned Lord Byron into a misogynist. There was something to the drunk's theory, for, quite clearly: if one removed the temporality from Linz Street, there would be nothing left but matter which now and then enjoyed transmuting itself from the Cambrian Era into Vienna's second longest street ... 'Where're we now' a voice asked with effort. 'On Linz Street,' I answered, annoyed. 'Not again!' came the reply ... It would seem that one has to be pretty full of dry wine to discover the law of the eternal recurrence of the identical. Wise or mad, mad or drunk — what's the difference? Can it be that the wisdom of the great philosophers is not so amazing, that the bacillus which brings about wisdom is in the end not so very different from others, less celebrated ... or are the orphic primal words of the lords of the universe just that much truer because they can flow forth at the drop of a hat from the unrestrained

Albert Ehrenstein / TUBUTSCH

subconscious of a person blasted on wine? ... This marvellous stranger stopped and tried to prevent a lamp-post from falling over ... Fool that I am, I carried on — although I later regretted not having got involved in an instructive conversation with him, so as to have at least found out how he had come to the assumption that Linz Street doesn't exist. At that moment, however, joyful that someone had deemed me worthy of such a conversation, joyful about, by my standards, a great event, I quickly made my way home ... perhaps because I was afraid of being caught with a drunk by the police and arrested as a thief.

No policeman appeared. Out of prudence. For there were tramps strolling about, brushing against me none too considerately, and since the evening had been bristling with adventures, I had grown accustomed to the idea of a nocturnal hold-up and had already decided to outwit the first threatening figure by voluntarily handing over my wallet and watch, with the request that he should feel free to avail himself of them in the future ...

It would not have been easy for me to part with my watch, the source of countless small pleasures. How often have I been in a park and grown tired of observing some ageing gent who watches the children playing with their balls and diabolos ... where time has started to congeal and seemed to circle in eternity above; how often have I approached one of the lads and coaxed him with the words: 'Do you think you could be kind enough to ask me what time it is?' ... I don't believe one could be politer. The old gentlemen expressed their consternation by waggling their walking sticks, but their conduct didn't bother me in the least, for they were my rivals when it came to offering to tell the time ... and when a plucky lad fulfilled my wish, which sometimes happened ... I flipped open the lid and reported with chronometric accuracy just how far the day had progressed ... and my pleasure was no less than that of a child at its confirmation, who for the first time is able to function as a teller of time ... So, one can see just how unwilling I was to give away my watch, an essential item for the running of my business ... Quite possible that the vagrants had absolutely no such intentions: passing street-cleaning carts and their drivers, to whom I had kept close by, brought me to safety and obviated the execution of my plan ...

Once a day has begun eventfully, it generally carries on being every bit as lively: sewermen lifted the manhole covers and, Herculean, started to descend into the underworld. An old wound opened at the sight of them, the insatiable desire to be a sewerman's wife awoke in me. The majority of other women commit adultery by day, but they can go about their business at night without fear of being caught. I recommend that our playwrights turn their attention to this theme. Generously offer it to them. In the same way that I am always ready to help all our local industries ...

No, the housekeeper who always keeps me waiting so long won't have any more reason to complain about me. Once as he read what I had written on my registration form: 'Religion: "Greek-paradox". Occupation: "My desire is to have a small part in the Chorus Mysticus",' he apparently broke out with: 'Oh, we've not had the likes of that living here in The House of the Three Steeds as far as me and my missus can remember.' He won't have any more reason to gripe. With the street directory in my hand, I am going to devote myself to preparing for the cab driver's exam. Or better still: I'm considering joining the ranks of the inventors. What have I invented? I shall patent my inkwell as a flycatcher. I at once told my housekeeper of the change I had undergone. He looked at me drowsily, uncertain, but receiving his tip as he unlocked the door, he actually bade me 'Good night!' before hobbling off in his slippers to bed. But written on his thinker's brow was: 'What's with you then? Go and sleep it off first!' ... Inventor? That doesn't exclude the possibility that tomorrow I'll wake up clad in the clothes of a cabby or a Slovakian cauliflower dealer who is out to make the acquaintance of a sewerman's wife and put her marital fidelity to the test ... No, I'd never do that, I no longer feel I've the strength for that. The

Albert Ehrenstein / **TUBUTSCH**

housekeeper's doubting look has robbed me of all my energy. And as I looked at the visiting card which adorned the door of my one-windowed room complete with separate entrance by the light of the waning wax-candle, and read that I was Mr Karl Tubutsch, I quietly said to myself, dismayed, no more than: 'Not again!' ...

I often wake up at night with a start. What's up? Nothing. Nothing! Doesn't anyone want to break in? Everything is planned in advance. Oh, I wouldn't like to be the person who broke into my room. Quite apart from the fact that there is nothing to be had beyond Philipp, my boot-jack, and maybe a street directory, I confess in all honesty: I haven't the slightest clue who the intruder might be, but I have every intention of sending the poor devil to his death. My penknife lies open and ready for murder on my bedside table. Philipp, my boot-jack, keeps watch below, ready to be thrown ... doesn't anyone want to break into my room ... I'm longing for a murder.

If only I had toothache. Then I could say 'Abracadabra' three times; the holy word 'Zip-Zip' would also probably have the same magical effect ... and even if that didn't make the pain go away, I still wouldn't go to the dentist, no way, rather nurture and cherish the pain, not let it fade, keep fanning it back to life. At least that would be a feeling! But my health is unshakeable.

If only some sorrow would grasp me in its talons! ... Only others, my neighbours, are blessed by this rarely appreciated fortune. Here in this house lives a comfort-loving couple, both well off, she is the head saleswoman in a large fashion store, he is the chief inspector at the post office, they have an only child and don't begrudge themselves a thing. Not long ago the man's father died, he had lived with them for twenty years. It happened during their holidays, so they had time to deal with it. And these monsters set the funeral for the morning and get up at the crack of dawn so that they can take the tram to the cemetery before half past seven when it only costs sixpence!

If someone were to die on me, someone who would give me the right to go into mourning, I would allow myself a cab at the very least. But that's the way it is: relatives go and die on the people who don't want to go into mourning ... but me ... I'm not allowed to experience a thing, am, as it were, a person who just floats in the air ...

Six children are sitting around, contentedly munching their sandwiches and admiring a pavior busy at work — three to the right and three to the left — I would also like to sit with them, if only to enjoy the consternation and embarrassment it would cause the dear old streetworker. Quite impossible. Given the present state of medical science, my very modest pleasure would certainly be interrupted by a small spell inside ...

Every day I eat my lunch in a sausage shop. And more or less the same sharply cut faces keep coming in, clerks in a hurry, a cigarette dangling from their mouths, milliners in such haste that they don't even drop their handkerchiefs at the appropriate moment ... poor elderly people, travellers or strangers, all of them with at least one part of their bodies which has to make regular visits to the hospital ... almost all of the visitors know me now ... all apart from the hunchbacked pedlar who occasionally comes hawking matches, pencils, cuff-links, writing paper and trouser presses from table to table. As I say, the people all know me, but does one of them think to ask me why I eat my lunch wearing red kid gloves? I only wear them so that someone will ask me why, and I can answer: 'I'm somewhat absent-minded and have a tendency to bite my nails, so I wear gloves to stop myself, so that my nails can grow in peace and attain perfection ...' I've bought the gloves in vain. They all think I'm crazy, or too lofty for them to dare to ask ... Nobody sounds me out, not even Thekla, the wan waitress with the black curly locks who asks me every day whether I would like gherkins, mustard or horse radish with my sausages ... Thekla, to whom I always slide a few pennies, not even she lifts me out of my mood by asking such an obvious question, although she is more or less duty bound to do so.

I'm afraid that I'll come to a sticky end one day. I slip slowly down into ever more ambiguous spheres. Naturally, people who are blessed by moral insanity — criminals from that great cannibal Napoleon to the small child who steals a plum and gets chased by the grocer's little son, first shouts 'Mother!' and then sticks his booty in his mouth just to hide it — are all of them beings whom nature has rightly favoured and usually protected with an armour formed of a lack of conscience and a faulty memory which precludes regret; also that, which a certain dim-wittedness, which is such a far cry from Darwin, refers to as the materialism of our times, namely Americanism — even these admirable defenders of the corporate trusts are as morally justifiable as the consumption of oxen and the existence of camel-riders when rideable camels are at hand. But what one cannot defend is stealing other people's precious time and causing harm without personally being able to gain from it. I have gone and applied for jobs advertised by businessmen just out of boredom, so as to be among people and get to know them ... jobs as errand boys, secondary school teachers, bookkeepers, engravers, correspondents, private tutors, valets etc. And after a long and vague to and fro, talking away until the people were totally confused, I always took my leave with these words: 'I should like to think it over and perhaps come back for another interview.' From a lenient standpoint, one might view this as a harmless prank. But it is far more mean, despicable and insidious to sit deliberately on one of the benches consecrated to courting couples, acting quite contrarily, reading the newspaper if it is still light and compelling the desperate couples to leave ... hated alike by the leagues of Czechoslovakian wet-nurses, on account of the limited number of suitable seats, since they only allow themselves to be impregnated on the benches along the Kaiser-Wilhelm Ring ... and held in fear by the tall Bosnians from the Votive Park and the German champions from the Augarten ... they carry on their games into the depths of the night. Ostensibly so as to collect statistical data on the length of time between the first kiss and the final embrace ...

It may be asked why I don't forget these shallow diversions and indulge myself in something more entertaining? While there is a lot to be said for being a dog-owner, given the large number of time-filling chores one must attend to, how much more are the simple and harmless pleasures occasioned by the tending of a piteous animal outshone by the company of a woman. To which I might add: When even a Homeric hero can have too much of 'sleep and love, song and merry-making' what depths of emotion and exhaustion would the likes of me start to register? My ears are still resounding with the cries of the Viennese ladies, gasping in the moment of rapture: 'Ah!' 'Oh!', 'Christ!' and 'Do you really love me as well!' — If they were poetesses they would presumably say: 'Tandaradei!' ... and I can still hear the 'Hoo', 'Hah', 'Hoh' of the Hungarians when I hold my ears. The girl from Berlin says 'Hmmm, tasty!' The only ones who didn't say a word were the Gypsy girls; but take my advice, leave your watch at home when making amorous advances to them ... and call yourself lucky if Trántire and Chnarpe-diches don't name you as the father of their children, who by right should resemble the whole of the officer corps from the local garrison ... Yes, another one was sensible to hold her tongue ... Marischa, the wife of the village judge of Popudjin. She made love the same way she would cut herself a slice of bread. Every one of her movements had a machine like assurance. Truly, I shall never forget how we chanced on one another that first time. It was the morning after her wedding, which I was unaware of. She, a stranger to me, was mowing the meadow which glistened with morning dew, her hips swaying as she moved forwards ... her short

Albert Ehrenstein / **TUBUTSCH**

skirts for ever swinging around and revealing her calves ... I sauntered past and could not resist leaning over to stroke the blossoming chin and cheeks of such a lovely, fresh woman. She blushed but didn't rebuff me: death stood behind me, the farmer with his scythe. And I just had enough presence of mind to say: 'So, my woman, I can come by your vineyard this afternoon and pick up the mulberries.' The farmer stared like an ox. She, bending down even further, as if she wanted to help me find something which had fallen on the ground, said yes, and that afternoon there were not just mulberries to be had in the vineyard ... And later on she informed me that her husband and mother had gone on a pilgrimage to Sassin, and I crept into her room where she lay waiting with her scent of stables, then returning home in the dark — taking care not to step into the dung heap to the right of the yard or fall into the cess-pit on the left — to sing the joys of the perilous love between Jehangir Mirza and Maasumeh Sultan Begum ... But my enthusiasm was soon to become paralysed by the oppressive conflict between such petty fortunes and the monstrous feelings and imaginings which accompanied them; indeed, in the long run it is an economic impossibility to manufacture ambrosia while having to eat filth oneself ... Apart from which the unfortunate gift of being able to see the skeleton inside even the most beloved woman, which can sometimes make an embrace all the more heart-rending, but in the end I was bound to be cut off from womankind by an immeasurable horror ... enough of all that love business! I'd much rather have a dog. The housekeeper's childless wife has got one which I think very highly of. A young toy bulldog, it holds court before the children in the yard; if they bring it turnips, calf's liver or sausages, it will answer to Fido, Bonzo, Fifi or even worse. But the little devil ignores any name under the sun if you only want to be nice to him, and should one become more insistent, perhaps like an old widow who once wanted to tie a pink bow around its neck, it growls a warning and then snaps. Its limitless power of reaction, its fresh and youthful bull-like charges at any scrap of paper or handkerchief held in front of it, and last but not least its exemplary self-sufficiency, have made it my ideal. It is able to lie about for hours on end hypnotising the self-same bone without a trace of boredom, and doesn't see any need for change. It doesn't need any teacher to tell it ironically: 'That's going to get you a long way!' — it knows that so deep in its bones that it is no longer conscious of it: no one can get further than to their own self. I, on the hand, when I find it too dull just being 'me', am forced to become someone else. Usually I am Marius and sit among the ruins of Carthage; but sometimes I am Prince Echsenklumm, entertain relations with an opera singer, gladly grant the chief editor Armand Schigut an interview on the trade deal with Monaco, forbid my valet, Dominic — played by my boot-jack Philipp — to allow anyone to see me except Baroness Toothscale ... and no sooner has this eternal yes your highness, no your highness got on my nerves, than I turn into a celebrated diva, give my miserable director the slap round the chops I had been longing to give him for ages, or set about him with a chair. I was just about to transform myself into the poet Konrad Rarehammer and silently smoke a cigarette in Café Symbol in order to restore myself from these unaccustomed exertions, when my boot-jack interrupted me. He was fed up with always playing the servants, directors, Carthaginian ruins, and cigarettes, and longed just once to be a prince, a heroine, or a playwright. 'Boot!' ... I said to him, 'Boot! Pride comes before a fall.' 'Master,' came the answer, 'Master, I'm no ordinary boot-jack.' 'That's perfectly obvious. Any boot-jack in my service is *eo ipso* no longer a normal boot-jack.' 'I didn't mean it that way.' 'Is there divine blood in your fibres? Are you an enchanted princess or perhaps even the boot-jack with which Zeus ingratiated himself with Hera?' 'No, no, but all the same, from an old family. Listen: I am descended in a direct line from the boot-jack that Mithridates swallowed in order to immunise his stomach against all poison.' 'He must have plagued his master as much as you to end up being used

Albert Ehrenstein / TUBUTSCH

like that.' Philipp forbade any such allusions to the fates of personal ancestors who were no less illustrious than meritorious. 'Or else I shall be ruthless and hand in my notice. Not for nothing am I being considered for the presidency of the forthcoming First International Boot-jack Congress in America. Roosevelt will personally ...' 'Roosevelt?' 'I mean Roosevelt's boot-jack. We call him Roosevelt for short ... has invited me to preside ... and just because of my position as the descendant of a famous ... or do you think that Mr Tubutsch's boot-jack ... ?' 'Yes, well, how are you going to get to America, oh boot-jack of my soul?' 'My body, my mean form, will remain here, while my spirit soars up, flies off, crawls into a power line and is over there in a jiffy. In the old days it was a lot more bother. You couldn't always find a bolt of lightning and there was no relying on that vagabond of a wind, it would always set us down just where we didn't want to be ... on Lake Tanganyika or the Fiji Islands ... where there was not a fellow soul to be found far and wide ...' I felt flattered to be in contact with an entity which in a way put me in very close contact with the President of the United States, so we made a pact whereby from now on we alternated the lead roles. He was the grocer who said: 'Today we've gotta luvverly cheese from Prims!'; I the customer who tries a taste with a shrug of the shoulders. Then again I was the elephant baby ... running around in circles ... and he the child shouting: 'Oh! How sweet!'; finally he was the tree trunk with a hat on one branch, coursing down the Danube to the Black Sea, and I was the oarsman who had fallen into the water and was cursing him, the water rat which housed between his roots, or the otter checking the validity of the tree trunk's ticket. Until my fun was spoilt by the impossibility, even with the greatest exertions of my will, of transforming myself into Prince Echsenklumm or the water rat sufficiently so as to be externally visible to myself and others. 'Philipp!' I said. 'Come here.' Philipp came, if somewhat reluctantly, as if he sensed the worst. I wrapped him up carefully in brown wrapping paper and went for a walk. But none of the passers-by wanted to ask me what was inside my little brown packet. And I had already prepared a short speech: 'Ladies and Gentlemen! Here you are looking at something quite out of the ordinary! A talking boot-jack! He is descended from the boot-jack to his Asiatic Majesty, King Mithridates of Pontus ... shortly he will preside at the First International Boot-jack Congress. Roosevelt himself ...' Nobody showed the slightest curiosity and I didn't want to be pushy ... That I remained unquestioned might still have been tolerable ... but Philipp went into a huff because I had been so faithless, had sought to profane his secrets ... his soul had emigrated to America for good ... I was alone again ...

I used to dream of fame. It was never allotted to me. And what remained were sarcastic remarks directed at the more fortunate. I had always shown a talent for this. When I had eaten myself to the core, I would start on others. But now I have become weaker, milder. As I said, I write in pencil. My food is as delicate as an invalid's. Recently I spent a whole morning watching a general who stopped in front of every shop window on Mariahilfe Street, regardless of whether it was a lingerie shop or a hairdresser's. It was just after the manoeuvres. I experienced neither malicious joy nor commiseration; I simply stood and watched until I myself was the general and felt ready to take over the role he had to continue playing. The way in which he lifted his sabre so that it wouldn't drag along the pavement, normally a reflex, was unspeakably sad ... The next day I meditated just as long on a jackdaw which was hopping back and forth, restlessly back and forth in front of a florist's in Weihburg Lane. Broken, its clipped wings dragged along the dirt of the cobblestones. And just a few days before it had circled round the spire of St Stephan's cathedral or been in command of a brigade ... I would have dearly loved to have arranged a meeting between the general and the jackdaw. But I no longer dare to carry out such great undertakings, since my last venture went so awry ...

Albert Ehrenstein / **TUBUTSCH**

On my travels I often passed an inn whose landlord's first name was Dominik. Now the Christian name Dominik is not uncommon among landlords. But why? This is an unfathomable mystery; but because of the regularity with which I have to walk past the sign outside the wine tavern, a relationship had gradually established itself between myself and the proprietor. Not that I had ever seen the landlord. Heaven forbid! Such realistic prerequisites are quite unnecessary where I'm concerned ... But looking at the calendar one day, I saw that it was his Saint's day. 'Today you must at last go in and visit him,' I said to myself, and put on my red kid gloves. I entered. None of my expectations came into being. I was served by a man in a blue apron, the porter, a duster over one shoulder. I keep waiting and waiting so as to catch sight of the esteemed gentleman. He doesn't arrive. Nothing of the kind. I get impatient and want to leave soon, so I ask the porter where his master has got to. The lad hesitates, I tell him to his face that the landlord has presumably got to pay the brewer that day and has done a bolt. And so it all came out: the host had treacherously gone off to the vintners' inns to taste the new wine, had gone away on his name-day to booze with another landlord, in his own company, as it were. There can be no doubt, the idea is as funny as can be and would make a fine subject for a Dutch painter: a landlord who goes for a drink at another landlord's; but I had sacrificed both time and money and had not found the fulfilment I had longed for. As if a mocking fate, which dearly loves to take everything from the little man in order to heap even more on the greater, wanted to rob me of this meagre event of mine, the staggering sight of a landlord celebrating his Saint's day! Odd, but typical, for tricks of this sort are for ever being played on me. Perhaps in order to put me out of the running, unviable creature that I am, by checkmating my every move. I won't even mention how, as I still had acquaintances, I would often not see them for months, only to see them all during the one day on which they had presumably agreed to congregate, with the aim of giving me — at the very least — a paralysed arm by continually waving at me. There are better examples.

Years ago, when I was somewhat more full of the joys of life, the shattering death of the two Pollak flies having not yet occurred and thus not warned me to maintain a calmer relationship with fate, in those days I bucked myself up, overcame any misgivings and bought myself a cane. In order to set out on adventures. That's not on without a cane. Just as a knight could not have battled with giants, dwarves and dragons for the sake of a virgin without his targe or with an undubbed saddle.

One Sunday I knotted my tie for the first and last time with a care which can only be compared, if at all, with that which the prophets must have spent girding their loins, and took the tram to Sievring. No small pleasure to whizz past the stops while others had to wait stiffly at them. Unfortunately a distant cousin boarded at Billroth Street, a snob of the first order with a volume of Balzac jutting ostentatiously out of his pocket. I jokingly admonished him for lugging bound books into the open countryside, particularly those which would soon be in everyone's pockets, pointing out that it was only truly worth his while to hawk books which weren't yet modern. He, however, misunderstood me completely and drew me into a lengthy discussion. About Balzac's end, how Friederike had supposedly betrayed Goethe like Sand betrayed Musset, and Oh, the idyll at Sesenheim! As a vicar's daughter she would have brought the theologist's child into the world as a matter of course — which is to say, when one leaves Lenz and a few French immigration officers to one side ... truth and poetry! We talked about woman and how every being, male or female, which bears the weight of reason or imagination, is more or less bound to be jealous and moreover cannot avoid suffering under the jealousy it has inherited from its animal forebears ... and one subject led to another and only when it was too late — the forest had already swallowed us up — did the pitiable wretch open his mouth to

Albert Ehrenstein / **TUBUTSCH**

tell me that I had missed the most important thing! An attractive young miss had been sitting in the tram, listening to my witticisms and resting her gaze on me all the while, and afterwards had even followed us a good way, but in the end, since it was difficult for her to speak with me, had dropped behind. I had been talking about woman until life, laughing, swaying and skipping and blossoming in all its glory just two steps away, had gone and left me! ... As if that wasn't enough, as we tried to make way for a unit of lovers to pass by on a narrow path, the female part of it stepped onto the cane I was elegiacally dragging behind me: the cane broke — a clear sign of Providence that I should at once leave the path I had scarcely set foot on ... On a nearby meadow a slender sixteen-year-old girl in the company of her mummy could find nothing better to do than pluck the autumn crocuses. I followed her example ...

I always live in expectation of something astounding which should come, enter, and break in on me. Such as an orang-utan, a wood grouse with eyes aglow, or best of all a raging bull. But then it occurs to me that he couldn't even get through the door, and I let my inflated hopes fade ... When someone rings, all of the neighbours peer out of their doors and I also go immediately to the threshold of my one-windowed room complete with separate entrance ... ready, should it be one of my old friends looking me up, to wrap myself in my overcoat and accompany him on a walk or, should he prefer, to show him the points of interest in my room: my boot-jack Philipp and — in sepulchral tones — the two Pollak flies ... I expect the astounding, or at least something pleasant: when I open up, the bell is usually for next door. Or it's a beggar. I don't give them anything. Firstly because I've nothing myself, and secondly if you give them something they leave at once, leaving you standing. And that is not my intention ... Unfortunately other people are also equally inconsiderate, they ring and go at once when they have received their information. A case recently ... there is a ring in the early hours, in a flash I am half dressed and have opened the door, standing in a draught: there is a man outside who asks me if I am the gentleman who ordered the crystal oil? Anyone else would have slammed the door in his face with a curse, I'm polite, rashly answer with: 'No!', but be that as it may, indicate my readiness to allow myself to be drawn into conversation ... simply on account of the strangeness of his profession. Crystal oil vendor ... however, he turns around brusquely, turns his back on me, and stomps off up the stairs ... and I have to pull myself together so as not to crack up under all the disappointments I have suffered ...

Jehangir Mirza says: 'I wave back and forth like a bodiless shadow, and fall flat on the ground if there is no wall to support me.' I have no wall to support me. It seems that something like a fall on the ground is also going to happen to me ... No, I can't take it any more! What's still keeping me? Schnudi, the toy bulldog, is no more. An old man with a fierce, bristling beard and a bundle over his shoulder ... Ahasuerus ... entered the courtyard, cried out his 'Any old rags and lumber?' The stranger's arrival seemed to confuse the dog, it let fly. The hawker shouts once, twice: 'Scram, won't you?' The dog doesn't hear, snaps at the intruder's legs. He in turn spits demoniacally between its eyes and the dog spins around like a mad thing, trying to remove the foreign object above its nose with its short tongue. He doesn't manage it, the hawker leaves, the dog carries on spinning, its eyes no longer see a thing, are blinded by the wild chase. Schnudi, Schnudi with the pink bow, keeps on turning and turning ... until he has to be shot ... Now I have nobody left. I even looked at a cabby's nag in the hope that it might want to talk with me ...

I bet it just didn't want to be seen talking with me. I'm sure that with a bit of effort it would have managed to talk if I were someone else ...

Albert Ehrenstein / **TUBUTSCH**

What stops me from making an end of it all, finding eternal rest in some lake or inkwell or solving the question: Which crazed god or demon owns the inkwell in which we live and die, and to whom in turn the crazed god belongs? Would it really be such a joy to slip up to some Marischa, and be she what she may, at any rate a whore or loose woman or adulteress, watching out all the while for the dung heap to the left, the cess pit to the right ... then to return home and sing the joys of the passionate love between Jehangir Mirza and Maasumeh Sultan Begum ... would it really be such a joy to manufacture ambrosia while having to devour filth oneself? And if one were a poet, one would still be no more than a born animal imitator. And even if you are a master of the word, who has found words as resonant as the roaring of a bull, you are still just a beggar and your sounding forth is no more than an imitation of the voice of the prince who rules the horses, and of the butterfly which wings its way to the light from out of its black chrysalis, assuming it's not just the voice of some other poet — yes, you imitator of animals, you let every conceivable voice ring out from you in order to drown your own emptiness, the lack of a voice of your own ... What am I waiting for? Off! Before I turn into a palsied cobbler ... Why keep on choking back the enervating conflict between petty fortunes and vast feelings and concepts?

Life. Such a magnificent word! I imagine life as a waitress who asks me what I want with my sausages, mustard, horseradish or gherkins ... the waitress's name is Thekla ... the possibilities are limited, but always these magnificent words! A discrepancy for many. Once I was invited to watch a famous chess master play a game of simultaneous chess. The assembly hall a stuffy, oppressive room full of tobacco smoke. Suddenly a cry rang out: 'The master's coming!' Who enters? A gormless looking individual with thin protruding ears in a worn out suit. But his short, blue jacket was certainly no more worn out than his face. Ha ha! The master is coming ... What else was there left to do? Not a lot. Once I had an acquaintance who in turn had a chum who had been in the fourth class with him at school. But did my one-time acquaintance's friend get taken out of the school and stuck behind a butcher's block or in a cobbler's shop because he lacked the application to become a blockhead like the rest and gain the teachers' approval? No, by chance he landed in a wine merchant's. A few weeks later he met my acquaintance on the main street — Waldemar Tibitanzel was his name, and he wrote unpublished poems — and he kept on boasting that after what was only a short apprenticeship he could already manufacture hundred year-old Bordeauxs within a few minutes. It is regrettable indeed that a young man who inspired such hope could also lose his footing in this career with a dream-like rapidity. Doubtlessly with his genius he would have soon been able to serve us a Bordeaux from the dawn of time, or at least from the Cambrian Era. He did nothing of the kind. The shape-shifter turned up in the Burg Theatre as an archangel. Shortly afterwards my acquaintance saw him again by the cathedral. Viewed artistically, Waldemar Tibitanzel's beard was the exact meeting point between Christ's and a young girl's, and a keen observer would have uttered the surmise, which was near to the truth, that he hadn't shaved. The black lacquer had flaked from the buckles of his shoes, revealing the yellow of the brass, and likewise the smallest details revealed the desolate state of his finances and his Austrianness. The archangel, seemingly engrossed in his clean-shaven face, ignored the unpublished writer who, a day later, complained to me bitterly. And before yet another week had run its course, Waldemar Tibitanzel had died in the middle of a five act tragedy. And if tomorrow I call this unknown wine adulterer and cod-actor to account for bygone deeds, then I do it out of a sort of solidarity, or to put it briefly: this is purely a matter of principles ... and not just empty wishes ... Then I, my God, even in the old days as I was still the king and many a person hankered after my greeting, I only bestowed it with irregularity. Sometimes I would give a

Albert Ehrenstein / TUBUTSCH

double greeting with a deep bow and the next time, afflicted by a sort of paralysis of the will, none at all, and when the populace wasn't content to put the double portion together with the non-received and divide it all by two, grumbling instead at my uncouthness, I didn't give a tiny damn for these flies. And if tomorrow I send my seconds — and lacking anyone else, then my fellows in fate and elective comrades, the old cobbler and the hat-maker, up to the archangel — then that is a completely different matter. I want to die and so eliminate a second person whose nothingness I have seen through, just as one eliminates a poisonous gas by turning off the tap and Ahasuerus eliminated Schnudi, the inferior toy bulldog ... Should I remain alive, which I hope I won't, I shall nevertheless bequeath my boot-jack and a certain inkwell to anyone who turns up: and should several contenders prove to have the same qualifications, then perfumed policemen will have priority. But before I crank the engine into action and go flying out of the curve to smash against a milestone, before I set off for that distant land ... close the shutters for the last time and deprive myself of my view of Linz Street, I want to make a last effort and bark an answer to the pinscher nervously pacing back and forth on the roof of a van, sit with the six children looking at the street worker, ask the cobbler Engelbert Kokoschnigg why he displays the sign 'The Two Lions,' and the greengrocer woman whether she is a widow and, if not, why she tolerates the pea-picking sparrow — I envy him in his care-free existence — I shall try to clap my eyes on landlord Dominik, observe myself in the lame-winged raven in Weihburg Lane, and should I be in a suitable mood, I shall solve the problem with my own ears as to whether poetesses really do say 'Tandaradei' in a particular situation. This life grants us no other joys than these ... Am I taken for a merry soul? Yes! Heartrendingly merry! This is all just gallows humour. And fear. And if life seems to consist of just such trifles, as I propose, then what if death choses to play a befitting role just to make fun of me? Disappoint me. Death, once the farmer with his scythe, an oaf to be sure, but even then a respectable personage accredited by countless paintings from notable artists, takes on increasingly ludicrous forms in my imagination. I don't picture him as the Black Knight, he appears as the approaching chess master, or a clown turns up, sticking out a tongue which grows into infinity and stabs me through ... I see him as a tram-conductor who clips my ticket, tells me it's invalid and won't wait for the next stop before insisting I get off ... with a few indispensable words in a Czech accent ... I see him as a young ruffian nailing up bats by their wings, a student kicking out the street lights, a minister who dissolves parliament and recently I even saw him as a bus driver. 'The driver is not permitted to talk with the passengers.' The parallel is obvious ...

I don't think I could bear it if even Death should fob me off with yet another disappointment ...

I have sunk into a deep apathy and listlessness, my soul is unable to take wing, I have avoided reading Goethe for a long time now because deep down I feel myself unworthy of him. And now will glorious death elude me too? My friend the reaper be reduced to a caricature? Would that be fair? He can look after himself, I've no alternative but to take my leave from earth, this one-windowed room complete with separate exit! Abandoned and forsaken ... What's so exceptional about that? Shutters fall ... nothing can be seen of the streets ... how I look forward to it! Why be afraid? I'll take a run-up and jump out. Or should I stay after all? Everyone's doing just fine. There are Dalmatian wines in the grocer's window. That didn't use to be the case. But I don't have anything at all, nothing which could make me happy deep inside. As I said, I've nothing except for — my name is Tubutsch, Karl Tubutsch ...

Carl Einstein

HERR GIORGIO BEBUQUIN

(1907)

I

The shards of a yellow glass lantern clattered to a wench's voice: would you like to see your mother's spirit? The shifty light dripped onto the delicately marked bald pate of a young man who anxiously deflected a question which might start him thinking about the consistency of his own person. He turned away from the Hall of Distorting Mirrors, which give more food for thought than the words of fifteen professors. He turned away from the Circus of Suspended Gravity, even though he admitted to himself with a smile that by doing so he was missing the chance to find the solution to his life. He avoided the Theatre of Mute Ecstasy with his head sunk in pride — ecstasy is unseemly, makes our abilities look foolish — and entered the Museum of Cheap Torpor with a shudder. The hazy form of a stout woman was sitting naked at the till. She was so broad in the beam that she wasn't so much sitting on a chair as on her melancholy, extremely ample derrière. She was wearing a yellow feathered hat with a broad-sweeping rim and emerald green stockings with garters that reached right up to her armpits and decorated her body with none too thrilling, vibrating arabesques. Red rubies stared up vertically from her sealion-hands: Evening, Mr Bebuquin, she said. Bebuquin entered a wearily lit room where a mannequin was standing, slightly plump, covered in rouge, eyebrows pencilled in and blowing the same kiss it had done for the entirety of its existence. Heartened by this lack of artistry, he sat down a few paces away from the doll. The young man didn't know what it was that drew him to the Philistine. Here was a quiet, friendly painlessness, which nonetheless left him cold. But what kept bringing him back was the peculiar fact that this calm, conventional smile could make him lose consciousness. The calm which surrounded every inanimate object outraged him, for he had not yet become sufficiently deadened to count as a pleasant person. He screamed at the mannequin, railed at it and threw it once again from the chair and out of the door, where the fat lady picked it up with a slight look of concern. He turned around in the empty room: I don't want a copy and no influences either. I want me, something absolutely unique must come out of my soul, even if it's just a vacancy stared into some private space. Things mean nothing to me, take one thing and you're committed to every other. It's there in the flow, and the infinity of a point is horrifying.

The fat lady, Miss Euphemia, returned and asked him to continue, when a stout gentleman addressed him sharply: Young man, take up the applied sciences. The tallow light of a realisation lit up painfully inside him: he had expected to watch a play but had ended up acting a part for another. He screamed: I am a mirror, a motionless puddle which gives a reflection and glistens in the light of the gas lamps.

Carl Einstein / **HERR GIORGIO BEBUQUIN**

But has a mirror ever reflected itself? The corpulent gentleman looked at him with commiseration. He had a small head and a silver brain pan with wondrously enchased ornamentations in which were set fine, glittering panels of gems. George wanted to get away; Nebukadnezar Böhm screamed at him in a rage: What are you doing jumping around in my atmosphere, you monster?

Pardon me, sir, your atmosphere is the product of factors which have no bearing on yourself.

All the same, Nebukadnezar replied kindly, it's a question of power, a matter of nomenclature and self-hypnosis.

Bebuquin straightened himself up. You must be from Saxony and have read Nietzsche, who went mad because he wasn't entrusted with a job in the police department and ended up having to write psychologically astute books to make ends meet.

Miss Euphemia asked the gentlemen to treat her spirit in a more rational manner, and said she would like to visit a dance hall. The two of them nodded and stamped off down the wooden staircase. Euphemia fetched her stole, and Nebukadnezar grabbed a megaphone and barked up at the wide, unrolling Milky Way: I am searching for the wondrous. Euphemia's lap dog fell out of the megaphone; Euphemia returned with a pleasant smile.

Dear friend, Nebukadnezar addressed him, eroticism is the ecstasy of the dilettante, but I shall put in a good word for you in my next review. Women are so irritating because they always give us the same thing. We, on the other hand, never want to admit that two completely different bodies have the same centre.

Adieu, I don't wish to keep you from proving your observations by deeds.

Euphemia asked the fat man to go and fetch something to eat and drink from a hotel, and turned back to tend to her dog as she had heard about its attack of dropsy. The fat man grasped at a tree and painfully at his throat. Then he also left, to tend to the dog. Nebukadnezar bowed his head over Euphemia's massive bosom. A mirror hung above him. He saw how her breasts divided into a multitude of strange shapes in the finely cut gemstone panels of his head, sparkling into shapes which no reality had previously ever been able to give him. The engraved silver refracted and refined the glittering of the forms. Nebukadnezar stared into the mirror, greedily enjoying the fact that he was able to dismember reality, that his soul was the silver and gemstones, his eye the mirror. Bebuquin, he shouted and collapsed; for he was still unable to bear the soul of things. Two arms dragged him back up, pressing him onto two firm, full breasts, and long tresses of hair fell over his silver cranium and every hair was a thousand forms. He recalled the woman and he realised, somewhat uneasily, that he was no longer able to penetrate through the flashing of the gems to get to her, and his body almost burst in the battle between two realities. But at the same time he was overcome by a wild joy because his silver brain virtually granted him immortality, for it raised every appearance to a higher power and he was able to switch off his thoughts, thanks to the precise cut of the stones and the thoroughly logical engravings. By means of the patterns of the engravings he could create himself a new logic whose visible symbols were the fissures in the capsule. It multiplied his powers, he believed himself to be in another, perpetually new world with new desires. He no longer apprehended his form through touch, had almost forgotten it as it writhed in pain, for the visible world no longer concurred with it.

Please don't abuse me, Bebuquin's reedy voice sounded from the mirror, don't get so het up about objects; it's all just combination, there's nothing new. Don't run riot with means which are out of place; where does that lead you? We can't stand outside our own skins. The whole business runs strictly according to causality. Yes, if logic were ever to let go of us, neither of us could say at what point it might come back into effect. That's the snag, my friend. You were almost starting to be original as you nearly went mad. Let's strike up the song of collective loneliness. Your addiction to originality results from your disgraceful emptiness; mine too. I shall take my leave from you without more ado. Then you can mirror yourself in your self. You see, that is a point. But objects won't get us any further either.

Lace curtains are drawn together.

II

Bebuquin tossed about on his pillow and suffered. First of all he set about trying to discover what 'suffering' is, and what purpose and reason suffering might still hold for him. But he came up with none; for as often as he dissected his pain he came across causes, or more precisely transmutations, which were everything else but suffering. He recognised that suffering is a stimulus for joy, a pleasant letting-go, and told himself that pain is nowhere to be found, and that all in all there's a ridiculously naïve mix-up at the bottom of this nomenclature; he realised that it's all just a fake tidying up, because the logical has nothing to do with the mental. He felt that logic was as bad as an artist who does a painting of a blonde wench and calls it virtue.

The problem with the logical is that it doesn't even hold on a symbolic level. You fatheads, you've simply got to see that logic should never be allowed to be anything but style, without ever touching on reality. We must make logical compositions, using the forms of logic like a decorative artist. We've got to realise that logic is the most fanciful thing of all.

He was seized with horror as he thought of the objects which were forever trying to suck him up, the way he annihilated objects with his symbolism, and how everything only exists by annihilation. Here he saw a justification of all that was aesthetic; but at the same time he also saw that since he could no longer see an ultimate purpose for the whole, he had also to deny it in the individual case. He longed for madness, but his last untamed remnants of humanity were too scared. His only hope seemed to be a respectable boredom; but not in order to slyly justify a system as the ebullient Schopenhauer had done, though it became clear to him that there was a stylistic factor of the first order lurking in boredom.

He leafed through a few maths books and it gave him a lot of pleasure to juggle about with infinity, just like a child with hoops and balls. But in so doing he did not believe that he was transposing himself into things, he noted that he was inside himself. He saw that it was inappropriate to call himself a poet, for in this art he would never get further than being intoxicated by the symbols. It in no way sufficed that the technique of poetry is symbolic, thus lending its objects a completely different sense; he still felt that spoken representation was just an imperfect art when measured against music. He cursed the scientists' efforts to reduce music to concrete physiological processes. But he felt decidedly pleased at the fact that they would interpret their digestion while being certain to give anything to do with the arts a wide berth. He was glad to see the confirmation of an old opinion of his, that the parts have absolutely nothing to say about the whole, that the synthetic is the unconscious pre-requisite for logical analysis and that the main issue would thus certainly be avoided, just as the psychologists did.

He cried out sadly, what poor material I would make for a novel, for I shall never accomplish a thing, just keep turning inside myself; I'd love to say something witty about human action, if only I just knew what it was. One thing's for sure, I've never acted or experienced.

Or enjoyed, you idiot, Nebukadnezar hissed into the room before slamming the lid of the commode shut again. Small shining clouds started to glow and a gauze curtain adorned with dainty blossoms was drawn open.

Sir, you were just wittering on about a clean separation from your ego. I see that you are seeking God. Yes, well, I admit that it is hard to see how the relative can become absolute through pleasure and other such passive intoxications. Just now you failed to forget the road to things; but in the end the results are all the same, you babe with your thinker's brow, he shouted with a raised index finger. I never worried about what I enjoy, but the fact that I enjoy was always of the greatest importance to me.

Sir, you are searching for aims with your belly. Away with you. And by the way, your transcendental pleasure machine was dangerous. Remember, I was witness to your blessed departure.

You still won't admit that it was simply my nerve chords which snapped. My ornamented brain was far more durable. It's simply outrageous how your trying seriousness keeps inspiring me to make bad jokes. And now your own unique reflection is gone. He got into bed next to Bebuquin.

Bebuquin, he began kindly, you're still a human being. Try out a few variations, you monotonous clod. Permit me to tell you the story of the curtains in the Garden of Signs. You Narcissus, you unproductive wretch you.

Giorgio lowered the blanket from his ears, stuck a biscuit in his mouth, and Böhm started up:

III

The Story of the Curtains

I stood before a large piece of sacking and screamed: You're nothing but knots.

Must you always be so abusive?

Don't interrupt me. I need to attest to myself. Soon I noticed that the sacking was nobody else but myself. It was my first knowledge of myself, but I forged on. There was an enormous rumbling. A storm tore me apart. I screamed in agony. I saw that the greater part of the sacking was done for. But at that moment I was totally dazzled by myself. Just imagine, I was a steely mountain range standing on its head. Tender blossoms of the soul concealed the ravines which even half a gross of cushions wouldn't have filled. I understood the whole nonsense and realised that a grain of sand is far more valuable than an infinite universe. I could also fathom the infinitesimal, the wonder of quality which cannot be annulled by historical or any other means. In any case, I noted that it all boiled down to the greatest possible ease of movement. I admit that here logic is inadequate, for every axiom disproves the next. Remember that proceeding from the proposition of causal thought one comes precisely to the acausal, but I am directing myself to the main issues with naïve devotion. I said to myself, Böhm, get rid of yourself. Anything personal is unproductive. Just be curtain and tear yourself to pieces. Insult yourself long enough that you turn into something else. Just be curtain and theatre play at one and the same time. You must always do the opposite if you feel a desire, or else you'll soon be up a gum tree. I have always said that doing the opposite is just as correct. And why keep on walking on two legs. Why not amputate one of them under the bedclothes in a fit of heroism?

Pleasure demands self-control and agony.

Basic tenet: avoid equilibrium.

As you see, my silver brain pan is asymmetrical. That's the root of my productivity. With the ever changing combinations one loses one's wretched memory of things and that embarrassing penchant for finality. Which you've not dared to think about to this day. The world is the means for thought. It's not a matter of knowing, that's a tautology void of any fantasy. But rather of thinking. Thinking.

And that puts the whole business in a new light, good sir. Geniuses never act, or they only appear to act. Your aim must be a thought, a newer one, indeed the very newest. Do you now understand the great Napoleon, Sir? The man wasn't ambitious. That is a projection of the dilettantes and university intriguers. The man tried every new means to help himself think; but he was something of an ideologist. Now here I must insist on one thing: don't lump me with the mawkish sentimentality of the pantheists. Those people could never grasp a good image; that's their problem. They are unconcentrated high-school boys who consequently never get beyond concepts, and they are precisely what I disown. The concept is just as much nonsense as the object. We'll never be free of combinations. The concept yearns for the things, but I want just the opposite. I direct my attention to pleasure. Now you can see that my end can almost be described as tragic. But put on your clothes. We're going to attend a hypothetical action, namely the mass for my death.

IV

Bebuquin had been staring at a corner of his room for weeks now, trying to bring it to life with his own being. It was horrifying for him to be dependent on the incomprehensible, never-ending facts which negated him. But his spent will-power was not even able to create a speck of dust, and with his eyes closed he could not see a thing. It must be possible, just as one used to be able to believe in a god who created the world out of nothing. I find it so embarrassing that I shall never be perfect. And why haven't I even the illusion of perfection? But then he noticed that a certain ability to picture the real still resided within him. He regretted this, however much everything seemed to him to be a matter of indifference. It was not that his basic instincts had extinguished. He said to himself that value is something quite alogical, and he did not want to construct a logic out of that. He didn't feel enlivened by this contradiction, had rather a feeling of suspension. Of rest. It was not negation that brought him pleasure. He despised these pretentious malcontents. He despised this impurity in the dramatic human being. He considered whether it might not be his own laziness which forced him to this viewpoint. But reasons were only side issues for him. It was a question of the thought, which was logical, and was also the source of its causes.

Böhm greeted him quietly and warmly. He had been taking care of himself since his death, for he had yet to find out anything definite about immortality. It's very gentlemanly of you to struggle with logic, with such mortal contempt. It does you credit. But unfortunately you're not going to have any success, for you only assume one logic and one non-logic. There are many logics inside us, my friend, logics which fight one another, and out of their battle arises the alogical. Don't let yourself be fooled by a few inept philosophers who keep rabbiting on about unity and the relationships of the parts to one another and their involvement in the whole. We are no longer so lacking in fantasy as to uphold the existence of a god. All that brazen twisting together of everything to form a whole only appeals to the laziness of one's fellow man. Look here, Bebuquin. First of all, people haven't a clue about the constitution of the body. Think of the broad cloaks of light the saints wear in the paintings of old, and please take it literally. But all that's just commonplace remarks. What you're lacking, my friend, is the wondrous. Do you see now why you've never got to grips with things and objects? You are a fantast who is lacking in means. I also once searched for the wondrous. Remember Melitta who fell out of the megaphone and what a fool I made of myself. The one thing women are good for is making a fool of yourself. It's the one form of selection which is just, because women are just full of idiocy. Thus one talks about woman's possibilities and in the end believes that she is fantastic. I've understood at least one thing since my blessed departure. You are a fantast because you haven't got it in you to be anything more. Without doubt the fantastic is just as equally a question of matter as it is of form. But you mustn't forget one thing. Fantasts are people who can't get to the bottom of a triangle. Not that one should call them symbolists. But in Heaven's name, you quite simply need this dilettantism. You've never ever seen a handful of people, or a leaf. Think of a woman standing under a lamppost, a nose, a belly of light, and that's all. Light, intercepted by people and houses. There's something else I'd like to add to this. Guard yourself against quantitative experiments. In art both number and size are completely irrelevant. If they play any role at all, it can only be a derivative one. It's pure dilettantism to work with infinity. Here I must give you another piece of advice which may inspire you later. Kant will certainly come to play a large role. But watch out. His seductive importance lies in the fact that he managed to create a balance between object and subject. But he overlooked one thing, the most important: what the subject — the practitioner of the theory of knowledge — does, which actually determines the subject and the object. Is that a psychic Thing in Itself then? There's the catch — the reason why German idealism could exaggerate Kant to such an extent. The uncreative will always waste their energies on the impossible. Be unable to recognise the boundaries, how much of the spiritual the objects can bear and assume. All this piffle about infinity comes from unformed and unapplied mental energy. It is the expression of potential energies, which is to say the concern of powerful inability.

Gustav Meyrink

THE RING OF SATURN

(1908)

The youths came groping up the spiral staircase step by step.

A darkness filled the laboratory, and the light from the stars trickled in thin, cold streams down the polished brass of the tubes of the telescopes, down into the round room.

By turning slowly from side to side and allowing one's eyes to wander, one could see the rays of light as they splashed onto the metal pendula that hung from the ceiling. The darkness of the floor swallowed up the glistening drops as they fell from the smooth, gleaming machines.

Gustav Meyrink / THE RING OF SATURN

'Today the master is going to study Saturn,' said Wijkander after a while, and he pointed his finger at the large telescope which stretched down from the night sky like the stiff, wet horn of a giant snail. Not one of the youths contradicted him; they were not even amazed when they approached the lens and saw that Axel Wijkander's words were correct.

'This is all a puzzle to me — how can anyone in semi-darkness tell which star the telescope's pointed at, just by its position?' one of them asked in admiration. 'How can you know so exactly, Axel?'

'I can feel it, the whole room is full of Saturn's suffocating influence. Believe me, Doctor Mohini, the telescopes — they suck at the stars at which they are pointed — are like living funnels which draw the rays, both visible and invisible, down into the vortices of their magnifying lenses!'

'Anyone who like myself has spent years keeping watch through the nights, his senses always at the ready, learns to feel not just the fine, imperceptible aura of the stars, and to perceive their ebb and flow and how they seize hold of our minds with a silent grip, undoing our resolve in order to slip new ideas in their place; how these malicious powers wrestle with one another in grim, hate-filled silence to gain the upper hand and steer the ship of our fates — he also learns to dream in wakefulness and see how, at certain hours of the night, the soulless phantoms of dead heavenly bodies slip into the realms of the visible, greedy for life, and exchange mysterious understandings through strange, halting gesticulations which awaken an indefinite, nameless horror in our souls ... But let's turn on the light. We could easily disturb the objects on the table here in the darkness, and the master dislikes things being moved from their place.

One of his companions went over to the wall and groped for the electric lamp. The quiet hiss of a searching finger could be heard moving about the alcove, then all of a sudden there was light and the bright yellow bronze of the pendula and telescope shone out gaily into the room.

The night sky, which had just snuggled its velvety skin up close to the window, suddenly recoiled and hid its countenance far, far away in the icy space beyond the stars.

'There's the large round bottle I was telling you about yesterday, Doctor,' said Wijkander, 'the one the master used in his last experiment.

'And if you look up there on the walls you will see the metal rods which produced the alternating current, the so-called Hertzian waves, which enclosed the bottle in an electric field.

'Doctor, you have promised to keep absolute silence about everything you are about to see and experience, and to do everything you can to help us in your capacity as a psychiatrist.

'Do you really believe that when the master arrives and, believing himself to be unobserved, starts to perform certain operations which, although I can obviously give you a hint of, it is impossible to reveal in any greater depth, that you will be able to remain uninfluenced by his external actions and grasp the core of his being and tell, just by observation, whether one can rule out insanity?

'Will you be able to suppress your scientific prejudices to such an extent that, should it come to it, you will openly admit that it is indeed an unknown mental state, perhaps similar to the deep sleep known as the "Turya trance" — that it is something which science has never encountered, but which is not insanity?

'Would you have the courage to admit that, Doctor? You see, only our love for the master and our wish to protect him from his downfall has given us the courage to take this step, to bring you here and have you see things which have perhaps never been seen by an uninitiated eye.'

Doctor Mohini gazed in front of him. 'I will honestly do all that I can, and will respect your requests and all the confidences with which you entrusted me yesterday; but when I think it all over carefully, it's all too stupid for words. Can there really be a science, a truly hidden knowledge which is supposed to have investigated and mastered an enormous range of phenomena whose very existence we have never even suspected?!

'You are not just talking about magic, I mean black and white magic. I've heard you talking about the secrets of a green, hidden realm and the invisible inhabitants of a violet world!

'You say that you yourself practise ... violet magic, and belong to an age-old brotherhood which has preserved these secrets and arcana from the grey pre-dawn of man.

'And you talk of the "soul" as if it were something *proven*! It's supposedly a fine, material vortex, the bearer of an exact consciousness?!

'And not just that: your master is supposed to have trapped just such a soul inside that glass container there, by keeping the bottle bathed in the waves of a Hertzian oscillator!? I can't help it, but that's really, God knows, the greatest ...'

Axel Wijkander shoved back his chair with impatience, walked up to the large telescope and peered in, disgruntled.

'Yes, but what else should we say, Doctor Mohini?' asked one of the friends at last. 'That's just how it *was*; the master *did* keep a human soul isolated here in the bottle for a long time. He had released it from its restraining wrappers, one by one, like removing the layers of a sea onion; had refined its powers and — one day it just disappeared, had penetrated the glass wall and the isolating electrical field, and escaped ... !'

At this moment a loud cry from Axel Wijkander interrupted the speaker, and everybody looked up in astonishment.

Wijkander gasped for breath: 'A ring, a *serrated* ring. With white filigree, it's unbelievable, unheard of!' he screamed. 'A new ring, a new ring around Saturn has formed!'

One after another they looked into the lens and could hardly control themselves for amazement.

Doctor Mohini, who was not an astronomer, could neither understand the significance of such a phenomenon as the formation of a new ring around Saturn, nor appreciate its immense consequences. He had hardly begun to form a few questions when a man's heavy footsteps were heard coming up the spiral staircase.

'For God's sake, back to your places, turn that light out, the master's coming,' ordered Wijkander in great haste. 'And you, Doctor, stay hidden in your alcove, no matter what happens, you hear! If the master sees you, everything's lost.'

A moment later the observatory was once more in complete darkness and still as the grave.

The steps came nearer and nearer. A figure in a white silken gown entered the room and lit a tiny lamp on the table, which gave out a narrow, dazzling circle of light.

'It tears my soul apart,' whispered Wijkander into his neighbour's ear, 'the poor, poor old master, how deeply grief has furrowed his brow.'

The aged man walked up to the telescope, took a long look into it, then stumbled back to his table like a broken man.

'The ring is growing by the hour – now it's even growing points as well. It's ghastly,' the adept's despairing moans could be heard, and he buried his face in his hands in searing pain.

He sat like that for a long, long time, and the youths sobbed quietly in their hiding-places.

At last he sprang up in wild resolve, rolled the bottle over to the telescope and laid three objects of indeterminable shape beside it on the floor.

Then he knelt down stiffly in the middle of the room and formed curious poses with his upper body and arms resembling geometrical figures or instruments; simultaneously he murmured monotonous sentences which from time to time turned into long drawn out howling vowels.

'All merciful God, protect his soul, it is the invocation of the typhoon,' whispered Wijkander to the others, appalled. 'He wishes to force the escaped soul back from outer space. If he fails, he forfeits his life by suicide. Brothers, give me all your attention and when I give the sign, seize him. And hold on tight to your hearts, for the proximity of the typhoon alone is enough to burst their chambers!'

The adept remained kneeling and motionless, and his vocalisations became louder and more wailing.

The small flame on the table cast a murky glow and began to swell, smouldering like a glowing eye through the room, and it seemed to gradually take on a greenish violet colour in small, barely noticeable spasms.

The thaumaturge's murmuring had completely ceased, but, at long regular intervals, his voice rang out, cutting the air with bloodcurdling cries.

Otherwise not a sound. A silence, as alarming and terrible as the gnawing pains of death ...

A feeling descended on them, as if everything around had fallen to ash and the room were sinking at breakneck speed to somewhere or other that lay in an inexplicable direction, ever deeper down and down into the suffocating realm of the past.

Then suddenly comes a groping, slimy splashing as if a wet, invisible creature was rushing through the room in short, hasty jumps.

Violet shimmering handprints appear on the floor, slither and grope indecisively back and forth, trying to rise up as bodies from the realm of surfaces; they fall back down, powerless. Pallid, phantom-like beings — the brainless, horrifying leftovers of the dead — have separated themselves from the wall and glide about, senselessly, aimlessly, half conscious, with the reeling, swinging movements of idiotic cripples, their cheeks blown out by mysterious, half-witted smiles. Slowly they drift, very slowly and furtively, as if wishing to cloak some inexplicable and ruinous design, or they stare malevolently into the distance, only to suddenly shoot forward a short distance, with the lightning speed of vipers.

Bulbous bodies fall silently from the ceiling, roll up and creep about — the white, ghastly spiders which inhabit the spheres of suicides and weave from mutilated cruciforms the web of the past, which grows and grows ceaselessly, from hour to hour.

Icy terror blasts through the room — the ungraspable, lying beyond all thought and understanding, the strangling fear of death, which has no roots nor origin in any cause: the formless brood animal of horror.

A hollow sound of something falling resounds across the floor, Doctor Mohini has collapsed dead.

His face is thrown right back, his mouth gapes wide. 'Hold on to your hearts, the typhoon! ...' Axel Wijkander's shout can be heard, and then a flood of unbound happenings breaks in from every side, one crashing in on top of the next. The large bottle explodes into a thousand strangely shaped splinters, the walls give out a phosphorescent light.

An alien putrescence infiltrates the edges of the skylight and window alcoves, turning the hard stone into a swollen mass like bloodless, denatured gums; eating into the walls and ceiling with the speed of licking flames.

The adept has sprung up, reeling; in mental confusion he has grasped a sharp pointed sacrificial knife and plunged it into his breast.

The youths have seized his arms, but can no longer close the deep wounds from which his life oozes.

The bright beams of the electric-light are victor once more in the round room of the observatory, and the spiders and phantoms of foulness have disappeared.

The bottle, however, lies smashed, clear scorch marks cover the floor, and the master bleeds to death on a mat. They have searched in vain for the sacrificial knife. Mohini's corpse lies on its chest beneath the telescope, limbs cramped together, and his upturned face grins at the ceiling with a grimace twisted by the horror of death.

Gustav Meyrink / **THE RING OF SATURN**

The youths surround the master's couch, and he gently resists their pleas for him to spare himself. 'Allow me to talk with you and forget your sorrow. Nobody can keep me alive, and my soul is full of yearning to finish that which I was unable to do in my bodily form.

'Did you not see how the aura of decay walked through this house! Just one brief moment more and it would have become material-like fog precipitating into hoar frost – and everything inside the observatory, you and I, would just be mould and putrefaction.

'The singe-marks there on the floor, they originate from the hate-filled inhabitants of the pit, who vainly grabbed for my soul. And just as their marks stand here burnt into the wood and stone, their other work would have become permanent and visible, were it not for the courageous way you threw yourselves between us.

'For everything which is "permanent" on the earth, as the fools put it, was previously spectre; spectre, visible or invisible, and there is nothing more than spectre *solidified*.

'Thus whatever it be, beautiful or ugly, noble, good or bad, joyous with a hidden death in its heart, or sad with a hidden joy in its heart – there is always something of the spectre in it.

'Even if only a few can feel this ghostliness in the world, it is there all the same, eternal and everlasting.

'The basic lesson of our order is that we should climb the sheer walls of our lives and reach the peak of the mountain, where the gigantic magician stands, and with his dazzling mirror, conjures the world below out of its deceitful reflections!

'You must understand that I have wrestled for the highest knowledge, have searched for a human existence to kill, in order to investigate its soul. I wished to sacrifice a human being who was truly useless on earth, and I mixed with people, among men and women, and imagined that such a one would be easy to find.

'With the joy of certainty, I visited solicitors, doctors and the military – I nearly succeeded among the high-school teachers: nearly!

'But it was always nearly, for there was always a small, often just minute, secret sign on them, which forced me to let them go.

'Then came the day when I at last hit upon it. Not just a single creature, no, a whole stratum.

'Like unintentionally finding a troop of woodlice when picking up an old pot from the cellar floor.

'Vicars' wives!

'That was it.

'I had listened in on a whole gaggle of vicars' wives, how they ceaselessly went about "making themselves useful"; holding meetings "for the instruction of the domestics"; knitting warm, disgusting socks for the poor little negro children who enjoy running around naked as God intended; distributing public morals and protestant cotton gloves. And how they pester us, poor, plagued humanity: one really should collect silver foil, old corks, paper scraps, bent nails and other rubbish, so that "nothing goes to waste!"

'And as I saw how they set about hatching up new missionary societies and diluting the mysteries of the holy books with the dish-water of "moral" enlightenment, the cup of my wrath was full.

'I had one already under my knife, a strawberry-blonde, "German" beast, a genuine product of Wendian-Kashubian-Obitritian blood, when I saw she was blessed with child, and Moses' age-old law commanded me to stop. I caught a second, and a tenth and a hundredth, and they were always blessed with child!

'So I went on the prowl day and night — like a dog after crabs[1] – and at last I succeeded in fishing one out from her lying-in bed at the right moment!

'She was a Saxon woman with blue goose eyes and a greased-flat parting.

'For nine months I kept her locked up, out of conscience, just in case something might appear after all, or a sort of virginal multiplication occurred, like the deep sea molluscs which multiply by segmentation or such like.

'In the unwatched moments of her imprisonment she secretly wrote a thick tome entitled: *Words from the Heart as a Dowry for German Daughters upon their being received into the Circles of Adulthood*'!

'But I caught the book in time and incinerated it in an oxy-hydrogen blow-pipe ... !

'At last I separated her soul from her body and held it isolated in the glass bottle, when one day the inexplicable odour of goat's milk led me to suspect the worst, and before I could put the Hertzian oscillator – which had clearly failed for a moment – back into operation, the disaster had already occurred and the *anima pastoris* had flown, never to be brought back.

'I immediately resorted to the strongest bait, laid a pair of ladies' knickers made of pink fustian (registered trademark 'Lama') on the window sill, an ivory backscratcher, yes, even an album of edifying verse in poisonous blue velvet with golden abcesses. All for nothing! I turned to the laws of occult Telenergy which govern the operation of magical charms at a distance — all in vain!

'A distilled soul is simply not to be caught!!

'Now she is living in outer space and teaches the unsuspecting planet spirits the infernal arts of female handicraft.

'And today she actually managed to give Saturn ... *a new crocheted ring!!*

'And that was too much for me.

'I have thought of just about everything and cudgelled my brains; there remain but two ways; either to apply an irritant, that's Scylla; or withhold the irritant, that's Charybdis.

'You know Johannes Muller's brilliant teaching. He wrote: "One may illuminate the retina of the eye, or variously exert pressure or heat or apply an irritant, but regardless which, the objective stimulus is never perceived as the corresponding pressure, warmth or electricity. Rather it is always just perceived as visual sensation. Moreover, when one illuminates the skin, or applies light, pressure or electricity, this will never be experienced as anything other than tactile sensation, with all that that entails."

'And this relentless law governs out there as well, for — if one *applies a stimulus or irritant* to the essential core of a vicar's woman, regardless what, *she crochets,* and if she stays *unstimulated* ...' the master's voice became quiet and unearthly, 'then ... then ... *it just ... reproduces itself.*'

The adept sank down dead.

Shaken to the core, Axel Wijkander folded his hands:

'Let us pray, brothers. He has entered the realm of peace – may his soul be happy for ever and ever!'

Georg Heym

THE DISSECTION

(1911)

The dead man lay naked and alone on a white table in the large theatre, in the oppressive whiteness, the ghastly sobriety of the operating theatre in which the screams from never-ending tortures still seemed to reverberate.

He was bathed by the noonday sun which caused the livid spots to awaken on his forehead; it conjured a bright green from his naked belly and swelled it up like a large water skin.

The body was like the iridescent calyx of an enormous flower, a mysterious plant from the Indian jungles which someone had shyly placed before the Altar of Death.

Magnificent reds and blues grew along his loins, and the large wound beneath his navel slowly burst open in the heat like a red furrow in a field, emitting an awful smell.

The doctors entered. A group of amiable gentlemen with white gowns, duelling scars and golden pince-nez.

They walked up to the corpse and looked at it with interest, immersed in scientific discussion.

They took their dissecting instruments out of the white cabinets, white chests full of hammers, bonesaws with sturdy teeth, files, terrible batteries of forceps, small cases bristling with enormous needles which seemed to be eternally screaming for flesh like twisted vulture beaks.

They started their appalling handiwork. Like dreadful torturers, blood streaming over hands which thrust ever deeper into the cold corpse, drawing out its innards, like white cooks gutting a goose.

The intestines coiled round their arms: greenish-yellow snakes, and the excrement dripped down their gowns, a warm, putrid liquid. They lanced the bladder; the cold urine glistened inside like a yellowish wine. They poured it into large bowls; it smelt harsh and pungent like ammonia.

But the dead man slept. Patiently he allowed himself to be tugged back and forth, to be wrenched from side to side by the hair, and slept.

And while the hammer blows crashed down on his head, a dream, the remnants of love, awoke in him like a burning torch shining out into his night.

A great, broad sky opened up in front of the large window, filled with small, white clouds floating in the light, like small, white gods in the quiet of the afternoon. And the swallows circled high above in the blue of the sky, quivering under the warm July sun.

The black blood of death ran over the blue putrescence of his forehead. It evaporated in the heat and formed a terrible cloud, and death's decay crept over him with its brightly coloured claws. His

Georg Heym / THE DISSECTION

skin started to flow apart, his stomach turned white as an eel's under the greedy fingers of the doctors, who bathed their arms up to the elbows in the moist flesh.

The putrefaction twisted the dead man's mouth apart, he seemed to smile, he dreamed of blissful stars, of a sweet-scented summer eve. His melting lips trembled as if from a fleeting kiss.

'How I love you. I've loved you so deeply. Shall I tell you how much I love you? As you walked through the poppy fields, yourself a fragrant poppy-flame, you had drunk the whole evening into yourself. And your dress billowed round your ankles like a wave of fire in the setting sun. But your head was inclined in the light and your hair kept burning, flaming from all my kisses.

'And so you left and kept turning to look at me. And the lantern in your hand continued swinging in the twilight, like a glowing rose, far into the distance.

'I shall see you again tomorrow. Here beneath the chapel window, here, where the light falls from the candles and transfigures your hair into a golden forest, here, where the daffodils nestle up to your ankles, tender as soft kisses.

'I shall see you again every evening at the hour of dusk. We shall never forsake one another. How I love you! Shall I tell you how much I love you?'

And the dead man trembled quietly in rapture on his white dissecting table, while the iron chisels in the doctors' hands split open the bones of his temples.

Ferdinand Hardekopf

THE MENTAL LINK[1]

(1912)

Something one knows well: when the desired state of drowsiness, a profound stupor as is induced by mocha, snaps back closer to consciousness with a brusque jerk? When sadly we are flung higher, towards the light? The bed and feeling of ease are still so soothing; but now we are less distant from our responsibilities, we are quietly appalled because we feel we cannot slip back into those imaginary corridors. (O, such comfortable ones!) That luxuriousness came without our command, without payment. Now it is gone. We are still beneath the threshold of wakefulness — but now this extreme is also imminent. Just one thought, too full of concern, none too willing to depart, was to blame for this dis-illusion, dis-satisfaction, this désenchantement.

Then I awoke. The window was wide open — on the far side of a wilderness of women's clothing. Moonlight crept in from outside, cream and green, along with soft bundles of these perfumes: myrrhs, which the rain has coaxed from the trees on the boulevards by evening; an erotic sort of petrol which powers certain sorts of car; every vegetable from the breathing ground; the naïve pungency of the street; the inner mysteries of woman; and the silent skirmishes at the outposts of fear. But fine perfumes calmed me in my bedroom, along with the white mirrors, soft-yellow pillows, so much pampering sumptuousness — yet as if forbidden and paid for by acts of decision which no one would acknowledge, not even you, you waifs, scarcely ... I spotted mama, so sweetly mirrored inside the angelic chalky frame.

'Darling, you're already awake and it's still only early evening?' she said.

Not everything became recognisable at once. Every sleep falsifies the world anew — or (less deceitful) some sleeps summate, some eliminate the woken experience. Mama stood there, almost fully dressed, but once again her breast was so lightly covered, and it must be chilly outside — the long velvet wrap, which had no trim, was still nestling round the arm of the chair — so frail, so aware of the effect which had to be achieved. Mama dabbed the powder puff in her compact, the silver ... and lipstick and make-up could only cast suspicion on this countenance: this stage of never-ending love.

At this point I understood my torpor, and also the disjointedness of the lyricisms. Yes, I — *I* was allowed to be weary all the time. She, all the more beautiful, I, all the more tormented ... But I knew that already, it could not affect me, I sent it packing. Managerial problems. There was no passion to keep me any longer from my duties, or the perception of sensations ensuing from this attitude.

The citizens, doctors, dramatists, parliamentarians had paved one province after another with trashy terrors. I rejected it outright.

Mama's lips blossomed strawberry-red. Her gaze glowed from blue ice. She came (ah) from the winter, it was long since springtime. A doe. My love for her was unbounded.

'And you promise me –' I said.

She, in the doorway: '– that I won't feel anything? Please darling, must I tell you again, you know I won't.'

She was already gone ...

Should I go to the café with a book? That afternoon there had been a smart lady in Café de la Métempsychose — in the soft colours of the late Renoir. No doubt she deserved to be adored. And my nerves had been ready to launch out into this great intoxication; but I, an experienced rough-rider, bridled them. One must be cold if one wishes to savour chaos. Every rapture must be prepared, just as the Compagnie Générale du Travail prepares a strike. The lady's hands disclosed that she was the daughter of a railway baron. She must have made a lot of delightful, quite exemplary mistakes. And to the question as to whether she believed in God, she would have answered: 'That all depends on whether God believes in me.' Perhaps I would find this billionairess once more and be allowed to put pretty words in her mouth from a provocative distance ...

I didn't go to the café. Mama returned late that night. Accompanied.

'Darling, I want to — '

I finished it off for her (for my nerves already knew as much) — 'introduce you to your new father.'

'Yes.'

My, was she sweet.

A decorous bow from Mr Frock Coat, now almost in possession of his privileges. Doubtless a civil servant, a philosopher, a person who coined necessary phrases about nationalism and dishonour and traditional capabilities.

Ferdinand Hardekopf / THE MENTAL LINK

That which was about to take place was surely the holiest of holies — that, which I *knew and took back*, — like a creator who *sucked* his universe *back* inside himself —

... But here this true story takes two directions. The more repulsive reading has shots being fired from somewhere or other: Mama is dead. A wire frame has (in a last scrap of respect) conserved her figure, and lends expression to my vain, fumbling despair. Mama is dead for Mr Frock Coat and, in the best respects, for me too — that was to be expected.

In contrast to this an idyll, a friendlier, more Germanic version of the story. He became the most loving Papa to me. He read every wish from my mama's (long since unpainted) lips. From time to time she leant over him roguishly and whispered sweet nothings into his ever attendant ear. Then she would bury her bashfulness in his broad chest. And bit by bit my sole rulership was usurped by countless hordes of, admittedly anaemic, siblings.

Wassily Kandinsky

BASSOON

(1912)

Very large houses suddenly collapsed. Small houses remained untouched. A fat hard egg-shaped orange-cloud suddenly hung over the town. It seemed to hang from the pointed peak of the tall, lank tower of the town hall and radiated violet.

A naked, spindly tree stretched its twitching and trembling long branches into the depths of the skies. It was completely black, like a hole in white paper. Its four small leaves trembled a long time. Although the wind was calm.

Yet when the storm came, felling many a heavy walled building, the thin branches remained motionless. The small leaves became stiff, as if cast in iron.

Wassily Kandinsky / BASSOON

A flock of crows flew through the air in a straight line over the town. And suddenly everything was still once more.

The orange-cloud disappeared. The sky turned a sharp blue. The town a yellow that moved one to tears.

And through this calm came just one sound: the clatter of horseshoes. With that everyone knew that a white horse was wandering all alone through the desolate streets. This sound continued for a long time, for a very, very long time. And for that reason no one could really tell when it stopped. Who can say when silence begins?

Then everything was gradually turned green by the lingering, attenuated, somewhat expressionless, impassive, long-drawn sounds of a bassoon which wavered for a long time in the depths of empty space. At first deep and somewhat grimy. Then increasingly bright, cold, poisonous, even brighter, even colder, even more poisonous.

The buildings grew taller and became narrower. They all leaned towards a point to the right, perhaps to the coming day. Something like a striving towards the morning became noticeable.

And then the sky, the houses, the cobblestones and the people who walked upon them became even brighter, even colder, even more poisonously green. The people walked onwards, ceaselessly, unremittingly, slowly, constantly looking ahead. And always alone.

But correspondingly a large, opulent crown now flourished on the naked treetop. Up there on high, the crown had a compact, upwards-curving sausage-like form. This crown was itself of such a garish yellow that no heart would be able to endure it.

It is good that none of the people walking below saw this treetop. Only the bassoon attempted to capture this colour. It rose ever higher, its tense tone became shrill and nasal. How good that the bassoon never reached this note.

Mynona

A CHILD'S HEROIC DEED

(1913)

Christian, a pavior from the vicinity, left the open countryside and set off to a small chamber where his bride awaited him. In such circumstances every moment is precious; Christian hurried himself and surprised his lass in a situation which, although it did not cool his love, caused the girl a great deal of shame and embarrassment. Christian grew coarse: 'Shut your fuss!' There was an exchange of words, with the result that the situation found its ultimate conclusion. Christian had been kept on short rations. With that the two of them went to bed, the sun sank a bloody red and a lukewarm summer night suffused through the window, conjuring up a dreamy atmosphere.

Mynona / A CHILD'S HEROIC DEED

Exactly nine months after this blood red sunset, poor Mathilde brought a monstrosity into the world: a creature as red as a hard-boiled crab, with spiny outgrowths instead of hair. But nonetheless it managed to live, and was known throughout its life as the red hedgehog.

Now it happened that the director of a natural history collection in the neighbouring town got wind of this event and made up his mind to take a look at, and maybe even custody of, the red hedgehog. He travelled to the simple, open-hearted folk and encouraged them to hand over the red hedgehog to his collection on payment of a tidy sum:

'Where have you stored him?'

'Aaah, well,' replied Christian, 'he's still alive and kicking!'

'What!' the curator was astonished, 'I thought I would be correct in assuming that you had him preserved in alcohol.'

At that moment the red hedgehog came up to them and cast each of them a perky look. The director took an exceptional liking to the young lad. 'A lovely example, could be my greatest catch,' he thought. 'Your boy has just one shortcoming, he's *alive*. Only dead monstrosities are of use to me.' With that he departed, leaving Christian and Mathilde painfully disappointed. Both of them looked irritably at the red hedgehog.

'Father, would the gentleman put me in alcohol if I was no longer alive?'

'Yes, you miserable wretch, and give us money to boot, so we'd be a lot better off than having you around.'

'Hmm, mummy,' the red hedgehog inquired further, 'wouldn't you be sad if I were dead and swimming about in alcohol?'

Mathilde denied this at once. 'What? When you could at last help us earn a decent penny! On the contrary, you scumbag!'

Scared away by his parents' coarse natures, this thirster for knowledge toddled off down the village street when, lo and behold!

the director drove past in his trap. 'Sir, sir!' the boy called. The director recognised him and halted with interest: 'What can I do for you, young man?' 'If I were dead, would I end up in a jar?' 'In a beautiful, clean glass container full of the purest alcohol, my dear sweet child. Stuck on it would be a dainty label, on which: "Abortus VIII, Class B, Example 454" would be written in the fairest of hands.' 'Oh, dear sir, please write that down for me.' The director obliged with a smile: 'Here you are, you strange little lad!'

The strange little lad went to his parents: 'Stop being so sad, it can all still turn out for the best.' His father and mother pricked up their ears eagerly. 'Just bring a glass container large enough for me to get into,' said the boy. Father fetched one. 'Now fill it with pure alcohol,' the child decreed. The father complied with an air of joy, for he suspected the best. Meanwhile the boy asked Mathilde to stick the label with the director's writing onto the glass.

The boy undressed himself, and before the delighted parents could give him a helping hand, he dived head first into the jar. The parents shed tears of joy, and took it down to the post office. They received a letter of thanks from the director, saying that the dispatch was perfectly in keeping with the regulations regarding oddity.

Later, when of a summer night the sun set once more a bloody red, Mathilde and Christian would sink in speculative dreamings and think of their heroic red hedgehog.

... Oh cowardly times, when so many twins still fail to find the courage to grow together at their backsides.

Hans Arp

WINTERGARTEN[1]

(1913)

B lossoming branches covered with shining lamps are growing from the stars. Wine is flowing in streams from the stars' eaves. Mr Archie A. Goodale wanders between the stars with his head hanging in the depths. Sometimes he sways pensively, like a heavy grape.
   The voice of the lady singer let forth at full belt, right at the start of the gruesome tragedy. As if she wanted to drown the murderous whirling and swirling with her song. She sang in the loudest fortissimo. There was no estimating the extent of the tragedy. The tremendous roar of the blood merely seemed to spur the singer to

carry on with undiminished force. She sang on undaunted, even though every attempt failed to put a stop to this monstrosity with its dark fluids of murder, madness and dreams.

The man's transparent skin allows a clear view of his innermost being. Everything twitches and jiggles and jerks inside him while he sprawls out langorously with his clockwork, his framework and canals. The red, yellow and blue cords which perform the twitching, jigging and jerking, intensify the horror which seizes the spectator at the sight of all live bodily existence. Thus, given the complexity and unreality of our flocculent being, from now on we would prefer to represent this anatomy primitively, like the folds in the raiments of the saints of old.

Iridescent skulls, blond hides, filled with hairs, animal fruits and needles. Helmets made from bright fuzzy hairs in front of black paper shades. Out of moss and down shimmer dewy fauns and classical vices.

Eternity smokes our inner joy and suffering, as if in a pipe. We recompense ourselves with our dream, with good old drink. We slurp down the dream in long swigs, until the day wakes us with its shrillness and tears us back from the other side. Helpless and quaking, we are forced to resurrect once more. A number of eyes are filled with the darkness of theatre boxes, with their little erotic expedients. But the song of the parturient woman continues to ring out from behind natural flowers.

The sparkling nickel-plated trapezes sway and swing out — flashes of sheet lightning at the back of the stage. Rosy spheres have made a big show on them. Now they draw away into the gloomy distance. Bye-bye, bye-bye. All too soon their skills will be forgotten. One won't remember the tip of the tiniest nose or even the teensiest pinkie belonging to those rosy spheres. A surge of handkerchiefs and glassy gems sinks down majestically from the balustrade. Golden lion-skins ferment in a net. O the astonished faces of the geraniums and housewives!

Hans Arp / **WINTERGARTEN**

Genuflect before the diamond altars in the gardens of blossoming crucifixes! A heart perishes on a brazen mouth. It breathes and trickles and solidifies into silver threads. A dream forms lines full of the most subtle power, such as are to be found in the finger arrangement of the Buddhas and whose pride and definitive explanations are squandered on such trifles as suns and stars.

Rajahs before the painted backdrops of European minds, intoxications full of Guys'[2] grace smelling sweetly of oriental perfumeries. Pirouettes from the days of gallantry. Good-natured dream-beast masks from a mid-summer night's haunting, pervaded by a girly loveliness in a shimmer of pearls. Salons, whose figures have been influenced by the freshness of meadows, turquoises, gauze. There's a rustling in these salons as from green, evergreen treetops. And full of proud friendliness, their figures sing like water-springs in lace-trimmed nests. The conventions of a more intimate manner of painting and a more secret style force their way through a couple of small blue rents, into the bird-hearts of these salon figures.

Feelings whose heavens bear blazing hearts and whose people have stars in their breasts. Mix-ups between women and plants. Cages full of flowers. Twilight-circuses. Metamorphoses of night-blossoming tree-crowns into book-cover caryatids. Curious blendings of natural juices and remote artificialities.

Alfred Wolfenstein

FAR GREATER THAN EVERY MAGIC

(1913)

T he small fat book drew the student's eye downwards in a zigzag — and then up to a new, foreign side. But he suddenly stopped, jumped dreamily way up high, like a burglar through a dormer window, bringing all reality hot on his heels in pursuit across the dizzying heights, dogs whistling over the tops of the chimney-pots — he leapt through the air but the law book in his hand kept lecturing him out loud.

Franz shook himself and rapped his knuckles on the pages, taking another look inside: it wasn't on. These sentences couldn't grab his attention. These sharp hacking sentences wanted to be grabbed, but

Alfred Wolfenstein / FAR GREATER THAN EVERY MAGIC

the sight of them merely made him think — about his own thoughts. Sitting conscious and detached in his chair with the clock on the wall ticking as loud as his heart, he felt himself soaring impassioned through space. The palms of his hands became so dry that he was tormented by the constant need to breathe on them.

But all the same — desert! he cried and he stared at the book, I will, I shall master you! You trickle through my brain and lodge there like sieved sand — I will get you, I must. He leaned back with tears in his eyes, threw himself forwards again, his forehead in his hand, landing with his elbows on the table. Oh — even when he makes progress, all he learns is despair, for it is not his mind but his feelings which resist, the inexpungeable form cast by his childhood. He is gentle, he is philanthropic, he is unsure, full of yearning, he comes from the provinces. That's why he cannot conquer this realm of power, the law book comes from the city.

He stared into thin air — ghostly threads wriggled in front of his eyes, clauses tangled — the long spirits of law struggled above the book, filed through one another vacantly, impassively swapped places for and against — and their piercing declamations trickled away silently, as barren as sand. In their midst rose the unapproachable pyramid, manned with ever loftier authorities in black array, sitting one above another on rigid seats and dictating the law with lips of knifes. On top one man who, puffed up by his underlings like the mighty base balancing on its tip, whispered: On all the laws lies peace[1].

Franz, annoyed by his constant drooping, stood up, sending his chair back into the room with a hefty jerk like an eavesdropper at a keyhole. Leaning out of the window into the dusk, he felt the house tremble under the menacing city, the pavements shook between underground rumbling and black visible bustling. But the roaring omnibus cut a clear path for itself through the masses, the power of the gigantic vehicle raged on quite unfettered and Franz watched with admiration as the driver steered coldly past. Another appeared from the other side with a thunderous boom, disappearing with a motionless statue-profile on his quivering seat. They drove through the town imperiously, their route like a steel cable passing through its clutching eye, unswerving as they let the giant city unroll beneath the gorging and belching of their racing steeds.

That was the city of legislation, the man-eating towers filled with laws, that was the city which he had not yet penetrated: How was he going to master the laws there, spontaneous generations from its stony body! Souls, piled on high like mountains of corpses, automaton-heads, networks of nerve-rails, order upon order, that was the first step to mutual dominion. Step right up if you want to make progress!

But he still concealed himself. He was the provincial town. Its childlike contours circumscribed his spirit. One step idyllically following the next, like rows of wooden-framed cottages, his face disappeared among the masses, just as when one peeks over the sill of the barrack-room window and sees without being seen. The boundless will which he had brought to the city was a boundless mist over fields and meadows. He looked at authority's nakedness in astonishment, but kept adorning it with veils. Then he swelled his chest again in rage — but his *childhood* imposed its dimensions on the vaults of all his plans like a small tinsel star.

Destroy it! was his constant thought now — turn the past into a mere accident, whirl up into the air and discard everything that is superfluous to rootless flight!

He threw himself onto his chair and looked over at the green book. He carried the chair back to the table on his backside. Tired, he rested his temples in his hands and looked down at the book which was slowly turning white, like closing eyelids —

It was quiet — until he suddenly heard a piano playing in the distance, dispassionate playing — a new neighbour. The top notes rose up in frenzied passages, higher after every descent, a dancing voice burying the heavy undertow of the bass notes, reaching ever further beyond the keys into the icy beauty of a flaming sonority, as if on a more majestic piano — and yet reaching ever closer — until a voice spoke in the midst of their flight:

I'd be pleased to help.

Franz looked up and thought that there was a mirror in front of him: a white face with dark hair was studying him closely, yet hollow and drawn with cutting lips. But beneath, rectangular like a book, groaned a heavy green torso covered with large print, its short legs resting on the table. Lacking a neck, the head stuck out like a bony bookmark. The corners of the grinning mouth sliced the narrow face right into thin air, so that the creases seemed to vanish in the far distance. — And Franz felt himself being grasped under his arms — lifted away — wind rushed past him, he travelled along something endlessly wide — he heard deafening ringing, cold and melodic like high piano notes, from ahead.

The moon appeared and Franz saw himself riding along the road on a steam roller. At first it appeared to be an omnibus, then an iron wall swelled up, blaring and resounding, beneath him — and he grew with it, legs stretching out like flying buttresses, encircling the roaring roller which was so large it hardly moved. He sat there tall and erect, the driver waving assurances back at him, this cool master of the monstrous wheel who drove through the empty streets of the empire as if it were a bus which passes every hour — to familiar cottages.

The machine drew into the sleeping home town with a whistle. It plunged on through clear air full of stars and gardens, its wheels on either pavement — bay windows sprang forwards and smashed, piles of needlework baskets crashed down — shop windows shot across the street, the department store burst apart, emptying its entire stock so that the air was filled with glittering gifts, calendars, slippers, shop displays, herrings, plush furniture. They cascaded through the whirling mayhem of mown down lampposts and trees, down onto the square which trembled at the dreadful sight — He knew every window here — every pane shattered. The lemonade stand from his schooldays was blasted aside. Peering down at the cobblestones around the collapsing street corner was a matrimonial bed, hanging from the ribs of the balcony. And new corners kept exploding from the unbridled journey, sleepyheads fled from the multitude of heaped-up beds, but nowhere a pair of lovers.

Then the church bells began to clamour, while the rosy dawn approached. The driver winked over his shoulder, his laughing mouth cut through his head — and he no longer kept to the delicate line of the streets but rammed the walls as he swung the roller to the left and the right. The houses tumbled onto the cobbles like matchboxes, sitting rooms with loose covers, spindly steps with gates, enamel stoves, water pumps, outhouses with heart-shaped windows. In their midst grew the firework of strange objects which had imprinted him deep and afresh on even the shortest of walks — and which he had been unable to cast from his memories till now: and now in a matter of seconds a monument with sword and palm frond, the bill-boards, taxi stand, local bank, villa whose construction had always been a source of surprise when out for a Sunday walk — a village was establishing itself as a suburb — toppled over.

But now, with the greatest joy, straight into the people who, shrieking and straying among the ruins, had once stood with their hands in their pockets in front of occasionally tinkling shops, sat in front of coffee services on porch benches, cosy together in their effortless gossip and poisonously distant to other peoples' worlds: broken at last, they were describing enormous curves through the air — the petty-minded, prying guardian; the stupid stuck-up mayor; the unsuspecting schoolmaster who had inspired inextinguishable awe since earliest memory and tugged at the hair on temples or cowardly rapped fingers or pinched biceps; pupils giving their never-ending greetings from one end of Cavalier Street to the other without a trace of self-disgust; adolescent friends with faces rapidly robbed of youth by fatherhood; girls rapidly engaged and plump.

Alfred Wolfenstein / FAR GREATER THAN EVERY MAGIC

The small town was a pulp of flesh and debris. Just a few last horrified spectres scurried between the silhouettes. They dismounted, the steam roller sank with a roar, and shot flames into the expanse of ruins which melted away in the fire — the wind whipped past — all that was left was an empty plane.

Oh glorious emptiness! Franz sank to his knees in gratitude — liberty, release, there was an enormous free space in his soul! But now — may a new content arrive! A different life in the space freed within! — They were already flying back along high pitched whirring notes which leapt between ever higher explosions in the aether — until the sky was filled by the dazzling light from the town — Franz leaned back in his chair, hordes of giant grazing steam rollers rumbled past beneath the windows — He looked in anticipation at the mouth — which spoke:

Yes — now I shall teach you power — and like an echo, the humming slowly faded: Easy — There lies the city of power — but you don't have to lift a finger — I shall bestow you with its essence — and you shall rule.

He raised his eyebrows with a laugh. They sailed over his clear, glassy forehead, tracing a line through the walls of the room to the horizon. He disappeared. Then sparkling music entered from far away, a shadowy hand groped round the door and dragged him down gloomy corridors. At the far end was an opening — shining opaline towards him — and a voice screamed as he crossed the threshold: *Learn to be aware!*

He closed his eyes, but the dazzling light pierced his lids — he found himself in a towering hall with a ceiling made of opaque panes which dripped water — they were made of ice and dripped wherever he went. At the same time there was an incessant hissing — the frosted drops as they fell onto the burning floor tiles, red from an invisible fire. They produced no steam, but rather a wraith of light which seemed to take on shape, then lurched round the room, thrusting its stony, protruding teeth down into its heart in furious battle. Countless naked faces were staring as if out of bulbous cells along the walls, which stretched to the horizon. Their ghastly chins, cut off by curtains, jutted out fiercely into the hall, and over them grew bloody mouths, thick as coconuts, while their foreheads shrunk back into the depths of the curtains. Moving on the floor between the ridges of their chins, which crossed in the middle of the hall, was a spume-white bed:

The other man stood in front, concealing it, dark and green, with the broad tome of his torso ...

He whispered: open your eyes!

He screamed: and behold my desire!!

Franz gave a start: he saw an eye glisten in the middle of the crooked, cartilaginous triangle of the legs — a tender gaze — and then a naked body with a soft sheen ... The gazes rained down, the curtains rose — billowing up in front of the figures which now crept towards her. The other man pointed at the woman with a grinning, open hand, and as he looked around, as if amidst the crowd in a conjurer's booth, his clothes flew away. He displayed his revolting nudity to Franz and, turning in a circle, to the standing men — as if he was including Franz among their ranks. Then, slowly kneeling, he lowered himself onto the prostrate figure. But his face seemed to peer through the back of his head, kept staring at Franz with a flickering tongue.

And Franz, already falling under the spell, looked at the spectators: as if beneath wintery suns, there were icicles hanging from their drooping jowls. Their lips were two question marks rising up into nothingness, kissing themselves with a lonely kiss, twisted into a knot of legal articles.[2] A blue, glassy, empty sphere extended round their heads, and as it sucked up the life around it, the fat green torso appeared mirrored in its coldness, then falling on the bed like an open book, its nerves a-flutter. And Franz felt the horrifying power of the lonely, barren, ice-fire spewing stiff, lascivious swelling around him, the hushed chorus of lust, the zenith of the most terrible, bleak, lovelessness: more chilling than to lack love — to look on and watch love! And with a last glimmer of awareness he felt that anyone who is capable of that is cut off from love for ever — has the keenest weapon, has only weapons and nothing else, and can do what they will with the world — stronger than Napoleon —

Now the last white distance from the bed had to be eliminated. Shaking himself, he raised his arms, grabbed the icy light and smashed through the grinning face on the back of the head into thin air.

And felt himself buckle under his own blow — and touch a wonderful human body — a spark flashed out and melted the icy inferno with a deafening noise. Closing his eyes he saw the edges of the yawning ravine crash together — And he opened his arms and pressed a heart to his own, feeling the flame of closeness — the flame of closeness blazing thousandfold. He felt how every path was a devilish detour, a false turn, false desire, empty forms which disappeared to leave one single path shining forth to humanity — A human mouth approached and suddenly he saw a red winged heart start to glow in the skin of his breast — a glowing heart forced its way right to his head and vanquished freezing authorities. A human mouth gave new birth to his heart, so that it might rule at last!

His shoulders rose once more in order to sink down into the raptures of closeness with even greater passion and intensity ...

He looked up — at the bright sunlit table where a pale lamp was still glowing weakly. His neck was stiff; he looked sideways out of the corners of his sore eyes and saw himself sitting at the edge of the blue sky, filled with the clamour of day.

It was morning. He had woken up.

His arms lay hard as stone in front of the book on the edge of the table — He grabbed it with every sinew of his body, jumped up rejoicing, and cast it out of the window —

Love!

Far greater than every magic: love!

His childhood is destroyed — but now youth can begin! May authority roll no longer through your ravaged space — may your feelings blossom! But mighty, open to all the world!

That book is for the old and blind! Wishful dreams stared at him from the night, the break of day and from all eternity — God, the dawn of every barren torment, had looked at him — and given him knowledge!

His heart opened in the sun's rays: Oh humanity, scarcely are you born than you are killed by the tortures by which you are taught, trained and drained! Your ways conjure up staircases and banisters — right up to the rooftops, but no further. But love is greater than that, it soars above learning on roaring wings, resounding with humanity.

Turn back to humanity — to the world — to love! Become gardeners — whatever you want! — become nothing ! — and the whole of space will be free for you.

Paul Zech

THE TERRACE AT THE POLE

(1913)

I have christened Potsdam Square 'Pole'. People will smile. Smile at this name. Smile pityingly at me. But creating norms out of a defect is a deadly serious matter. Thus to make it more explicable: now and then a seed, a synthesis, extracts itself from the causes behind appearances and their magic — which are visibly represented as the centre of a circle, and in which all the streams of life meet. Syntheses also emanate streams of high tension far and wide.

But the Pole, as something new and elementary, is at the same time high tension.

What do our terms for energies mean when everyone smells, tastes, sees and assimilates them into their feelings in different ways? Tensions are media though, throbbing deep down as if a mysterious hand had fitted a new mechanism to the very source of our blood.

I experience all things in such a way that my experience broadens out like a bleak plane: with that I become receptive to materials, which are primordial sounds.

But primordial sounds are knowledgeable. They know about energies which contain gateways. They surge up to them and quiver inside, filling gaps which have separated minds for so long. No event remains unmoved by their cool caresses. They light up even the darkest corner. Every radiance sparkles towards them. Mountains split wide open. The seed banishes the damp grey fears of the wakefulness free of dreams: I am. These are words which visibly bear every occurrence on their foreheads like brands. Words which cast ghostly shadows on the others, the shadows of the primal meaning of their futures, of their possibilities of being, and of their conclusions. But one thread of this shadow turned into a knowing, primordial sound: I am! Am part of this circle, which has cars, battles, tumult, and children's screams.

And this terrace is an island, shaded by noises, bathed in primordial sounds, dazzled on every side by appearances. And every step from this point is towards destinations which everyone suspects, marvels at, yet none can construe. And yet everything which has come into being here will become the path to its own end. The vessels of life flow over.

This terrace at the pole is an island. All the four winds, which have met elsewhere, spread out their plunder for me to see. The cars are making their din and disgorging the smell of the suburbs like bad breath. They are brightly loaded with red, blond and gold, black, brown and blue. The frosty and the hot-headed, laughing and laughed at, crippled and whole ... many multifarious masks occupying narrow windows which flash by in a trice. The ringing of their housing estates wafts over to me like the buzzing of insects.

I feel the pulse of engines and can interpret their comings and goings by the rhythm of its beat. Who can talk of unhappiness when a will, turned into the momentum of wheels, brushes the weak aside — to land where all weakness meets its end? And will is a resounding of ministries, hunts, courts of assizes, nights of passion. Pleasure trip by aeroplane. In the guise of freedom the will rolls over every beaming point of the star.[1]

And a man is standing there, like a tree, casting the star in shadow with two branches, which are his hands. Signpost hands. I watch these twitching hands for a long while. With every new minute the tree-man's head whips to one side. Now to his right shoulder, then to the weaker one, the left. But a voice emanates from him, as if from Jericho.

I see the teeming of the timid and the striding of the indifferent. Each has his profession and the remains from eating houses, pale ale cellars, coffee houses and milk bars lodged in their garments. What sleight of hand causes a person's fears? Who inoculated that other fatalism into their mortal juices? Many are fetishists by habit: looking at this life through a prism. And I look with amazement at the people groomed for the world, or uniformed or steeled by sport. And then the nimble white butterflies, the speckled hyenas, the black panthers escaped from the jungles of lasciviousness. At every turn the reflection of the coming downfall which consumes so many, startles so many — but destroys neither the strength of their muscles nor desiccates the marrow of their nerves to dust and cinders. Eyes closed, they stamp, surge and caper over the trap-doors of the traffic. They, the new-pious, the new-strong, the new rabble-rousers and underminers.

There is a cool afternoon breeze and an eddy from the east which gathers the withered leaves from the nearby boulevards against the sides of the curbstones. Colours from asters and carnations blaze through the gaps in the stampede of cars. Many are they who carry these parting summer's greetings, hawked by a few poor women, to the twilight darkness of their apartments. And the chosen helper, this splash of colour, will it outblossom the greyness of discord, the black of mourning and the white of restrained emptiness? Act as a bridge: which reconciles, beautifies, tames or heals?

The dogs, tied to leather leashes or ornamental chains, are still wearing their muzzles. Breath of their repressed desires turns to foam, stiff as chalk. People enveloped in commiseration and others chilled by loneliness wrap silken glitter or silver filigree around their shaggy, swollen necks. And these animals are slaves of a high life which already out-trumps the horizons of the world beyond.

And this one freezing here, with the white, clouded gaze of the blind, is a prop. A speck on the stage backdrop. The sceptic sniffs and tastes it with the stupidity of the glutton, for he believes he is entitled to investigate and fathom the origins of their being. Quite different from he who really knows. Perhaps he has the automaton cracked open and transforms mechano-plastic art into gushing fountains. Exudes murmured sounds which expose and cut apart every fibre of the soul. And a face forms. Its expression one of patient waiting. A play of sunlight, somehow come into being, blossoms on the deeply rutted chin. Raises it up into an indefinite universe lying far away. And the speck becomes a planet and has sun and moons and eclipses.

And a ragged figure appears at the parapet of the terrace. The clamour of dazzling dress and pressed suits highlights the misery of his motley coat, the moss-filled furrows from care-worn years, with glaring repulsiveness. His trembling hand, which skewers newspapers fresh from the printing press, shadows the purpose of his life. He is nothing but a paper which one purchases for a nickel. The whole created in the image of God: a present in return for a round metal disc.

The lowly must not be humiliated any longer! Those who reduce them to specks on the walls of the world are roused to the heights of conceit by the appearances in this world.

And conceit is the image of feelings which have all but stopped resonating.

Fine rain falls distraughtly. Fairy lights bob up and down. White spheres soar into the sky like cast falcons. Eyes bulge, yellow and white, from precipitous walls. Jagged gables and slanting rooftops start to dance. Streams of sparks wrap themselves around the rhythm of their twists and turns. Wheels of fire circle round the lifeless rigidity of their foreheads and lust after the thoughts of the resourceful who know their public, making new assaults and blazing onslaughts. The call of their instincts directs the music: to me! And casts itself into the darkness.

There is no echo.

Shadows, eerily extending the madness, come and disappear; confident and smoothly. A pandemonium of weariness, love of adventure, theft, hate, lies, carnality and lust to kill. A glittering from the depths of the streets sends waves of phosphorescences round the hurtling appearances. Their origins and a sensual sighing dream lie in the tempo of the footsteps.

However, the machines are pounding away in the vaults, stretching wire cables along tunnels. Energies from the beyond flash along the plaited copper threads. The ebbing of their magic would unleash indescribable darkness, fire and brimstone, madness and plundering mobs. Signals of subversion beat in every wayfarer's veins. The mind of the assembled mass smoulders. Ostracism is the one thing the agitators stole from Hellas. The thought is ruthless and strangles its begetter. Everything spiritual is seen as fanaticism. Every change boycott. Completion is a gateway which opens onto tangled paths, sweetly shaded by ornamental trees, which lead to the very heart of the jails. And every leader is a warden for those jailed for life. But the hoofbeats of the Huns' steeds are already sounding in the distance. Troops from the east and north, countless as the grains of sand. And bloated faces stare, their eyes the livid green of putrefying fish, through the barred windows of the theatre as if ringed by moon craters, puzzling out the never-ending confusion of voices from the Tower of Babel.

But machines, still churning underground, send up white showers of ashes. Like sperm. And there are seeds inside, they have all they need. And sire mouths. Scarcely born, they jump over and under one another, fleeing and crossing themselves. Repel themselves, outdoing every revulsion with another. And roar together like thousands of kisses, which are the sea.

My neighbours at their round tables arm themselves with sensational astral occurrences. They encroach on biblical gardens and bask in the cold flames of their moods. Beautiful ladies set fire to their hair. And their breasts all harbour a wakeful secret which leaps out and incites men's thoughts.

Oh, eyes meet yours, racing like comets: this way and that.

The expressions of the besieged waiters reflect dignity and well-being. They are allowed to have a heart and exchange it for money, to go dancing once the arc-lamps have been extinguished.

What a safe world!

And now this motion from the hundreds of skulls. The music of their breathing. The thunder of their vocal chords. Every gesture has a practical cause. Every scuffling of small feet ends up imaginary. The deed has had its purpose forestalled and has been conned with an outcome, sale and purchase: the objectivisation of the life of appearances. And the whole affair is high-handed and no longer bears the truly freezing colours of the individual.

But I don't want to grow poor. Although I sense the final poverty all too well. I sense the ways of its brothers and sisters and want to stop my life from flowing into that bloody sea of kinship. It calls loudly to me and never answers.

But the life beneath me is no longer that multifarious life of old. There is no resonance!

Someone extinguishes the rays of the pointed star. The speck on the stage scenery gave birth to thousands of others. Their life is now nothing more than immaculately functioning business. The black panthers run around tame as pets. One can catch them and spend a soothing hour just stroking them.

But the terrace doesn't finish asking its question. It hangs there, as if strangled. White shattered crockery yawns with boredom. The remnants of bright temptations bellow from crumpled papers. And the rows of seats still feed on a warmth called greed. But the material from which it is gained is missing.

And the observer who has long presided over his pen, curses his hand and promises himself he will forget its existence. Crippled, he thinks himself back in his home, while his spirit strives for new forms. Never had his wrath been so radiant. For now his blood — just as long as it could feel, was set in motion by a cause — saw the existent and the transcendent with the power of the synthesis of feelings and deviations from the norm.

One laughing and one laughed at. One burning with attraction. One repelled, turned to ice — just like the world.

Else Lasker-Schüler

IF MY HEART WERE HEALTHY — CINEMATICS

(1913)

I f my heart were healthy, I would first of all jump out of the window; then I'd go to the picture palace and never appear again. I feel exactly as if I'd drawn first prize in the lottery and not yet been paid, or won a nag in a sweepstake and can't get hold of a stall for 'nothing'. Life is after all a play set on a spiral staircase, going forever upwards in circles and coming back down again, forever turning around itself as the stars do. I feel a happy despair, a desperate happiness; I'd like most of all to spring to my death or play a prank. My friend Laurentia boozes like a young student, she studies the languages of the old masters, I mean Greek and Latin,

Else Lasker-Schüler / IF MY HEART WERE HEALTHY

and is making good progress. But what's all that to me? I don't want to know a thing, nothing. If only it wouldn't keep pounding like that!

My brain gets completely churned up, the pounding from below doesn't just come every Friday and Saturday — sending every speck of dust whirling through the air — it also comes on the other weekdays because I live here between the inner and outer houses and have to suffer the brutality of the courtyards between. I always sit with the windows closed and won't see anything of the summer; I can't go out, I write ghost stories; I have debts. And there's a draught if I leave the doors open behind, and to the left and right of me. I've worn a cat's fur ever since I've been in this flat; when I'm invited somewhere in the evening I am beset by a terrible anxiety that I might start to miaow! I've absolutely no desire to carry on living, even if people still want to read my verse; anyone who enjoys reading it should write me a nice letter sometime. You see, I have to bathe in salts of sorrel on account of my illness, so that people won't make any faux pas concerning me. And I always get so bored in the bathtub and enjoy reading flattering letters about myself. How annoying a bad review can be! One feels an immediate fondness for someone who writes a few pleasant words. There are some really likeable people in the world. It's just pale faces I can't stand, I distrust light. So I only employ black maids and servants. I have two Negroes and two Red Indian girls: sometimes Tecofi's chieftain father comes to Berlin and performs with his troupe in Chât Noir. Whenever his father comes to Berlin, Tecofi asks me whether he can come and live on my balcony. I have no objection. My Somali Negro is of royal descent. His father owns flocks of mutton-sheep near Tenerife. Sometimes he sends me a couple of skinned sheep, they arrive here as haut-goût ragout. Osmann, the younger of my two Negroes, looks like a meditative gorilla in a flower tub. Wicked species, wonderful to look at, but one must leave him in peace; recently I also stopped whistling to him whenever I wanted him to bite off someone's head. He's too good for that, too valuable to obey anyone, even me. My two Red Indian girls are very industrious, I've employed them to pick up the threads of my logic, the logic of my livelihood. Sometimes they search the whole night long, I fear that one day they'll suddenly hang themselves on the main thread. One has to accept that. Dark people make bad sleuths, they can't find a thing in the night of their skin. Hallo! What would I do if my heart were healthy? Do I even have a heart, or at least something similar? I must cry at this intermezzo in the programme — good that there's such a thing as nut bars, they're a comfort, likewise peppermints in small wooden boxes. I don't believe that my heart is made of flesh and blood, its walls are badly cracked; it has less transitory value than eternal value and so I am completely useless for the passer-by. I am only of interest to the researcher. The phone always rings at the most impressive moments. 'This is 3524, who's that?' 'Doctor Nikito Ambrosia, is that Else Lasker-Schüler?' 'Unfortunately.' 'Please don't jump for joy, Madam, but may I be humble enough to ask whether you would consider an engagement at the Wintergarten for 10,000 marks a month? That makes roughly 100,000 a year?' 'You must be joking, sir, it's not usual to engage an artist at the variety for more than a month.' 'But it is our every intention to tie you to our variety, Madam.' 'I take it you're interested in my Arabian number, Doctor Ambrosius?' 'Quite right! Where you sit high above Thebes on your camel.' 'Sir, I know you, there's nobody else at the variety with such an unvarnished basso. You're Professor Gellert, the last scion of the Hohenzollern dynasty.' End! My letter: my sweetest darling heart in Adrianopolis! You see, he asked me whether I still love him, urging me not to lie. But I'm not going to give him any material for his verses (he is a poet), 'I love him then! And that's that!' If I could only get to Turkey for a while, especially since my ancestors were all carried around in sedan chairs. That's why I have difficulty walking. When your soles have already cooled off, mine are still aglow. If my heart were healthy, what would I do?

Else Lasker-Schüler / IF MY HEART WERE HEALTHY

Just a moment please! I would strip off naked as the day and throw myself into a freshwater lake inhabited by gentle fish, although I can't stand scales. Or I would go to the South Pole and warm myself good and proper, or at any rate I'd have an anthracite stove brought to the ice zone. What *else* should I do? Remain standing *directly* on the Tropic of Capricorn, *out of spite*. I would paint moustaches on the signs of the zodiac. Isn't it a heavenly shame that my heart is not healthy? Heart ailments, or rather neuroses, come from the moon. Every disease comes from above. It's very pleasant down here. That's why so many aviators plummet from the sky; it's not that the airplane explodes, rather they all get the falling sickness as they suck in more and more of the astral bacilli. What the aviators look like: like birds — their noses are beaks and they stretch their heads up high. A new breed of humans. Once I had lunch with a glider pilot, he hacked away at his meat like a goshawk, tore at his schnitzel like an Egyptian vulture. Karl Vollmöller's wonderful *Katherine von Armagnac*[1] is the world's first aviatrix. Everyone is flying at the Aerial Navigation Exhibition in the Union Theatre by the zoo. I can watch for nothing, I've promised to write all about it. I haven't a penny but that's no reason to cut myself off from the rest of the world. And I'm even supposed to take over the government in Thebes, I already rule there pro forma. The people of Berlin say that I have an *idée fixe*. An *idée fixe* is a perfectly natural thing: nature which enslaves laws. I am the Prince of Thebes. Only Kaiser William can understand me here in Germany when it comes to ruling. And I have a colourful people. At night I lie on the roof and during the day I sit beneath my palm-tree and rule. I am responsible for everything; my people still squint with uncertainty, they think I am playing a joke, but for me even jokes are deadly serious. I have no preferences — just people. I am unjust because I have taste and artistic judgement; when I address my people I don't come to any conclusions because I don't want to be tied down. I am most tolerant when it comes to myself, I am lenient to myself, I agree with myself, out of diplomacy, because my people must stick with me. I just think a great deal, too much, very direct, I allow all my thoughts to come up very close to me so that they will learn to lose their fears. If only I wasn't always disturbed in the early morning by so many Moslem barbers wishing to tattoo me, by western artists who want to paint my portrait. At night I am always roused from my rooftop slumbers by my pashas who are unable to contain their enthusiasm about my accession to power. But they always forgot to raise one question during the audiences I grant, a pressing one at that. Since I have been elected the ruling Prince of Thebes, a large number of ambitious souls walk along the city's streets with the same traditional costume and mien, striving to be my equal. My emulators! The thing is that ruling is also an art, an aptitude, just like painting, poetry and music. Emulation, however, is an activity, and thus emulation produces something, just like work. I never work, I hate writing-desks — admittedly I have one myself — but it's never been fully intact. Last night, as my Negroes were asleep, the pashas forced in the gate to my roof on account of the postage stamps. During the night my profile was photographed in fullest colour (profile suits me better than *en face*), wearing my turban and royal robes; every letter now distributes Me, the highest of the high, around my city.

Georg Trakl

DREAM AND DEMENTIA

(1914)

In the evening the father turned into an old man; the mother's face turned to stone in dark rooms and the curse of the degenerated lineage weighed heavily on the young man. Sometimes he recalled his childhood, filled with sickness, dread and darkness, hidden games in the starry garden, or how he had fed the rats in the dusky courtyard. The slender figure of his sister stepped out of the blue mirror and he toppled, as if dead, into the darkness. At night his mouth split open like a red fruit and the stars shone forth above his mute grief. His dreams filled the old house of his fathers. In the evening he liked to walk through the ruined graveyard, or view the corpses in the twilight of the morgue, the green patches of putrefaction on their lovely hands. He asked for a piece of bread at the cloister gate; the shadow of a black horse jumped out of the darkness and startled him. Lying in the cool of his bed, he was overcome by inexpressible tears. But there was no one to come and lay a hand on his forehead. As autumn arrived he, a clairvoyant, walked across the brown pastures. O the hours of wild rapture, the evenings by the green river, the hunts. O the soul which quietly sang the song of the yellowed reed; fiery devotion. He looked long and silent into the starry eyes of the toad, felt the coldness of the ancient stones with shuddering hands, and incanted the hallowed legend of the blue fountain-head. O the silver fish and the fruit which fall from stunted trees. Chords rang from his footsteps, filling him with pride and misanthropy. On the way home he came across an empty castle. Dilapidated gods stood in the garden, filling the evening with their sorrow. But he felt: I have dwelt forgotten years here. An organ chorale filled him with the fear of God. But he spent his days in a gloomy cave, lied and stole and hid himself, a flaming wolf, from his mother's white face. O the hour in which he fell to the ground with a mouth of stone in the starry garden, and the shadow of the murderer descended on him. He went to the moor with purple brow and the wrath of God scourged his metallic shoulders; o the storm-tossed birches, the dark animals which avoided his benighted paths. His heart burned with hate, wantonness, so that he violated the silent child in the verdant summer garden, recognised his benighted countenance in this radiant creature. Woe, as in the evening a greyish skeleton, death, stepped up to his window from the purple flowers. O you towers and bells; and the shadows of the night fell on him like stone.

No one loved him. His head burned with lies and debauchery in dusky rooms. The blue rustling of a woman's gown froze him to a pillar, and in the doorway stood the nocturnal figure of his mother.

Georg Trakl / **DREAM AND DEMENTIA**

The shadow of the evil one rose to his head. O you nights and stars. In the evening he went to the mountain with the cripple; the rosy gleam of the sunset covered the icy peak, and his heart sounded quietly in the twilight. The stormy pines sank over them heavily, and the red huntsman came out of the forest. And with the night his heart broke like crystal and the darkness struck his forehead. With icy hands he strangled a wild cat beneath bare oak trees. The white figure of a lamenting angel appeared to his right, and the cripple's shadow grew in the darkness. But he picked up a stone and cast it at the man, so that he took flight, wailing. And the gentle countenance of the angel melted into the shadows of the tree with a sigh. For a long time he lay on the stony field, marvelling at the golden canopy of stars. Chased by bats, he dived off into the darkness. He entered the ruined house, breathless. A wild animal, he drank from the blue waters of the well in the courtyard until he froze. Feverish, he sat on the icy steps, railing against God in the hope he might die. O the grey countenance of terror as he raised his rounded eyes to the severed throat of a dove. Scurrying up unfamiliar steps he encountered a Jewish maid, and he snatched at her black hair, taking her mouth in his. Animosity followed him down dark alleys, and a clatter of iron tore at his ears. He, an altar boy, quietly followed the silent priest along autumnal walls; intoxicated, he breathed in the scarlet of those hallowed vestments beneath withered trees. O the wasted disc of the sun. Sweet torments ate at his flesh. His bleeding form appeared to him caked in filth in a desolate mews house. His love deepened for the stone's sublime forms; for the tower with its diabolical gargoyles which storms the blue starry sky by night; the cool grave in which man's fiery heart is preserved. Woe to the unspeakable guilt which the grave proclaims. But as he walked beneath the bare trees to the autumnal river, in contemplation of ardour, a flaming demon in a coat of hair appeared to him: his sister. The stars extinguished above their heads as they woke.

O the accursed lineage. When that fate is consumated in sullied rooms, then death enters the house with mouldering steps. O if only it were spring outside, with a sweet bird singing in the blossoming tree. But the sparse greenery shrivels up grey at the night-walkers' windows and the bleeding hearts continue their contemplation of evil. O the contemplator's springtime paths at dusk. He is more innocent in his enjoyment of the blossoming hedgerows, the farmer's newly sown fields and the bird in song, God's gentle creation; the Angelus and the friendly congregation of the people. That he might forget his fate and the thorny barb. The brook turns green, unrestrained, where his feet wander silverly, and a whispering tree rustles above his benighted head. Then he raises the snake with a slender hand, and his heart melted away in fiery tears. Sublime is the forest's silence, the green clad darkness and the mossy wildlife, fluttering up as night falls. O the horror, that his guilt is known by all, walks thorny paths. Then he found the white figure of the child in the briar, bleeding for the cloak of its bridegroom. But he stood before her, mute and suffering, buried in his steely hair. O the radiant angels, scattered by the purple night-wind. He dwelt the night long in a crystal cave and the leprous scales grew, silver on his forehead. A shadow, he walked along the bridle path beneath autumn stars. Snow fell and blue darkness filled the house. His father's harsh voice sounded like a blind man's, and summoned the horror. Woe to the stooped figures of the women. The fruit and tools decayed under the bony hands of the appalled lineage. A wolf tore the first-born apart and the sisters fled to bony dotards in dark gardens. A benighted seer sang this tale beside decayed walls and his voice devoured God's wind. O the rapture of death. O you children of a dark lineage. The blood's evil flowers shimmer silver on his temples, the cold moon in his cracked eyes. O the night-wanderers; o the accursed.

Deep is the slumber under dark poisons, filled with stars and the

Georg Trakl / DREAM AND DEMENTIA

white face of his mother, the stony face of his mother. Death is bitter, the nourishment of those burdened with guilt; the earthen faces crumbled, grinning, in the brown branches of the family tree. But he sang quietly in the green shadow of the elder tree, wakened from wicked dreams; a sweet playmate approaches him, a rosy angel so that he, a gentle stag, would sleep for the night; and he saw the starry countenance of purity. The sunflowers drooped golden over the garden fence, for it had turned summer. O the industry of the bees and the green foliage of the nut tree; the passing thunderstorms. Silver blossomed the poppy too, bore our nocturnal stardreams in green pods. O how quiet was the house as the father stepped into the dark. The fruit ripened purple on the tree and the gardener set-to with his hardened hands; o the signs made of hair in the radiant sun. But with evening the shadow of the departed quietly entered the bereaved circle of his relatives and his step rang crystal over the greening meadow before the forest. They gathered, hushed, around the table; dying people breaking the bread, the bleeding bread, with waxen hands. Woe to the sister's stony eyes, for her madness settled on her brother's nocturnal brow during the meal, and the bread turned to stone under the mother's suffering hands. O the putrefied, for they kept silence about hell with silver tongues. Then the lamps extinguished in the cool chamber and the suffering people looked at one another silently through purple masks. Rain teemed the whole night long, refreshing the pastures. In the thorny wilderness the dark one followed the gilded path through the corn, the song of the lark and the gentle quiet of the green boughs, in search of peace. O you villages and mossy steps, blazing sight. But the footsteps wobbled bonily over sleeping snakes at the edge of the forest, the ear forever following the frenzied scream of the vulture. In the evening he found a stony wilderness, a dead man's funeral procession leading into his father's gloomy house. Purple clouds darkened his head so that he pounced silently on his own blood and likeness, a lunar countenance; sank stonily into emptiness, there in a broken mirror — a dying youth — appeared his sister; the night devoured by the damned lineage.

Alfred Lichtenstein

CONVERSATION ABOUT LEGS

(1915)

I

I was sitting in a railway carriage when the man opposite me said:

'No one can tread on your legs.'

I said: 'Why?'

The man said: 'You don't have any legs.'

I said: 'Does it show?'

The man said: 'Of course.'

I took my legs out of my rucksack. I had wrapped them up in tissue paper and taken them along as a souvenir.

The man said: 'What's that?'

I said: 'My legs.'

The man said: 'You're taking your legs in hand but it still

doesn't get you anywhere.'

I said: 'I'm afraid you're right.'

After a pause the man said: 'What do you really think you're going to do without legs?'

I said: 'I've still to think that one over.'

The man said: 'Without legs you couldn't even commit suicide without a lot of difficulty.'

I said: 'That's a very stale joke.'

The man said: 'Not at all. If you wanted to hang yourself, someone would first have to lift you onto the window-sill. And who would turn on the gas tap for you if you wanted to gas yourself? You could only get hold of a revolver if you arranged it slyly with a porter. What would happen though if the shot strayed? To drown yourself you'd have to take a taxi and have two attendants carry you on a stretcher to the river which was to despatch you to the shore beyond.'

I said: 'That's for me to worry about.'

The man said: 'You're wrong. From the moment I saw you I've been wondering how one could get rid of you once and for all. Do you think that a man without legs is a pleasant sight? Or even has the right to exist? On the contrary, you're a considerable disturbance to the aesthetic feelings of your fellow man.'

I said: 'Allow me to present myself. I am professor of ethics and aesthetics at the university.'

The man said: 'How are you going to manage that? Present yourself? It's perfectly obvious that you haven't a clue just how unpresentable you are.'

I looked glumly at my stumps.

Alfred Lichtenstein / CONVERSATION ABOUT LEGS

II

Straightaway the lady opposite said:

'It must be a strange feeling not to have any legs.'

I said: 'Yes.'

The lady said: 'I couldn't touch a man with no legs.'

I said: 'I'm very clean.'

The lady said: 'I have to overcome an enormous erotic revulsion just to talk to you. Not to mention look at you.'

I said: 'Ah well.'

The lady said: 'It's not that I think you're a criminal. You may well be a very clever and once likeable person. But with the best will in the world I couldn't have anything to do with you because of your missing legs.'

I said: 'One gets used to everything.'

The lady said: 'A person without legs produces an inexplicable sensation of the utmost horror in any woman with normal feelings. As if you had committed some revolting sin.'

I said: 'I'm quite innocent though. The first leg got lost in the excitement as I took up my first professorial chair. I lost the second while I was deeply wrapped in thought and came up with the important law of aesthetics which led to sweeping changes in our discipline.'

The lady said: 'How does the law go?'

I said: 'The law states: It all depends on the structure of the mind and soul. If the mind and soul are nobly formed, one must find the body beautiful as well, quite regardless of how hunched and disfigured it might be outwardly.'

The lady lifted her dress ostentatiously, revealing a pair of gorgeous legs right to the top of her thighs. Wrapped in a wealth of silk, they stretched down from her succulent body like blossoming branches.

With that the lady concluded: 'You may well be right, although one could equally argue the opposite. In any case, a person with legs is something quite, quite different from someone without.'

And with that she strode off proudly, leaving me sitting.

Theodor Däubler

THE PROPELLER

(1915)

T he stars are the propeller's forerunners: man's first acknowledgement of the stars also spelt existence for the propeller. The first star is nothing less than man's desire to fly: and that which is written bright above us on the heavens is merely the prototype of the propeller. The fair appearance of the pointed stars can fly across the universe. The stars remain waiting above the smithies of the past. There are stars with many wings, for the wing count varies since it determines facts. The stars fly up to our eyes, often the same star with five, seven, six and even less or more pulsating points; diamonds vibrate as a result of the dew and moonness or an unsuspected between-heaven-and-earthness through which it, the darling star, has to fly in order to reach a human being. Likewise the propeller: it has varying wing counts, for every beat of its blades is also a Yes which corresponds to, and consequently upholds, its purpose. But the mill-wheel, which is also a star, has the form of the cross; it is nothing less than the cross which turns, for its aim is to supply the holy bread for the Christians.

The windmill is mystic; the creaking of its vanes attracts the ravens and shies them away. Old mills are haunted, often by the dead miller himself; also the Evil One has his hand in this because the wind plays jokes on the cross, spinning it round and turning it on its head; but the mill's aim is to supply Christendom with holy bread.

The moon can do the mill little harm, for then it mostly remains still; yes, it appears to be a house full of sorcery which crosses itself at night so that the ghosts have to carry on past. Just the miller often returns in person, once he has grown too old and had his cross turned upside down and placed on its head too often. Then he is seen by both horse and donkey, dogs too. Incidentally, the donkey has the step, gait and soul of a selenite; like the moon it also knows every ghost story by heart. With its strong religious disposition it is retarded and is particularly well matched to the mill.

Above the smithy stands a star in the higher plane of poetry, and moons rise and set above it alternately. Above the mill the Milky Way flees to the sea, above the mill rages the Great Bear because the swift provider of the flour is Nordic. And every turn of the wheel signifies another star, and the mill calls every life of a hundred years the Milky Way.

And now mankind is promising a constellation of its own: every whirl of the propeller means star-birth: each and every flight across the ocean means star-birth: the beats of our blades through the air mean star-birth. Now it is the warmth which is ready and waiting for the propeller. The constellation will be a southerly one. It has already been preceded by a nebula somewhere or other; the heart-beat of all humanity had fixed it to the heavens, for the heart is a star, and the temperature of blood is the maid and harbinger of its

Theodor Däubler / THE PROPELLER

birth; that is why the cluster of stars has risen to the south. And once the cold constellation has become incarnate, thus preparing and presaging its immortality, the secret curse of ardour and passion will have been removed; hell extinguishes with every heartbeat. Now we are also helped by the clear-cut star-birth provided by the propeller.

The invention of the propeller has put a finishing mark on mortal fear.

The propeller-driven ship tows the very essence of a foaming comet in its wake; who can believe that the hope from such motion could get lost? The setting in motion and holding in suspense of the great tide by warm ardour kindly lays the way for new zoogenesis. The propeller has made an end of both the swan and the spider. The sailing ship, the swan-birth and swan-form, spinning its way back and forth against the wind to far off destinations, will certainly preserve these two animals for us, but with the propeller-ship comes the dawn of a new form of being. Both swans and the sail have come to us from the moon; the spider remains a star, but its spinning instinct makes the moonbeams its own, for webs are the moon's work. The sail imitates the quarter moon, the boat is the very first moon-birth among humanity. The propeller remains a star and, giving birth to stars, can outstar every moonness; for the propeller ship, laden with its fruit, also bears the surging comet — far brighter than the sailing ship — across the seas. Do the pilots allow the air to get an impression of their comet? Of a very special one? Should conscious streamers come into being? Must the genesis of two entities divide there? The one into sounds, the other into motion? And our excitement, our anticipation and assiduity before a flight, hasn't this inspired the genesis of new souls in mankind? Won't the ultimate question, the question about our age, be a fieriness?

The stars cast their seed across rich countries, onto the dead sea; it is accompanied by a shower of shooting stars so that we really see and believe it. Plants come into being, trees believe, there where the stars have made pastures fertile; the birds chirp, learning to sing, around the forest where the trees have been made fertile by the stars. And from the forest grow stars which are eyes, primal star-clad animals catch the scent. Hence the animals of the zodiac above. Man rises when the stars arrive at the glaciers, germinating the loneliness of the individual. Gods arrive unendingly when the stars stride across the deserts; yet the stars on the ancient sea teach the animated pastures prayer, prayer to the gods, begging for woman.

The earth is mankind's wish: and mankind's wish is itself lively and animating, easily aroused and fickle: there is no such thing as the earth, just an earthquake. But the silent star insists on this desired being, which is our own selves. Summoned by our own wishes, we drift up to it in the distance, encircling the star with our ardour, inwardly silent. Every star-boat journey into the heavens travels and sparkles onwards with but one single wish, illuminated by the shining star of our destination. But it still trembles inside one's self. That is why every circular hike simply leads back to the hiker. Let your kites fly, give yourselves up to pilgrim song! That which you release, wants to return home to the star because it is born of wishes, and the star is your promised destiny deep in your self.

Heinrich Nowak

THE SOLAR PLAGUE

(1915)

I

I live in the city of Littehota, which nestles beside the bay where the Minaulka opens onto the ocean in a broad estuary. Actually it consists of two parts: Manahota, which lies on the coast, and the villa district called Littequar which stretches right into the renowned, fertile Grotaqua region.

For some fourteen days the city with its four and a half million inhabitants has been suffering from an incredible heatwave. The mercury in the thermometer has risen to an incredibly high level.

During the day Littehota lies in the scorching sun like the rotting corpse of a great, antediluvian animal. Thousands of human maggots start moving inside it in the cool of the evening.

The only possibility of sleep is outdoors, and anyone who does not have to stay in the city has long since fled to the countryside.

II

I must mention a particularly strange occurrence.

Today I met a doctor I know well, a brilliant specialist in throat complaints.

The following dialogue ensued:

I: 'What do you think about this new disease which is scourging our city?'

He looked at me with a large question mark written over his face.

I: 'I mean the solar plague!'

The specialist: 'What do you mean?'

I: 'The solar plague! What! You haven't heard about the new disease?! Then listen to this! They've just discovered a completely new sort of bacillus, they're often referred to as solar bacilli. They only exist under abnormally strong heat. Normally they stream into the human body on the warm air, entering by the ears, nose, mouth and eyes. Then they make their way into the brain and cause absolute chaos. The outcome is always fatal, within two to three hours. A cure can be virtually ruled out, an antibacillus must be found first.'

The specialist smiled and excused himself.

III

I met Mará.

She is a Malay and works for the Luna Limited Company which has a chain of fun-fairs in all the major cities of America and Europe. At the moment Mará is appearing with her eight tame panthers at the Luna Park in Littehota. For the show she wears a red dress with a French cut which does not suit her at all. Her cats jump through fiery hoops, run along the tops of champagne bottles, some of them can walk along a tightrope, and others use their teeth to catch the burning torches which Mará tosses to them with unintelligible calls. For the finale they form a pyramid with the help of a couple of wooden stands, and T'ho, the youngest of the eight cats, is lifted onto the peak by its mistress.

IV

The Luna Park has been closed for an indefinite period. There have been no visitors as a result of the enormous heat.

All the same I went there this morning. The attendant, who knew me, let me in and I had the opportunity to see how Mará feeds her cats. I also got to know Signor Vasco Taddio (he performs with a half-tamed Bessarabian lion and lives in constant danger).

Mará told me that he is her protector.

Taddio's first words to me were 'Oh Signore, you 'ave a ssigarette for me?'

Then he went off to his Bessarabian lion and left me alone with Mará. Today she wore a loose, silken gown in reddish violet which revealed her brown arms and strong, naked legs.

We sat in one of the airy pavilions in the park. The heat sucked at the pores of my skin.

Mará (smiling): 'I won't have to come here for a long time now!'

She stroked T'ho, the young panther who was lying on her lap.

T'ho growled contentedly.

Mará rolled herself a cigarette.

V

I've just read in the newspapers:
'FREAK HEATWAVE, 65 SUICIDES.'
(Steam-roller driver let himself be crushed.
Eight suicides in the subway!)
The details were given in the text below.

I lie naked in bed, an ice compress on my forehead.

I think and my mind conjures up faces — alien experiences. I crawl into someone else's psyche, just as one can crawl into the skinned hide of a slaughtered animal.

A tarmacked street.

Fresh gravel is scattered on top, I must press it flat with my machine.

Eight metres forward ... eight metres back.

I don't have to do a thing, the vehicle is set for this distance and automatically switches between the forwards and backwards motion at the appropriate moment. I just have to keep my eye on the manometer.

The mercury column sinks, the pressure in the boiler is an eighth of an atmosphere too low. I call the stoker who is sleeping in the shadow of a tree on the side of the road. He jumps on while we are still in motion and throws a few shovels of coke into the furnace box.

I am engulfed from head to foot by the blazing heat. The coals glow yellowish white.

The furnace box is closed again, the stoker jumps off and lies back in the shadow of the tree.

The sun burns down on my head.

Heinrich Nowak / **THE SOLAR PLAGUE**

The mercury column in the manometer slowly rises once more.

If only I could get away from this tiresome machine!

But the heat's the same everywhere ...

Drowsy ...

Tired ...

Mac, the cobbler, looked by this morning, just as I was leaving. He told me that he would bring me my mended wellingtons. He came just as I was about to leave ...

The manometer rises: the pressure is too high. I must let off steam.

The heat is unbearable and it's only eleven o'clock. Still one hour to go to the midday siren.

I've been married for three weeks now ...

The cobbler arrived just as I had to leave.

If only I could have a lie-down like the stoker!

A new stretch of road must be rolled flat. I must alter the mechanism. Now sixteen metres forward ... What a noise the gravel makes beneath the roller! I wouldn't like to have my head under that ...

Eight metres forward ... Eight metres back ...

The dial on the manometer quivers gently.

The stoker has gone and fetched beer. It is strictly forbidden to drink during working hours, but the heat gnaws cruelly at our throats.

How cool the liquid runs through the body ...

I must ask Olga what Mac, the cobbler, has been telling her. Odd that he came early in the morning, just as I had to leave.

The sleeping stoker has a jug of beer by his side, I could jump down and have a drink. But it is strictly forbidden to leave the vehicle while in motion.

Another three quarters of an hour till the midday siren ...

Then comes the endless journey back home ... and I have to bolt my lunch so that I am back here on time.

Tired ...

Drowsy ...

Once I get back I really must ask Olga what Mac, the cobbler, really wanted ...

Olga used to go around with Mac a lot when I knew her as a young girl. More than with the other fellows.

Back home I'll have her rub me down with a piece of ice.

In fact my wife could easily cheat on me ... She knows exactly when I'm away from home.

But what does it matter to me in the end ...

Tired ... heat ...

I'm starting to believe that the heat wants to crush my head ...

I've a sharp pain behind my ears.

If at least that would stop!

Eight metres ... seven metres ... four metres ... three metres ... Now the machine will stop for a moment and immediately start back again.

What's it matter to me, Mac can lie on Olga if he likes!

I just want a drink!

Jump down.

My legs wobble.

Why bother to drink ...

Take the trouble to go the twenty steps to the jug? The hell with it all.

How nice it is to lie on the gravel!

I wake up from my doze. The newspaper lies in front of me. The headline screams:

'FREAK HEATWAVE, 65 SUICIDES!'

I crawl out of the foreign psyche as if out of a hide.

Evening has arrived at last. I want to dress and visit Mará.

VII

I have rented a large, isolated villa in the Grotaqua forests, and am living there with Mará and T'ho. Twice a day a large, dark blue automobile drives up to the gate and takes us to eat at the hotel some three kilometres away. There's nobody living here, just a wily looking gardener in an adjoining building. We've fled from the heat in the city and will try to outlive it here.

Mará doesn't talk much on the whole, she is almost always busy with T'ho. T'ho hates me, snarls at me whenever I pass by and looks as if she would like most of all to jump at my throat.

I feed T'ho bloody calf meat which is still warm, secretly, so that Mará doesn't notice. It's very difficult to get hold of.

For Mará once told me:

'Panthers turn wild again if they get to eat raw, bloody beef, and can't be tamed again.'

I secretly feed T'ho with red, bloody calf meat.

I hate T'ho.

VIII

At sunset I walked deep into the prairie. Night fell and devoured the last remains of the day at a furious speed.

Now the blue, tropical starry night stretches above me.

Sultry ...

My head pounds.

The blood hammers at my temples.

Mará ...

I walk back home. A large, heavy gate closes behind me. I walk through black, dead rooms.

Sometimes there's a creak.

I call quietly: 'Mará!'

No answer.

I think: Mará or T'ho could jump at my throat at any moment.

I call again, quietly: 'Mará'

No answer ...

Perhaps they're upstairs or on the flat roof.

I slowly walk up the stairs. I know that there are twenty-two steps. After I've climbed about half way, something spits at me.

Four green eyes sparkle in the darkness.

Mará and T'ho are lying on the cool stone tiles. Mará is wearing a transparent, filmy green gown. She has two heavy gold bracelets on her legs. They jingle quietly with a light, metallic sound when she walks.

I: 'Are you there, Mará?'

I: 'What are you doing here in the dark?'

My voice has a strange sound which is completely alien to me.

Mará: 'T'ho has become much wilder since we've come here. She no longer follows me like she used to.'

I (casually): 'That must come from the change of air. And apart from that she no longer has to spend the whole day on show behind bars. She's beginning to enjoy herself.'

(At the Luna funfair the animals are on view to the public during the day.)

Mará rolls herself a cigarette.

'A card arrived today from Vasco Taddio, he has handed in his notice to Lunapark Limited. In three weeks' time he'll be appearing at Barnum's in New York.'

I: 'He also hit you and your cats often enough: now at least you'll be able to recover!'

Mará scratches her brown legs.

I am exhausted from the heat, go to a room and throw myself on the bed.

Mará plays with T'ho.

I: 'Leave the cat alone, lock it away somewhere!'

Mará: 'I can't sleep without T'ho!'

She lies next to me with T'ho.

T'ho brushes her tail across my face.

IX

Today I took a newspaper from the hotel which the large, dark blue automobile takes us to twice a day.

I lie in one of the rooms in our villa and read:

'FREAK HEATWAVE, 49 SUICIDES.'

(Lurking burglar throws himself from tenth storey —

16 hang themselves.)

The report followed underneath.

Mará lies next to me, toying with my neck. I feel that I'll fall asleep soon ...

Mará has very beautiful brown arms ...

Her hands are as soft as a child's ...

Mará ...

T'ho is lying asleep on the floor.

I read the newspaper:

... a large number of burglar's tools were found on the man as he was picked from the ground. A second vagrant, the dead man's accomplice, tried to escape while the roof of the building was being searched. But he was successfully apprehended. During the preliminary exami-

liminary examinations he stated that they had intended breaking into a jeweller's shop situated in the building. They had crept onto the roof unseen in the early morning, intending to carry out their plan undisturbed by night. But suddenly his friend, who was normally one of the most daring, was beset by a mad fear. Seeing that there was no way back during the day-time, he jumped over the side at once ...

How lovely Mará is with her silent caresses ...

Her brown hands are resting on my neck.

I see her in front of me, and a question torments me: do you love me? I possess her, no question, but ...

Vasco Taddio had doubtlessly received her love ...

I'll fall asleep soon.

It's wonderful to possess a woman completely ...

One just has to have enough money, then one can buy them. One can have everything for gold and diamonds. And women's hands are so soft and warm ...

Although warmth can sometimes be fatal.

Like the sun, burning down on the roof ...

'Ric, have you got any whisky left?'

Hopefully the pawnbroker's will be worth the effort ...

Ah, Mará, the tip of your tongue on my neck!

You want to bite me?

You've learnt that from T'ho!

Tired ...

Drowsy ...

If only it wasn't for this heat ...

'Mará, please give me some water!'

Peculiar, what an odd, bitter flavour the water has!

T'ho growls, rolls over onto the other side, and carries on sleeping.

'Good night Mará, I feel sleepy!'

I think and my thoughts form themselves into visions. Mará is lying next to me, naked, brown and cool. Perhaps she'll fall asleep soon. Her hands rest on my neck.

Heinrich Nowak / **THE SOLAR PLAGUE**

One gets so thirsty, and I've only just had something to drink. A glass of champagne would be excellent right now! One would feel the bubbles right down into one's stomach. But one needs money for that ...

Not a stitch of my clothing is dry ...

God, the roof's hot ...

'Ric, give me some whisky!'

Just one day of torment and tomorrow will be better, tomorrow we'll have money and will be sitting in cool baths with beautiful women.

'Do you think they might catch us, Ric?'

'We'd be done for if someone sees us here by daylight: there's no going back, we'd fall right into their hands ... and the neighbouring roofs are much too high! ...

It's not even noon ...

God! The tin roof's blistering ...

We can't edge along to the shade of the chimney stack, because sooner or later we'd get spotted by the policeman down there on the corner!

Ric, what time is it?

What, only half-past eleven?

Look, Ric, the policeman ... I'm sure he keeps looking up at us. Maybe he's already seen us!

Does your head also ache as much, Ric?

It hurts most behind my ears!

I'm so tired ... I'm going to sleep, Ric ... keep an eye on me so I don't fall over! ...

I'm completely done in! ... aren't you in pain too, Ric?

Tired ...

Drowsy ...

Ric, the policeman's looking!

You think I'm mistaken? Take a look yourself!

Ric, give me a swig of whisky!

Look, the policeman's looking again ...
My head aches.
The policeman's crossing the street ... he's entering the building ... he's coming to get us ...
The roof's so hot, I can't stand it any more ... The policeman's coming up ...
I've got to hide in the gutter ...
The policeman's coming ...
Ric, my head ...
I can't take it any more! ... Let go of me, Ric!
What are you doing with my throat? ... Ric, your teeth are so strange.
Let go of me, I can't stand the pain any more.
I want to jump over.
The policeman's coming.
Ric, you've turned into a cat.
Let go of me then!
Ah ...

X

'Mará, you've bitten me in the throat again, and why do you let T'ho lie on my chest?'
Mará smiles.
T'ho curls up in a corner of the bed.
I run my hand over Mará's black hair.
Mará: 'I love you!'
I: 'Get T'ho out of here!'
Mará: 'I can't sleep without T'ho!'

She hums a negro song and strokes T'ho with her right hand, her left one resting on my chest.

XI

Twice a day the panther, T'ho, travels with us to the hotel in the large, dark blue automobile. She always sits very obediently on her chair while we eat, sometimes purring quietly. Today she suddenly jumped up from her chair and, snarling and hissing, tried to bite the waiter's leg as he was serving us.

Mará paled. Her brusque shout frightened the animal off.

When we arrived home I saw Mará beat T'ho for the first time with a thick leather whip.

And the tears streamed down her face.

XII

I hate T'ho, she robs me of a part of Mará's love. Mará isn't as totally wrapped up in me as I would like. A part of her feelings is always absent, a part of her inner being which is stolen from me by T'ho.

Yes, I actually think that T'ho has the larger share of Mará. Mará can't sleep without T'ho ...

Mará once said to me: 'If panthers get to eat raw, bloody meat, they turn wild again and can't be tamed.'

I secretly feed T'ho with raw calf meat which is still warm.

XIII

Tonight the fever hit me for the first time and wouldn't let go.

We're stuck in the middle of a heatwave which has enveloped half of the continent, and I'm shivering.

Mará gave me some of her chocolate pastilles containing quinine. She is very tender to me.

T'ho lies in the corner, fastened to an iron chain.

Mará: 'You mustn't get ill, I'll be sad if you get ill.'

I: 'It's nothing much, Mará, just a touch of fever!'

She places a chocolate pastille between her white teeth, kisses me and pushes the pastille into my mouth with her tongue.

Mará: 'T'ho is ill too!'

I: 'Perhaps she's got the fever as well!'

Mará walks over to T'ho, she talks to the cat and strokes her. The cat growls contentedly. Then the chain rattles, and T'ho pads around the room on her soft paws. She lies down next to my bed — by Mará's feet. Mará strokes her with the soles of her feet.

Mará (taking a close look): 'Your lips are pale! Mará is sad!'

I: 'Yes — '

Mará: 'I don't want you to be ill!'

She buries her head in my chest and hides her face.

Mará (after a very tender kiss): 'What does a white woman do when she loves a white man?'

I: 'She fulfils all of his wishes!'

Mará: 'And when a white man loves a white woman, what does he do?'

I: 'He tries to fulfil all of her wishes!'

Mará scratches her brown legs. She smiles mysteriously. She bends over me.

Mará: 'When a brown girl loves a brown man, and when a brown

Heinrich Nowak / **THE SOLAR PLAGUE**

man loves a brown girl, they go and make a sacrifice together to the god of war.'

Mará kisses my neck. Her body nestles up to mine.

Mará: 'White women don't know what love is!'

T'ho jumps onto the bed to Mará.

XIV

The fever has subsided.

I walk through the tropical night. The light of the stars illuminates my way.

I think about Mará.

Before I left she kissed my eyes in a wonderfully tender way.

I'm very tired, but I don't want to return home yet: it is nicer to think about the one you love from far away.

Mará kissed my eyes in a wonderfully tender way.

The night loves me.

The world loves me.

XV

T'ho and Mará are asleep.

I get up quietly and fetch my Browning. I place the barrel to T'ho's head. One squeeze of the trigger and T'ho would be dead. Then Mará would belong to me alone. To me alone! Then I would no longer have to share Maráʼs love.

But Mará would be deeply wounded if I shot Tʼho, and her thoughts would centre even more on her.

No, I mustnʼt shoot Tʼho.

She must die by accident.

But Tʼho must die!

XVI

Noon.

The large, dark blue automobile will arrive in ten minutes.

The heat crushes all life to the ground.

Drowsy . .

Tired ...

My hands play mechanically with the Browning.

Mará and Tʼho are in the next room.

If I now fired a bullet at my head, Mará would get a shock and rush up to me with Tʼho.

Perhaps she would even scream.

Perhaps she would cry over my body!

Tʼho would certainly lick my blood!

I place the barrel of the Browning to my temple.

Mará is singing her negro song in the next room.

A scream is waiting in my throat: Iʼm completely insane.

Why do I want to shoot myself?

The large blue automobile drives up.

XVII

I am sitting in an almost inaccessible thicket in the jungle.

My heart is ready for battle: I love Mará!

I have carved myself a club from an ash tree which was uprooted by a gale.

My heart yearns for battle!

My heart loves Mará.

I swing the club through the burning air.

My muscles tense. My body sways: my body yearns for Mará!

A sand viper glides over my foot. Now it coils itself, rises up in front of me and flashes its venomous tongue.

I swing my club ...

The sand viper gives one last twitch and is dead.

My heart is warlike!

I love Mará!

XVIII

The fever has seized me again. Mará gives me her quinine pastilles. T'ho flashes her eyes at me, cruel and cold.

My mind is beset by the most terrible thoughts.

A glowing sand viper wriggles up me and coils round my throat. My fingernails bore into soft flesh. I smell the stench of rotting and decay.

A grey animal stretches out its six long tentacles at me. Mará pulls a knife on me. T'ho sits on my throat. The sand viper's tongue flickers round my jugular veins. I want to grab my club ... My hands reach into emptiness ...

T'ho is on the prowl for my blood. T'ho hates me!

I grab hold of my Browning.

Mará stabs a knife into my chest — I fire — A bang —

Mará screams.

The gun smoke slowly disperses. Mortar crumbles from the wall.

T'ho arches her back in a corner of the room. Mará stands beside me, rests her hands on my forehead and tenderly removes the revolver.

I'm lost: I've got the solar plague!

Perhaps in two hours I'll commit suicide.

'Mará, save me!'

XIX

An insidious fever drains me and completely unhinges my mind.

I have spent two hours of dread, waiting for the moment of my suicide. The sound of the automobile horn saved me.

The solar plague has passed me by this once.

An automobile's horn set my thoughts back in their normal course. The clamour of reality destroyed an insane vision.

XX

It is the dead of night.

Mará and I want to sleep. Mará's brown body lies beside me. T'ho crouches at the foot of the bed.

I: 'Mará, get T'ho out of this room!'

Mará: 'I can't sleep without T'ho!'

She strokes T'ho.

I: 'Mará, get T'ho out of this room!'

Total silence. Two bellicose eyes stare at me.

I: 'I want you to lock T'ho up in the next room!'

Mará: 'Then you must lock up Mará as well, Mará can't sleep without T'ho!'

She smiles.

I: 'T'ho must go!'

Mará: 'I can't love you without T'ho!'

I get up, grab the snarling cat by the neck and drag it into the next room.

Mará creeps along behind me, goes over to T'ho in the corner, crouches and strokes the animal.

I: 'Come on Mará, I'm locking up now.'

Mará: 'Mará is staying with T'ho!'

I want to shut the door. In this moment two eyes bore into mine. Mará stands up, naked, brown and loving. She opens her arms to me.

And the door is locked.

XXI

I'm afraid of the solar plague.

I'm going to have to drive to the city to a famous psychiatrist. Probably I'm only in the middle of a very bad neurosis.

Up until now, everyone who died of the solar plague was also insane.

I know these psychiatric conditions, I know why they all commit suicide. My knowledge of my condition will save me, it will be the antibacillus for the solar plague.

XXII

During the sunset, on the flat roof of our home.

Mará: 'Yesterday you left me alone the whole night long!'

I: 'You said you simply had to sleep with T'ho.'

Mará: 'I love you! — We still haven't made a sacrifice to the god of war!'

I: 'A few days ago I was sitting in the forest, I carved a piece of ashwood into a club. And my heart thought of you! It yearned for war. A poisonous, grey sand viper crawled over my foot and I killed it with my club. My heart felt you'

Mará: 'I know that you hate T'ho, but I don't want to be with you without her! My heart yearns for war as well, it loves you! I knew that you would leave me on my own for the whole night, and I still went to T'ho. My body yearns for you, my body thirsts for battle!'

I: 'T'ho takes away a part of my possibilities for your love, that's why I hate T'ho!'

Mará: 'T'ho is a wild panther which lusts for blood. That's why I love her!'

I: 'T'ho is our fate!'

Mará: 'T'ho is war!'

XXIII

The bellicose episodes in our love are almost enough to steel me against the sun, but all the same I shall drive to Littehota soon and visit a psychiatrist. Mará will have to remain here alone with T'ho for two days.

Today I spent a long time standing with the gardener who was working in the garden. His expression, which is normally just sly, had something cruel about it.

The gardener: 'Your panther has killed my goat!'

I: 'You'll be compensated!'

The gardener: 'The animal was set at my goat, my wife saw it!'

I (seemingly indifferent): 'Aha ... probably out of boredom.'

XXIV

Mará is in the next room, asleep with T'ho.

I am alone, the window is open and the tropical summer night streams in.

I feel that I will fall asleep soon.
I still think: If only Mará were here ...
Long after midnight:
I am woken from my sleep by a soft snarling. I want to jump up. I can't — T'ho is sitting on my chest. The cat stares at my throat. Thirsting for blood.

I mustn't make a move. One move and I'm dead — I can't even call Mará — Not a sound — just lie there quietly —

The Malay peers through the crack of the door. I guess what's happened: she has placed T'ho on my chest. Now she is observing me.

T'ho sits on my chest, ready to pounce.

I mustn't even twitch, otherwise I'll lose Mará and my life.

The clock creeps slowly forwards.

Mará sees that I am awake. I feel how much she loves me now. And T'ho is sitting on my throat.

I forget the danger. Mará, I love you!

The day starts to grope slowly through the window.

Mará shouts: 'T'ho!!!'

T'ho looks at me once more, springs off my chest and slinks over to Mará.

Mará comes over to me, brown and naked.

Mará: 'I love you!'

She lays down beside me. Her hands clasp my throat.

Mará: 'I loved your throat as T'ho threatened it!'

Our nerves tauten and our blood screams:

War! War! War!

XXV

Once again I am in the throes of the fever. I shiver under the boiling sun.

My fear of the sun is madness ...

This abnormal heat has lasted nearly three weeks now. And no end in sight!

If the fever subsides I shall drive to Littehota tomorrow morning.

XXVI

Rioting in Littehota!!!

Crowds are streaming down the streets and yelling. Sweat trickles down their foreheads. They're building barricades.

Soldiers on the march.

Trumpets ...

Drums ...

A madman stands on the curb. The people are bawling all around him. He screams:

'We're dying from the heat! We can't work any more! We're starving! The government must organise rain for us!!!'

Soldiers.

A lieutenant in command.

The crack of a gun salvo.

The madman springs from the curb with a flic-flac.

Someone wants to get to the front.

With a club against the soldiers.

A stray shot!

He makes a deep bow, claps his hands to his body and dies.

Someone leaps at the lieutenant, tears away his sabre, punches him in the face.

A bayonet ravages his belly.

XXVII

More crowds.

Armed against the soldiers with clubs, staves and Brownings!

War in Littehota!!!

Shots — Bayonets in the guts — one of them springs into the air like a shot hare. Turning a double somersault.

The soldiers flee!

Canon!

Collapsing houses — screams — flames — war — war — trumpets — shots — murder —

People drag a captured canon behind them, singing.

They aim it at the sun and shoot at the blazing fire.

Within two days Manahota lies in ruins.

Littequar is in flames.

Littehota died of the solar plague.

XXVIII

I returned to Mará. I was gone for one and a half days.

I row across the lake which separates our villa from the Grotaqua forests. The sun burns down on my head. The water in the lake is lukewarm.

I stand up in my canoe in the middle of the lake and scream to the world: 'Mará!'

'The war is being conducted by two different races. If you were a man, I would have to kill you. But because you are a woman I must love you. Our love is the love and hate of two races! T'ho is our fate!'

XXIX

The battle revolves around T'ho. Hard and silent. Every day I secretly feed T'ho with warm, bloody meat.

T'ho is no longer allowed to walk around freely; she is always fastened to an iron chain.

Today we went swimming in the lake. T'ho lay on the shore, chained. Mará stepped out of the water and went to T'ho. The panther snapped at Mará's brown legs.

As we arrived home, T'ho was chained up.

Mará took her thick leather whip.

Thick red blood trickled down T'ho's head.

Mará came to me, she took my head in her hands and cried.

Mará: 'Soon it will all be over, T'ho's head is bleeding!'

XXX

Thousands of stars are floating in the dark blue sky.

I've fled into the night-time prairie, away from the reality of eros. My body has the grotesquely angular movements of a tomahawk-wielding Red Indian. My feverish hands grasp at phantoms: fantasms of a female body.

The intellect trembles off over the heavens.

I observe the feeling of my love and love it.

I observe the feeling of my hate and hate it.

I talk to the blades of grass and say: you!

I talk to the heavens and say: you!

My feverish thoughts are burning for war.

My thinking has turned into a wild animal which wants to leap at you.

Drunk, I drag myself onwards.

I know that in ten minutes the intoxication will be over and I will collapse in exhaustion.

XXXI

The tropical frenzy is destroying me.

Mará had hurried after me and found me lying in the prairie. She screamed as she spotted me.

She ran back. The gardener dragged me to the villa.

Febrile delirium.

T'ho must come to me! I want to stroke T'ho. Mará, our love

won't die, T'ho lets me stroke her.

Mará cried, I noticed even though she tried to hide her tears from me.

XXXII

Mará lies naked in front of me — on the flat roof of our villa in the scorching heat of the sun.

She looks out into the far distance.

Mará: 'I've arranged to have the other seven panthers come.'

She kisses me.

The sun will kill me!

XXXIII

Mará's cats were delivered in a heavy wooden cage. We've locked them in an empty room. T'ho is with them and is glad.

Mará (smiling): 'Go into the room with the cats and fetch T'ho for me!'

I open the door and enter with echoing steps. Mará half closes the door behind me and peers through the narrow crack.

My voice rings out commandingly: 'T'ho!'

The animal slinks up to me with its paws outstretched, almost on its belly, and snarls at me. I pick her up in my arms, my hand stroking her coat smooth, and carry her out singing a tune.

The other cats hiss and snarl.

Mará has opened the door for me, I hand her T'ho. She kisses the cat's head and presses it to her breast. Then she lets T'ho slip to the ground.

Her eyes pierce mine. She comes up to me and places her brown hands round my shoulders. I feel her fingernails in my flesh.

Love, love grows into the immeasurable.

XXXIV

I can't live in this heat any more, I want to get away from here, to the coolness of the ocean.

The threat of death has hung over me for four weeks now.

Mará smiles at everything.

Her body is cool and brown.

Suddenly I am struck by an insane idea. It might save us, but it's mad all the same.

What if an enormous fire was started!

Hundreds of square miles of countryside must catch fire. The combustion would produce steam, and then rain, rain, coolness! A thunder storm would burst …

It would be cool, perhaps only for a short while, but it would be cool.

I carry on contemplating the fire … The Red Indians knew how to use fire in times of drought, in order to summon the rain.

But this idea is madness …

XXXV

The hotel where we eat is almost completely uninhabited. Everyone has fled to the ocean.

We are sitting in a fairly empty dining room. The waiters' footsteps echo, long and clear.

A Negro stands in a corner, operating a bellows which stirs the hot, muggy air just enough to produce a cooling breeze.

T'ho no longer travels with us.

Mará sits pensively in front of her plate. Then:

'Vasco Taddio has written to me, telling me I should also quit Lunapark Limited and go and join Barnum's with my panthers.'

Later: 'From now on I will only be able to perform with seven cats, T'ho is no use any more!'

I think: I'll be able to think more clearly once the burnt forests have relieved me of my torment. But the forest fire is pure madness ...

Thus my precondition for clear thought is insanity!

Mará ponders over her plate ...

XXXVI

I paddle across the lake.

Mará is swimming. Her dark brown body disappears further and further into the distance.

My canoe reaches the distant shore. I chain it up to an ancient sycamore tree.

I walk into the depths of the jungle. I pass the spot where I slayed the sand viper and quietly sang a song in honour of Mará. I pass by trees under which I had fantasised feverishly. I arrive at the spot where I had formed Mará's body, brown, naked and slender, in the soft earth.

I walk deep into the jungle.

The evening closes in around me. Then the night quickly stretches out its black hands towards me.

I sit down beneath a Durmast oak. Fever begins to run up and down my skin. I shiver.

My mind creates grotesque images.

Then someone comes up to me and says a peculiar word:

'Gloráqualioréma!'

I reply:

'The wildness which warm, bloody beef produces in panthers is terrible. By the way, Sir, you can still experience your miracle!'

The stranger shakes his head in thought and says 'Gloráqualioréma!' once more.

I start to smile:

'Yes, the lion tamer who used to work in the Luna Fun Fair now performs at Barnum's. I also have something I'm burning to tell you: the forest is burning! — The sun is shining! — I always had to make up pure, simple sentences like this when I was at school. I was still a young boy when my father died!'

An automobile comes racing up, skewers the man with the penetrating rays of its head lamps and drives off.

There's not a people in the whole world which doesn't see the sun as a circular disk, and that is also the origin of the great heat ... great heat ... great heat ... great heat ...

I'm startled by my delirium.

Tired ...

All around me is the dark blue starry night. I can't go any further for fear of losing the path.

I shall spend the night here!

I light a cigarette. Cast the glowing match over my shoulder.

Heinrich Nowak / **THE SOLAR PLAGUE**

Today, while walking at the height of noon, a large, brown death's-head moth came fluttering up and alighted on my shirt, just where my heart beats.

I look into the depths of the dark blue forest.

Silence.

Blue.

Suddenly I see a red, glowing point: it grows larger and larger. Flames lick upwards.

The glowing match has set fire to dried leaves on the ground! The forest is going to catch fire!

I stand up and talk to the flames: sweet fire!

The flames spill over and flow along the floor, licking broad tree trunks.

I jump across a stream of flames. It flows after me, I start to run.

The forest is in agony.

Dear forest, you must die!

You must die so that it will rain!

The forest night burns bright-red behind me. I leap over toppled trees. Sometimes my feet get tangled in creepers. I fall flat on the ground.

Automatically I think:

Find safety from the fire! ... It's going to rain! ! ...

Find safety from the fire! ... It's going to rain! ! ...

I must get across the lake! ...

The fire is running faster than me! ...

The sycamore to which my canoe is chained is burning, a blazing torch in the glare of the fire.

The lake is lit bright red. I travel through bloody water. I paddle away from the forest fire towards the shelter of the rain.

I'll be able to think clearly again. Mará, I shall be able to love you without this torment!

The paddles grow heavier and heavier in my hands. If only I was already there on the shore! ...

Tired ...

Drowsy ...

I want to sleep, deep, sound and untroubled! Dreamless! My wishes are fulfilled: it's going to rain. I shall be able to love Mará without torment.

Ah, Mará

XXXVII

My canoe hits the shore. I hear the keel scrape on the sand.

Evening, the sun sets. I have a sluggish feeling as if I had woken from a deep sleep. I get up from my lying position and notice that my clothes are still damp in places.

Ah, I've been lying unconscious in the boat, drifting round the lake. The paddles are gone and the bows singed from the fire.

How many hours have passed since the forest fire?

I look round at our villa, it's quite far away, reddened by the setting sun.

I attempt to propel myself with the boat-hook, to get back to the house.

My clothes are damp! So it *has* rained!

A light cloud of smoke climbs over the mountains, it's probably still burning there.

Mará ...

XXXVIII

I crawl onto land with effort. I'm overcome by dizziness.
 Groaning, I reach the room in our house.
 I whisper:
 'Mará!'
 I call with a moan:
 'T'ho'
 The floor where I stand has been sanctified by Mará's brown legs. I lay flat on the ground. Mará will come and find me lying on the ground. T'ho will sniff at me.
 My consciousness fades. My eyes grow heavy. Bright colours stream out of the nothingness.

XXXIX

 I awake from my faint and my flight from the burning forest.
 Night.
 I try to orient myself and light a candle.
 T'ho is lying not far away, a bullet hole in her head.
 Next to her my Browning and a scrap of paper. Written in a clumsy child's hand is:
 'T'ho had to be put down — she bit Mará — Mará has gone to Vasco Taddio.'
 T'ho, our fate ... Ah! our love! ...
 I lie back on the floor and nestle my head on T'ho's stiff body.
 The stars shine into the room. But my eyes see the sun and my body feels its heat.
 Time whistles through my ears.
 Mará is gone.
 My hands stroke the Browning, my lips kiss the barrel. It is cold.

My tongue plays along it. The putrefaction stretches out its arms to me.

I think:

My mind is reeling. The logic of my feelings is becoming murderous.

Eros has made peace with me!

The reality around me becomes imaginary. All the images become blurred and swim into one another.

Mará's brown legs are travelling on the train.

The sun wants to play football with my head. My Browning has turned into a little animal, it creeps into my mouth and licks my tongue.

I am standing on the verge.

The wild animal in my head, the wild animal of the passing seconds, will devour me yet.

Ah, Mará!

Gottfried Benn

THE ISLAND

(1916)

Rönne, a doctor, could justify the orderliness imposed on his days by the authorities, the approval which had to be gained from the state, even the rules affecting his calling, by assuming that this was life.

Did it matter that the island was small, could be viewed in its entirety from a hill, a strip of rock between the seagulls and the sea — there was the prison with its convicts to which he had been appointed as doctor, and then there was a beach, a large meadow full of shrubs and twittering, a refuge for the birds, and further below a squalid village with fishermen, but that demanded closer investigation.

A throat had to be painted, a perjurer's knee massaged, and then Rönne got up and left the walled farmstead. In front of it was the white beach covered with blossoming oats and thistles. For the summer had arrived from across the sea like a squall: the sky thundered with blueness, it teemed warmth and light.

Wrapped up in thought about how best to employ the time available to him after finishing his duties, and what this meant with regard to the state and the individual, he walked off. He took deep breaths of the clear sea air, cleansing his narrow chest, opening himself willingly to the wholesomeness which it is so well known to provide the wanderer. He felt at one with the spirit which had summoned and appointed him, which had decided without hesitation to safeguard this forward-looking bourgeois institution which deserved the protection of the public at large in repayment for its vigorous efforts, namely to weed out the vermin without, however, disregarding the intrinsic humanity of the fallen. Thus in a sort of tacit acknowledgement of the all-embracing bond of the psychic, the spirit was against their extermination and provided the doctor instead.

And now the gaunt shingled roofing of the first huts, was it not shelter from storm and rain, defence against hardship, a cover for warmth and cosiness? The net carefully spread out over post and stone by the husband returned from the catch, was it not wrapped in the smells of the abode where the natural, the supremely healthy took place? And now a gust of wind blew against a sou'wester, and an arm grabbed the brim: Truly, here stimuli were responded to by the organic; its symptoms powered by drives: metabolism and reproduction; the reflex arc ruled, one could relax here.

Men were sitting in front of an inn. Their intention? To sit there! Not walking about, saving their energy. Drinking out of pots! Purely for pleasure? No way! The nutritional value could not be overlooked. And if so? Communal recreation? Swapping tales?! Confirmations!!!?

And the sullen man to one side? The brooding man who took himself more seriously? Didn't the more complete act, the greater

Gottfried Benn / THE ISLAND

superstructure, the bringer of light into possible chasms, also blaze on his forehead, penetrating the demonic, pitched against the gods?

Put shortly; perceptions which should bring satisfaction. Nowhere a disturbance, everywhere sunshine and a clear course of events.

Rönne sat down. I have some free time, he said to himself, to think things through. Good, an island in a more or less southerly sea. There are none here, but there could be: cinnamon forests. It's June now, so the bark would start to peel and a twig might break off in the process. A truly delightful fragrance would be released, an aromatic event just by tearing off a leaf.

Then all in all: shrubs four to six feet high, soft, green leaves like laurel with yellow tinted pistils. The gathering begins as soon as the sprout is as thick as a thumb, demanding many hands, baskets, billhooks, bark and bast; much has already been proven by these words, but only once inside the hut is the bark peeled.

Yes, that was an island lying in a sea off India. A ship approached, suddenly entering the wind which had embraced the land, and now it stood in the breath of the brownish forest. The cinnamon forest, thought the traveller, and the cinnamon forest, thought Rönne. The ground was white as snow, and the brushwood full of sap. And he walked across the island between rye and vine, detached and isolated by stillness. His judgement is desire, the syntax forming opinions. But he ponders on the pollen of a plant, for he is ready to scatter it. Long gone are the days of mourning when he had travelled here with the ladies in the railway carriage: isn't it pretty here, the mother said to her daughters, just look! And then from the windows of the carriage they took in the row of hills, dim in the blue mists, before it the valley and a town sinking behind woods and clover; for, as Rönne always concluded, the slopes would not have taken place if the mother hadn't mentioned it.

But here life was not greeted with such vague exclamations. Here everything which met the eye was accepted. A net, the sight of a lobster pot, were assimilated quite matter-of-fact. Even when he was thinking something, as just now, something quite different was there, not an enrichment, more a dream.

He sat, pale, on the beach. He felt light and transparent and seemed to be no dirtier than a stone in motion, than a rounded boulder kept in place by a fragile arrangement.

And if he had been motivated to come to the island by the feeling that he had a duty to do, to test his conceptions on objects which were, as far as possible, isolated and subject to scarcely changing conditions, then he now sensed something like fulfilment. It seemed to him that his concepts were slipping away. The way, for instance, 'sea' had been for him — a linguistic given cut off from the bright waters, mobile, but at most as a ferret for the system, the result of a process of thought, a highly general term. But now it seemed to him that it was wandering back to where there had been vast waters to the south and brackish tides to the north and waves salted the unsuspecting lip. The urge to establish it more clearly, to outline it more unassailably against the dunes and the sea, vanished quietly. He felt himself quietly forget it, letting it return to the substance, to the gull and the seaweed, the smell of the storm and the inquietude ...

Rönne lived a solitary life, absorbed in his development and working hard. His studies were devoted to the creation of the new syntax. The aim was to complete the view of the world which the work of the last century had created. It seemed truly necessary to him to eliminate the familiar 'you'[1] form in grammar, because the address had become mythical.

He felt committed to carrying out this development, whose history stretched back thousands of years.

The restructuring of movement into teleological action lay in the mists of man's origins. That much was certain. Also that man had opened his eyes in many spots: at the bright sky, across deserts, on the Nile, and at the fiddle-players by the myrtle lagoons — but here in the North a decision had to be made: the third drive had entered between hunger and love. It had grown out of the bad breath of the ascetics, from exhausted sexualities beneath the thick air of the foglands, the realisation, hecatombs groaning for the unity of thought, and the hour of fulfilment seemed to have arrived.

If Descartes once assumed that the pineal gland was the seat of the soul because its appearance, yellowish, elongated, mild but nevertheless threatening, was apparently like God's finger, then the physiologists of the brain had determined that sugar appears in the urine after puncturing the brain matter, as indicated by the appearance of indigo. Yes, the correlates for the occurrence of salivation. Psychology had recognised the symptomatic nature of the emotions stemming from sensation, set down their rightful general values in exact curves as a defence against damaging influences, and with that the ability to determine individual differences was complete. The theory of knowledge had finalised its breakthrough by reviving Berkeley's ideas to yield a new panpsychism, which assigned reality the status of condensed concepts meaningful to the environment, particularly the sexual, which promoted the perpetuation of the species.

We can take this as a settled matter, Rönne said to himself. This has now been taught and accepted for almost two decades. But what had become of the individual's self-appraisal, where did that take place? Its expression, the spoken word, where did that occur?

Wrapped in thought, he walked beside a field with a man he had taken along from the institution.

'Poppies, the distended form of the summer,' he cried out loud, 'Omphalic: connecting a belly-like part, dynamite of dualism: here is a colour-blind person, the reddened night. Ha, how you rattle along! Tumbled into the field, you serrate form, you corner-stone of stimulation, washed into the weeds — and all the sweet noons when my eye fell asleep on you, last, silent slumbers, faithful hours

— blue shadows on your stigma, leaning on your fluttering conflagration, warmed, comforted, sunk in your fire: brought to blossom!: now this man — you too! You too! — All my misfortunes playing along my edges in the broad spread of summer — and now: where am I not?

Where am I not, he thought and turned towards the institution, and when does an event fail to intrude upon the given? Down below are rooms. Men, directors and administrators are sitting at tables, the toothpick moving to and fro between each new intellectual stimulation.

The psychic complex revolves around the day's events and the racing results. It touches on the disconcerting, the anomalous, even attunes itself to the contradictory. The attempt to unravel the unexplained, to preserve the doubtful, is awakened in the mental processes — the word is there to bridge the discrepancies. Experience is brought forth, proof and defence furnished; and must an observation, made here and there, even if not conclusive, be completely invalid? The darkness is already receding. The muddles are already being ironed out and the blue of the heavens descends so that there can be no more contradictions.

The blueness of something always descends, sooner or later — of roast veal, for instance, which everyone knows. He suddenly walks up to a table of regulars, and their unique individualities wind themselves around him. Geographical peculiarities, oddities from the realms of taste emerge, the urge for nuances encircle him. Argument and detraction, attack and reconciliation, will surge around the roast, the unleasher of the psychic.

And who does this morning mood encounter? A woman who rises exceptionally early; all the coldness and dew flow into that being walking there. Transmission occurs, a call will ensue, a stock of tales about past walks is formed. The storehouses for assimilating events are everywhere, and what was and will be has long since occurred.

When was anyone last in the midst of the stream? I must think it

Gottfried Benn / THE ISLAND

all over, must make a synopsis of it all, nothing eludes logical association. Beginning and end, but I occur. I live on this island and think cinnamon forests. Reality and dream intertwine inside me. Why does the poppy bloom, only to loose its redness; the lad speaks, but the psychic complex is still there, even without him.

The competition between the associations, that is the ultimate self, he thought, and he walked back to the institution which stood on a hill by the sea. If a newspaper, a phenomenon ensuing from bookshops, juts out of my pocket, it provides a link for a chain of movements towards fellow beings, to an event, as it were, between unique individuals. Should my associate say 'might I have a look', then although there is a stimulus which has an effect, a will directed at something, motoric competitions, there is still always the pattern of the soul, the vital arrangement which sets the traps.

We've reached the end, he felt, we've conquered the final organ. I shall walk down the corridor and my steps will echo. Shouldn't my steps echo in the corridor? Yes indeed, that's life, and a small quip while passing the lady administrator? Yes, that too!

The ship landed, as it did every week, and with the passengers disembarked a woman who wanted to stay for a while.

Rönne got to know her, why shouldn't he get to know her: a bunch of secondary sexual characteristics in anthropoid formation.

But soon he asked himself uneasily: I want her company, but not her powers of intellect, so what then? She is medium sized, blonde, bleached with peroxide, and greying at the temples. Her eyes focus on the distance, her pupils the unchangeable grey of the mist — but I sense it as flight, I must formulate it.

Her nature: she loves white flowers, cats and crystals and she cannot sleep alone at night because she loves to hear the beating of another heart, but where should I apply the principle to integrate it all? She never demands affection, but when one approaches her one is in the palace of love, and suddenly she stands over me, tall and unmoving in a pose which must hurt her — what appalling confusion.

Scenting danger, hearing a distant current babbling on its way to engulf, to dissolve him, he cast his sociological framework aside.

What, the millet on the neighbouring island had gone mouldy? Had the little man been treated fairly? What had become of honesty and brotherly love? What would be left if they vanished? Or: truly a slave to his customary quantity of tea leaves, shaken in a bottle, filled, stoppered and shaken again, then handed over to an acquaintance, the neighbour, or someone who wants to know more and has honest intentions and a helpful nature, what could still be employed to tempt him? He, amalgamated into the state as the plain and simple bearer of its shame. Perhaps there'll be peace at last, right?

But the lure was there once more, the woman, the flowing nature. Released, he whispered to the nurse who had arrived: a bad knee! How does this precipitate into reality. What a powerful formula! Officially obliged to recognise it because of my position! Knee ailments, swellings, spreading inflammations. — Firm ground — Masculinities!

There again, every appearance has its organising principle, and he walked to the beach consoled; the important thing is to ascertain which one applies to her; the system is all-bounteous, it contains her as well. It also contains her who, unconscious of fidelity and broken promises, cannot come right now because the fisherwoman was carrying a rod and the salps were glistening — collect experiences, make deductions, his calm sky above her too! But her hips, when she walked beside him, rustled like the senseless, and round her shoulders was a mane of chaos.

He plunged deeper into his books, forging his world. But how? Hadn't articles of this peculiar sort recently been given space in the most respected natural science journals, even been discussed with interest?

The work of an unknown Jewish doctor from Danzig, who literally said that feelings reach deeper than intellectual faculties? That

Gottfried Benn / THE ISLAND

feeling is the greatest secret of our lives and the question of its origin unanswerable? To think it through to its perfect conclusion: that feeling no longer belongs to the sensations?

Did the author know what that meant? When he said that feeling is no longer dependant on stimulus, as he, Rönne, had learnt? When he named it the dark stream, which gushes out of the body? The incalculable?

Did the man really know the questions which would arise as a consequence of his new teaching, did this complete unknown understand the true gravity of his assertion which he simply sent into the world in a book with a dull grey cover, without any announcement, not even making it clear on the title page? Did he know perhaps that he was answering the question as to whether novelty can come into being?

Rönne drew a deep breath. Was this some sort of new science which would supersede him? That every insemination bore the seed of something unbelievably new, that the uniting of elements was continued in the following generations in the form of bisexuality, and it was this which had to be recognised as the mighty creative force which had raised life to its heights?

Rönne shuddered. He looked once more at the journal which had reviewed the book, at the name of the man who had signed the article: it was his former teacher.

Creative man! A new shaping of the concept of evolution from the mathematical to the intuitive — but what was to become of him, the doctor, locked in the quantitative, the confirmed professional empiricist?

If he came across a throat with a dangerous swelling — could he subdue it intuitively? Wouldn't he be forced rather to concentrate his mind on analytic phenomena, empirics, purposeful gestures, on the whole horror of affirmed realities, to a hypothesis about reality which he could no longer defend epistemologically, for the sake of the child which was already blue as a result of its throat, which was suffocating and brought him his money. And that because of his position?

He suddenly felt extremely tired and a poison in his limbs. He went over to the window which looked out on the garden. The blossoms stood there, shadowless white beside the magnificence of the hedgerows; something trembling hung from every blade of grass; the evening mingled with the scent of shrubs, which gleamed limitless and eternal.

For a moment something brushed his head: a relaxation, a soft rattle of an explosion, and an image entered his eye: bright countryside vibrating with blues and glowing fire and cleft by roses, a pillar in the distance, its base overgrown; and there he was with the woman, two lost animals silently expelling juices and breaths.

But it was gone in an instant. He ran his hand across his eyes. The band closed quickly back round his forehead and coolness returned to his temples: what was going on here? He had lived with a woman and had once seen her gather the withered petals from the edge of a colourful stone-topped table and form them into a small pile; then she sat down again, lost to the sight of a bright shrub. That was all he really knew about her; for the rest he felt estranged from himself, there was a rustling and he bled — but where did that get him?

His gaze hardened. He forced his way into the garden, steeling himself, tidying the bushes, pacing out the path. And now it hit him: he was standing at the exit of a millennium, but the woman was a constant; he owed his development to an epoch which had created a system, and whatever might happen to it, he was that!

He cast his gaze challengingly into the evening and lo, the intrinsic nature of the hyacinths formed a blueness under the fragrant curves of pure formulae, uniform consistencies in the space of the garden; and an old hag on her last legs, a match-seller, plodded up the steps of the institution beneath the conflagration of calculable rays from a sun setting perpendicularly to the earth ...

Hans Flesch-Brunningen

THE METAPHYSICAL CANARY

(1917)

The seven-headed family was sitting at their midday meal. The plain linen table-cloth had a lot of stains, brown, red, and green from the spinach. The limping cook, who only possessed one tooth, had just served the fourth course. It was ovaries, which Papa had brought home fresh from the Institute of Anatomy, and blood dumplings. Aunt Johannes, sitting as guest of honour at the head of the table, served herself first. Aunt Johannes came from Reichenberg in Bohemia, and was a hermaphrodite. She had green hands and knew the Odyssey by heart. As she poked about in the blood sauce she said 'Eggcellent!', and her nose drooped. The red canary sent a cry over their heads and swung about in its little house, which was mounted on a cheap stand. Aunt Johannes looked up and said 'Fine then!' And the six remaining middle-class noses held their breath. It was, as it happens, a canary from Kamchatka and an offspring of Tiki-taki who had always accompanied Napoleon on his travels and is in fact said to have already steered the course of history under Frederick the Great. An Eskimo had slipped him to Aunt Johannes at the Brussels World's Fair just as the exhibition hall had started to burn, with the words 'Sapli rumpala menti ghinkwa wh!', which is to say: 'Close, open, shake, so that it shines!' So now he hung there in the middle of the Weinschweisser family with fourteen eyes glued to him, while the ovaries turned cold on their heavy, earthenware plates. Aunt Johannes carried on: 'And because I don't just love you as my relatives, but also admire you as bastions of the solid German family and of the good, free, prudent, German home, I've come and brought this animal with me, which I've charmed and cast a spell on so that it will work for our well-being. Last night it whispered to me that it would send us money, as much as anyone could wish for, and there'd be no end to our riches. Maybe I didn't cast the spell correctly.' A wave of astonishment washed over the dishes of the family's soul. Meanwhile Sunday's leftovers had arrived, crystallised earlobes, — and the father took his turn to speak; with his frank, masculine forehead, his bushy beard and the ribbon from the student fencing club he wore on his waistcoat, this was the man who was accustomed to cutting up corpses. 'Good, money — very good, money. We'll donate it to the Institute for a new building. And another bit for charity.' He stroked his beard. 'One could also go to Italy, to the immortal sites.'

But then mother Eulalia spoke up. Still young — she didn't give birth to the children, she's stepmother and soon enough the gallant sleeping partner of father and sons alike. So she spoke, with her tightly squeezed-in neck and her opulent bosom which swelled up for the occasion, catching a meat dumpling in the process: 'Good, money. The household can be increased. And the Housewifes' Institute and the Elizabeth Society can have a share, something to put the name Weinschweisser in the papers.' She calmly revealed a set of perfectly white teeth. 'And a car of some sort, a reddish Fiat, and hats from Drecoll.' She went off into a dream in Aunt Johannes' thin head of hair. But the canary let out a cry from above, and Aunt Johannes held out her greenish hand for it to feed on, picking and pinching as she murmured a few words. Frederick, a stern youth, twenty-four summers old and with a taut struggling expression around his lips and a head of blond, backwards-combed hair, threw aside his cup of chicory coffee causing his father to give him a stern look, and crying out 'Hail! Hail!', he started to sing the 'Wacht am Rhein,[1] a patriotic song which was forbidden. But Frederick was dreaming: 'Hail? The school society — German youth — the inquiring spirit — legal digests — journeys to Greece — the grounding of clubs — national — liberal — Hail!'

Adolf, the free-spirit and social politician who was cooing with cousin Mathilde — she showed him her boots made from the skin of little children, and played the coquette with the youth who was wearing his departmental insignia to one side — was a member of the Academics' Association, and was a poet whose ideal was a mixture of Karl Kraus, Frank Baum and Treumann. And so the youth kept cooing: 'Money — Oh money! I'll give it all to you, my sweet little silk stockings, dearest cousin, jupons. We'll travel away. See the world. And dream fairy-tales in sleeping cars. The Riviera, Paris.' He shuddered as he thought of all the flirts that he'd encounter there. Mathilde shouted 'Whoopee!' and threw a rose out of the window in youthful exuberance. It fell onto the nose of a senior school master, Max Hindleg, who, turning his nose up with a sniff, carried on walking. But the canary turned pale at the shout of 'Whoopee' and clattered its wings. And Aunt Johannes said warningly: 'Keep quiet, my little ones! He's about to reveal something.' But seeing that all except for little Otto, the seventeen year-old, were busy, she turned to him, and out of the confines of her false teeth came: 'Well, and you?' This lad with his protruding ears and hideous skull carried on lightly brushing out his dandruff onto the linen table-cloth, and then shouted out clearly: 'You're all the most insufferable idiots!' Father Weinschweisser looked over, troubled, and the red bird started to drop something as Otto carried on: 'A dozen' — and he pointed at a place in the newspaper — 'and then Mentscher. Is the best …' — And he turned to the window and spat out into the blue spring day.

All of a sudden Aunt Johannes called out: 'Look!' The magical canary had shrunken in size, slipped out of its house and settled on Aunt Johannes's shoulder beside her ear. The Weinschweissers sat up and listened. Aunt Johannes had turned pale, and there were carmine blotches on her hands. Someone in the street below called out a street cry for old clothes, without giving a good reason why. The air in the room suddenly turned green and started to shake to and fro in layers. The red canary was whistling: 'Come my lovely, come, to the park at half-past eight …' Aunt Johannes cried: 'That's it!' and her eyeballs disappeared behind the thinly dispersed lashes of her eyelids. The cook burst in. Her tooth started to waggle up and down with inquisitiveness. Father Weinschweisser stroked his beard in excitement and called: 'Ha well — ha well.' Then look, a penetrating stench had spread out around the world. Everything turned as black as night. One could hear wing-beats and cries and Aunt Johannes's ecstatic voice. By popular request, the Universal Orchestra was also now playing 'Come my lovely —' to the accompaniment of thunder and lightning. This lasted four minutes. As the light returned, the earth was barren and empty. The world was dead. Two canaries rose up into the aether, out of the rubble of the Weinschweisser house. One of them was Aunt Johannes who, keeping her half of the promise which the magic bird had whispered

Hans Flesch-Brunningen / THE METAPHYSICAL CANARY

into her ear and which would release her from her hermaphroditism, hadn't spoken her magic spell and was now flying off to Sirius with Tiki-taki's mighty offspring to carry out her final work and set up a race of birds on the earth. Apart from them Father Weinschweisser was the only one to rub the sleep from his eyes. All that he found of his wife was a stocking, from the cook a tooth, and from the rest of the family, just gaseous bulges in the air, which was now brown with lilac stripes. Apart from which, he found that his beard was now just a pile of cuttings. So, he shook his castrated head, bent over, belly to the ground, murmured something like 'Oh hallowed earth of the homeland'— and bought a fourteen heller transfer ticket for the last train and travelled to Mars to look for a job. However, he was sent back by return of post, and since then he's been vainly trying to populate the world with new Weinschweissers by budding. Recently he's been contemplating approaching his sister Kanari, nee Weinschweisser, with a petition to populate Europe with immigrant canaries. Maybe he'll succeed …

Hugo Ball

GRAND HOTEL METAPHYSICS

(ca. 1917)

The birth of Dadaism. Mulche-Mulche, the quintessence of the phantastic, gives birth to young Mr Foetus high above in that region which, encircled by music, dance, foolishness and divine familiarity, distinguishes itself quite clearly from its opposite.

No one got so hot under the collar about any of Messrs Clemenceau's and Lloyd George's speeches, or one of Ludendorff's[1] gunshots, as they did about the small fluctuating bunch of dadaistic itinerant prophets who preached childishness after their own fashion.

Hugo Ball / GRAND HOTEL METAPHYSICS

Mulche-Mulche made her way to the observation roof of the Grand Hotel Metaphysics in an elevator made of tulips and hyacinths. Up there awaiting her were: the Master of Ceremonies, whose duty it was to arrange the astronomical implements, the Clague-ass, who was greedily regaling himself with a bucket full of raspberry sherbet, and Musicon, Our Lady, built solely of passacaglias and fugues.

Mulche-Mulche's slender leg was completely wrapped in chrysanthemums, so that she could only manage a modest step when walking. Her rose-petal tongue fluttered briefly between her teeth. Golden rain hung from her eyes and the black counterpane of the four-poster which had been prepared for her was painted with silver hounds.

The hotel was constructed of rubber and was porous. The gables and eaves of the upper storeys jutted out far over the front. Once Mulche-Mulche was undressed and the sparkle of her eyes was colouring the heavens — hooee, Clague-ass had already drunk his fill. Hooee, he shouted his welcome with a voice heard far and wide. The Master of Ceremonies gave a number of expansive bows and edged the telescope towards the parapet in order to study the celestography. However Musicon, a golden flame dancing incessantly round the four-poster, suddenly raised her arms, and behold, violins rained shadows across the city.

Mulche-Mulche's eyes blazed to ashes. The replenishment of her body was conducted with so much corn, incense and myrrh that the bed covers rose and bulged. The freight in her belly was increased by all manner of fruit and seed, then bursting the wraps in which it was bound with a crack.

At this the entire rachitic populace from the neighbourhood set about hindering a birth which threatened their barren land with fertility.

P.T. Bridet, the flower of death tucked in his hat, swelled on his wooden leg, wailing. A hog-wash smile had embossed itself across his chops. He raced up grimly from the parlour of the departed, ready to deal angrily with this unheard of business.

And there came Pimperling with his unscrewable head. The tympanic membranes hung crumpled from his ears at both sides. He wore a head band of Northern Light, latest model. Specimen of the mud-swamped mass-graver who, coated with saccharine and incensed by the rat he smelt, set about safeguarding his good odour.

And there came Toto, who had nothing except for this name. His steely Adam's apple purred smoothly in the wind when he walked into the nor'-easter. He had girded his Jericho stomacher about his waist, that the fluttering rags of his guts might not get lost. The Marseillaise, his Shibboleth, beamed red from his chest.

And they besieged the gardens, posted the sentries and shot at the roof terrace with big guns from the movie world, thundering day and night. They sent the violet-radiating 'Potato-soul' floating upwards as a sounding balloon. 'God save the King' or 'The family that prays together stays together' was written on their signal rockets. And they had 'We are being consumed by our fear of the present' shouted up at the terrace through a megaphone. At that moment the deity up above was busying his fingers, vainly trying to lure young Mr Foetus from out of Mulche-Mulche's rumbling body. It had already reached the point where he cautiously peered out of the gaping maternal portal. But he withdrew with a blink of his cunning fox face on seeing the four of them, Jopp, Musicon, Deity and Clague-ass, assembled to receive him with butterfly nets, sticks and staves and a wet dish-cloth. And haughty squirts and spurts of sweat gushed out of Mulche's reddened body, sousing everything far and wide.

The people down below fell into a quandary as to what should be done with their rusted film artillery, and whether they should clear off or stay. And asked the advice of the 'Potato-soul' and decided to storm the charming scene at the Grand Hotel Metaphysics with violence.

They rolled up the first of the catapults — the Idol of Fashion.

Hugo Ball / GRAND HOTEL METAPHYSICS

This is a low-browed pin-head, which sparkles under its burden of rhinestones and oriental gewgaws. It can be called the Funless Idol because it has been carved from head to foot out of wooden fibs and wears an iron heart on its chest as a watch charm.

It towers up, black-throated and bedecked with bells, the tuning fork of vice raised on high in its right hand. But painted over and over with characters from the Qabbalah and the Talmud, it stares quite affably with its child's pupils. With its six hundred self-swivelling arms, it twists both facts and history. It also has a tin box with an oxy-hydrogen blowpipe fixed to its hindmost vertebra. Thus when the unguentary evacuation takes place, generals, gang leaders — scarcely human forms — are expelled abaft to drag their faces through the filth.

But Jopp, aided by Musicon, lowers the fuse into the depths of its stomach and, since it is loaded with hepar, salfurio, aconitum and vitriol, they blow it up and thwart the assault.

The second idol, the 'Bearded Dog', is wheeled up in order to wash away the tender anecdotes from the terrace of the Grand Hotel Metaphysics with its primordial roars and rancour. The bedrock of the religions is prized up with crow-bars, so as to open up a way and a path. The 'Ideological Superstructure' shares fall rapidly. 'Oh no, the collapse into bestiality!' Bridet whines. 'The magic printing works of the Holy Ghost are no longer enough to impede the end of the world.'

And it was already hissing up, coupled in front of a church on casters — worried priests, prelates, deacons and the Summi Episcopi keeping look-out behind its curtains. Five-ridged back-bones are dragging along its mangy hide, which is tattooed with troops. Its receding brow crowned with the likeness of Golgotha. Up until now it remained in the stable of allegories, fed with a chaff made of lines of force. Now it is rolling forwards, to puff its astonishment against Musicon's melodious voice.

But its rage outdoes itself. Before its breath can reach the ridge of the roof, it crooks its body and lets out the seeds of its manhood, smelling of jasmine and water lilies. Enfeebled, the monster's knees tremble. It lieth its head on its paws, whimpering submissively. With a lash of its own tail it smashes apart the wobbly holiday church, which belonged to the public guardians who had been pulling it. So this onslaught failed too.

And while Musicon's golden flame danced along the airy observation roof, umbala oh-oh, the last idol is brought up: Puppet Death made of stucco, stretched out lengthways in the truck ready to be hoisted up on its strings. 'Long live the scandal!' called Pimperling in greeting. 'Poetic friend,' said Toto, 'there is a sick and mangled cadaver about thy head. Thine eyes are coloured cobalt-blue, thy forehead pale ochre yellow. Hand me the suitcase. Selah.' And Bridet: 'Verily, discretest master, thine odour is not bad for thine age. This is going to be tremendous fun. May each let down his locks and shake a leg which he hath torn off of the other. Let us build a triumphal arch, and where thou placeth thy foot, might thou be accompanied by joy and well-being!'

With that Death gave a nod and took their experiences from them in the same way one accepts a letter of submission, then offering his head to the noose which was to convey him to the roof. They hooked the bobbins onto him, turned the handles and guided him up. But the burden was too great. He had already reached three quarters of the way, swinging and swaying and livening to the prospect of scaling the roof ridge. The ropes tautened, whistled and sang, the hawser crowed, and he crashed down from the dizzying heights, landing with all his weight on Pimperling who, honest to the core, had expected ought but such a jostling. They carried him, dead thrice over and five times slain, wrapped in a handkerchief to one side, where they feverishly attempted to pull the dislodged timberwork of the rear of his head back into place. But there was no helping him. And even Death had come asunder during Pimperling's death by Death.

Then Mulche-Mulche suddenly let out twelve piercing screams, one quickly after another. Her compass-leg rose up to the edge of the heavens. And she gave birth. First a small Jewish lad wearing a tiny coronet on his purple brow, who at once swung up onto the umbilical chord and started to perform gymnastics. And Musicon laughed, as if she were his cousin.

And forty days passed, and Mulche stood with chalky countenance by the parapet. Then she raised her compass-leg a second time, high up into the heavens. And this time she gave birth to a large amount of dishwater, scree, gravel, rubble, mud and lumber which showered, rattled and thundered down over the parapet and squashed the plantigrades' lust and limbs. Jopp was pleased with this, and the Deity lowered his butterfly net and looked on in amazement.

And another forty days passed and Mulche stood lost in thought and with large devouring eyes. Then she raised her leg a third time and gave birth to Mr Foetus, as described on Folio 28, Ars magna. Confucius had praised him. A sparkling border adorns his back. His father is Plimplamplasko,[2] the lofty spirit, addicted to miracles and drunk with love.

Conrad Felixmüller

MILITARY ORDERLY FELIXMÜLLER, XI ARNSDORF[1]

(1918)

Here I am, military orderly Felixmüller on sick bay duty. Emphasis however on 'Felixmüller' and 'sick'. First I want to examine myself and my patients. Summon up warmth, goodness and feeling. Still got enough heart and soul to feel. It's night-time. Stretched out around me are twenty sick soldiers. Sick in their minds, epileptic, mad, crippled, wounded. All people like me. Flesh, bodies, legs — strange shapes, some soft, some hard. Pain everywhere, mainly in their heads (me too, three days ago a doctor

Conrad Felixmüller / MILITARY ORDERLY FELIXMÜLLER

shattered my head with his little hammer — i.e., I'm suffering from pain after being smashed to pieces). Everything oozing with blood. Red and glowing like molten iron. Lungs, chest, the whole body packed full with capillaries, these minutiae. Distended belly criss-crossed by the blues and reds of these seeping capillaries. Green sulphurous glistening guts, endlessly long and filled with flatulent filth, made of flesh, like my flesh, bestial and teeming with blood. Swells up repulsively (feel the fullness) — repulses me — want to vomit — can't. A cart rolls over my limbs.

And strain myself to serve other, similar bodies — the sick, wounded, mad — with this, my body. Bodies stretched out on twenty beds. Suddenly all these people stand in front of me with their bloody, pussy bandages, hazy, sometimes disappearing, in a cloud of carbolic. Have myself only just reached the point where I can help and understand: am sick, wounded, crazed, have fever and receive ice-packs for my legs. Got a red burning rash all over. Grows palpably, from the size of a spot to the size of my hand. In the end I'm just one burning rash. I can't lie flat, can't sleep. Waking dreams. First in the fray, loaded with bullets, almost buckling under the weight — and shortly after in the speeding Red Cross express. Thundering along. Lying in ghostly white. Red Cross nurses, white-gowned attendants and doctors in front of my fat swollen face — swelling as all feeling disappears. Soar into the depths, dark eternity. Just hear a lovely crunching like glass from knives cutting through skin into flesh, slicing tendons like leather. Sawing leg bones like wood — Timber! — Blood spurts a red curve through the window across towns, villages, fields. Fields of tattered bandages fly up, bandage my stump. And soar with the train into a dark red tunnel. Even deeper — watch out — head gone — torn off — plummet into the abyss until — feel my bed. Convulsed by shock. Shadows on walls melt into departing nurses (Red Cross). My comrade plays with a glowing cigarette in the dark, and I brood — where could they have chucked my leg? Into pussy, blood encrusted bandages:

into shit, pungent urine? — Where, where have they chucked that greenish-black shimmering, glibbery-gellyish trembling leg? Dead leg — cut off. What if I don't find it, what if the attendant won't tell me — you wretch — what if I attack you in a rage, smash the window with my fists or tear off your leg! Even if you're not listening, I can still see through the window — blue window, looking on dull moon over snow covered field! (Recognising wondrous-blue steel colour — window! You! Mine! Steel ingot!) Would so love to cast myself through the window into cooling snow, if only it weren't nailed shut. One ought to make steel nails out of my ingot. Foot-long, like those used to crucify Jesus. Even longer (why is my comrade screaming in the orderly's room — is he being nailed to the cross with my lovely nail?) I could find a better use for my blue, foot-long, sharpened nail. Already held it in front of me for ages, while reflections from the hospital across the way flicker through the window over my outstretched hands. My fingers have calluses on their tips, and can't really feel the sharp edged surfaces. Holding the nail against my head — at my temple — stroking it very soft and ticklish — ah — how nice its tip pricks my red and blue veined temple! Presses into my skin and thin skull. The thick, two centimetre-square silver-steel nail pierces! How accurately I locate the painful spot in my brain! The one the doctor touched delicately with his little hammer — thrust through to the other side and pull out — covered with shreds of brain and veins —! Blood trickles down both temples — trickling red drops onto my throat.

Can blood be that beautiful —?! Can flow and drip so beautifully!

What — if — I — now — gave — all — twenty — comrades — the — same — pleasure with my silver-steel nail? Gave them the same pain-relieving delight? Extinguish their consciousness as well? If I was to pierce their temples one by one with my silver-steel, blue, now bloody-red, nail?!

Why on earth not? I've not spilt any blood! Have yet to thrust a bayonet into gut-entwined bellies! Smash skulls with rifle butts?

Conrad Felixmüller / MILITARY ORDERLY FELIXMÜLLER

Right, I'll do it at once. If only they were all sound asleep. They'll all have a nice surprise tomorrow. Each one lying in his little pool of blood.

It's good that the night's drawn to an end — and our comrade attendant is telling us it is time to wash.

I'm going to have a warm wash — because I'm freezing cold and have a headache. And slowly get up — to wash.

And now I'll watch out that they don't slip me a sedative (I'm supposed to take drops).

Wrecked from the restless night. The whole night one raving fit. First one bed — then the couple next to it — then four beds — then every bed and the chief attendant — raved.

Two days ago they put a comrade in the cell — now they're bringing him back, still completely doped with cocaine. I go up to him. Give him cigarettes and ask them to play the gramophone. A music hall song: 'Malongo from the Congo' — he must be cheered-up after vain attempts to escape. He told me of his discovery of the fireside window — window bars which loosened with a heavy tug; flight after climbing down on bed sheets! I would flee with him. I'm not crazy!

Since yesterday they suspect I suffer from fits of rage because — well — a patient was raving and smacking his face against the wall and Nurse Emma said: 'The chief attendant can't be everywhere' — and I screamed: — I want to get out. In order to tell you all that highly valuable humans are getting tangled in bleak, black bars. Throttling their helpless innocence with their nerves, in complete despair. This throttling is symptomatic. Tell how face to face combat turns into madness and raging comrades beat up their attendants, wanting to kill without stopping — burn out, then to weep like babes.

I've told the doctors: 'Leave them be — let them rage — kill, for all I care — it's better that they throttle the guilty who are indolent, irresponsible, unwilling to help — for you've sentenced yourselves to death with your guilt, by refusing to be brothers to these men who rage, rave and smash open their skulls! Just because of you: because you don't try to stop them!'

Everyone would be healthy and happy at once, if someone said: 'War is over,' told them: 'We gave ourselves to save you from it — because we now know and realise that each and every one of you is our brother, who has swallowed our guilt for us, is mad and raging.' — If someone said to them: 'We love you, fellow men, — and will put an end to it.'

O — I know what I have to do in order that everyone, thanks to my insignificant person, realises his fortune at being here on this earth — I must speak!

Regardless of my flow of words which is now coming into full swing and which — even if it consumes me — must grab you!

Melt the ice-cold walls of hearts with love! Smash the bull-headed egotism of capitalist hacks for these people here in this cess-pit of Europe.

No-one is your enemy — you must recognise your fellow man, your self, in even the most deranged bloody stump — for it's you who is deranged, raving, raging, the murderer at war!

Heinrich Schaefer

TWO SKETCHES

(1918)

Head

Fall dead? Me? Dead! Me! Oh, rise in my throat, brazen laughter, and swirl your swords above it! Is it not the way of all things that every person yellows, parchment-like, on the approach of death, feebly croaking his last, while clutching his chest? And I? I, a gigantic monster bursting with pistons?! My breast: giant rocks which know no crumbling. It scarcely bends to them, my breast scarcely knows my head which is sharpened by the winds aloft, my defiant head in black, billowing clouds, my transfixing stone face which is there to lure the whole caustic, cutting rabble. It is cold and hard, cold and hard to the caves which glow beneath in its own stone. It, too, was once a glowing lustre and was a blazing laughter as it wound its way out of the ground and shook the earth from itself. Now it is a frozen laugh and guards its power in the stone edifice. Behold this rock-hewn head of the sphinx. Nobody knows whether its eyes are extinguished or their light hidden. — Is it not replete with every possible deed? Does it not seem to succumb to an inner slumber and think of its deeds and rest on them and know and know —

But sometimes, after many years, there is an urge from within and it looks up at my bright empty sky. Superabundant is the earth. My body is the earth. My head towers high above the earth in solitude. Then rising up the tube which passes from my body through my head comes a roar! I roars! I roars! First with girl-like shrillness, then a manly bass, then bestial and alien and more bestial and more alien. From a hard tree, it falls asunder, bursts apart and extends into a cloud and the cloud rains down clouds. Suddenly my roar has torn itself free and is a living being in itself, occupying every inch of the unvaulted space above me, lying above me as my second self, my great friend who enclasps my head. Its rust-brown fur shines greasily over me with green eyes —

Remembering

I have grasped every thought and slid down its incline until it found its siblings. I have helped demonstrate the rounds danced by each and every thought. I've reached my end. I wallow in disgust. I am in the calm before all thoughts —

Imagine a golden staff, standing here in the ground. I have seen this staff in the glory of the sun, admired it and bedecked it with plagues inscribed with dithyrambs. I have stroked it like a pussy-cat and kissed it like a baby's head. Looked as the rain flowed down it,

Heinrich Schaefer / TWO SKETCHES

cold and bleak. I have blinked my eyes and thought about all the years it has stood there, and thought nothing more. It filled me with anger, but I can't say why, I had slept badly. And then I started to sing about it once more. I have abused it and decried it and hit it, smashing it and trampling it to dust, and was unable to tolerate even the dust. I have thought about it in tears and woefulness. I have ridiculed and bitterly derided it. I have spoken honourably of it, just like an elder who can talk about everything with composure. It all ended in utter foolishness, and I yearn my way deep, ever deeper, inside it. Nothing is left except my body and the tangible things around it and what I sense of them. Nothing exists but this — and this final form, in which I stand — a sensitive idiot — ah ba bi quo qua qua bi ba ba — What more?

Wieland Herzfelde

STRENGE FROM LEIPZIG

(1919)

I am sitting in the theatre with two girlfriends after a successful argument with the doorman who didn't want to let us in without tickets. Else Lasker-Schüler's *'Wupper'* is playing.[1]

But we are being shown a film version of *'The Wupper'*. I am sorry about this because it means that my two companions can carry on talking without stop. Soon they will quarrel, I can sense this although there are no real indications to suggest anything of the sort ...

Wieland Herzfelde / STRENGE FROM LEIPZIG

For a long time now we have been sitting at a table, sorting all manner of magazines in the most circuitous way. There is something very tortuous about the way we are sorting them. All three of us are fully aware that there must be a simpler way of doing it, but we haven't a clue how, all the more so because the copies keep getting mixed up and we have to start sorting them all over again. Later on we continue our work in a sanatorium, where we are all lying in bed. First together, then in a pair, and in the end myself alone, forever engrossed in these magazines which are spread out in front of me on the duvet.

Now and then a doctor appears, who puts me in a very bad mood. I start to suspect that the sanatorium is a secret prison.

While sorting through the magazines I chance upon a new one (which does not exist in reality) published by Insel Verlag.[2]

'It is similar to the magazine *Hyperion*, but better produced,' I say to myself. Leafing through it, I discover various reprints of publications from my own publishing house. Above all poems from the book *Sulamith*. I am glad about this, but want to travel to Leipzig to find out why I hadn't been told. Then one of my two girlfriends, the one with the black hair, returns and gives me a sealed letter which simply bears the inscription 'To Harry Count Kessler.' I am politely asked to await the Count's answer and then take it with me directly to Leipzig. Even though it's sealed I open the letter, but cannot read a word because it's written in code (very clearly and pleasantly, similar to Latin). Now I see that the correspondent is one Strenge from Leipzig. 'Ah, the famous communist who was the target of so many attacks in the papers,' I say out loud.

Now I know for sure. The sanatorium is guarded like a prison. It occurs to me that I have often dreamt that I can fly. I want to see whether I can manage it while awake. I bob up and down on tiptoe and without any effort I float quite quickly through the open window, across the street to a balcony.

But now I doubt whether this is all not just a dream after all. In order to convince myself of the reality of my flight, I walk through the glass doors of the balcony into the unfamiliar flat, into what is clearly the dining room. I pull all manner of faces in the large mirror there, still wondering whether I am dreaming or not, then I snap my fingers next to my ear. No, I can hear it, so I must be fully awake.

A table spread with tastily filled rolls attracts my attention. I devour a whole load of them without more ado, and with this my last suspicion that I am dreaming disappears. I am now filled by measureless joy; it's true then, I can fly! Except I also feel rather uneasy about the rolls I have just eaten.

And as I look round the room shyly, there, lying on a silken settee, is a young, naked woman with a smile which says: 'I've been watching you from the very start.' Her beauty is inviting and the curves of her hips seem to perfect the curves of my flight. I approach her with a mixture of extreme awkwardness and unabashed desire, reach for her hand and grasp it as if requesting forgiveness and surrender. With this her smile broadens, she presses my hand to her right breast — so elastic, soft, that I claw at it in mad desire (as in a game with young kittens). She wraps her left arm round my neck and presses my face into her lap which, instead of having pubic hair, is decorated with a bouquet of dark violets; I breathe in their perfume, mixed with the humus smell of the woman's flesh, taking long, deep breaths — until I am gradually overcome by a feeling of complete contentment, and my fingers slowly loosen themselves from the slightly cooled breasts. But my breath remains scorching hot, and soon the violets in the woman's lap have withered beneath my lips. Then I straighten up and see —

That I must have been dreaming, that I have fallen asleep on a settee which is patterned with bouquets of violets. And now I doubt once more whether I can fly; want to try at once, but no longer have the slightest idea how to start.

Then I am in Leipzig. I am strolling along one of the main streets in a bad mood, past tall grey administrative buildings, when unexpectedly

Wieland Herzfelde / STRENGE FROM LEIPZIG

I hear the voice of a man I cannot see — presumably from a window or a balcony on the first floor in front of me — moaning in self pity:

'Oh it's dreadful — a scandal — the very thought of it — what a way to treat someone! That could only happen here. What barbarians — mistreating their prisoners like that! God I'm done in! Mentally and physically wrecked!'

Meanwhile the man has come down the veranda stairs to the street, still lamenting the disgraceful treatment of the arrested communists. Then he comes up to me with a slight limp (which appears to me to be solely the product of his imagination). Straight away I say to myself: 'That's Strenge, the communist leader.' I am disappointed by his appearance: fat, pot-bellied, broad-shouldered. With a goatee beard which is starting to turn bushy, boils on the back of his neck, he is dressed rather like a city councillor or juror; but he's much livelier.

'I must give him the answer to his coded letter!'

'You must be Mr Strenge?' 'Of course I am,' he answers, seemingly insulted that I even ask. I hand the answer from Count Kessler. His son puts it into his pocket for him, unopened. The son is slim. His thighs are too large for his tight trousers, he acts as if secretly he's got belly-ache. I can't stand him. He edges up too close to people. Strenge immediately starts telling me how he had been played around with in prison. But as I interrupt him — I had also been held in custody in Berlin, we had a lot worse to contend with there — he drops the subject and starts talking about communism. I no longer know what he said ... During the conversation the fact is also mentioned that almost all communist leaders are foreigners, or at least of foreign descent. 'Yes, right,' says Strenge, 'there's no such thing as a pure German revolutionary.' I agree with him, but think to myself: 'If only he didn't look so damned German himself; and that's the sort of revolutionary he'll be.'

As if guessing the train of my thoughts, he suddenly explains (and in this moment his suit turns cobalt-blue and his face chrome-yellow, his son's face also turns yellow, but only partly because some patches remain pink and covered in blackheads) — that he's actually a foreigner too, coming in fact from Argentina.

With these words he pulls a concertina postcard from his jacket pocket and lets me look at the rows of photographs of Argentine landscapes, etc. The first two pictures depict goats in the meadows; one of them costs 450 marks, the other 1000; that's written underneath. I am surprised at the enormous difference in price, but Mr Strenge explains: the expensive goat has a few bunches of hair on its rump which are made into a particularly valuable type of wool. In fact this sort of goat is not a goat at all, but rather an Argentine sheep. I take a close look, and actually discover the bunches of hair. Whereupon Mr Strenge junior tells me without any warning that he's blind. As I hadn't noticed this until then, I asked him in what way. He tells me he cannot read Argentine. 'Symbolic,' I say to myself, and find him even more dislikeable. Now I attempt to decipher the captions beneath the cards on my own, and notice that they are not in Argentine or Spanish, but in Portuguese. On closer inspection, this Portuguese is scarcely any different to German.

I am no longer with Mr Strenge and his son. Nor in Leipzig, but rather in Argentina, where I am being driven in a dog-cart, carried across the Argentine countryside at full gallop by two small horses. Sitting beside me in the carriage is my friend. The highway is as straight as an arrow. The scenic landscapes are only to be seen on the right, there is absolutely nothing to the left except, perhaps, an abyss. I am looking at constantly changing motifs which open up one after another, just like the concertina postcard: now bushes like rubber plants, glazed dark-green, then giant conifers, now meadowlands with complicated drainage systems and foreign looking cattle, there a red church (just like the one on Ludwig Church Square in Berlin-Wilmersdorf), then once again maize fields which have sprung up so high that they look like a prehistoric horse-tail forest, and now — very nearby — a monstrous whale in the middle of the countryside, obviously stuffed.

But a tall wooden hoarding has been erected on the back of the whale, painted with the elegant forms of gentlemen — adverts for a tailor's in the capital. I ask my friend (who must live on one of the farms here, or at least during his holidays), what it's all about, why this fish has been brought on land, whether it has been stuffed, and why a tailor was advertising there. My friend laughs mischievously: hadn't I realised that everything I'd seen along the highway was just an advert? And what's more for the railway?

All these wonderful landscapes and arbours and installations which we had driven past had been artificially built by the Argentine Railway authorities, who for the present were building highways instead of railways, to give the traveller a taste of Argentina's charms. No one would use the roads if one simply let them run through the countryside according to the dictates of nature.

While he gives me this peculiar explanation we have long since left the whale behind, and now to our right there is a river with absolutely parallel banks, almost a canal. Strange: all at once this river is criss-crossed by tightly packed pipes running from one side to the other, rather like the rungs of a ladder. I can find no explanation for this. The pipes become ever more densely packed. I am about to open my mouth to ask my friend what it all means:

When the light flowed rapidly and yet quite gradually into my eyes, and I noticed that I was staring at the central heating radiator next to my bed.

Kurt Schwitters

THE ONION
MERZPOEM 8

(1919)

T he day on which I was to be slaughtered was a highly eventworthy one. (Do not be afraid, just have faith!) The king was ready, the two assistants waited. The slaughterer had been ordered to appear at half-past six; it was a quarter-past six, and I saw to the necessary preparations myself. We had chosen a spacious hall so that as many spectators as possible could participate in comfort. A telephone was not far away. The doctor lived in the house next door and was on call in case one of the spectators should faint. (Mementoes from the confirmation.) Two enormous pulleys hung from the ceiling so that I could be wound up afterwards, if it was decided to

Kurt Schwitters / THE ONION MERZPOEM 8

gut me. Four strong lads stood at the ready to lend a hand, former Russian prisoners of war — broad, bony figures. (Journal for Land and Property Owners.) Two excellent girls were also at the ready; spotlessly clean wenches. I found it a pleasant thought that these two lovely women were going to whip my blood and clean and prepare my innards.

The hall had been swept clean and washed. I had two well scrubbed tables set against the wall to one side, set with various bowls, knives and forks. I now had a towel, a bowl and a jug of water brought to me, and a piece of soap (Sunlight). The two girls, Anna and Emma, brought a tub and a whisk. It certainly is a peculiar feeling when you're going to be slaughtered in ten minutes. (The Sacrifices of Motherhood.) Up to now I had never been slaughtered, not in all my life. That's only for grown-ups. Yes indeed, things are bad when the potatoes have to be dug up and the oats are gone. We've not really had a proper summer at all. Ten minutes can seem a very long time. (Faith, Hope and Charity.) (Ducks goosing about on the meadow.) Everything was organised down to the last detail.

And the princess arrived as well. She was wearing a short, white skirt which was slightly skew-whiff, but that made her look very graceful. The church spire is very steep, you know. Spring pastures, dedicated in friendship. King's daughter-legs skip daintily with a hop. I love these dainty kicking hoppitykinglydaughterlegs. Tail wags sour cream. She presented herself ink-pot to me and asked clear as a bell white sharp clean: 'Are you to be slaughtered today?' Hot fishing — knife shooting blood. I lowered my eyes and rejoiced at her greeting. 'What a handsome man you are, Alves Brumstick, what a handsome man!' she said red lips vein cooking blood, Bon Voyage! Saucy needlepoint nose: 'I bring you the world's last greeting. You must become a nun! (My house is your world.) (Leather without the head.) Tanned leather measured to navel size. You're certainly in a great hurry these days, getting everything ready for this momentous day. (Peace be with you.) How quickly you've matured, ripened, over-ripe!

With what joy can you look at your ripeness! May it always make you happy! How nice that the weather has held for your slaughterday, so that the slaughterer can come by bike.' (Genuine Brussels Handiwork.) Health is its own blessing. 'Allow me, my princess, to make a telephone call. It is already half-past six and the slaughterer still hasn't arrived.' 'Hallo! Is that the slaughterer in person? The spectators are getting impatient, why aren't you on your way? (From here to eternity!) 'Please start with the festivities! I've just speared my sister on the church spire as a weather-cock. The church spire is very steep, you know, and spikes fish up above in the lashing air. The lightning conductor was very rusty and didn't really want to stab my sister through the belly. But fish spikes bright in the whip-stench. Please begin with the formalities!'

I had the king summoned. 'Your Majesty, I place my handsome figure at your command! I put my corpse at your disposal!' (The millimetre line for six columns costs 20 pfennigs.) The king beckoned. (Fortuna Grinding Machine.) The two seconds in black frock coats and black gloves, top hats and black ties, placed themselves at the king's side. A black dog flew past croaking. The king beckoned again. The four Russians, Anna and Emma, readied themselves to give a hand. The king beckoned again. The seconds approached me, introduced themselves and asked for my last wish. (Look up at the star!) I asked that the princess might sing the great Worker's Song and then kiss me. (Headless necks, sole leather.) A lady in the king's company fell to the floor in a faint. The doctor was called. Firm whips heartfelt. The princess sang: 'Worker trumpets

> c sharp d
> d sharp e
> i sharp e
> thee thou thy thine,'

the great Workers' Song in its entirety. Lamp-post trumpets kissing broad skirts billowing white needle-pointed kiss. Wrap arms broad skirts billow neck needle-points warm hose smooth sleek fish carps,

Kurt Schwitters / THE ONION MERZPOEM 8

carps, carps. (Prière de fermer la porte.) Please, please, close the door. Oh you, you, you! I love you so! (The world with its sins.) Now slaughter me!

The king beckoned once more, the slaughterer stepped forward. The house is silent. Pro patria est, dum ludere videmur. (The blue-red-yellow girls' company.) (No smoking, as well as holding-in-the-hand of non-burning cigars.) Two servants wheel away his bicycle. (Imperial emergency relief tax.) A servant brings a cudgel, large balloon lemon-pale. (Hold on to what you have got!) The slaughterer has a blue striped overall waving cloth. (Sugar-beet girl.) October wanes ceremony rivals seconds. — Go! — I urchin! — The slaughterer bends back, head inclined, the cudgel up behind. (The greatest joy and delight, a cosy home life!) The slaughterer jumps up, (Such is love!) swings cudgel descending descending heavy heavy tenderly whips descending heavy heavy very very very. — My skull split open.

Now I had to collapse; so I collapsed collapsed collapsed, flat. Aaaaa aaaaaaa aaa aaaaa b. (Applause from all sides.)

What was going to happen now? My arms and feet were tied to the hoists, hoists hoist me up. Lowering coils up flat spread out-crooked. (Appeal to all mental and manual workers.) I was stabbed in the side. Blood guttered bucket blue jet red thick whip. Turn maids whisk up wheels railway engines whisking Emma Anna. (Thine innocent heart dedicated this day in holy wedlock!) The king wanted something to drink. Blue singed flame murder a lot a lot. Empty burns the stomach flame sulphur blood. Since then the king has no longer a beard. Stay true to your duty, be faithful. (Handed on by the Editors.) For everything has its science. (Amplificatores, Worker's Council for Capitalist Development, Berlin.)

The decision was made to gut me. (New Mocha Bonbons, the latest thing.) Transfer ticket travellers travel knives slit tremble intestines. (Peacetime goods.) It was a very entryworthy garden restaurant. I felt a thousand joys saviour morning twenty. The entity nurtured in the greenhouse had only given blossom to three lusters. (Thunderous applause.) Mooncalf shines inside softly pulled intestines fat pain softly disanaesthetised. (Everything for the Red Army.) Clean, clean, be clean. Girls, clean when washing, so that nothing burns. (May God protect you.) (May God protect you.)

Hot flame, hot flame! Earthworms played inside, gently in my belly, a quiet tickling. The king hungered for my eyes. Princess, fetch me John's eyes! (Today you are going to leave your parental home!) Round spheres with slippery slime inside leapt out of the sockets right into soft hands. The eyes are served on a plate, knife, fork. (Free help and advice for soldiers who are deaf or hard of hearing.) Slippery slimed oysters eyes drop heavy stomach. Children under twelve will only be admitted when accompanied and supervised by an adult. In addition, children under eight must be taken by the hand if requested. (Entrance fifty pfennig per person, total at least one mark.)

'Poison!' the king shouted and he rolled on the floor. (Place the cradle up on high, so the world will multiply.) 'Sweet dreams, I've been poisoned.' (August has thirty-one days, the days shorten by one hour and fifty-six minutes.) Yes, it is terrible. 'Lord, I trust in you, I raise my hands up high!' Two toadstools grew upwards eyes stalk smooth tuber sap and bored two holes in the king's belly. Eyes eyed stalk-eyed. King chalk started silently. The princess had terrible palpitations. (Acetylene removes the smell of bodily excretions.) She felt so dreadfully sorry for her father. The doctor was called and attended the holes in the king's belly. (Veritas vincit, with Anna Blume in the lead role.) The old king had fainted. Fear climaxed silver strings stone to stone. The princess beckoned and commanded that I be put back together. (That is how bed feathers are cleaned, dusted, washed, steamed and dried.)

They started to put me back together. First my eyes were put back in their sockets with a gentle push. (Do not be afraid, faith, hope

Kurt Schwitters / THE ONION MERZPOEM 8

and charity are the stars.) Then my innards were fetched. Luckily nothing had been cooked or chopped up for sausages. (Vaincu, mais non dompté.) But one is happy if the autumn is fine. No sooner were they reinserted than my innards snapped back snug and firmly in place. The result of my own inner magnetic currents. (The art of leading a happy life in marriage.) A few problems had to be overcome when ordering the intestines for they had got slightly entangled. (Saint Florian[1] has moved into the German theatre. Gales of laughter every evening.) But I realised what the matter was and steered my electric currents back and forth, crisscross, one two one two one two one of the sound of churned beams in the eye. I pulled and wrenched magnetically at my intestines until they all lay correctly in their normal place. My knowledge of the inner man served me well here. (One year probation, then permanent placement as a Prussian civil servant.) Right you are! In the meantime my solid parts had been put back together, and only the blood was lacking. (Borden's sweet milk chocolate.) The maids held the bowl full of blood under the gash in my side and whisked in reverse. The king gave a loud groan. With the help of my magnetic currents, a thick stream of blood rose up from the red surface and entered the wound in my side. (What every woman should know should not be said to a girl.) My arteries filled slowly, my heart was full, my innards soaked up blood. But my heart still failed to move, I was still dead. (Freshly painted.) The slaughterer touched the wound in my side with his knife, gave a deep stab before withdrawing the knife and — the wound was closed. (Detach here and send to the address above.) Every woman should inform herself about this, at the latest after finalising her marriage. I now had all my parts back together, there were just a few gaps because a couple of scraps had remained sticking to the knifes. Both the wish and the need are present, but the opportunity is lacking. There was also quite a lot of blood missing because the king had drunken it. (For the ideals of Socialism.) Ever since then I've been somewhat anaemic. Take the cage back home and buy yourself a bird. The hoists were lowered, the pulleys hoisted down. Now I felt that I had to stand up straight, and so I stood up straight, very quickly at first, and then getting progressively slower, until I was standing. (My heart and mouth have grown mean.) In the Burgundian Empire grew a lass; I am but a woman. O child, be mindful where you go! Learn to be good and pious! Remain pious, O child, venture into life without shyness! (Vote Socialist.) The two seconds took their places willingly next to me and grasped my hands. (Prescriptions filled out for every medical insurance.) The joys of childhood trickled away, the struggles of life started this day. I was very eager to know how they were going to bring me back to life. (Ism file from Jefim Golychef.)[2] It is strictly prohibited to touch the exhibits. I was dizzy. (Quietly undermine Strindberg Stramm.)[3] Our good old teacher liked to add a dash of humour to his lessons, and that was not a mistake. (Sunny view.) I believe in nothing whatsoever. (Trombone party.) Turned out right! An appeal in these dark times to all Protestant teachers who believe in the Bible! (What the husband should know about pregnancy and birth!) Your mouth is a saw. (Mr Sunshine dentist.) The slaughterer picked up his cudgel (The tragedy of the Incarnation.), stood in front of me (The conduct of the husband during pregnancy.) and laid the cudgel gently on my split skull. (Rudolf Bauer *is* an artist.) Lilac-blue roses waiting for Anna Blume shooting thorn gap field bed. (Ready to be plucked, tenderly united.) A partial explanation misses the point. Then the slaughterer leapt back with a mighty jerk. (The colonel is and remains a gentleman, even when he is an idiot.) The wife must know everything. There was an enormous crash as the cudgel freed itself from my head. Here is the opportunity for a job solely intended for women. Contents: 1. How to win love. 2. The tamed shrew. 3. What young women value in men. 4. A few words about kissing. 5. How to make an impression. 6. On receiving a refusal. 7. Is reluctance to marry justified? 8. The origins of chastity. 9. Older opinions. 10. How can

Kurt Schwitters / THE ONION MERZPOEM 8

one achieve moderation? 11. A word of advice. 12. Is love blind? 13. How does one recognise true love? 14. The man's former life. 15. The most intimate of questions. 16. The new belief. 17. The dark star. The slaughterer jumped back and returned to his original starting position. (He should be your master.) However, the mainstay of the firm remains nicely well-behaved. (Jamais embarassé.) The pieces of my skull flew back together, I was more or less in one piece again. (Sweet moment.) You don't like 'taters, and gherkins are too fatty fer ye. The theatre is only there for people who are not in any way people. Dispatch upon receipt of payment, the book is richly illustrated. It was quite a peculiar feeling to be alive again. Selter's water-sail light up Maria's scent. I felt I ought to strike a bit of a pose, so I struck a bit of a pose. (The king died at this moment.) With a grand gesture I went up to the king's daughter and silently gave her my hand. (Kiss me!) The princess dropped before me, onto her pretty lace-pointed knee. (From the narrow limits of one's homeland.) Meanwhile the doctor was gnashing a knuckle of pork. More vacancies in the supplement. She now implored me to save her father. (Happiness in the house on the heath.) I knew that this wasn't the time and place to be good-natured, one can recognise the stupid by their good-naturedness. (Anna Blume remains hard.) (Dangerous age.) 'Your father,' I said, 'the king, the king stays dead.' (Buffing leather made of sealion's fur.) The doctor fell in a faint. I had two yellow wax candles stuck in the holes in the king's belly and let them be lit. (Stamps will be taken in payment.) The king exploded as the flames licked down through the holes into his belly. The people, however, broke out in cheers for me. (Socialism means work.)

Franz Kafka

THE VULTURE

(1920)

There was a vulture pecking at my feet. It had already torn open my socks and boots and was now pecking at the feet themselves. It kept striking away, then it would fly off, restlessly circle me a number of times, and then continue its work. A man walked up, watched for a little while, and asked me why I put up with the vulture. 'I'm quite defenceless,' I said, 'it came and started pecking at me, naturally I tried to drive it away, even attempted to strangle it, but an animal like that is very strong, it even wanted to spring at my face, so I preferred to sacrifice my feet. Now they're almost in shreds.' 'Why do you allow yourself to suffer like that,' the

Franz Kafka / THE VULTURE

man said, 'one shot and a vulture is over and done with.' 'Really?' I asked, 'and would you arrange that for me?' 'With pleasure,' said the man, 'I just have to go home and fetch my gun. Can you wait another half an hour?' 'I don't know,' I said. I stood for a while, paralysed with agony, and then I said: 'Please, try it in any case.' 'Good,' said the man, 'I'll hurry.' The vulture had been quietly listening to our conversation, letting its eyes wander between the man and myself. I now saw that it had understood everything, it flew off and, bending right back to gain enough momentum, it thrust its beak like a spear thrower into my mouth, deep inside me. Falling backwards, I felt myself released as it drowned helplessly in my blood which was filling my depths and bursting every bank.

Iwan Goll

THE EUROCOCCUS

(EXTRACT)

(1927)

After crazed wanderings through the dream of reality, I ended up, I can't say how, at the Bar de l'Ennui at exactly five o'clock. In contrast to the other bars of its kind, it was renowned as a moral establishment. It was managed by an Armenian, Dr Syrianx. A born spiritualist, fakir and pearl dealer, Dr Syrianx had realised that it was essential to open this bar as the best possible means to advertise his main professions: he wanted, as it were, to bestow the world with a recumbent trust *en miniature* by not only providing his bar guests with drinks, but also with the necessary dreams. In addition the trust received a further, far greater significance because

Iwan Goll / THE EUROCOCCUS (EXTRACT)

Dr Syrianx was the proud father of three daughters. With the aid of the bar he could assure their livelihood for the time being.

The daughters were called Li, La and Lu: they were respectively blonde, black and red-headed, twenty-one, seventeen and fourteen years-old, and had three different mothers: Li's was a Swedish painter, La's a Romanian queen, and Lu was one of the authentic daughters of Toulouse Lautrec's Goulue and had been raised by the Assistance Publique until Dr Syrianx had suddenly remembered her. Lu wore her hair *à la garçonne*, La had a Grecian topknot *à la Sappho*, Lu a tennis champion's bob.

Li had an artistic streak, La a maternal soul, and Lu was simply a virgin.

As I entered Dr Syrianx received me in a purple robe. He excused his daughters who would be returning from a lecture at the Sorbonne at any moment. In the meantime he showed me photos of them in various poses and draperies, asking me to take my pick.

'If you like sport, then Li, my good Sir. She won the three hundred metres sprint. She is well behaved, and if you were a poet you would compare her thighs with an antelope's. La, on the other hand, is as warm as the shores of the Mediterranean. She'll take good care of your soul. She'll put a better knot in your tie: she'll just give you a maternal kiss on the forehead. And she writes reviews for the Nouvelle Revue Française. But Lu, ah! The lily in the crest of France, Jean d'Arc without armour. Genuine freckles on her temples. And you heard how old she is!'

At last I managed to introduce myself: 'I am a friend of d'Anglade who asked me to come and visit him here.'

'Then please take a seat, La and a sherry!'

And Dr Syrianx disappeared behind the bar. But he returned immediately:

'I could see it at once. La's the woman for you. No! Don't argue. This bar is a humane institute in which the buds of France's most brilliant heritage will be brought back to blossom: I want to marry love with the spirit. Tell me, where can one still find that in Europe!'

I replied that he was running a truly marvellous, exemplary enterprise, and asked him whether his daughters agreed with his principles. Dr Syrianx sadly admitted that he had been unable to exert much influence on their characters, but had done all that was necessary for their development in the field of love and spirit: first of all they had been brought up in a convent school, and then by Dalcroze. La had studied and written a doctorate on Madame Pompadour, Lu had won first prize for typing.

Dr Syrianx kept looking at the door. They still hadn't arrived. Then he brought more photographs: the gallery of their lovers. He particularly drew my attention to the pictures of Bela Kun, Oskar Kokoschka and Clémenceau.

Finally La appeared, dressed magnificently. She gave her father her hat and college book, and me a quivering kiss on the lips. I realised that the only way to master the situation was to overtrump her, and told La that I had just flown in from London in order to inspect the shape of her famous breasts. After this I told her that I had been in Saloniki, where the trees cast purple shadows; in Leningrad, where the people suddenly stop dead in the street, fall to their knees in front of one another and weep; and in Berlin, where the eighteen year-old youths already have bright red bald pates. Last of all I confided to her that I was one of Anatole France's twenty-seven illegitimate sons, hence my talent!

But La was not to be outdone: she at once compared me with the seraph in the novel *La Révolte des Anges* and ran her hand through my curls. Just as I tried to grab it and press it to my lips, La quickly pulled it away and laughed:

'I can't stand old Grandpa France, and his grandchildren will have to suffer as a result. You've chosen a bad godfather there. All you young men who nowadays want, as it were, to defile his corpse in public are his congenitally afflicted offspring. Your impatience these days, your scepticism, your nihilism, are not the slightest bit

Iwan Goll / THE EUROCOCCUS (EXTRACT)

different to his old sterile irony. France and Dada are all part of one family, he before and you after the war. D'Anglade, for example ...'

Her talk didn't displease me. The hetairai are today's guardians of the arts, without the aftertaste of the *Précieuses Ridicules*. Poetry is better in their hands than in those of bourgeois wives. But doesn't art then end up being nourished at the expense of love? The spirit is a strong narcotic for the heart. I tried in vain to catch hold of her fingertips. Her thoughts on the contemporary novel were too clever by far. She resisted long enough for me to fall deeply in love with her. The longer we talked the more solemn her voice grew, the purer her body seemed to be. Soon I no longer dared to even brush against her dress. And a glorious feeling burnt my throat.

'What is love?' She suddenly started to expound on a question I asked. 'Love is when my friend, the painter Giacomo, travels across Europe for years on end with his young wife and three year-old daughter, following a Polish actress who doesn't pay him the scantest attention. He has scarcely a penny, boards in the smallest hotels, cooks the meals for the three of them himself and now and then sells a strange looking landscape. He, his wife and his little daughter travel behind the troupe to Barcelona, Dieppe, Southampton, Oslo, Smolensk, and there's always a small, cheap inn opposite the theatre where his loved one is playing. Giacomo's little wife spies on the actress and finds out all she can about her, telling him how a passionate letter was received, how the applause was, and when they will be moving on. She stands by the window on rainy evenings next to her love-torn Giacomo and waits until the artistes leave and she passes by. One morning at eleven o'clock the family trinity was leaning dreamily against the hotel window and the little daughter was in her father's arms, playing with the trailing autumn foliage which draped the house. Then suddenly, quite unexpectedly, she walks down the street: with her elegant antelope gait, with her storm tossed locks and her fur jacket — out of shock Giacomo drops the child from the second storey onto the street. Blood flows from her tiny head. She's dead. But Giacomo doesn't scream, doesn't run down the stairs, his eyes are spellbound, wonder at the movement with which his beloved is now reverently bowing down over the child's body, and he trembles, because now he will be able to speak with her for the first time ...'

But me, can I love? Have I ever had the feeling of being three times as large, three times as beautiful, three times as strong as every other man in the world because there were a golden pair of woman's eyes at my side which constituted my superhuman worth? Now I know why up until now I have remained so impoverished: because I had no one to whom I could give my self, my world!

I want to love La! I love La!

Her hair illuminates Paris like an unexpected sunset. The velvety alto of her voice drowns the wailing of the iron, the poverty and the sick. What she says is the pure truth, the profoundest wisdom. Yes, how could I have believed I lived before I knew La! La is a new era: she completely overthrows the Gregorian calendar. La refutes every chart of the heavens which the astrologers have ever drawn up: La, the most important constellation of all, and which no one had ever discovered! La dictates a new book of civil law!

What am I without La! Or France without La! The blue month of April has been invented in her honour, the Eiffel Tower decorates itself with red tulips in her honour, the kid-goats are sacrificed at Easter in her honour.

La has a neck made of mother of pearl, blonde down on her crimson lip, her eyelids open like sunshades. She smiles and asks me if I would like another port. Yes, dear La, I'll have another port. La strides slowly and majestically across the room. She is a perfect work of art. Her movements are as certain and smooth as a Rolls Royce, rapid and faultless. Such perfection is almost frightening, like an Egyptian statue. Does she lack humanity?

Iwan Goll / THE EUROCOCCUS (EXTRACT)

All the same, loving this woman makes me strong, almighty perhaps. Women never used to look at me like now. They never noticed me. But now that I am rich and handsome, because I love, every eye will search me out. Women turn instinctively to look at me as they enter the bar, like flowers to the light. Only the rich can reap the rewards. Only the man with fortune on his side is trusted by the world. Love is a halo around our hat which we ourselves don't suspect, but which is our real power.

At this moment I felt an inexplicable urge to kneel. It pulled my limbs, my whole ego, down to the ground. I no longer wanted to find fault with the world, wanted to say yes to everything, be amazed at myself again and admire everything and love, love, love.

Without any warning Henry d'Anglade entered the door and transfixed me with his gaze. The feeling which had hardly time to spread its wings flowed back into my inner, most hidden self. La sipped her drink, tugged her hair. D'Anglade didn't even take the time to hang up his hat, or to kiss La's hand: the voice was deadly sad which sat next to me:

'Well? The result? Is it the beginning? Is it the end?'

By which he meant the tragedy of Europe. La and I understood him at once. A silence descended, as if the fate of the entire human race depended on me. It was my duty to give a precise report to this person who that morning had shown me the way to a new perception of the world. I related every step and every thought from the day gone by in the minutest detail. I made my report about the discovery of the Eurococcus. La snuggled up to me warmly. D'Anglade nodded in a friendly manner. As I was finished he said:

'I am pleased with you. You belong to us. A number of young men who, like yourself, bear the knowledge of the great death within them, are forming a closed, secret sect which only admits the chosen few. We are against everything because everything has become futile: we deny work, every action and every feeling, progress, beauty and love. We are finished, done for, empty-handed heirs. There is nothing left for us but to strike. Just like the prison inmates who have recently gone on hunger strike, we are striking against love, thought and morality. The European epoch is dying out. There's no more point in saving anything. Decline is also a form of voluptuousness, just like growth. Autumn is just as sensual as springtime. There is as much greatness in dying as in procreation.'

D'Anglade's face was a ghastly mask of despair. La ran a silver hand through his hair. Was the bar so small? Was there a thunder storm lying in wait in the sky outside? I suddenly felt I could no longer breathe, that I was suffocating. Now, here in this atmosphere for the first time, something inside me, a last stirring of youth, seemed to baulk at the inevitable. And I, who had previously announced my own decay and the great importance of the existence of the Eurococcus, started to oppose these truths and resist them.

A new thought flashed through my mind:

'Agreed,' I said, 'the Eurococcus is devouring us. It's a disease, but doesn't every disease have a cure? Mightn't one be discovered tomorrow or the day after? Why despair completely? And America? Hygiene? Radio? Tennis? Petrol? The flight to the moon? ... I've got it! Couldn't we use the Americoon against the Eurococcus? Won't it all end up in one enormous scientific battle?'

'No, no, no!' D'Anglade was getting heated and angry. 'We've known about the Americoon for a long time now. It's a quack remedy. It is a bright poster pasted on the crumbling cloister walls of Paris. An Americoon pill manufactured out of corned beef and Waterman's ink is a useless medication for our headaches and in the long run damages our heart. It just disturbs the circulation and no longer eradicates the Eurococcus. We want to die our own death, not someone else's. That is Europe's heroism. It fights with its spirit, whose weaknesses it has already recognised, alone, isolated, misunderstood, but to the death, against the transatlantic demon, the metallic colossus, the new Egyptians. It fights by striking, by refusing, with

Iwan Goll / THE EUROCOCCUS (EXTRACT)

ridicules and smiles. It fights with decay. It fights precisely with the help of the Eurococcus. There's no point in easing the task of the new, bull-like, primal strength of these demons, the Americans. They want to colonise Europe? The spirit makes itself scarce for those unworthy of it. They should start by draining the marshes, like every beginner.'

D'Anglade spoke with such conviction and passion that I was already ashamed I had contradicted him. He was right. Hadn't I myself spent the whole day just gathering arguments for his thesis? Why was I resisting now? Perhaps simply because the revelation of love had chanced to descend on me the moment he had entered? And because I now regretted having to die and renounce, just as a suicide suddenly starts to swim in the coldness of the river?

I groaned in agony, quietly, almost inaudibly:

'But I love La!'

With which La tore away her soft, her warm, her silvery hand which I had taken hold of, directing a peal of laughter at me:

'You're absurd, my little darling! You don't know what love is! A kiss is a craving for the gates of heaven and the discovery of a small mouth which quickly tires. It's all so boring, nothing but boredom!'

'What's not boring then?' I asked naïvely.

'Everything is boring,' d'Anglade quickly explained in order to forestall any new eruption of love which might embarrass him. 'Boredom is the other epidemic which is making Europe ripe for decline. Boredom is the end product of each and every civilisation. It is the arteriosclerosis of the great thinking peoples. The moment always arrives where even God, whether he's called Zeus, Zebaoth or Zoroaster, has finished creating his universe and asks: "What's the point of it actually?" He yawns and chucks it aside. Mankind does the same with civilisation. Boredom is the condition of a people which no longer believes but all the same is doing just fine. Boredom is when every clock in the country is predestined to be correct. When the same naïve flowers blossom again in the month of March. When every day the deaths of good family fathers are announced in the papers When a war breaks out in the Balkans. When poems go on about the stars. Boredom is a symptom of ageing. Boredom is the diagnosis that talent and virtue are slowly being spent. Boredom is the life-long damnation to a form of being which has worn itself out.'

These words seeped into me like coal gas creeping into the open lungs of a sleeping man.

Henry continued:

'Out of contrariness I, for example, have chosen the hardest profession of all: doing nothing! I do nothing out of principle, asceticism even. Doing nothing is the hardest torture that a person can put himself through. For he is always brought face to face with his own self, which demands that he gives account for the sun which he uselessly squanders, for the springs of energy in his organism, the gold of wisdom in the mines of his brain. The masses work, slog, forget. They drink the alcohol of their sweat. Work is a flight from responsibility and God. Since the mystic beliefs were banned from Europe, pillars of glory have been erected to rationality in order to put something in place of the cross: the French Revolution named its goddess reason, the Russians named their Moloch work. But the machine called Europe is running idle: it fills stomachs with fake bread, builds artificial houses with iron paper, the products are bad, the pay meagre, and at the end of the six holy work days is the unholy Sunday which one sleeps through out of fear of the great boredom which is infecting Europe. Sunday, the day of idleness, is nowadays a punishment for Christianity, the cities collapse into soulless ruins, nature is just the backdrop for dusty sports. Doing nothing out of principle, my dear, is nowadays the most violent form of revolt!'

At this I dropped my head. Hadn't I felt exactly the same as I had been running around Paris all day? Humanity regimented by its doing, and found it all laughable? Worked, and hadn't my work become the source of infinite disgust?

Iwan Goll / THE EUROCOCCUS (EXTRACT)

'Long live the Eurococcus!' I shouted and swigged down my glass of port. I now no longer protected myself with healthy, unrefined optimism, I killed the hypocritical illusion of youth within me: I felt how ill I was, seriously ill, and I no longer wanted to hide it.

There it was, dear professor, the Eurococcus! Here beneath my skin, here behind La's beautiful eyelashes, here beside Henry's appalling smile: it had already eaten away our souls and we were now leather puppets living solely by force of habit. There it was, the Eurococcus, in our hearts which stood alone like a plundered castle, the gates forced open, where every passer-by lay down for a night and then left, eaten away by vermin.

There was no love any more. La was right. And what I had earlier sworn had been old reminiscences.

A clammy boredom was chloroforming us.

'We don't know!' a humanitarian philanthropist had erected in gigantic letters across the boulevards.

'What shall we do?' I asked tonelessly across the table.

'There is absolutely no reason to complain,' Henry explained, 'we're just fine. We only need to be inwardly consistent. We must uphold the having of no ideals as our ideal. The lack of an ideal, however, brings us the greatest well-being on earth, whose attainment was the one reason for creating every single ideal in the history of mankind. Namely, freedom, absolute freedom ... But I would prefer to explain this theory in more suitable surroundings. Come to the Bar de la Mort this evening.'

Henry had probably noticed how my features contorted. I was fighting an inward battle, the final battle with all the ancient spirits which still peopled me: with the eyes of my mother, with the angels from holy paintings, with the revolutionary phrases on the goodness of man, with the articles of the law books. And I felt forced to make yet one more attempt to save myself from the ghastly sickness of this emptiness: to cast myself into the purity of nature, to believe in the naïvety of God-given bounty, where there is no thought or interpretation or smiling, just the sun and the wind constantly proclaiming God's eternal will.

It was the month of May. And soon the sweet port wine was flowing — a sunset over the western skies such as I had not seen for ages. Oh to feel the May like the copper beetles, the glistening pikes, the small pink trees. It was May in the asparagus fields of Lorry, May in the daffodil covered hills of Vevey, May in the acacia lined avenues of Odessa, the May of the sloe, May of the weasel, May of the larks, May in the whole western world!

I left Henry and La, my mouth trembling. A taxi brought me to the Gare St Lazare. I hurried through the viscid mass of travellers like a man in despair who has just received a telegram calling him to the death bed of his distant bride. I bought a ticket to the death bed of the bridal forest in St Cloud. Squashed between unsuspecting bank clerks and pillars of civilisation who were avidly devouring the details of the murder on the Marseilles Express and my flight in the papers, I reached the gateway to nature at last. Here I would once more take death to task, before imposing witnesses.

Nature: perhaps this one last time you were still the emergency exit from the human calamity! Nature, lowliness and scene of frenetic dramas, world of primordial passions, full of old loves and jealousies and hate and fear and awe, full of all that was foreign to us empty casks. World of grasses, liverworts, dandelions, larkspurs and sorrel which still know shock and despair with their flower cups and stamens and anthers, world of stag beetles, newts, the silvery fish in the brook, the velvety martens, the blazing squirrels, the drunken privet moths, all the wonders of the season and zoology! To you! I wanted to save myself by coming to you and throwing myself at your feet with the last remnants of my devotion!

And I hurried off to the hills, across highways which still concealed the echoes of royal coaches. The evening descended and the

Iwan Goll / THE EUROCOCCUS (EXTRACT)

sun behind the already shadowy trees hung in the branches like the wild flight of golden feathers from a shot pheasant. Then suddenly I saw it, a shock turned my eyes to glass: I no longer cast a shadow! A new Peter Schlemihl,[1] I had lost my shadow! I stepped to the side like a person who thinks he's standing in someone's way or treading on the tails of their coat: but no, there was no shadow there. I was beingless, no longer connected with space and earth, unreal, inauthentic. But more terrifying than this was that the trees, the statues and the lanterns also cast no shadows, even though the gold of the sun streamed out of the crucible of the heavens, soft and runny!

The alders, beeches and oaks no longer had the support of their shadows and resembled the charred remains of a great firework display which had taken place the evening before. The firework of a collapsing Europe! Nothing wed the things to the earth any more. The rays of the sun shone through the hole-ridden, transparent tree trunks, just as on the stage.

Was the whole of nature also nothing more than a backdrop, scenery, illusion? The Musée Grévin of a mouldy world? The black swans no longer cast reflections on the poetic pond, but they sang, their voices were the last for far and wide, ringing agonised like the wails from hospitals. A few amazons were galloping across the distant horizon on mahogany horses: were they living forms or visions? One could not hear the clatter of hoofs on the stony path or the bright cries of the women's laughter: and naturally not even they cast shadows. Two deer watched me calmly from a blackberry bush as I gesticulated desperately on the main road. But they didn't run off, they carried on sniffing as if I didn't exist ...

Yes, do I still exist? I ran my hand over my forehead and limbs but could not feel myself. I was seized by a mad fear. I ran back, running over slopes, banks, over artistic beds of flowers and lakes. I ran past cycling park keepers who tried in vain to stop me, knocked over a pram, tore my sleeve on a fence, ran and ran to the station and onto the train which was already pulling out. And to the inquisitive question from a passenger, I could only breathlessly whisper that one word:

'The Eurococcus!'

This strange behaviour must have raised enormous suspicion. Doubtlessly the park keeper, who had seen me running through the evening forest with such a bad conscience, and the station master whom I had pushed aside without showing my ticket, had immediately phoned Paris and given my description: 'tie askew ... eyes reddened from reading and crying ...' Thank God I no longer had my lemon-yellow gloves.

Back at the station in Paris I instantly saw that my neighbour in the train was keeping hard on my heels: his gaze grabbed my collar firmer than a fist.

We collided with the great hasty mass of people who were seemingly occupied with just one single collective thought, for at that moment everyone without exception was reading the thick black headlines of the latest evening edition:

'NEW CLUES ON THE THIRD BANDIT'

There it was! They had telephoned! Now I had to believe it! I was almost glad, I saw my impending arrest as an act of mercy. For I would no longer be personally responsible for the trials of my soul. The prison cell beckoned to me as if it were the only place of sanctuary where my unbridled fate could be tamed ...

But how was I suddenly able to slip through the exit unnoticed, without even being asked for the missing ticket, and was free once more to move among the seething tide of humanity?

I was free, but what was I to do with myself? Inconsolable, inconsolable and blind, I ambled on. But where to? Where?

Back to the only people who had already learnt to live without a

Iwan Goll / THE EUROCOCCUS (EXTRACT)

shadow, without love, without fear, without illusion! I made for the Bar de la Mort. Written on the door in red enamel letters was:

'THE WORD 'HEART' IS FORBIDDEN ON PAIN OF DEATH!'

The bar was no larger or more brightly lit than a diving bell which had been sunk to the deepest chasms of the Parisian ocean. The inhabitants were clearly breathing something other than oxygen and nitrogen: the modern opium of total pessimism. They performed very weary, very casual, very melancholy movements, while claiming to be in the throws of an orgy. A Hawaiian perched on a stool in the corner, ventriloquising with his banjo. High above on the piano sat Paris's most celebrated poet, legs dangling, black angels fluttering round his forehead. He imitated the pose of a Greek shepherd boy and drew androgynous notes out of an ocarina, half like the wailings of a woman, half like the laughter of clowns. Delos-New York.

On the table in front sat a boy, his cheeks were milk, his eye a girl's and his heart that of a brazen knight. He acted as if he were bewitched by the flute. In reality he was already riding on an eagle to Zeus, his long-since elected Ganymede.

There was also a painter, a born crusader, who nurtured his cultural decadence like a carbuncle. A musician, fat and cosy like a well-to-do notary, plucked at his nerves as if on the strings of a mandolin. And how many other youths, lax and relaxed, words falling from their lips like ripe fruit. There they would become old men within a quarter of a year, while precocious bashfulness still rested on their eyelashes.

They all had spirit, the primacy of the spirit over the world, and yet how bored they were! They had the ancestral spirit stamped on their foreheads and in their passports. They had Voltaire in the creases of their mouths, Renan on their temples, Rabelais in their ravening hearts. But they had had the words: 'THE WORD 'HEART'

IS FORBIDDEN!' written on the door. The word 'heart' was out of date. When one of the uninitiated spoke it, the whole bar fell silent, outraged, annoyed, insulted, like an English dinner party when the word 'stomach' is spoken.

And there was Henry, sitting next to La who had been so astonished at the word love. He quickly pulled me over to his table, ordered a chrysanthemum cocktail and without further ado returned to the conversation which had been interrupted that afternoon:

'What did I tell you ... quite right ... it is our lack of ideals which creates the highest good for which mankind is constantly striving: freedom! Absolute freedom is our first and last law. The freedom of the self comes before morality, friendship, and God. We've nothing else to lose anyhow. We are outside the law and the only punishment which threatens us is death, such as threatened the outcasts in the middle ages. So we possess the freedom of the poorest of the poor, those who have no longer a mother to revere, no fatherland for which they want to die, no more ambition (after all, every reporter from the north and south American press has already interviewed and photographed us), we don't even admire art any more because we are the ones who make it. We having nothing left to fear, our history is now in the past. And we are only still alive because of a moratorium.'

'A tiny company, 'the aware', we have taken up civilisation's fiercest weapons to fight against the dark army of the masses, whose leaders are hunger and stupidity. These weapons are the *smile* and the *lie*.

'We are the prophets of suicide, but on the largest scale: we take occidental culture to the point of absurdity. We have declared it bankrupt. We ridicule the wonders of technology, the doctor's inventions, the successes of the slave workers and the plant physiologists.'

'We live haphazardly, like the cavemen and Red Indians, and answer every question with What For? We're living it up in smiles

Iwan Goll / THE EUROCOCCUS (EXTRACT)

and lies, then there is no God or dictator who could manage to forbid our smiles and lies.'

'The smile is civilisation's finest adornment. It signifies the will-power and duty to fashion mankind's coexistence as quietly and agreeably as possible so that it will always appear friendly. For it is all a matter of appearance. The smile is culture's diploma: it is the diplomat's badge. I have accustomed myself to folding my face into fine creases which flow round my eyes and lips like rounded waves. My face is as sensitive as the surface of a lake: a person approaches and casts his gaze into it like a pebble and I respond at once: I smile. I veil myself. One can no longer look into my depths. No one recognises me any more, no one knows what I am thinking. How few are the Europeans who know how to smile: a few elderly French ministers, a couple of Italian financiers, three English lords. Someone recently claimed he had never seen a German smile. Some skins just aren't suited for it. But the people of China, with their four thousand year-old culture, receive a wonderful schooling in smiling. Then it is nothing more nor less than a discipline. Smiling is a regime like marching on parade. Why always make a serious or angry or sad or disappointed face? Why bare one's soul in the open? But a people that smiles does not prove that it is the slightest bit happy, on the contrary. The majority of those who smile are poor laughers. For they know! They burden themselves but alleviate the lives of their fellow man. Smiling should be the first requirement of culture.'

'But this external smile has a step-sister: the *lie*! I am proud of the smile as I would be of a difficult art which has to be learnt for years on end. But only proud. Whereas I love the lie dearly. It is like a beautiful sister who would spell incest if one approached her. Just the thought of her is punishable. But that makes her charm all the greater.'

'The lie is also a part of culture. The Negro lies from his disposition, the woman out of sexual necessity. But the conscious person lies out of superiority. Lying is not a sin, since there has never been a law-maker or philosopher who could determine what truth is. I lie for the fun of it. I lie for fear of the gravity of life. I lie out of boredom. How can anyone who has more fantasy than the Catholic evening paper get by without lying? I lie permanently, like the permanency of the Pope's blessing. I lie because the women I seduce want to be lied to. I lie because the policeman on the street forces me to lie with his truncheon. In short, I lie because I am honest, I lie to you. And most of all I lie to myself ...'

Henry downed his chrysanthemum cocktail in one.

Paris's most celebrated poet was still sitting on his piano, looking on at the world contemptuously with a towering, irregular head which looked as if it had been chiselled by Lehmbruck.[2] The blossoms of European civilisation sat at the tables, deliberately doing precisely the opposite to the three-hundred years of style, esprit and good behaviour with which they had been inoculated. These tender youths cursed each other in the foulest way. They treated their women with coarseness and cynicism. They deliberately talked banal nonsense. They killed everything which they should have honoured. They killed themselves with their sheer genius: they slowly tore out one another's teeth, thighs, hair and hearts. It was a glorious, collective, suicide.

They no longer wanted to think, no longer wanted to know. They lived and talked and moved about the smoky Bar de la Mort nonchalantly, as if in slow motion; the bar looked like a basket full of live crabs which, unconsciously crawling in and out of one another, had strayed from the ocean's current!

They were all pale and empty: but that came, as I knew, from the European sickness. The Eurococcus was even more endemic here than in the old books, the stones of the Gothic cathedrals and the bones of the poor old donkey who had to cart off the excrement from Paris at five o'clock in the morning. And who knows whether or not it was this elite which had brought the bacillus with them!

Iwan Goll / THE EUROCOCCUS (EXTRACT)

The boredom of healthy youngsters was the result of the Eurococcus epidemic.

The women, ravaged by the Eurococcus, had no more love to give.

These people had even given up thinking. They were afraid to think about themselves.

A bright, silvery, starry night formed a canopy high above this gloomy sepulchre, and the salty wind sang its cosmic song as ever. But not far away, one street to the left, was a ghastly night shelter, the invention of a terrible social phantasy: here aged beggars could cling onto a thick rope for ten centimes and, standing there under the eye of the snoring republic, fall asleep. Here gin flowed in streams beside tears. And it was all one. The incurable illness ravaged humanity. It ravaged buildings, animals and nature's works. My reasoning reared up against this ghastly vision. Was there no escape? I knew that there were the same youths, the same beggars, in Genoa, Liverpool and Charlottenburg. I knew that no doctor would bring a cure now: not Freud, not Vornoff, not Zinovieff.

La had undressed and was dancing on the piano.

Then three policemen entered the doors and pointed at me.

I jumped at once into the middle of the bar and screamed the three forbidden words of this age: 'My heart! My God! I love!' into the commotion of the bar and was glad that someone believed that I had the daring and will power to be a murderer — when suddenly the police officer signalled to his men that they should let go of me and excused himself to the proprietor: there had simply been a mistake!

Robert Musil

THE GIANT AGOAG

(1929)

When the hero of this little tale — and a hero he was! — pushed up his sleeves, two arms as thin as the sound of a musical box came to light. And the women praised his intelligence warmly, but they 'went' with others of whom they did not speak quite so well. Only once did a woman of appreciable beauty show, to the surprise of all, a deeper interest in him; but she had loved casting fond looks at him while simultaneously shrugging her shoulders. And when the brief toing and froing over the choice of nicknames, which generally takes place at the beginning of a love affair, had come to an end, she called him: 'My little squirrel!'

Robert Musil / **THE GIANT AGOAG**

That's why he only read the sports section of the newspapers, preferring the boxing news and above all the news on the heavyweights.

Although his life was not a happy one, he did not slacken his attempts to climb the path to physical strength. And since he hadn't the money to join a body-building club, and since, according to recent ideas, sport is the triumph of morale and spirit, rather than some despicable propensity of the body, he attempted this ascent alone. There was not a free afternoon on which he did not go out for walks on tip-toe. And when he was sure that he was alone and unobserved in a room, he would stretch his right arm over his shoulder in order to reach the parts on his left side, or vice versa. He made dressing and undressing a mental challenge by seeking the most strenuous ways of performing them. And since every muscle in the human body is paired with an abductor muscle, such that one extends when the other contracts, or contracts when the other extends, he managed to create untold difficulties for himself with each and every movement. One can safely say that on good days he consisted of two completely alien people who did unremitting battle with one another. But when he retired to bed after just a day, used to the full, he would simultaneously distend every muscle he could muster one last time; and there he would lie amidst his own muscles like a piece of alien flesh in the talons of a hawk, until, overcome by tiredness, its grip would relax and drop him vertically into sleep. It was inevitable that with this lifestyle he would end up invincibly strong. But before this was to be, he got into an argument on the street and received a hiding from a fat slug of a person.

His soul was injured by this ignominious fight; nothing would ever be quite the same for him, and for some time it was quite debatable whether he could even endure a life so void of hope. But then he was saved by a large omnibus. He was a chance witness to an accident: a large omnibus ran over a young man of athletic build, and, tragic though this was for the victim, for him it was to become the starting point of a new life. The athlete was, as it were, pared from his life like a wood shaving or an apple peel, while the omnibus, merely embarrassed, pulled to one side and, coming to a stop, stared back from a large number of eyes. It was a sad sight, but our man was quick to see his chance and clambered aboard the victor.

That was the way it was, and from then on it was to remain that way: whenever the mood took him, he could pay fifteen pence and creep into the body of a giant which sent every sportsman leaping for safety. The giant's name was Agoag. Which meant perhaps All-glorious-omnibus-athletic-group; then anyone who still wants to experience fairytales these days can't afford to dither when it comes to using their brains. Our hero sat upstairs where he was so large that he lost all feeling for the dwarfs who teemed about on the street. Impossible to imagine what they found to discuss with each other. He was delighted when they jumped aside in fright. He darted at them when they crossed the road like a full grown tyke chasing sparrows. He looked down at the roofs of the smart cars, which had always intimidated him with their poshness, but now with the awareness of his own destructive power, rather like a person who looks, knife in hand, at the dear little chickens in a poultry yard. He didn't need much imagination for that, merely logical thought. For if it is true that clothes make the man, why shouldn't an omnibus be able to do the same? One wears, or is girded by, its enormous strength, just as another dons a suit of armour or slings a rifle over his shoulder; and if the pantheon of knightly heroes allows itself to be wed to a suit of protective armour, then why not to an omnibus? And then consider the great pillars of strength in world history: was it their weak bodies, cosseted by the comforts of power, that made them so terrifying, or did their invincibility rely on the apparatus of power with which they cloaked it? And how is it, our hero wondered, enthroned now in his new realm of thought, with all the nobility of the sporting world

Robert Musil / THE GIANT AGOAG

who attend the kings of boxing, running and swimming like courtiers, from the manager and trainer to the man who removes the blood-filled bucket or places the bathrobe round their shoulders; whence comes the personal dignity of these present-day successors to the Lord High Stewards and Ganymedes of old? From themselves or from the rays of some alien strength? The accident, as one can see, had honed his intellect.

He now used every free moment not for sport, but for omnibus rides. His dream was a comprehensive season ticket. And if he has obtained it and has not died, fallen to his doom, been crushed to death, run over or flung in the mad house, then he is still riding in it today. However, on one occasion he did go too far and allowed a girlfriend to accompany him in the expectation that she would be able to appreciate man's intellectual beauty. And inside the giant's body there had been a tiny parasite with a bristly moustache who had given his girlfriend a cheeky smile which, almost imperceptibly, she had returned; indeed, he even chanced to brush her as he got out and seemed to whisper something to her in the process, while at the same time excusing himself chivalrously to all the passengers. Our hero seethed with rage; his first impulse was to leap at this rival, but as small as the man might have appeared outside the giant Agoag, all the larger and broader he seemed inside. So our hero remained seated and only later showered his girlfriend with reproaches. And lo and behold, although he had let her in on his view of things, she failed to respond with: I haven't the time of day for strong men, I only admire strong omnibuses! but simply disavowed it.

Since this intellectual betrayal, which can be attributed to woman's lack of mental daring, our hero somewhat curtailed his journeys, and when he did board a bus, it was without female company. He sensed a little of the truth about the fate of the male which is contained in the saying: the greatest strength lies in solitude!

Hermann Ungar

SOMETHING BEHIND THIS

(1929)

Leopold stood outside the front door of the house he had just left, and thought. He had the feeling that he had forgotten something. He turned round slowly and climbed back up the three steep stairs to the musician.

'Excuse me', he said, and entered.

Inside the room he saw the painting at once. He had only seen it fleetingly in the past. He also knew now that what he had forgotten had been his memory of this picture.

'A peculiar painting,' he said and he looked at it perplexed. 'A very peculiar painting indeed.'

'Yes,' said the musician. He was astonished that Leopold had nothing more to say.

Leopold turned round in the doorway.

'I'm going to Wilhelm Rau's Restaurant in Brunnen Street. You know where I mean. I'm to be there until ten o'clock. Then I'll go home.'

The musician didn't ask: why are you telling me that?

The musician was young and unassuming.

The thought of the painting oppressed Leopold. It was a painting in a simple frame. One could see a table top. A man with bony hands unfurled on the table was counting silver pieces. His hands were thin and the fingers long. Beside him sat a woman whose loose smock did more to reveal her hanging breasts than hide them. Her hands were also unfurled. A liquid had been poured over the table, quite clearly a sticky fluid. The faces were white, angular and gaunt. They were bony faces, slender, suffering and unfurled like the hands.

Leopold thought that this painting might be called the 'Last Supper' or the 'Host'. It reminded him of things it certainly had nothing to do with, as little as it had to do with the Last Supper. It was essentially a profane painting. It was the hands which made it holy, and the eyes.

The hands were unfurled. That was the astonishing thing about it. Leopold had never heard this word used quite like that before. But it was a familiar, holy word. Perhaps it came from a long forgotten hymn.

The musician started to play. Leopold heard it because the musician's window was open wide. The street was deserted.

It occurred to him that he had promised the musician he would meet him in Brunnen Street. It was possible that the musician would come and look for him. It was nine o'clock.

Leopold hastened his step.

The thought of this painting was oppressive. It now seemed to

Leopold that the liquid which had been poured onto the table was not wine or schnapps, as he had originally thought, but blood. Although the picture had created the impression of being only in black and white, the damp patch on the table seemed to be red and sticky and not yet dry. He felt it clearly with his fingers, it was not at all like schnapps or wine. He felt that the stickiness did not originate from sugar, that it was the stickiness of blood. It seemed to have flowed from the bloodless fingers. But perhaps the stickiness had been there before. The landlord, who came to wipe it away from the table, stepped back because Leopold wouldn't remove his fingers from it, left his beer untouched and gave the landlord an unfriendly look.

Without doubt everything would be cleared up shortly: as soon as the musician who owned the painting arrived. He could explain what it all meant.

Leopold straightened up, and his elbows distanced themselves from his body. But he kept his fingers unfurled. He was shocked that the blood was there on the table, and looked at the door which should have opened. There was no one in the inn besides the landlord.

Leopold ran his hand over his forehead, for the thought of the painting was oppressive. He wanted to forget the thought.

But the money, he thought. What's happened to the money? There's something behind all this. 'Something behind all this,' he said out loud, and the words seemed incomprehensible, foreign, almost unbearable.

He left without drinking his beer. He thought how much money it would cost and how the woman was starving. But he had given his promise to the musician. And now he hadn't come.

As he stepped onto the street it struck ten. Then he started to walk.

The woman sat in a smock in the room. He saw her hanging breasts, which the smock revealed more than hid. It was not quite a month since the child had died.

Leopold now placed the money from his pocket on the table in front of the woman. Six silver coins which he had received from the musician for writing out music.

There was a smell of fresh meat. The meat lay in a bowl by the window.

'Moritz?' Leopold asked.

Moritz had been the name of the black tomcat.

He took the meat from the bowl, brought it over and placed it on the table top.

'Let's eat,' he said.

They ate and threw the bones into the corner. Nothing remained of Moritz except for a damp patch on the table. They sat next to each other.

'The guests will arrive soon,' he said.

They waited for the musician to arrive.

As morning approached she loosened her smock, and her breasts, which he knew, hung over the table. They were meagre, empty breasts. They were gaunt and unfurled.

Blood had flowed from her breasts instead of milk as she had suckled her child. He looked at her breasts. There was a terrible stain on the table.

The blood killed the child, he thought.

They are lovely breasts, he thought, empty, unfurled breasts. Did blood still flow from them? Into her smock? In the end there's a crust of blood stuck to the smock. Such oppressive thoughts in one's head, such oppressive thoughts.

Perhaps, thought Leopold, if the musician comes and sees it all, the breasts, the stain, the money and the smock, the empty bleeding lovely breasts, perhaps he will be able to tell me what's behind it all. It's there. But incomprehensible, foreign and almost unbearable, Leopold, oh Leopold.

NOTES

Albert Ehrenstein *Tubutsch*

1   1848, the year of the March Revolution which, among other things, brought about the downfall of the Metternichs in Austria.

Gustav Meyrink *The Ring of Saturn*

1   Elsewhere, Meyrink elucidated this as follows: 'There once was a dog who had to mind twelve crabs wrapped in a handkerchief. But one of the crabs tore its way out and, although the dog managed to get it back to the

NOTES

handkerchief, in the meantime two others had escaped in different directions. The dog didn't stop for breath as it brought these two back, but now four had escaped etc., etc.'

Ferdinand Hardekopf *The Mental Link*

1 The original title 'Der Gedanken-Strich' is a wilful writing of the word 'Gedankenstrich', meaning a dash, as in a sentence. By adding his own hyphen, the author has split the word into two and thus created a new field of associational possibilities: 'Gedanken' means thoughts, while 'Strich' means, among many other things, a pencil stroke or line, a prostitute's pitch, or even a 'cut', as in 'a cut in a text'.

Hans Arp *Wintergarten*

1 The Wintergarten was a famous revue theatre in Berlin which also inspired, among others, Ferdinand Hardekopf.
2 Constantin Guys (1805–1892), French illustrator and artist renowned for his delicate portrayals of ladies and dandies. He inspired Baudelaire's study on dandyism.

Alfred Wolfenstein *Far Greater than Every Magic*

1 A parody of the opening line of Goethe's famous poem, Wanderers Nachtlied: 'On all the peaks lies peace'.
2 The original, 'schlangenparagraphen' ('snake-articles'), alludes to the appearance of the German sign for a legal article: §

NOTES

Paul Zech *The Terrace at the Pole*

1   Potsdam Square is at a star-like junction of six roads.

Else Lasker-Schüler *If My Heart Were Healthy*

1   *Katherine von Armagnac*, a play by Karl Vollmöller, dandy, archeologist, author and builder and driver of sports cars and aeroplanes.

Gottfried Benn *The Island*

1   Here, as in archaic English, the German language has two 'you' forms for addressing an individual: *Du* (*Thou*) used when addressing friends and children, and *Sie* (*You*) when addressing anyone else. Here the Du form is being referred to.

Hans Flesch-Brunningen *The Metaphysical Canary*

1   'Wacht am Rhein', a German patriotic song dating from the French invasion.

Hugo Ball *Grand Hotel Metaphysics*

1   Erich Ludendorff, a Prussian field marshall who commanded beside Hindenburg during the First World War in true sabre-rattling fashion.

NOTES

2   Plimplamplasko, a character from the book *Plimplamplasko, the Lofty Minded* by Friedrich Klinger, 1780, which makes fun of the cult of genius. In the middle of 1917, Ball planned to use this title for a collection of his poems which never came into being.

Conrad Felixmüller *Military Orderly Felixmüller, XI Arnsdorf*

1   Arnsdorf, the psychiatric hospital near Dresden where Felixmüller worked during the 1914–18 War.

Wieland Herzfelde *Strenge from Leipzig*

1   *The Wupper*, a play by Else Lasker-Schüler. The Wupper is a river in Lasker-Schüler's hometown, Wuppertal.
2   Insel Verlag, a major German publishing house from the 1890s to the present day.

Kurt Schwitters *The Onion*

1   Saint Florian, patron saint of firemen.
2   Jefim Golyscheff, Berlin Dadaist.
3   August Stramm, influential early Expressionist poet.

Iwan Goll *The Eurococcus*

1   Peter Schlemihl, the title character of the novella by A. von Chamisso, a patient person who, dogged by misfortune, sells his shadow.

NOTES

2 Wilhelm Lehmbruck, a German sculptor who after formative years in Paris, dedicated himself largely to gracious, Expressionist female nudes.

The Periodicals

Among the wealth of periodicals which appeared during the Expressionist era, three major magazines which are mentioned frequently in the introduction and biographies deserve a word of their own. *Die Aktion*, a weekly which started in 1911, combined revolutionary politics and the demand for a revolution in art and literature. Vigorously anti-war from 1914 to 1918, it later hailed the Russian Revolution and continued solely as a political journal for the Anti-National Socialist Party. The second major periodical, *Der Sturm*, founded in 1910, was more avant-garde in the literature, music and art that it published. From about 1917 onwards there was a strong emphasis on concrete poetry, the so-called 'Sturm poetry'. Both magazines were centres for many of the best writers of the time, and both published their own books. *Die weissen Blätter*, started in 1913, was a purely literary monthly which was important for its publication of novella and book length works. In 1915 it moved from Leipzig to Zurich in order to escape the censors during the war.

BIOGRAPHIES

FRANZ HELD (pseudonym for Franz Herzfelde): (B. Düsseldorf, 1862. D. Munich, 1908.)

A firebrand socialist full of heady ideas for world unity, his modern ideas obviously influenced his two important sons, W. Herzfelde and the photo-monteur John Heartfield. Along with Panizza, Held was involved in the free theatre clubs which provided a stage outside the control of the Wilhelminian censors, and which foreshadowed the Expressionist clubs and cabarets. His own Fresco Theatre in the 1890s rejected trivialising realism: he envisaged a theatre in which 'broad-ranging conceptions of life are personified in their immensity by gigantic characters, who are driven swiftly towards destinies of enormous significance with great passion ... Just sharp contours and convulsive scenes can offer a basis for this raging stream of modern humanity's ancestors as it bursts the banks of conventionality.' A better definition of Expressionism would be hard to find!

Held was sentenced to imprisonment for blasphemy in the same year as Panizza, but he managed to escape to Switzerland and then Austria. In the summer of 1899 he disappeared, ending up in the same mental hospital as his wife, and his later years were spent in senile dementia. This piece was first published during the late 1890s, and was reprinted in *Die Aktion* in 1914.

OSKAR PANIZZA: (B. Bad Kissingen, 1853. D. Bayreuth, 1921.)

Panizza first studied music and philosophy, then medicine, and after a spell as a doctor in a mental hospital he became a full-time writer and publisher. He was very active in the Modern Movement in Munich (along with Franz Held), writing reviews, social commentaries, short stories and plays. It was the play, *The Council of Love*, which earned him a year's jail sentence in Munich for blasphemy in 1895. On release he emigrated to Switzerland, and then to Paris. The last sixteen years of his life were spent in a German mental institution.

His philosophical treatises on psychosis and solipsism aroused the interest of Mynona and later Michael Foucault and Vienna Group member Oswald Wiener. His prose won the admiration of the Surrealists and more recently the German playwright Heiner Müller, who wrote 'Panizza is a terrorist; anyone who wishes not to be a German would do well to read him.'

BIOGRAPHIES

ALBERT MOMBERT: (B. Karlsruhe, 1872. D. Winthertür, 1942.)

Mombert, the self-named 'divine drinker', was a leading member of the 'cosmicist school', and an important forerunner of the Expressionists. His work was published in major Expressionist periodicals, including *Der Sturm*, and as late as 1918 the Expressionist Ludwig Meidner dedicated his book *Im Nacken das Sternenmeer* to him. Mombert's writing centred round the creation of cosmic myths set in visionary landscapes, which can be seen as a renewal of the Gnostic tradition. This piece was written in 1902 for a children's book published three years later. Mombert died shortly after being rescued from the concentration camp Gurs in Southern France.

PAUL SCHEERBART: (B. Danzig, 1863. D. Grosslichterfelde, Berlin, 1915.)

Publisher, inventor of 'perpetua mobilia', visionary, anti-materialist, anti-militarist, advocate of glass architecture, agent provocateur against petit-bourgeois seriousness, astro-metaphysician who believed in the life of asteroids and planets, Paul Scheerbart was much loved by the Expressionists, and just about everyone else. He in turn loved a good glass: Scheerbart was a member of the alcoholically enthused literary circle which met in the Black Piglet (Schwarze Ferkel) in Berlin in the 1890s, perhaps the one true bohemian/decadent German-speaking group, centred around Przybyszewski, Strindberg and Edward Munch, to name a few. Scheerbart took his own life in 1915 as a protest against the war.

ALFRED DÖBLIN: (B. Stettin, 1878. D. Emmendingen, 1957.)

One of the major German writers of this century, Döblin was an early contributor to the Expressionist periodical *Der Sturm*, and was an important theorist, but later grew critical of the movement. His literary output embraced numerous novels, the most famous being *Berlin Alexanderplatz* in 1929, plays, essays and a large number of short stories.

First published in 1910, but written some six years earlier (before the inception of the first Expressionist art movement), 'The Murder of a Buttercup' was an extremely important work for Expressionism. Showing the influence of Italian Futurism in the jagged syntax, it marks a break from Döblin's earlier neo-Romantic style. In this coolly observed psychotic episode, which can be seen as a parable of the destruction of the father in the form of the eternal petit-bourgeois philistine, he forgos any psychological explanation or comment, showing the central character caught between his own thoughts and his unreflected actions. As Döblin wrote: 'Psychology in the novel … is a purely abstract phantasmagoria' and: 'Just understanding everything means humiliating everything.'

Döblin's life showed a number of swings between extreme poles: as a young man working as a psychiatrist he wanted to side with sobriety and reason, but caught in the chaos of life he began to develop an anti-rationalist standpoint. The socialist and 'grand inquisitor of atheism' in the twenties, succumbed to a nature mysticism which led to his conversion to Catholicism whilst in exile in 1941.

ALBERT EHRENSTEIN: (B. Vienna, 1886. D. New York, 1950.)

'It's perhaps in slightly bad taste to mention this, but anyway, I was impertinent enough to commit the crime of not allowing Jesus Christ to go first by entering the world on 23 of December', wrote Albert Ehrenstein in a letter to Karl Kraus at the end of 1911. It was a comment which could have come anywhere in the pages of the novella *Tubutsch* which was published that year and brought him instant fame; a book which blends a poor man's megalomania with a sulphurous whiff of humour which verges on the uncanny. The

BIOGRAPHIES

quote is also particularly fitting for one who has often been referred to as a literary Ahasuer, and who worked the character into several of his works. For despite his early successes as a wild, scathing Expressionist poet, further crowned by *Tubutsch* and over twenty other major publications, and his intense political commitment (he was a member of the Anti-Nationalist Socialist Party in 1918, and later the left-wing 'Gruppe 1925' with, among others, Brecht and Döblin), Ehrenstein was a restless individual who rarely held down a job for any length of time and was constantly on the move, travelling to Moscow, Usbechistan, Prague, Berlin, North Africa, finally to flee from 'Barbaropa', as he called the European continent, to New York. However, America was also not the 'land flowing with cream and honey melons' he had expected, and after a decade of growing isolation and embitterment, he died poverty-stricken in a charity hospital. But even in death the 'Tubutsch' in him would have had cause for a bitter laugh at the way the Jewish Ehrenstein was dressed-up for his burial, being given the blond hair and rosy cheeks he had never had in real life!

Tubutsch was written in a week in 1907, and published in 1911 with twelve illustrations by Oskar Kokoschka.

CARL EINSTEIN: (B. Neuwied, 1885. D. Pau, France, 1940.)

It would be hard to overestimate the importance of this writer as both a novelist (*Bebuquin*) and literary theorist, and as an internationally reknowned art theorist and critic. *Bebuquin* was the first trump of Expressionist prose writing and shortly after, his seminal work *African Sculpture* put him firmly on the map as an art critic. After work on *Die Aktion* and *Die weissen Blätter*, he teamed up with the Berlin Dadists, editing several periodicals.

During the following twenty years he was involved in Constructivism, Surrealism (including work with Les Ballets Suedois), collaborated with Bataille and Leiris (*Documents*) and Eugene Jolas

(*Transition*), and with Jean Renoir on his film *Toni*, which heralded French neo-Realism. He even received a grateful mention in *Finnegan's Wake*. After fighting against Franco with the Durutti Column, he fled to France, was arrested, fled again and committed suicide in the Pyrenees as the German troops invaded Southern France.

Although the completed *Bebuquin* first appeared in 1912, the first four slightly different chapters included here were published separately in 1907 under the lengthier title. The complete work was dedicated to André Gide, with whom Gottfried Benn compared the author, saying that *Bebuquin* and Gide's *Paludes* were 'absolute art'.

GUSTAV MEYRINK: (B. Vienna, 1868. D. Starnberg, 1932.)

A man with an aristocratic bearing and a slight limp, a duellist, dandy, misanthrope, unsuccessful banker (his career ended when he was charged for influencing his customers, particularly the women, to make bad investments by occult means!), Meyrink was also the inventor of the hanging incandescent gas light and the man who translated Dickens into Bavarian dialect. His pen produced one of the most important occult novels of all time, *The Golem*, and a series of fantastic grotesques which did not leave his own interest in the occult and Buddhism untouched. Although he was more strongly rooted in the neo-Romantic movement, a late symbolist off-shoot, a number of his contemporaries (especially publishers and critics) were keen to dub him as an Expressionist, and he was also published in the Expressionist periodical *Die weissen Blätter*.

GEORG HEYM: (B. Hirschberg, 1887. D. Berlin, 1912.)

Although Heym is rightly remembered as one of the first writers to give Expressionism a poetic voice, writing black visions of the coming cultural catastrophe and the harsh desert of the city, his

BIOGRAPHIES

prose typically incorporated fantastic themes, and his poetry was also often full of a grotesque, anarchic humour which reflected his own revolutionary longings. He would have loved to have been in the French Revolution and not, like Goethe, whom he hated, 'just sit there and not do a thing'.

Hugo Ball's wife, Emmy Hennings, described him as 'half rowdy and half angel'. One of the most gifted of the early Expressionists, Heym died in a skating accident while trying to save a friend.

FERDINAND HARDEKOPF: (B. Varel, 1876. D. Burghölzli, near Zurich, 1954.)

An early Expressionist poet active in *Die Aktion* circles, his slim oeuvre, capturing a sleazy world in sublimely grotesque, absurd images, is among the best written in the period. He had already started attacking the 'writing desk optimism' of the Expressionist activists in the early war years when he moved to Zurich in 1916 out of opposition to the war. But although he was intimate with the Dadaists, was read at their cabarets and published in their magazines, he kept his connections with the Expressionists through his interest in the magazine *Die weissen Blätter*, and by 1919 he had turned his back on Dada altogether, finding their inane jokes tasteless in the face of the realities in Germany. After the war he slipped into semi-obscurity on the French Riviera. During the occupation he was imprisoned in a concentration camp, before being released with the aid of André Gide. To his death he refused to take on a German passport.

WASSILY KANDINSKY: (B. Moscow, 1866. D. Neuilly-sur-Seine, France, 1944.)

A pioneer abstract painter, founder member of the Expressionist art circle the Blue Rider with Franz Marc, and later a teacher at the

BIOGRAPHIES

Bauhaus School, Kandinsky was a major force in rejecting representationalism in art. 'Bassoon', written in 1912 in German, is about as clear a precursor of Surrealist writing as one can find. Hans Arp described it as follows: 'a breath blows through eternally unfathomable depths'. It was part of a book containing both prose poems and wood cuts, a synaesthetic *Gesamtkunstwerk* entitled *Klänge (Sounds)*.

MYNONA (Pseudonym for Salomo Friedlaender): (B. Gollantsch/Poznán, 1871. D. Paris, 1946.)

While the Friedlaender part of him was a tireless philosopher, propagating a mixture of Stirnerian ideas and neo-Kantianism (his numerous philosophical publications included *Kant For Children*), his Mynona half (being the reverse of the German word for 'anonymous') wrote several novels and countless grotesques which were widely published in Expressionist periodicals. However, the two sides cannot be understood separately, for, as he wrote, 'above all, the grotesque humourist has the desire to refresh the memory of the divine, mysterious primal image of true life ...' Although friends with almost all the Expressionists and a star attraction at their readings, this bohemian writer and 'forerunner of the laughing Dada', as one Dadaist described him, was too 'uncomfortable' for many: he died in poverty in Paris after being refused help to emigrate to the United States by Thomas Mann.

HANS ARP: (B. Strasbourg, 1887. D. Basel, 1966.)

A bilingual artist and poet, Hans Arp made his first attempts to 'overcome the conventional art forms which have been instilled in us' between 1908 and 1910; a programme which took him through the Expressionist Blue Rider group, then on to Dada which he co-founded in Zurich, and finally to Surrealism. His painting turned its back increasingly on any form of representationalism, and his wonderfully facile Dada and Surrealist poetry and prose is still a joy to read.

'Wintergarten', which was written in 1913 and published in *Der Sturm*, is Expressionist in both style and choice of setting, albeit with a lingering hint of neo-Romanticism (and an early hint of Dada). Arp is one of the few artists or writers to have been involved with Expressionism, Dada and Surrealism.

ALFRED WOLFENSTEIN: (B. Halle, 1883. D. Paris, 1945.)

A lawyer and then full-time writer and important translator, Wolfenstein was one of the early generation of Expressionists, taking part in the cabarets in Berlin and working for a number of periodicals in Munich. After Hitler's rise he fled to Prague and then to Paris in 1934, before being arrested by the Gestapo. After his release he remained in hiding in Paris, where he became seriously ill and hospitalised, finally ending his life after his release.

A writer of great social commitment, he tried to combine political activism with the spirit of Christian socialism. The piece included in this anthology, written in 1913 but published in 1918, is an early example of the 'oh mankind!' type of Expressionist writing, albeit written with a seeming relish for the brutal negative utopia it portrays, and with a hero who remains somewhat ambivalent until the very end. This piece is also a good example of a story without any psychological interpretation, relying on a storm of images which tell their own tale.

PAUL ZECH: (B. Briesen, West Prussia, 1881. D. Buenos Aires, 1946.)

Although Zech was a pioneer of the literature about working life in the tradition of Zola's novel *Germinal*, and even worked for several years as a coal miner and metal worker, his writing has nevertheless an anti-realist, phantastic, mythical-animistic streak, producing a sort of mixture of Marx and Meister Eckhart. Indeed, his rather excessive phantasy also makes it difficult to confirm the details about his life — he was given to making rather fanciful claims, such as to a doctor's title and the authorship of several not-undisputed texts — a fact which also marred his position as a well-known Weimar writer. However, after two years industrial work he became an editor, dramaturgist, advertising manager and finally a librarian, before being thrown out of his job for being a member of the Socialist Party in 1933. He emigrated to Argentina, where he did odd jobs and transcribed South American myths and tales.

Normally a traditionalist in terms of narrative style, this piece shows the Expressionist love of heightened, plastic images and immediacy, combined with cognitive abstraction: the pursuit of the self as an antidote to the fascinating intensity and hideous senselessness of the city. Emphasising the contingency of his subjective perception on his surroundings and the fact that he has only one vantage point, the narrator abstracts his ego, creating a synthesis from feeling and knowledge. What he sees transforms into 'high tension', a high tension of defects which goes to form a norm. From this new standpoint he can see the basic patterns of life, so-called 'primal sounds', which spread out, forming the life he condemns with visionary judgement, perceiving that it is all directed towards enslavement, functionality, a life without feeling and mercy. The narrator sets himself apart from his subjectivity, rejecting a society which can only end in war.

ELSE LASKER-SCHÜLER: (B. Wuppertal-Elberfeld, 1869. D. Jerusalem, 1945.)

Somewhat older than the early Expressionists, Else Lasker-Schüler was acclaimed by them as the foremost woman writer of her times: Trakl dedicated poems to her, and her young admirer, Gottfried

Benn, said that she was the greatest woman lyricist Germany had ever had. Already in the 1890s, in the fold of the Berlin Bohème which helped her overcome her fear of her own feelings after a breakdown caused by her mother's death, she had made the break with the seductions of the intellect, a form of cowardice as she put it, and decided to live a second naïvety rather than go along with technical progress. To this end she styled herself as 'Prince Tino from Bagdad', living in a realm fused of her own magical reality and poetry which was populated by projections of her close friends, some of whom are still known by the names she created for them. As she put it, 'I would rather be a cannibal than chew the cud of sobriety.'

GEORG TRAKL: (B. Salzburg, 1887. D. Grodek, 1914.)

Trakl has a unique place in German literature, with his themes of transitoriness, dissolution, collapse, guilt and melancholy which he worked into an emblematic, acausal, associative world of images which reflected his own private life of morphine addiction and incest. He committed suicide, after the horrors of working in an inadequately equipped field hospital at the Battle of Grodek, by taking an overdose of cocaine. A writer who often recalls more of Hölderlin than the normal Expressionist heroes, Ehrenstein wrote that 'no one in Austria has written more beautiful verses'.

ALFRED LICHTENSTEIN: (B. 1889, Berlin. D. Somme, 1914.)

'A sad eccentric' and law graduate who became one of the first wave Expressionist writers, he contributed to both *Die Aktion* and *Der Sturm* before falling in the Somme during the opening months of the First World War. His sarcastic, curiously waggish production is colourfully dotted with syphilitics and suicides, forever underlining the black humour of our very existence, and the existential link this has to one's self. To this end he performed a Jarry-like split into Alfred Lichtenstein and Kuno Kohn, his literary creation, with a laconic comic objectivity. His work was an important influence on the later Dadaists Hans Arp and Hugo Ball.

THEODOR DÄUBLER: (B. Trieste, 1876. D. St Blasien, 1934.)

A giant of a man in all senses, Däubler was a true Bohemian who bore his habitual poverty like a beggar king. He led a restless life, travelling all round Europe, especially Italy where he had been brought up, and the then relatively unknown Greek Islands. Däubler was a highly popular figure who not only had an issue of *Die Aktion* dedicated entirely to him, but who was also taken under the wing of the Berlin Dadaists, but it is hard to tell whether his fame and popularity came more from his poetry or from his impressive presence. On the one hand the Expressionist painter Ludwig Meidner could write: 'Däubler, you old fatty, weighing three hundredweight but writing about flowers and rocks, clouds and sickle moons as no one else can'. On the other hand, his magnus opus, *Northern Lights*, which was published in 1910 and describes the creation of the universe and the birth of mankind from his own Gnostic standpoint in 30,000 verses, received very little reaction from critics and readers alike. Often considered a white elephant, it did however bring him posthumous acclaim from Arno Schmidt, who considered Däubler to be the most important writer of his generation. In later years Däubler established himself as a major art critic and champion of modern art, and he also became the vice-president of the German PEN club in 1928, although he himself was not even a member.

HEINRICH NOWAK: (B. Vienna, 1890. D. Zurich, 1955.)

His first book of poems in 1913 established Nowak as one of the leading early Austrian Expressionists. He was active in the

Akademischer Verband (Academic Society), the Viennese equivalent of the New Club, and also collaborated with Musil in a literary activist club (Die Katakombe). But despite publications in such important periodicals as *Der Sturm* and *Der Ruf* and his work as an editor for other magazines, he failed to consolidate his reputation. This was partly due to his uncompromising nature, and partly his interest in journalism. His slim literary production stopped in 1920, and attempts to draw interest to him in the last few decades have fallen on deaf ears. One of the best erotic writers in the movement, his close friend, Hans Flesch-Brunningen, wrote of him: 'One couldn't make out his sex life: all that can be established is that he got hold of the aether his mother used for cleaning, and then poured it over his sleeves and waistcoat so that he could brag that he had just come back from an aether orgy.'

GOTTFRIED BENN: (B. Mansfield, Westprignitz, 1886. D. West Berlin, 1956.)

Benn, a dandyish doctor specialising in skin and venereal diseases, was an important Expressionist writer and essayist who revealed a particularly choice world of putrefaction and sickness, writing collections of cruel, chilling poems and prose with such tasty titles as *Morgue*, *Flesh* and *Brains*. 'The Island' is taken from the latter. The public reaction was befitting: 'Disgusting!!' or 'What unbridled imagination, devoid of any mental hygiene'. Else Lasker-Schüler, however, wrote that: 'Each of his verses is a leopard bite, the jump of a wild animal. The bone is his stylus for waking the words.'

Benn's stance was strongly anti-rationalist, searching for a new myth and ways of overthrowing reason to allow one's inner impulses free rein. To this end he advocated drugs, championed the enfant terrible of the psychiatric world, Otto Gross, and later had a brief flirt with National Socialism. Benn is now often considered to be one of the major German writers of the century.

The book mentioned in the text is Semi Meyer's *Problems of the Development of the Mind*, which advanced the autonomy of feelings and the idea that evolution takes place in jumps.

HANS FLESCH-BRUNNINGEN (B. Brünn, Austria, 1895. D. Bad Ischl, 1981.)

Upon completing his law exams in 1919 Hans Flesch-Brunningen became a bank administrator, and from 1925 a full-time writer. After stays in Italy, France and five years in Berlin, he emigrated to England in 1934, where he worked for the BBC. He returned to Austria in 1963.

Flesch-Brunningen was active in the Viennese Expressionist circles where, as he later explained, disgusted with neo-Romantism, he went and wrote his first prose sketch 'on a piece of lavatory paper'. Heinrich Nowak wrote of him, 'Chaos has been revealed. The Dear Lord has locked up heaven and weeps'.

Hans Flesch-Brunningen's early writing exemplified the amoral, anti-bourgeois and anti-intellectual, and reflected his own somewhat androcentric vision of an eroticised world with free sex and state controlled bordellos, which he hoped would place the most important thing in life back in the centre.

'The Metaphysical Canary' was his first publication, originally appearing in *Die Aktion*.

HUGO BALL: (B. Pirmasens, 1886. D. St Abondio, Ticino, 1927.)

After studying theatre direction and being a dramaturgist in Munich, Ball attempted to set up an Expressionist theatre under the influence of his friend Wassily Kandinsky. Ball at first greeted the Great War, but then went into exile in Zurich where he worked in small commercial cabarets with his later wife, Emmy Hemmings, and then founded the legendary Cabaret Voltaire in January 1916, which was to become the cradle of Dada. Kandinsky's desire for a total, abstract theatre, as well as Einstein's call for an absolute, polycausal poetry, were major inspirations. However, Ball left Dada at the end of May 1917, later writing a lengthy work on Bakunin, converting to Catholicism in 1920 and devoting himself to psychology and theology.

His literary output consisted of several novels, a variety of Dada poems, and numerous social-critical, philosophical and theological works.

Tenderenda the Fantast, his most cryptic work which reflects Einstein's call for absolute poetry, is a collection of shamanic incantations, hymns and slapstick written between the years 1914 and 1920, but only first published in 1967. Described by Hans Arp as 'Dada's secret bequest', the novel follows his personal progression from Expressionism to an uncertain Christianity.

The text 'Grand Hotel Metaphysics', which was also the alternative title to the book, is a self-contained chapter which shows the birth of Dada as one Mr Foetus, the still-born successor to Christ (in the form of the little Jew, perhaps Tristan Tzara), much to the anger of the good citizens in the neighbourhood. These citizens (P.T. Bridet, Pimperling and Toto) contain sly references to the Expressionists: Pimperling has clear allusions to Däubler, and Toto to the Ehrenstein of *Tubutsch*. The piece was read by Ball in April 1917 at a Dada soirée, wearing fantastic costume, but there are indications that it may have been written earlier.

CONRAD FELIXMÜLLER: (B. Dresden, 1897. D. West Berlin, 1977.)

Born Felix Müller, in his new incarnation, Conrad Felixmüller, he was a founder member of two Expressionist groups in his home town of Dresden, where he also co-edited the magazine *Menschen*. A highly gifted painter, he was one of the most important artists of

BIOGRAPHIES

the so-called second generation of Expressionism, having his first exhibition at the age of eighteen and becoming a member of the November Group in Berlin. An active communist until 1926, when he left the party, after the Second World War he remained in Saxony as a Professor at the Martin Luther University in Halle, where his patience was repeatedly tried by the dogmas of Socialist Realism. His own work went through a number of more naturalist phases, and he later distanced himself from his early work.

The text in this anthology, his only prose work, is clearly based on his experiences when, as a conscientious objector during the First World War, he worked as a medical orderly in a mental hospital.

HEINRICH SCHAEFER: (B. Zabern, Alsace, 1889. D. Berlin, 1943.)

Very little is known about this genuine German *poète maudit* apart from the fact that he studied in Strasbourg and worked from the beginning of the war on *Die Aktion*, which also published his handful of short stories and one staggering novel. In 1918 he sided with the magazine's Anti-National Socialist Party, and in 1933, after his move to Berlin where he worked as a secondary school teacher, he was suspended by the Nazis.

WIELAND HERZFELDE: (B. 1896, Weggis, Switzerland. D. East Berlin, 1988.)

Taking after his father both politically and in his outspokenness (he was also charged with blasphemy), this founder member of the Berlin Dada went on to become one of the most innovative publishers between the wars (and then later in exile). His Malik Verlag, named after a character created by Else Lasker-Schüler, was the main publisher for Dada books, and also developed a policy of presenting socialist literature in a way that appealed to a wide audience, most importantly using the stunning layouts and jacket designs from his brother John Heartfield.

The book from which this story comes is a slender tome entitled *Tragi-grotesques of the Night*. A synthesis of dream and revolution, an 'absolute reality' such as Breton demanded and which foreshadows the surrealism of *The Communicating Vessels*, it was dedicated to his brother, John, with the hope that he would become a good socialist. The book was widely praised in the press, being seen variously as a collection of Expressionist prose poems or as quixotic satires. Herzfelde wrote that this particular dream was clearly influenced by his imprisonment during the White Terror in Berlin and Munich in early 1919, the counter-revolutionary offensive against the November revolutionaries in which they were mown down by mercenary troops employed by the Weimar government.

KURT SCHWITTERS: (B. Hannover, 1887. D. Kendal, England, 1949.)

A tirelessly innovative collagist, writer, performer and polemicist, he founded his own form of Dada, 'Merz', in the same year that 'The Onion', a nicely Expressionistic grotesque blended with Dada collage, was published in the Expressionist magazine *Der Sturm*. Although his later literary production became increasingly folksy, Schwitters never gave up his basic tenets, even working on an unpublished Dada magazine *PIN* with fellow Berlin Dadaist Raoul Hausmann in the forties, while living in dire circumstances in exile in England.

FRANZ KAFKA: (B. Prague, 1883. D. Vienna, 1924.)

Kafka's true stature was first recognised by Ehrenstein, while Musil rated his early works as those of a second rate Robert Walser! But despite a number of publications in such Expressionist periodicals as *Die weissen Blätter* before 1914, and the publication by an important house of several major texts including *Metamorphosis* and the *Trial* during the war, he was generally regarded as something of a curiosity during his life. Kafka was less formally experimental than the 'typical' Expressionists, and is more an Expressionist by import rather than conviction. However, the lack of psychologising, the uncanny grotesqueness and immediacy of his images shows much in common. This piece first appeared after his death in 1936.

IWAN GOLL: (B. Saint Dié, France, 1891. D. Paris, 1950.)

An Expressionist poet and playwright of great quality, and one of the movement's foremost theorists, he was also one of the first to proclaim that the movement had finally died after becoming too soft and sentimental during the war. But despite Tristan Tzara's attempts to woo him for Dada, he turned to Surrealism. Indeed, Goll was perhaps the first person to adopt Apollinaire's newly coined word 'Surrealism', in its German form 'Überrealismus', and he later wrote a manifesto calling for the artist to strip reality of its appearances to leave 'the supertemporal within the temporal', a chastised nature raised to the higher level of art. However, his manifesto was overshadowed by Breton's in the same year, and Goll's Surrealist phase remained little more than a footnote to the movement.

His novel, *The Eurococcus*, was written in 1927 under the banner of Surrealism, but shows considerably stronger Expressionist traits; isolation, decay, the city and the New Man. The extract chosen here is the concluding section.

ROBERT MUSIL: (B. Klagenfurt, Austria, 1880. D. Geneva, 1942.)

After studying philosophy and experimental psychology, Musil worked as a librarian in Vienna, where he started a literary career which was to bring him the Kleist Prize and international acclaim, particularly for his book *A Man Without Qualities*. A true Expressionist

BIOGRAPHIES

in his day, who also wrote for *Revolution*, he was active in the early cabarets and was published in the more outspoken periodicals. It was also during this period that he wrote his first novel, *The Young Torless*. During the Second World War he went into exile in Switzerland.

This piece was first published in 1936, in a volume of short prose texts entitled *A Legacy While Still Alive*, with the comment that they had all been written between 1920 and 1929. 'The Giant Agoag' is a good old-fashioned literary grotesque in the Expressionist manner.

HERMANN UNGAR: (B. Boskowice/Moravia, 1893. D. Prague, 1929.)

After completing his law studies in Prague, Munich and Berlin, Ungar spent the first two war years on the front, where he was severely wounded. Then, after almost a decade working in a bank, as a theatre dramaturgist and then as a civil servant, he decided to become a full-time writer, but died within a year from appendicitis.

Ungar's writing can be described as late Expressionist, although it also shows a clinical coldness more typical of New Objectivity. Apart from one comedy, his work revolves around nightmarish themes of sex, murder and disease, provocatively spiced with anarchic attacks on petit-bourgeois ideals.

ACKNOWLEDGEMENTS

Hans Flesch-Brunningen, 'Die metaphysische Kanarienvogel', from 'Das zerstörte Idyll', *Der jungste Tag* 44/45, 1917, reproduced by courtesy of Dr Hilde Spiel

Albert Ehrenstein, 'Tubutsch', from *Albert Ehrenstein, Werke, Bd. 2 Prosa*, Klaus Boer Verlag, Munich, 1989

Alfred Döblin, 'Die Ermordung einer Butterblume', from *Erzählungen aus fünf Jahrzehnten*, Walter-Verlag AG, Olten, 1979

ACKNOWLEDGEMENTS

Franz Kafka, 'Der Geier', courtesy of Martin Secker & Warburg, London, 1973

Robert Musil, 'Der Riese Agoag', from *Nachlass zu Lebzeiten*, Rowohlt Verlag GmbH, Reinbek & Hamburg, 1978

Wieland Herzfelde, 'Strenge von Leipzig', from *Tragikgrotesken Der Nacht*, Aufbau Verlag, Berlin & Weimar, 1972

Conrad Felixmüller, 'Militär-Krankenwärter Felixmüller XI Arnsdorf,' from *Menschen 1*, Buchverlag Der Morgen, Berlin, 1988, reproduced by courtesy of Titus Felixmüller

Mynona, 'Eines Kindes Heldentat', from *Aktion 3*, 1913, reproduced by courtesy of Herrn Hartmut Geerken

Kurt Schwitters, 'Die Zwiebel', from *Das Literarische werk, Bd. 2*, Du-Mont Buchverlag GmbH & Co., Cologne, 1974

Gottfried Benn, 'Die Insel', from *Sämtliche werke, Bd. 3*, Klett-Cotta Verlag, Stuttgart, 1987

Wassily Kandinsky, 'Fagott', from *Klänge* (1912), ADAGP, Paris and DACS, London, 1993

Hans Arp, 'Wintergarten', from *Gesammelte Gedichte, Bd. 1*, Limes Verlag in der F.A. Herbig Verlagsbuchhandlung GmbH, Munich, 1967

Else Lasker-Schüler, 'Wenn mein Herz gesund wäre', from *Gesammelte Werke in drei Banden, Bd. 2: Prosa und Schauspiele*, Kösel-Verlag, Munich, 1962

Alfred Mombert, 'Das Eis', from *Gesamtausgabe, Bd. 2* Kösel-Verlag, Munich, 1963

ACKNOWLEDGEMENTS

Gustav Meyrink, 'Der Saturnring', from *Des deutschen Spießers Wunderhorn*, Langen Muller Verlag in F.A. Herbig Verlagsbuchhandlung GmbH, Munich, 1980

Theodor Däubler, 'Die Schraube', from *Mit Silberner Sichel*, Hellerauer Verlag, Dresden-Hellerau, 1916

Alfred Wolfenstein, 'Über allen Zaubern', from *Erzählende Werke, Bd. 3*, Hase & Koehler Verlag, Mainz, 1985

Iwan Goll, *Die Eurococcus*, Argon Verlag GmbH, Berlin, 1988

Hugo Ball, 'Grand Hotel Metaphysik', from *Tenderenda der Phantast*, reproduced by courtesy of Atlas Press, London

Ferdinand Hardekopf, 'Der Gedankenstrich', from *Gesammelte Dichtungen*, Verlags AG Die Arche, Zurich, 1963

Hermann Ungar, 'Die Bewandtnis', Igel Verlag Literatur, Paderborn, 1989

Carl Einstein, 'Herr Giorgio Bebuquin Kapitel 1–4', from *Bebuquin oder die Dilettanten des Wunders*, in: Bd. 1, Carl Einstein, Werke, Bohman Druck und Verlag, Wien, Fannei & Walz, Berlin, 1980

Heinrich Nowak, 'Die Sonnenseuche', from *Die Sonnenseuche*, Medusa Verlag, Vienna-Berlin, 1984

Paul Zech, 'Auf der Terrasse am Pol', from *Das Neue Pathos*, Hefte 5 & 6, Berlin, 1913, reproduced by courtesy of Greifenverlag zur Rudolstadt, Rudolstadt

ACKNOWLEDGEMENTS

The publishers have made every effort to trace the copyright holders, but if they have inadvertently overlooked any they will be pleased to make the necessary arrangement at the first opportunity.

RELATED TITLES FROM ATLAS PRESS

Malcolm Green is the German books editor of Atlas Press which specialises in avant-garde and extremist literature from the 1890's to the present day. Atlas are the largest English language publisher of works relating to Expressionism, Surrealism, Dada and Pataphysics, etc. and have books in print, or forthcoming, from:

Achim von Arnim, Hans Carl Artmann, Konrad Bayer, Wolfgang Bauer, André Breton, Günter Brus, Pol Bury, The College of Pataphysics, Robert Desnos, Rikki Ducornet, Paul Eluard, Xavier Forneret, Carlo Emilio Gadda, Remy de Gourmont, Richard Huelsenbeck, Joris-Karl Huysmans, Alfred Jarry, Georges Limbour, Michel Leiris, Marcel Mariën, Harry Mathews, Bernard Noël, Montagu O'Reilly, Oskar Panizza, Oskar Pastior, Benjamin Péret, Grayson Perry, Raymond Queneau, Jacques Rigaut, Georges Rodenbach, Gerhard Roth, Raymond Roussel, Saint-Pol-Roux, Alberto Savinio, Jacques Vaché, Unica Zurn. Also, we publish a number of anthologies that contain selections from these and other related authors.

Many of these titles are only available directly from us by mail order. For a free catalogue write to (our full address):

BCM ATLAS PRESS, LONDON WCIN 3XX

• emissions of the anti-tradition •